"We need to un[illegible] about each othe[illegible] Otherwise, no one is going to believe we're legitimate."

"Why not?" Sam countered and placed a soft kiss on the inside of her palm.

"You don't need to do that now," she whispered, her voice no more than a breath in the quiet. "There's no one watching."

"It's a good thing, too, because what I want to do to you is best kept in private."

Her mouth formed a round O, and he lifted a finger to trace the soft flesh of her lips.

"We shouldn't..."

"I know," he repeated. "But I can't think of anything I want more."

"Me, too." She sat up and brought both of her hands to the sides of his face, cupping his jaw. "This isn't going to get complicated, right? It's all part of the show, pretending like we're in love. It ends when we both get what we want."

"That's the plan."

"Then it won't matter if I do this..." She brought her mouth to his.

A Pretend Groom

Michelle Major & Lee McKenzie

Previously published as *Her Accidental Engagement*
and *The Daddy Project*

 HARLEQUIN® MUST♥DOGS

ISBN-13: 978-1-335-04181-4

A Pretend Groom

Copyright © 2019 by Harlequin Books S.A.

First published as Her Accidental Engagement
by Harlequin Books in 2014 and
The Daddy Project by Harlequin Books in 2012.

The publisher acknowledges the copyright holder
of the individual works as follows:

Her Accidental Engagement
Copyright © 2014 by Michelle Major

The Daddy Project
Copyright © 2012 by Lee McKenzie McAnally

Recycling programs
for this product may
not exist in your area.

Printed in U.S.A.

CONTENTS

Michelle Major grew up in Ohio but dreamed of living in the mountains. After graduating with a degree in journalism, she headed west and settled in Colorado. Her life and house are filled with one great husband, two beautiful kids, a few furry pets and several well-behaved reptiles. She's grateful to have found her passion writing stories with happy endings. Michelle loves to hear from her readers at michellemajor.com.

Books by Michelle Major

Harlequin Special Edition

Maggie & Griffin

Falling for the Wrong Brother
Second Chance in Stonecreek
A Stonecreek Christmas Reunion

Crimson, Colorado

A Baby and a Betrothal
Always the Best Man
Christmas on Crimson Mountain
Romancing the Wallflower
Sleigh Bells in Crimson
Coming Home to Crimson

Visit the Author Profile page
at Harlequin.com for more titles.

HER ACCIDENTAL ENGAGEMENT

Michelle Major

To Mom and Dad: for your love, support
and the years of off-key harmonies

Chapter 1

Julia Morgan lit the final match, determined to destroy the letter clenched in her fingers. She was well aware of the mistakes she'd made in her life, but seeing them typed on fancy letterhead was more than she could take at the moment. She drew the flickering flame toward the paper but another gust of damp wind blew it out.

The mountains surrounding her hometown of Brevia, North Carolina, were notoriously wet in late winter. Even though it hadn't rained for several days, moisture clung to the frigid March air this afternoon, producing a cold she felt right to her bones.

With a frustrated groan, she crumpled the letter into a tiny ball. Add the inability to burn a single piece of paper to her colossal list of failures. Sinking to her knees on the soggy ground, she dropped the used matchstick into a trash bag with all the others.

She ignored the wail of a siren from the highway above her. She'd pulled off the road minutes earlier and climbed down the steep embankment, needing a moment to stop the panic welling inside her.

For a few seconds she focused her attention on the canopy of pine trees below the ridge where she stood, her heartbeat settling to a normal rhythm.

Since she'd returned to her hometown almost two years ago, this love of the forest had surprised her. She'd never been a nature girl, her gypsy existence taking her from one big city to another. Thanks to her beautiful son, Julia was now rooted in Brevia, and the dense woods that enveloped the town gave her the sense of peace she hadn't known she'd missed for ye---

The makeshift fire hadn't been much of a plan, but flying by the seat of her pants was nothing new for Julia. With a deep breath, she smoothed the wrinkled letter against the grass. She'd read it compulsively over the past week until the urge to destroy it had overtaken her. She knew the words by heart but needed the satisfaction of watching them go up in flames.

Unfit mother. Seeking custody. Better options.

Tears pricked the backs of her eyes. Burning the letter wouldn't change the potential it had to ruin her life. She'd tried to dismiss the contents as lies and conjecture. In a corner of her heart, she worried they were true and she wouldn't be able to defend herself against them.

Suddenly she was hauled to her feet. "Are you hurt? What happened?" A pair of large hands ran along her bare arms, then down her waist toward...

Whoa, there. "Back off, Andy Griffith," Julia sputtered as parts of her body she thought were in permanent hibernation sprang to life.

As if realizing how tightly he held her, Sam Callahan, Brevia's police chief, pushed away. He stalked several yards up the hill toward the road, then turned and came at her again. Muscles bunched under the shoulders of his police uniform.

She had to work hard to ignore the quick pull of awareness that pulsed through her. Darn good thing Julia had sworn off men. Even better that big, strong alpha men were *so* not her type.

Julia gave herself a mental headshake. "What do you want, Sam? I'm sort of busy here."

She could have sworn his eye twitched under his aviator sunglasses. He jabbed one arm toward the top of the hill. "What I *want* is to know what the hell you're doing off the side of the road. *Again*."

Right. She'd forgotten that the last time Sam had found her, she'd been eight months pregnant and had wrapped her ancient Honda around a tree trunk. He'd taken her to the hospital where her son, Charlie, had been born.

That day a year and a half ago had been the start of a new life for her. One she'd protect at any cost.

Sam had been new to Brevia and the role of police chief then. He'd also been a whole lot nicer. At least, to Julia. He'd made the rounds of the single ladies in town, but ever since Charlie's birth Sam had avoided her as though he thought he might be the first man in history to catch a pregnancy. Which was fine, especially given some of the details she'd heard about his history with women.

"Julia."

At the sound of her name, she focused on his words.

"There are skid marks where your car pulled off."

"I was in a hurry," she said and swiped at her still-moist cheeks.

His hands bunched at his sides as he eyed her bag. "Do I smell smoke?"

"I lit a match. Lots of them." Her chin hitched. "Wanna call Smokey Bear for backup?"

He muttered something under his breath at the same time a semi roared by on the road above.

"I didn't quite catch that."

Sam removed his sunglasses and tucked them into the front pocket of his shirt. He was almost *too* good-looking, his blond hair short but a little messy, as if he needed a trim. The effect softened his classically handsome features and a square jaw that fell just short of comic-book chiseled. His gaze slammed into hers, and Julia knew if ice could turn molten, it would be the exact color of Sam's blue eyes.

"You were on your knees," he said slowly.

Julia swallowed. "I lost a contact."

"You don't wear contacts."

"How do you…? Never mind." She bent to retrieve the bag of worthless matches.

His finger brushed the back of her arm. "What are you doing out here, Jules?"

Something about the sound of her name soft as a whisper broke through her defenses. She straightened and waved the letter at him. "I have a meeting in town and needed some fresh air to collect my thoughts."

"At the salon?"

She shook her head. "No. Hair dye doesn't require much mental fortitude. I have a real meeting, with an attorney."

He didn't ask for details but continued to watch her.

"It's about Charlie," she offered after a minute. "About

my custody." To add to her humiliation, she choked on the last word.

"You're his mother. Of course you have custody."

"I know." She lifted the letter. "But Jeff and his parents think—"

"Who's Jeff?"

"My ex-boyfriend." She sighed. "Charlie's father."

Sam's eyes narrowed. "The one who's never set eyes on him?"

"He's a college professor and travels the world doing research. His dad runs an investment firm in Columbus, Ohio, and his mom is a retired cardiologist. They're rich, powerful and very intellectual. The whole family is off-the-charts smart. I guess they have...concerns. For Charlie's future and my ability to provide the right environment. Jeff wants a new custody arrangement."

"Have Jeff's parents met Charlie?"

"No. They called a couple of times after he was born. They didn't approve of me when I was with Jeff, and since he didn't want anything to do with the baby..." She paused then added, "I let my mom deal with them."

That made him smile. "In my opinion, Vera is also off-the-charts smart."

Julia ignored the shiver in her legs at his slow grin. Her mother, Vera Morgan, was a pit bull. But also keenly intelligent. Everyone in her family was smart. Everyone but her.

"Jeff's mother is here with their family attorney to meet me. To make sure everything's okay—that Charlie is in good hands."

"Of course he's in good hands." Sam's voice gentled as he repeated, "You're his mother."

"I've done a lot of stupid things in my life, made a lot

of mistakes. Jeff knows the sordid details and I'm sure his parents do, too." Emotion clogged her throat.

Sam was not the man she wanted to have see her like this. She made a show of checking her watch. "What I could use is some damage control for my reputation. White picket fence, doting husband, pillar of the community stuff. It's a little late for me to join the Junior League." She shook her head. "Anyway, thanks for your concern today, but as you can see, I'm peachy keen."

"You shouldn't talk to anyone until you get an attorney of your own."

"Frank Davis said he would help me, but I hope it won't come to that. I'm sure the Johnsons want what's best for Charlie. I should at least hear them out. That boy deserves everything this world has to offer." She gave a humorless laugh and started back toward the road. "What he's got is me."

As she moved past Sam, his hand reached out, but she jerked away. If he touched her right now she'd be a goner, and she needed to keep it together. For Charlie.

"You're more than enough," he called after her.

"From your lips to God's ears, Chief," she whispered and climbed up to her car.

"Who are you and what have you done with my father?"

Sam shifted in his chair at Carl's, Brevia's most popular restaurant, still reeling from his unbelievable afternoon. From the bizarre encounter with Julia he'd been called to a domestic disturbance that ended up being a chicken loose in Bobby Royall's kitchen. It had made him almost thirty minutes late to dinner with his dad. Now he wished the bird hadn't been so easy to catch.

Joe Callahan adjusted his Patriots baseball cap and chuckled. "It's me, son. Only better."

Said who?

His father had been a police officer in Boston for almost forty years, most of which had been spent working homicide. Joe Callahan had dedicated his life to his career, and his family had suffered from the on-the-job stress and risks he took daily. Although it wasn't intentional, Sam had modeled his own life after his father's. Sam had put his job before everything and everyone in his life—just like Joe.

Recently, though, Joe had begun conducting programs for police departments on emotional awareness. Sam had resisted his father's repeated attempts to help him "get in touch" with his feelings. But now Joe was here and impossible to ignore.

"The boys down at the precinct loved my seminar. At least four of 'em were in tears by the end. I got thank-you notes from a half-dozen wives."

"That's great, Dad." Sam took a long drink of iced tea, wishing he wasn't on duty. A cold one would be mighty helpful tonight. "I don't see what that has to do with me or your unexpected visit to Brevia."

His father pulled a flyer out of the briefcase at his feet and pushed it across the table. "While I'm down here, I thought we could organize a workshop."

Sam glanced at the pamphlet. His stomach gave a hearty gurgle. *Law with Love, Presented by Retired Police Captain Joseph Callahan.* A picture of Joe hugging a group of uniformed officers filled the front page. Sam couldn't remember ever being hugged by his craggy, hard-nosed father. Holy mother of…

"I don't know. It's only me and one deputy on the force."

Joe tapped the sheet of paper. "It's for firefighters and paramedics, too. We could bring in neighboring towns—make it a regional event. Plus civil servants, city council. You're looking at a long-term reappointment, right? This could make quite an impression as far as your potential."

At the mention of his possible future in Brevia, Sam lost the battle with his temper. "My potential as what? I'm the chief of police, not the hug-it-out type."

His father's sharp intake of breath made Sam regret his outburst. "Sorry. You know what a small town this is and—"

Joe held up a hand. "Don't apologize." He removed his bifocals and dabbed at his eyes with a napkin.

"You aren't going to cry," Sam muttered, disbelieving. "You don't cry."

"Yes. I *am* going to cry. To take a moment and *feel* my pain."

Great. This was the second time today he'd brought someone to tears.

After a loud nose blow, Joe's watery gaze met his. "I feel my pain, and I feel yours."

"I'm not in pain." Sam let his eyes drift shut. "Other than a raging headache."

Joe ignored him and continued, "I did this to you, Sammy."

Sammy? His father hadn't called him Sammy since—

"When your mother died my whole world collapsed. I didn't think I could live without her. I didn't want to. It broke me a little more every day to see you and your brother that sad. I did the only thing I could to survive. I shut off my heart, and I made you do the same. I was wrong. I'm here to make it right again."

Sam saw customers from the surrounding tables begin to stare. "It's okay. Let's go outside for a minute."

Joe followed Sam's gaze and shook his head. "I'm not embarrassed to show my feelings. Not anymore." He took another breath, this one steadier. "Ever since the incident with my ole ticker." He thumped his sweat-shirt. "They say facing death can make you reevaluate your whole life."

"It was indigestion, Dad. Not a real heart attack. Remember?"

"Doesn't matter. The change to my heart was real. The effect on my life was real." He readjusted his glasses. "I want the same change for you. I want you to be happy."

"I'm fine." Sam gulped a mouthful of ice and crunched. "Happy as a clam."

"Are you seeing anyone?"

Alarm bells went off in Sam's head. "I...sure...am actually. She's great." He looked away from his father's expectant face, unable to lie to him directly. He glanced around the crowded restaurant and his gaze landed on Julia at a booth in the back. He hadn't noticed her when he'd first walked in, but now he couldn't pull his eyes away.

This must be the meeting with her ex-boyfriend's family she'd told him about. The faces of the two women seated across from her were blocked, but Julia's cheeks flamed pink. Her palm smacked the table as if she was about to lose control.

Easy there, sweetheart, he counseled silently.

As if she'd heard him, her eyes met his and held for several moments. His pulse hammered against his throat. Then she squared her shoulders and folded her hands in her lap.

He turned back to his father. "You'd like her. She's a real spitfire."

Joe smiled. "Like your mother."

Sam forced himself not to look at Julia again. "I was ten when she died. I don't remember that much."

"This one's different than your other girls?"

Sam caught the waitress's attention and signaled for the check.

"Because I think you need a new perspective. After what happened with…"

"I don't want to rehash my relationship history."

Joe reached across the table and clasped Sam's hand in his. "I know you want to find love and settle down."

Sam heard a loud cough behind him and found the young waitress staring. Her look could only be described as predatory. *Fantastic.* Sam had dated some when he'd first come to town but had kept to himself recently, finding it easier and less complicated to be alone. The way gossip went viral in Brevia, he'd have a fresh line of eligible women in front of his office by morning.

"I told you," Sam said, loud enough for the waitress to hear. "I've got a girlfriend. We're very happy."

The waitress dropped the check on the table with a *humph* and stalked away.

"It's serious?" Joe asked.

Sam's gaze wandered to Julia again. "Very," he muttered as she jabbed a finger across the table. This time his mental warning to not lose control didn't reach her. Her voice grew so loud that people at surrounding tables turned.

"I want to meet her," his dad said, rubbing his palms together, oblivious to the commotion behind him. "Why don't you give her a call and see if she can meet us for dessert? If she's so wonderful, I can help make sure you don't blow it."

At the moment, Sam wasn't worried about screwing up anything himself or producing a nonexistent girlfriend for his dad to fawn over. Instead he felt the need to avert someone else's disaster. "I'll be right back."

Joe grabbed his arm as he started past. "Don't be sore, Sammy. I was joking. You're a great catch."

Sam shrugged out of his father's grasp. "I need a minute. Stay here."

He darted around a passing waiter as he made his way to Julia, who now stood in front of the booth.

"You have no idea what I'm capable of," she shouted. All eyes on this side of the restaurant were glued to her.

Just as he reached her, Julia picked up a glass of water from the table. Sam leaned in and wrapped his fingers around hers before she could hurl it at anyone.

"Hey there, sugar," he said as he pulled her tense body tight to his side. "I didn't realize your meeting was at Carl's tonight. You doing okay?"

"Let go of me," she said on a hiss of breath. "This is none of your concern."

"Well, I *am* concerned," he whispered then plastered on a wide smile. "I haven't met your new friends yet."

She squirmed against him. "They aren't my—"

"Howdy, folks," Sam interrupted, turning his attention to the two strangers staring at him. "I'm Sam Callahan. A...uh...friend of Julia's."

The woman in the corner practically screamed "old money," from her sophisticated haircut to her tailored suit. A thick strand of pearls hung around her neck and a massive diamond sparkled on her left hand. The way her gaze narrowed, she must be Charlie's paternal grand-

mother. Next to her was a younger woman, tiny and book-
ish. Her big owl eyes blinked from behind retro glasses.
Faint streaks of color stole up her neck from the collar of
her starched oxford shirt as she watched the two of them.

"Friend?" The older woman scoffed. "Latest conquest,
no doubt." She nudged the woman beside her. "Are you
taking notes on this? She's now flaunting her boy toy in
front of us."

Boy toy? Sam's smile vanished and he worked to keep
his voice pleasant. "Excuse me, ma'am, you have the
wrong idea—"

She continued as if he hadn't spoken. "Can you imagine what my grandson's been subjected to when his
mother is obviously a tramp? When the judge hears—"

Sam held up a hand. "Wait just one minute, lady. If
you think you can waltz in here—"

Julia's fingernails dug into his arm. "I *don't* need your
help. Walk away."

He glanced down at her and saw embarrassment shim-
mering along with anger in her expression. And fear. At
the mention of the word *judge,* he'd felt some of the fight
go out of her. He wished he hadn't interrupted, that he'd
let her handle her own problems, the way she'd wanted
to in the first place. But a part of Sam needed to be the
hero just so he could feel something. It was what he was
used to, one of the few things he could count on. That
part of him couldn't walk away.

He released Julia and leveled his best law-enforcement
stare at the grandmother. As he expected, she shrank
back and darted a nervous glance at her companion. "I'm
Sam Callahan, Brevia's police chief." Hands on hips, he
held her gaze. "To be clear, I am *no one's* boy toy and
would appreciate if you'd conduct yourself in a more

civilized manner in my town. We don't take kindly to strangers spreading malicious rumors about our own. Do I make myself clear?"

Several beats passed before the studious-looking woman cleared her throat. "Mr. Callahan—"

Sam squared his shoulders. "You can call me Chief."

The attorney swallowed. "Chief Callahan, I'm Lexi Preston. I represent the interests of Charlie Morgan's father, Jeff Johnson, and grandparents, Dennis and Maria Johnson. My father is the Johnsons' family attorney and he asked me—"

"Get to the point."

"Yes, well…" Lexi mumbled as she shuffled papers around the table. "I was simply explaining to Ms. Morgan the facts of her case, or lack thereof, when she became hostile and confrontational. My client is not to blame for this unfortunate disturbance. We have statements from a number of Ms. Morgan's former acquaintances as to her character, so Dr. Johnson's assertion, while ill-advised, is not without foundation."

He heard Julia suck in a breath but kept his attention on the two women. "I don't care what your so-called statements allege. You're not going to drag Julia's name through the mud."

Preston collected the rest of the papers. "Why is Ms. Morgan's reputation your business? Is she under investigation by local law enforcement?"

"This can't get any worse," Julia whispered so low only he could here. "Go away, Sam. Now."

From the corner of his eye, Sam saw his father standing a few feet away, watching him intently. Sam was a good cop and he played things by the book, having learned the hard way not to bite off more than he could chew.

But some lessons didn't stick.

He peeled Julia's hand from its death grip around his upper arm and laced her fingers with his. "It's my business, Counselor, because I'm not going to let you or anyone hurt the woman I intend to marry."

Chapter 2

Julia thought things couldn't get worse.

Until they did.

She glanced around the restaurant, as dumbfounded as the people who stared at her from the surrounding tables. She recognized a lot of them; Carl's was a popular spot for Brevia locals.

Yanking Sam away from the table a few steps, she smiled up into his face, well aware of their audience. It took all her willpower to resist the urge to slap him silly. "Have you lost your mind?" she said, keeping her voice low.

The corners of his mouth were tight as he returned her smile. "Apparently."

"Fix this. You have to fix this."

"That's what I'm trying to do." He smoothed a stray hair from her cheek. "Trust me."

No way. Julia didn't trust men. She had a long line of

heartbreak in her past. Mountains of collateral damage that made her sure she was the only person she could trust to take care of her and Charlie. "Don't touch me," she whispered through gritted teeth.

His hand dropped from her face. "I'm going to help you. But you can't fight me. Not here."

She glanced over his shoulder at the attorney and Charlie's grandmother. For a fraction of a second, worry marred Maria Johnson's perfect features. Julia didn't understand the break in the ice queen's armor, but it must have had something to do with Sam.

"Fine." She reached forward and clasped both of his rock-solid arms, as if she could make him understand the gravity of her situation through a simple squeeze. "You better make it count. Charlie's future is on the line."

He searched her gaze for a long moment, then bent onto one knee. He took her fingers in his, tugging softly when she would have pulled away.

"I didn't mean..."

"Julia Morgan," he said, and his deep, clear voice rang out in the restaurant. "We've kept this quiet—no easy task in Brevia—but it's long past time to make things official." He cleared his throat, adjusting the collar of his starched uniform shirt. "Would you do me the honor of becoming my wife?"

Julia blinked back sudden tears. A marriage proposal was what she'd wanted, once upon a time. She'd wanted Jeff to see they could build a real life together. Foolishly sure he was the one, she'd been reckless and selfish. Then the universe had blessed her with a beautiful son. She was working day and night to make a good life for Charlie. Now that she wanted to do the right thing, she risked losing him.

Not for the first time, she wondered if he'd be better off with the Johnsons and the privileged life filled with opportunities they could provide.

She squeezed her eyes shut to clear her thoughts. She was Charlie's mother, no matter what, and wouldn't ever stop fighting for him.

Sam ran his finger along the inside of her wrist. "Are you going to answer the question? My leg is cramping."

"Oh, no. Sorry."

"No?" he asked over the collective gasp.

"I mean yes. Get up, you big oaf." Heat flooded her face and her stomach churned. What was she doing? She'd learned not to rely on a man for anything and now she was putting her entire future in Sam's hands. Impulsive as ever, she repeated, "Yes. My answer is yes."

He stood, rubbing one knee. "Cool it on the name-calling. We're in love, remember."

"You betcha, honey-bunny."

That produced a genuine grin from him, and she was again caught off guard by her body's reaction as tiny butterflies did a fast samba across her belly. Oblivious to his effect on her, Sam turned to the booth.

Before he could speak, an older man wrapped them both in a tight hug. "This is amazing."

Amazing? Not quite.

Sam caught her gaze, his eyes dark and unreadable. "I forgot to tell you earlier. My dad came to town today. Meet Joe Callahan, your future father-in-law."

Uh-oh.

Joe cupped her face between his large hands. "You're just what he needed. I can already tell." Tears shimmered in eyes the same color as Sam's, only sweeter and looking at her with such kindness a lump formed in Julia's throat. "You remind me of my Lorraine, rest her soul."

"Okay, Dad." Sam tugged her out of Joe's embrace. She took a step back but Sam pulled her against his side.

Joe turned to the booth. "I'll buy a round to celebrate. Any friends of…"

"Julia," Sam supplied with a sigh.

"Any friends of my future daughter-in-law are friends of mine."

"We're *not* friends," Lexi Preston ground out. "As I said earlier, I represent her son's biological father and his parents. They're interested in exploring a more viable custody arrangement. The Johnsons want what's best for the child. They can give him opportunities—"

"They want to take my baby," Julia mumbled. Sam's arm tightened around her waist.

If Joe was surprised to hear she had a child, he didn't let on. His posture went rigid. "That's ridiculous. She's the boy's mother."

"Dad, this isn't the time or place—" Sam began.

Joe wagged a finger at Lexi Preston and Maria Johnson. "Now listen here. I don't know what all this nonsense is about, but I can tell you my son will take care of that child and Julia. He's the law around here, for heaven's sake." He leaned closer and Lexi's nervous swallow mimicked Julia's. Joe Callahan might look like a teddy bear but he had a backbone of steel. "You'll have to come through both of us if you try to hurt her. We protect our own."

"I've had quite enough of this town for tonight." Maria pushed at the attorney, who stood quickly. "I don't care who you've got in your backwater little corner of the world, we're going to—"

Lexi put a hand on Maria's shoulder to silence her. "The less said tonight, the better. We have a court date next week." She gave Julia a curt nod. "Ms. Morgan, we'll see you then."

"Take care of the check, Lexi." Maria Johnson barked the order at her attorney before stalking out of the restaurant.

"Does that mean she's leaving Brevia?" Julia asked.

"For now. I'll stay for the duration of the process. The Johnsons will fly back and forth." Lexi leaned toward Julia. "I don't want to get your hopes up, but a stable home environment could change the situation." She clapped a hand over her mouth as if she'd said too much, then nodded to the group and scurried away.

Julia reached forward to hug Joe. "Thank you, Mr. Callahan. For what you said."

"I meant it. Sam isn't going to let anything happen to you."

Sam.

Julia turned, but focused her attention on the badge pinned to Sam's beige shirt, unable to make eye contact with him. Instead she looked out at the tables surrounding them. "Sorry for the commotion. Go back to dinner, and we'll get out of your way."

"Wait a minute." Sam's voice cut through the quiet.

Julia held her breath.

"As most of you heard tonight, Julia and I have something to celebrate." He grabbed her hand and drew her back to him. Her fingers spread across his broad chest of their own accord. "We need to make this believable for the gossip mill," he whispered against her ear.

A round of applause rang out in the restaurant followed by several clinks on glasses. "Kiss. Kiss. Kiss," came the call from the bar.

Julia froze as Sam gazed down at her, his expression heated. "Better give them what they want."

"It's totally unbelievable and I had garlic for dinner," she muttered, squirming in his arms.

"I'll take my chances," he answered with a laugh.

"Have it your way." Cheeks burning, she raised her head and pressed her mouth to his, a chaste peck fit for the balcony at Buckingham Palace. When she would have ended the kiss, Sam caught hold of her neck and dipped her low. She let out a startled gasp and he slid his tongue against the seam of her lips. Ever so gently he molded his mouth to hers.

A fire sparked low in her belly as she breathed in the scent of him, warm and woodsy and completely male. Lost in her reaction, her arms wound around his neck and her fingers played in the short hair along his collar. She heard his sharp intake of breath and suddenly he righted them both to a chorus of catcalls and stomping feet.

"That's what I'm talking about," someone yelled.

"Okay, folks." Sam's gaze swept across the restaurant and he smiled broadly. "Show's over. I'm going to see my lovely bride-to-be home."

Julia pressed her fingers to her lips and looked at Sam. The smile didn't reach his eyes.

When she turned, Joe watched her. "You're a breath of fresh air if I ever saw one," he said and gave her trembling hand a squeeze.

She led the group into the night but not before she noticed several members of the ladies' auxiliary huddled in the corner. They'd have a field day with this one. The salon would be buzzing with the news by morning. Her chest tightened as she felt Sam behind her, frustration pouring off him like a late-winter rainstorm. Maybe he'd already come to regret his stupid proposal.

This entire situation was his fault. She'd told him she didn't need a hero, and that was the truth.

Still, his announcement had rattled Maria Johnson and her attorney. She couldn't figure out how a fake engagement would benefit Sam, but he wasn't her problem.

Charlie was Julia's only priority. She'd do anything for her son.

Right now she needed time to think, to figure out how to make this bizarre predicament work in her favor. "It's been a long day, boys," she said quickly. "Joe, it was nice to meet you. How long will you be—"

"We need to talk," Sam interrupted, gripping her arm when she tried to break away.

"I thought I'd be around for a while. Give my boy some lessons in tapping into his feelings, finding his passion and all that." Joe gave Sam a hearty thump on the back. "After that little display, I think he may have wised up on his own. You're good for him, Julia. Real good."

Sam's hold on her loosened. He studied his father. "You mean one kiss convinced you I can do without a dose of your emotional mumbo jumbo?"

Julia swatted his arm. "That's your father. Show some respect."

Sam shot her a withering look. "I'll remember that the next time your mom's around."

Joe laughed and wrapped them in another hug. "Not just any kiss. It's different when you kiss *the one*. Trust me, I know. I bet they could see the sparks flying between the two of you clear down to the coast."

Looking into Joe's trusting face, she couldn't let Sam's father pin his hopes on her. She had to tell him the truth.

"Mr. Callahan, I don't—"

"You're right, Dad," Sam agreed. "It's different with Julia. I'm different, and I don't want you to worry about me anymore." He pinched the tip of Julia's nose, a little harder than necessary if you asked her.

"Ouch."

"Such a delicate flower." He laughed and dropped a quick kiss on her forehead. "What would I do without you?"

"Troll for women over in Charlotte?" she offered.

"See why I need her by my side?"

Joe nodded. "I do."

Sam turned to Julia and rubbed his warm hands down her arms. "Where are you parked?"

Julia pointed to the blue Jetta a few spaces down from where they stood, her mind still reeling.

"Perfect. I'm going to walk Dad back to the hotel and we'll talk tomorrow."

She didn't like the look in his eye. "I'm kind of busy at the salon tomorrow."

"Never too busy for your one true love."

Julia stifled the urge to gag. "I guess not."

"Get going, then, sugar." He pinched her bottom, making her yelp. She rounded on him but, at the calculating gleam in his eye, turned back toward her car. Sam and his dad watched until she'd pulled out.

Despite this peculiar evening, his announcement had served its purpose. Lexi Preston had said having Sam in the picture might change things. That could be the understatement of the year, but if it kept Charlie safe, Julia would make it work.

No matter what.

* * *

Sam took a fortifying drink of coffee and watched as another woman walked through the door of The Best Little Hairhouse. He knew Julia had worked at the salon since her return to Brevia two years ago, but that wasn't why he avoided this place like the plague. It was too girlie for him. The bottles of hair product and little rows of nail polish on the shelves gave him the heebie-jeebies.

The one time he'd ventured into the Hairhouse, after the owner had reported a man lurking in the back alley, he'd felt like a prize steer come up for auction.

He adjusted the brim of his hat, buttoned his jacket against the late-morning rain and started across the street. He'd put the visit off until almost lunchtime, irritated with himself at how much he wanted to see Julia again. Part of him wanted to blame her for making him crazy, but another piece, the part he tried to ignore, wanted to get close enough to her to smell the scent of sunshine on her hair.

He scrubbed a hand across his face. Sunshine on her hair? What the hell was that about? Women didn't smell like sunshine. She worked at a salon and probably had a ton of gunk in her hair at any given moment. Although the way the strands had felt soft on his fingers when he'd bent to kiss her last night told another story.

One he wasn't interested in reading. Or so he told himself.

Sam opened the front door and heard a blood-curdling scream from behind the wall at the reception desk. He jerked to attention. He might not spend a lot of time in beauty salons but could guarantee that sound wasn't typical.

"I'm going to choke the life out of her," a woman yelled, "as soon as my nails dry."

Nope. Something wasn't right.

He glanced at the empty reception desk then stepped through the oversized doorway that led to the main room.

A pack of women huddled around one of the chairs, Julia in the center of the mix.

"Is there a problem here, ladies?"

Seven pairs of eyes, ranging from angry to horrified, turned to him.

"Sam, thank the Lord you're here."

"You would not believe what happened."

"Congrats on your engagement, Chief."

The last comment produced silence from the group. He met Julia's exasperated gaze. "Not a good time," she mouthed and turned back to the center of the cluster, only to be pushed aside by a woman with a black smock draped around her considerable girth. Sam tried not to gape at her head, where the neat curls framing her face glowed an iridescent pink.

"There will be time for celebrating later. I want that woman arrested," Ida Garvey announced. Sam was used to Ida issuing dictatorial commands. She was the wealthiest woman in town, thanks to a generous inheritance from her late husband. Other than the clown hair, she looked like a picture-perfect grandma, albeit one with a sharp tongue and a belief that she ruled the world.

For an instant, he thought she was pointing at Julia. Then he noticed the young woman hunched in the corner, furiously wiping tears from her cheeks.

"Ida, don't be a drama queen." Julia shook her head. "No one is being arrested. Accidents happen. We'll fix it, but—"

"She turned my hair pink!" With a screech, Ida vaulted from the chair and grabbed a curling iron from a stand.

"I'm going to kill her!" Ida lunged toward the cowering woman, but Julia stepped into her path. The curling iron dropped, the barrel landing on Julia's arm before clattering to the floor.

Julia bit out an oath and Ida screamed again. "Look what you made me do," she bellowed at the now-sobbing stylist. "I burned her."

Sam strode forward with a new appreciation for the simplicity of breaking up a drunken bar brawl. Ida looked into his face then staggered back, one hand fluttering to her chest. "Are you gonna arrest me, Chief?"

"Sit down, Mrs. Garvey." He waved at the group of women. "All of you, back off. Now."

Ida plopped back into the chair as the group fell silent again.

Julia winced as he took her arm in his hands. A crimson mark slashed across her wrist, the skin already raised and angry. "Where's a faucet?"

"I'm fine," she said through gritted teeth. "Happens all the time."

"I sure as hell hope not."

"Not exactly like this. I can use the sink in back." She tugged her arm but he didn't let go.

"Don't anyone move," he ordered the women. "That means you, Ida."

"I don't need your help," Julia ground out as he followed her to the back of the salon.

"You aren't leaving me alone with that crowd."

"Not so brave now." Julia fumbled with the tap.

He nudged her out of the way. "I'll do it. Nice ring. I have good taste."

"I had it from… Well, it doesn't matter." Her cheeks flamed as she glanced at the diamond sparkling on her left hand. "I thought I should wear something until we had a chance to figure things out. Fewer questions that way. You know how nosy people are, especially in the salon."

They needed to talk, but Sam couldn't get beyond Julia being hurt, even by a curling iron. "Tell me what happened."

"Crystal, the one in the corner, is our newest stylist. Ida came in without an appointment and she was the only one available. When she went to mix the color, Ida started barking orders. Crystal got so nervous, she mixed it wrong. Instead of a fluffy white cotton ball, Mrs. Garvey's head is now glowing neon pink."

Sam hid a smile as he drew her arm under the faucet and adjusted the temperature. She closed her eyes and sighed as cold water washed over the burn. He drew small circles on her palm, amazed at the softness of her skin under the pad of his thumb.

After a moment he asked, "Do you want to press charges?"

Her eyes flew open, and then she smiled at his expression. "Assault with a deadly styling tool? No, thanks."

Her smile softened the angles of her face, made her beauty less ethereal and more earthy. God help him, he loved earthy.

She must have read something in his eyes because she yanked her hand away and flipped off the water. "I need to get out there before Ida goes after Crystal again."

"Did you hire Crystal?"

"About three weeks ago. She came over from Memphis right out of school to stay with her aunt and needs a break…" She paused, her eyes narrowing. "You think I'm an idiot for hiring a girl with so little experience."

"I didn't say that."

"Everyone thinks Val's a fool to leave me in charge. They're waiting for me to mess up." She wrapped her arms around her waist then flinched when the burn touched her sweater. "And here I am."

Sam knew Val Dupree, the Hairhouse's longtime owner, was planning to retire, and Julia was working to secure a loan to buy the business. She was acting as the salon's manager while Val spent the winter in Florida. "No one expects you to mess up."

"You've been in town long enough to know what people think of me."

The words held no malice, but she said them with a quiet conviction. Sam wanted to take her in his arms to soothe her worry and at the same time shake some sense into her. "Was it a mistake to hire Crystal?"

"No." She looked at him as though she expected an argument. When he offered none she continued, "She's good. Or she will be. I know it."

"Then we'd better make sure Ida Garvey doesn't attack your future star again."

"Right." She led him back into the main salon, where Ida still pinned Crystal to the wall with her angry stare. Everyone else's attention was fixed on Julia and Sam.

Julia glanced over her shoulder. "It's been twenty questions about our relationship all morning."

He nodded. "Let's take on one disaster at a time."

She squared her shoulders and approached Mrs. Garvey, no trace of self-doubt evident. "Ida, I'm sorry." She bent in front of the chair and took the older woman's hands in hers. "I'm going to clear my schedule for the afternoon and make your hair better than before. You'll get three months' worth of free services for your trouble."

Mrs. Garvey patted her pink hair. "That would help."

"Lizzy?" Julia called. A young woman peeked around the doorway from the front of the salon. "Would you re-schedule the rest of my clients? Everyone else, back to work."

"I'm sorry," Crystal said from the corner, taking a step toward Julia.

Ida shifted in the chair. "Don't you come near me."

Sam moved forward but Julia simply patted Ida's fleshy arm. "Take the rest of the day off, Crystal. I'll see you back here in the morning."

"Day off?" Ida screeched. "You're going to fire her, aren't you? Val would have fired her on the spot!"

Color rose in Julia's cheeks but she held her ground. "No, Mrs. Garvey. Crystal made a mistake."

"She's a menace. I knew she was doing it wrong from the start."

"She made a mistake," Julia repeated. "In part because you didn't let her do her job." She looked at Crystal. "Go on, hon. We'll talk in the morning."

"I have half a mind to call Val Dupree this minute and tell her how you're going to run her business into the ground."

"I'd watch what you say right now, Mrs. Garvey." Sam pointed to her hair. "Julia may leave you pink if you're not careful."

"She wouldn't dare." But Ida shut her mouth, chewing furiously on her bottom lip.

"Get comfortable," Julia told her. "We'll be here for a while."

She turned to Sam. "I think your work here is done, Chief."

He leveled a steely look at her. "We're not finished."

"Unless you want to pull up a chair next to Ida we are. The longer that color sits on her hair, the harder time I'll have getting it out."

"You don't play fair."

Her eyes glinted. "I never have."

Chapter 3

Julia rubbed her nose against Charlie's dimpled neck and was rewarded by a soft belly laugh. "Who's my best boy?" she asked and kissed the top of his head.

"Charlie," he answered in his sweet toddler voice.

"Thanks for keeping him today, Lainey." Julia's younger sister and their mother, Vera, took turns watching Charlie on the days when his normal babysitter was unavailable. "Things were crazy today at work."

She couldn't imagine balancing everything without her family's help. Two years ago, Julia's relationship with Lainey had been almost nonexistent. Thanks in large part to Charlie, she now felt a sisterly bond she hadn't realized was missing from her life.

"Crazy, how?" Lainey asked from where she stirred a pot of soup at the stove.

"Ida Garvey ended up with hair so pink it looked like cotton candy."

Lainey's mouth dropped open.

"She freaked out, as you can imagine." Charlie scrambled off her lap to play with a toy fire truck on the kitchen floor. "It took the whole afternoon to make it better."

"I thought you meant crazy like telling people about your secret boyfriend and his public proposal." Lainey turned and pointed a wooden spoon at Julia as if it were a weapon. "I can't believe I didn't even know you two were dating."

Julia groaned at the accusation in her sister's tone and the hurt that shadowed her green eyes. When she'd gone along with Sam's fake proposal last night, Julia hadn't thought about the repercussions of people believing them. Thinking things through wasn't her strong suit.

She didn't talk about her years away from Brevia with Lainey or their mother. They had some inkling of her penchant for dating losers and changing cities at the end of each bad relationship. When the going got tough, it had always seemed easier to move on than stick it out.

From the outside, Julia knew she appeared to have it together. She was quick with a sarcastic retort that made people believe life's little setbacks didn't affect her. She'd painted herself as the free spirit who wouldn't be tied to anyone or any place.

But her devil-may-care mask hid a deeply rooted insecurity that, if someone really got to know her, she wouldn't measure up. Because of her learning disabilities and in so many other ways.

Her struggles to read and process numbers at the most basic level had defined who she was for years. The shame she felt, as a result, was part of the very fiber of her being. She'd been labeled stupid and lazy, and despite what anyone told her to the contrary, she couldn't shake the belief that it was true.

Maybe that was why she picked men who were obviously bad bets. Maybe that was why she'd been a mean girl in high school—to keep people at arm's length so she wouldn't have a chance of being rejected.

She wondered for a moment how it would feel to confide the entire complicated situation to Lainey. For one person to truly understand her problem. She ached to lean in for support as fear weighed on her heart. But as much as they'd worked to repair their fractured relationship, Julia still couldn't tell her sister how scared she was of failing at what meant the most to her in life: being a mother to Charlie.

"I'm sorry. I didn't mean for half the town to find out at Carl's." No one in her family even knew about Jeff's interest in a new custody arrangement.

She stood, trying to come up with a plausible reason she wouldn't have shared big boyfriend news. "My track record with guys is common knowledge, and I didn't want Sam to have people beating down his door to warn him away from me."

Lainey's gaze turned sympathetic. "Oh, Jules. When Ethan and I first got back together I didn't want anyone to know, either. I felt like the town would hold my past mistakes against me and you were back and… Never mind now. I'm going to forgive you because it's so wonderful." She threw her arms around Julia. "Everyone loves Sam, so…" Lainey's voice trailed off.

Julia's stomach turned with frustration. "So, what? By default people are suddenly going to open their arms to me?"

Lainey shrugged. "It can't hurt. Do you have a date?"

"For what?"

Lainey pushed away. "The wedding, silly. You'll get married in Brevia, right?"

Julia blinked. "I suppose so. We're taking the planning slowly. I want a long engagement. It'll be better for Charlie."

"Sure." Lainey frowned but went back to the stove.

"Just enjoying each other and all that," Julia added quickly, guilt building with every lie she told. "So in love. You know."

"I want to be involved in the planning."

"Of course. We can have a girls' day out to look for dresses and stuff." With each detail, the difficulty of deceiving her family became more apparent.

She reminded herself that it was only for a short time, and she was protecting everyone from the stress of the custody fight. "I should go. Thanks to the commotion today, I'm late on the product order I should have sent. If Charlie goes down early enough, I'll be able to get it in tomorrow morning. A night full of numbers, lucky me."

"Do you want some help?"

Julia tensed. "I can handle it. I'm not a total idiot, despite rumors to the contrary." She saw hurt flash again in her sister's gaze and regretted her defensive tone.

She did most of the paperwork for the salon when Charlie went to bed to minimize her hours away from him. She spent many late nights pouring over the accounts and payroll information, terrified she'd make a mistake or miss an important detail. She was determined no one would ever see how unqualified she was to run her own business.

"No one thinks you're an idiot," Lainey said quietly. "You're doing an amazing job with the salon, but I know how things get when you're tired. I'm offering another set of eyes if you need them."

"I'm sorry I snapped." Julia rubbed two fingers against each temple, trying to ward off an impending headache. "I'll take it slow. It's routine paperwork, not splitting the atom."

"Could you delegate some of this to the receptionist or one of the part-time girls? Why does it all have to fall on you? If you'd only tell them—"

"They can't know. No one can. What if Val found out? The deal isn't final. She could change her mind about selling to me."

"She wouldn't do that," Lainey argued.

"Someone could take advantage, mix things up without me understanding until it's too late." Julia gathered Charlie's sippy cup and extra snacks into the diaper bag.

Lainey shook her head, frustration evident as she fisted her hands at her sides. "Learning disabilities don't make you stupid, Julia. When are you going to realize that? Your brain processes information differently. It has nothing to do with your IQ, and you have the best intuition of anyone I know. No one could take advantage of you—"

"Have you seen my list of ex-boyfriends?"

"—without you letting them," Lainey finished.

"Point taken." Even as much as Julia had wanted her relationship with Jeff to work out, she should have known it was doomed. He'd been the opposite of most guys she'd dated, and she should have known someone so academic and cultured wouldn't truly want her. They'd gone to museums and gallery openings, his interest in her giving her hope that someone would finally see her for more than a pretty face.

She'd craved his approval and made the mistake of sharing her secret with him. None of the men before him had known about the severe learning disabilities that had plagued her since grade school. She'd managed for years to keep her LD hidden from almost everyone.

Only her family and certain trusted teachers had known the struggles she'd faced in learning to read and process both words and numbers. She wasn't sure any of them understood how deep her problems were. The embarrassment and frustrations she'd felt as a kid had prevented her from letting teachers, interventionists or even her parents truly help her.

It had been easier to play the part of being too cool for school or, as she got older, not wanting to be tied down to a real job or responsibilities. Only for Charlie was she finally willing to put her best effort forward, constantly worried it wouldn't be enough.

"Are you still working with the literacy specialist?"

"Every week. It's a slow process, though. Between my visual and auditory learning deficiencies, I feel like a lost cause. Sometimes I wonder if it's even worth it."

"It's worth it," Lainey said as she lifted Charlie from the floor and gave him a hug before depositing him into Julia's arms. "LD is complex and I'm proud of you for everything you've accomplished despite it. I'm here if you need me. Ethan and Mom can take Charlie, so—"

"Mom's back?" Julia swallowed. She'd assumed her sister hadn't heard about the engagement. But their mother had her finger on the pulse of every snippet of gossip from Brevia to the state line. "She wasn't scheduled back until next week." Long enough for Julia to get a handle on her mess of a life.

"She flew in this morning. I can help contain her,

you know. You'll need reinforcements for damage control on that front."

Julia stopped in her tracks. Even though she'd worried about her mother finding out, hearing Lainey say it made her knees quiver the tiniest bit. "Mom knows? I thought she just got back."

"She knows," Lainey answered with an eye roll. "I think she's waiting for you to call and explain yourself."

Another layer of dread curled in the pit of Julia's stomach. Her mother would support her. Vera was a big part of Charlie's life and would fight tooth and nail to protect him. But she understood Julia's limitations better than anyone. Julia didn't want to know if her mom had any doubts about her ability to give Charlie a good life on her own.

Now was the time to come clean, but with Charlie in her arms, she couldn't bring herself to voice her fears. It might make them too real.

"I'll call her. She'll understand. I'll make her understand."

Lainey only smiled. "Good luck."

Julia needed a lot more than luck.

She tried to ignore the persistent knocking at her apartment door later that night. She hadn't called her mother and silently debated whether Vera would make the twenty-minute drive to Julia's apartment to rake her over the coals in person.

But Charlie had just fallen asleep after six verses of "The Wheels on the Bus," and Julia wasn't going to risk the noise waking him, so she opened the door, prepared for the mother–daughter smackdown of the century.

Sam stood in the hallway watching her.

Even better.

"Long day, Chief. I'll call you tomorrow." She tried to close the door but he shoved his foot into the opening. Blast those steel-toed boots.

He held up a white cardboard box and a six-pack of beer. "It's been a long day for both of us. We eat first and then dig ourselves out of this mess."

She sniffed the air. "Pepperoni?"

"With extra cheese."

She took a step back and he eased around her into the tiny apartment. It actually didn't feel so small with just her and Charlie in it. Somehow, Sam not only filled the room but used more than his fair share of the oxygen in it. Julia drew a shaky breath and led the way to the small dining area.

"Sorry," she apologized automatically as she picked macaroni noodles from the maple tabletop. "Charlie's been practicing his QB skills at mealtime."

"Nothing wrong with starting early. Where's the little guy?"

"Asleep. Finally."

Sam put the box on the table and handed her a beer as he cocked his head. "Is that classical music?"

"Beethoven."

"Sounds different than I remember. More animated."

She picked up a remote and pointed it at the television on the other side of the room. "It's a Junior Genius DVD."

"Come again?"

"A program designed to increase a young child's brain activity." She clicked off the television. "They have research to show that it works."

His brows rose. "I still hear music."

She felt color creep into her cheeks. "I play a Mozart disc as he falls asleep." She walked past him to the kitchen and pulled two plates from a cabinet.

"Are you a classical-music fan?"

She spun around and stalked back to the table. "Why? Do you think classical is too highbrow for someone like me? Would it make more sense if I was a Toby Keith groupie?"

He took a step back and studied her. "First off, don't hate on Toby Keith. Secondly, it was a question." He waved one hand in the direction of the bookcases that flanked the television. "You have more classical CDs on your shelves than I've seen in my entire life. It's a logical assumption."

"Sorry." She sighed. "I like some composers but it's mainly for Charlie. I figure he needs all the help he can get, living with me. You may have heard I'm not the sharpest knife in the drawer."

"Is that so?"

"It's a well-known fact in town. My mom will tell you I have 'street smarts.'" She met his gaze with a wry smile. "I'm sure any number of my former friends would be happy to tell you how I skated through school by charming teachers or bullying other students into helping me." She broke off as Sam watched her, worrying that she'd somehow given him a clue into her defective inner self. She plastered on a saucy smile and stretched up her arms in an exaggerated pose. "At that point my life's ambition was to be a supermodel."

"Personally, I wanted to be Eddie Van Halen." He shrugged. "Were you really a bully?"

"I like to remember it as a benevolent dictatorship. I had my reasons, but have discovered that the kids I ordered around back in the day have become adults who are more than happy to see the golden girl taken down a few pegs." She opened the pizza box and pulled out a slice, embarrassed at her silly adolescent dream. "I was the ring leader and the 'pretty one' in Brevia, but couldn't cut it in the big leagues."

"You started over. There's nothing wrong with that. People do it all the time."

"Right. I went to beauty school, dated a string of losers, partied too much and tried to live below my potential." She tipped her beer in a mock toast. "And that's pretty low."

"Somebody did a number on you, sweetheart. Because the way you handled that mess at the salon today took some clever negotiation skills. Not the work of a fool."

"We'll see what Val thinks once Ida spins it." She slid a piece of pizza onto his plate. "Sit down and eat. Unless the pizza was a ruse to get in the door so you could rip my head off without the neighbors hearing. Might be easier than going through with your *grand proposal*."

His knee brushed against her bare leg as he folded himself into the chair across from her. It occurred to Julia that she was wearing only boxer shorts and a faded Red Hot Chili Peppers T-shirt with no bra. Bad choice for tonight.

"Such violent thoughts," he said, sprinkling a packet of cheese flakes on his pizza.

She sat back and crossed her arms over her chest. As soon as she'd realized she was braless, her nipples had sprung to attention as if to yell "over here, look at us." Not something she wanted Sam to notice in a million years.

"Why did you do it? This crazy situation is your fault."

He frowned. "You weren't exactly convincing as the

levelheaded, responsible parent. You were about to dive across the table and take out the grandma."

"She deserved it." Julia popped out of her chair and grabbed a fleece sweatshirt from a hook near the hallway, trying not to let her belly show as she pulled it over her head. "But I didn't need to be rescued. Especially not by Three Strikes Sam." She sat back in her chair and picked up the pizza. "We're quite a pair. Do you really think anyone is going to believe you're engaged, given your reputation?"

"What reputation, and who is Three Strikes Sam?"

She finished her bite. "You don't know? Brevia is a small town. But we've got more than our share of single ladies. Apparently the long line of women you've dated since you arrived has banded together. The story is that you don't go on more than three dates with one woman. You've got your own fan club here in town. The ladies blog, tweet and keep track of you on Facebook. They call you Three Strikes Sam."

Sam felt as though he'd been kneed in the family jewels. Never mind the social-media insanity, what shocked him more was that Julia acted as if she knew the details of his dating history. That possibility was fright-night scary.

"You're making it up."

"I'm not that creative. You can log on to my computer and see for yourself. I only found out a couple of weeks ago, when Jean Hawkins was in the salon."

Sam swallowed hard. Jean was the dispatcher for the county sheriff's office. They'd had a couple of casual dinners last month but had agreed not to take it further. Or so he'd thought.

"She got a blowout and a bang trim. A 'wash that man right out of her hair' afternoon." Julia wrinkled her pert nose. "You know how it is—stylists are like therapists for some people. Get a woman in the chair and she has to spill her secrets."

"And *she* told you about this fan club?"

Julia nodded and took a drink of beer. "Three seems to be the magic number for you. You're a serial get-to-know-you dater."

Sam pushed away from the table and paced to the end of the narrow living room. "That's ridiculous." He ran a hand through his hair. "There's no arbitrary limit on the number of dates I'll go on with one woman."

"A dozen ladies claim there is," she countered. "They say you've more than made the rounds."

"I haven't dated a *dozen* ladies in Brevia. Besides, why would anyone gossip about dating me?"

"You've been in Brevia long enough to know how it works." She laughed, but he found no humor in the situation. Sure, he'd been on dates with a few different women. When he'd first come to town, it had sort of happened that way. He'd always been a gentleman. If things led to the bedroom he didn't complain, but he also didn't push it. No one had grumbled at the time.

He wasn't a serial dater. The way she said it made him sound like a scumbag. So what if he was a little gun-shy? Walking in on your fiancée with her legs wrapped around another guy would do that to a man. It had been almost three years now since he'd had his heart crushed, and he wasn't itching to repeat that particular form of hell. "You're telling me I'm a joke with these women because I'm not in a relationship?" His voice started to rise. "In case they haven't noticed, I have a serious job. One that's more important to me than my damned social life."

"It's not like that," she said quickly, reaching out to

place her cool fingers on his arm. A light touch that was oddly comforting. "No one is laughing at you. It's more like a challenge. Scary as it may sound, you have a town full of women who are determined to see you settle down. According to my sources, you're quite the catch."

He dropped back into the chair. "I came to Brevia because I wanted a fresh start."

"As Mick Jagger would say, 'you can't always get what you want.'"

"You think this fake engagement is what I need?"

"It was your idea to start. Plus, it's quieted the gossips, and your dad seemed to approve."

He nodded and took a long drink of beer. "My father loved you."

"Who can blame him?" she asked with a hair toss.

Sam smiled despite himself. "He wants to help me tap into my emotions."

She studied him as she took another bite. "Is that so bad?"

"I don't need to be more emotional."

"Your fans beg to differ."

"Don't remind me," he muttered.

A tiny cry came from the corner of the table and Julia adjusted a baby monitor. "I'm going to check on him." She padded down the hall, leaving Sam alone with his thoughts. Something he didn't need right now.

He preferred his emotions tightly bottled. It wasn't as if he didn't have feelings. Hell, he'd felt awful after calling off his engagement. He would have made a decent husband: loyal, faithful...

Maybe those were better attributes in a family pet, but he managed okay.

In Sam's opinion, there was no use wearing his heart

on his sleeve. The scraps of memory he had from the months after his mother died were awful, his dad too often passed out drunk on the couch. Neighbors shuttling Sam and his brother to school and a steady diet of peanut butter and jelly sandwiches. When Joe finally got a handle on his emotions, it had saved their family.

Sam would never risk caring for someone like that. Feeling too much, connecting to the feelings he'd locked up tight, might spiral him back into that uncontrolled chaos.

He looked around the apartment, taking in more details with Julia out of the room. The dining area opened directly onto the living room, which was filled with comfortable, oversized furniture covered in a creamy fabric. Several fuzzy blankets fell over the arm of one chair. A wicker box overflowed with various toys, most of which looked far more complex than he remembered from childhood.

In addition to the classical CDs, framed pictures of Charlie with Julia, Vera, Lainey and Ethan sat on the bookshelves. Sam had also noticed an impressive collection of books—several classics by Hemingway, Dickens, even Ayn Rand. For someone who clearly didn't see her own intelligence, Julia had sophisticated taste in reading material.

The baby monitor crackled, drawing his attention. He heard Julia's voice through the static. "Did you have a dream, Charlie-boy?" she cooed. "Can Mommy sing you back to sleep?"

Charlie gave another sleepy cry as an answer and a moment later Sam heard a familiar James Taylor song in a soft soprano.

He smiled as he listened to Julia sing. Classical for Charlie, Sweet Baby James for his mother.

Sam felt a thread of unfamiliar connection fill his heart. At the same time there was a release of pressure he hadn't realized he'd held. In the quiet of the moment, listening to her sweet and slightly off-key voice, the day's stress slipped away. He took a deep breath as his shoulders relaxed.

"I love you, sweetie," he heard her whisper, her tone so full of tenderness it made his heart ache all the more.

He understood in an instant how much it meant for Julia to keep her son. Knew that she'd do anything to keep Charlie safe.

Suddenly Sam wanted that for her more than he cared about his own future. But he was a man who'd made it through life taking care of himself, protecting number one at all costs. No matter how he felt about one spirited single mother, he couldn't afford to change that now.

Hearing footsteps, he quickly stood to clear the dishes from the table.

"I think he's back down," she said as she came into the kitchen.

Sam rounded on her, needing to get to the crux of the matter before he completely lost control. "You're right," he told her. "This deal was my idea and I'll play the part of doting fiancé because it helps us both."

"Doting may be pushing it," she said, fumbling with the pizza box, clearly wary of his change in mood. "We don't need to go overboard."

He propped one hip on the counter. "We need to make it believable." He kept his tone all business. "Whatever it takes."

"Fine. We'll make people believe we're totally in love.

I'm in. Whatever it takes to convince Jeff to drop the custody suit."

"Will he?"

"He still hasn't even seen Charlie. I get the impression his parents are pushing for the new custody deal. The attorney is really here to figure out if they have a viable case or not before they go public. Jeff didn't want kids in the first place. He'd even talked about getting the big snip. They probably think Charlie is their only shot at a grandchild, someone to mold and shape in their likeness."

"I don't think that's how kids work."

She shook her head. "I don't think they care. If we can convince Lexi that Charlie has a happy, stable home and that he's better off here than with Jeff and his family, that's the report she'll give to them. It will be enough. It has to. Once I get the custody agreement—"

"You'll dump my sorry butt," Sam supplied.

"Or you can break it off with me." She rinsed a plate and put it into the dishwasher. "People will expect it. You're up for reappointment soon. It should earn extra points with some of the council members. Everyone around here knows I'm a bad bet."

"I thought you and Ethan had been the town's golden couple back in the day."

"He was the golden boy," she corrected. "I was the eye candy on his arm. But I messed that up. My first in a series of epic fails in the relationship department."

"Does it bother you that he's with Lainey?" Sam asked, not willing to admit how much her answer meant to him.

She smiled. "They're perfect together in a way he and I never were. She completes him and all that."

"Do you think there's someone out there who'd complete you?"

"Absolutely." She nodded. "At this moment, he's drooling in the crib at the end of the hall."

He took a step closer to her and tucked a lock of hair behind her ear. "We're going to make sure he stays there."

Her lips parted as she looked up at him. Instinctively he eased toward her.

She blinked and raised her hands to his chest, almost pushing him away but not quite. "We have to establish some ground rules," she said, sounding as breathless as he felt.

"I'm the law around these parts, ma'am," he said in his best Southern drawl. "I make the rules."

"Nice try." She laughed and a thrill ran through him. "First off, no touching or kissing of any kind."

It was his turn to throw back his head and laugh. "We're supposed to be in love. You think people will believe you could keep your hands off me?"

She smacked his chest lightly. "I'm surprised your ego made it through the front door. Okay, if the situation calls for it you can kiss me. A little." Her eyes narrowed. "But no tongue."

He tried to keep a straight face. "Where's the fun in that?"

"My best offer," she whispered.

He traced her lips with the tip of one finger and felt himself grow heavy when they parted again. "I think we'd better practice to see if I'll be able to manage it."

He leaned in, but instead of claiming her mouth he tilted his head to reach the smooth column of her neck. He trailed delicate kisses up to her ear and was rewarded with a soft moan. Pushing her hair back, he cradled her face between his palms.

Her breath tingled against his skin and she looked at him, desire and self-control warring in the depths of her eyes. He wanted to keep this arrangement business but couldn't stop his overwhelming need. As out of control as a runaway train, he captured her lips with his.

Chapter 4

It should be illegal for a kiss to feel so good. The thought registered in Julia's dizzy brain. Followed quickly by her body's silent demand for more…more…more. Her arms wound around Sam's neck and she pressed into him, the heat from his body stoking a fire deep within her. His mouth melded to hers as he drew his hands up underneath her shirt.

A man hadn't kissed her like this in so long. As though he meant it, his mouth a promise of so much more.

A familiar voice cut through her lust-filled haze. "So, the rumors are true. Doesn't seem right your mother should be the last to know."

Sam's eyes flew open as he stepped away from her. Julia let out a soft groan.

"Ever think of knocking?" she asked, pressing her hands over her eyes.

"No" was her mother's succinct answer.

"Nice to see you, Mrs. Morgan." Although Sam's voice sounded a little shaky, Julia had to admire his courage in holding her mother's gaze.

Almost unwillingly, Julia turned and met her mom's steely glare. "I'm sorry, Mom. We wanted to keep things quiet a bit longer."

Vera Morgan was a tiny blonde dynamo of a woman. Her hair pulled back into a neat bun, she retained the beauty of her youth mixed with the maturity of decades spent overseeing her life and everyone in it. She crossed her arms over her chest. "Until you could announce your engagement in the middle of a crowded restaurant?"

Julia cringed. "Not the exact plan."

"I don't understand what this is about. It sounds like one of your typical impetuous decisions. Your father and I raised you to be more careful with how you act. I thought you'd have learned to be more responsible about the choices you make. Have you thought of Charlie? What's best for him?"

"He's all I think about and of course I want what's best for him. You have no idea…" Julia wanted to lay it all on the line for her mother—Jeff's family, the attorney, her fear of losing Charlie. She paused and glanced at Sam. He nodded slightly as if to encourage her.

How could she admit her years of bad choices could jeopardize Charlie's future? She knew her mother thought she was irresponsible, fickle and flighty. For most of her life, Julia had been all of those things and worse.

Her mother waited for an answer while the toe of one shoe tapped out a disapproving rhythm. Julia could measure the milestone moments of her life by her mother's slow toe tap. She swore sometimes she could hear it in her sleep.

"I don't expect you to understand, but this is good for Charlie. For both of us."

Vera's gaze slanted between Julia and Sam. "Having the hots for a guy isn't the same as love. From what I just witnessed, you two have chemistry, but marriage is a lot more than physical attraction."

Julia felt a blush rise to her cheeks. "I'm not a teenager anymore," she mumbled. "I get that."

"I worry about you rushing into something." Vera paused and pinned Sam with a look before continuing. "Especially with a man who has a reputation around town. I don't want you to be hurt."

"I know what I'm doing. Trust me. For once trust that I'm making the right decision." She hated that her voice cracked. She'd made some stupid choices in her life. So what? Lots of people did and they lived through it. Did she have to be raked over the coals for every indiscretion?

Sam's hand pressed into the small of her back, surprisingly comforting. "Mrs. Morgan," he began, his voice strong and confident. Julia wished she felt either right now. "Your daughter is the most amazing woman I've ever met."

Julia glanced over her shoulder, for a moment wondering if he was talking about her sister.

The corner of his mouth turned up as he looked at her. "*You* are amazing. You're honest and brave and willing to fight for what you want."

Charlie's sweet face flashed in Julia's mind, and she gave a slight nod.

"You're a lot stronger and smarter than you give yourself credit for." His gaze switched to Vera. "Than most people give her credit for. But that's going to change. I want people to see the woman I do. Maybe we shouldn't have hidden our relationship, but it wasn't anyone's business. To hell with my reputation and Julia's, too."

"I hear a couple town-council members are making a big deal about your single status as they're starting to review your contract. They think only a family man can impart the kind of values and leadership Brevia needs."

"Another reason we were quiet. I don't want to use Julia and Charlie to get reappointed. The job I've done as police chief should be enough."

He sounded so convincing, Julia almost believed him. At the very least, his conviction gave her the courage to stand up for herself a little more. "Sam's right. We're not looking for anyone's approval. This is about us."

"Have you set a date yet?" Vera asked, her tone hard again.

"We're working on that."

Sam cleared his throat. "I'm going to head home." He dropped a quick kiss on Julia's cheek. "I'll talk to you tomorrow."

"Coward," she whispered.

"Sticks and stones," he said softly before turning to Vera.

"Mrs. Morgan, I'm sorry you found out this way. I hope you know I have Julia and Charlie's best interests at heart."

Her mother's eyes narrowed.

"That's my cue." Sam scooted around Vera and let himself out the front door.

"I only want what's best for you." Vera stepped forward. "Your father and I didn't do enough to help you when you were younger. I won't make that mistake again." She wrapped one arm around Julia's waist. "I don't understand how this happened and I don't trust Sam Callahan. But I know Charlie is your number one priority. That's what counts."

Julia didn't want her mother to feel guilty. As a child, she'd tried to hide the extent of her problems from her parents, as well as everyone else. They weren't to blame. She let out a slow breath. "I'm doing this for Charlie."

"You love him?"

"He's my entire life."

"I meant, do you love Sam? Enough to marry him."

"Sam is a wonderful man," Julia answered quickly. "I'd be a fool not to want to marry him." Not exactly a declaration of deep and abiding love but it was as much as she could offer tonight. "I'm sorry you had to come over."

Her mother watched her for several moments before releasing her hold. "You're my daughter. I'll do anything to protect you. You know that, right?"

Julia nodded. Once again, she had the urge to share the whole sordid mess with her mother. She swallowed back her emotions. "It's late. I'll bring Charlie by in the morning before I drop him at the sitter's."

Vera patted her cheek. "Get some sleep. You look like you could use it. You can't keep up this pace. You're no spring chicken."

"Thanks for the reminder." That was the reason Julia wanted to handle this on her own. Vera couldn't help but judge her. It was in her mother's nature to point out all the ways Julia needed improvement. She'd have a field day with the custody situation. Julia had enough trouble without adding her mother's opinion into the mix.

She closed and locked the door behind her mother then

sagged against it. She'd done a lot of reckless things in her life but wondered if this time she'd gone off the deep end.

The baby monitor made a noise. Charlie gave a short cry before silence descended once more. Her gaze caught on a framed photo on one end table, taken minutes after his birth. She'd known as soon as the nurse had placed him in her arms that Charlie was the best part of her. She'd vowed that day to make something of her life, to become worthy of the gift she'd been given. While she had a difficult time tamping down her self-doubt, she never questioned how far she would go to protect her son. She'd do whatever it took to keep him safe, even this ridiculous charade with Sam. If it helped her custody case in the least, Julia would become the most devoted fiancée Brevia had ever seen.

That commitment was put to the test the next morning when a posse of angry women descended on the salon. Two to be exact, but it felt like a mob.

She'd swung by her mother's after breakfast then dropped Charlie with Mavis Donnelly, the older woman who watched him and one other toddler in her home. She'd gotten into town by eight-thirty, thanks to Charlie's propensity to wake with the sun. She wanted time to look over the monthly billing spreadsheets before anyone else arrived.

No one outside her immediate family knew about her condition, and she intended to keep it that way, afraid of being taken advantage of or thought too stupid to handle her own business. She put in the extra time she needed to get each financial piece right. Sometimes she studied the numbers until she felt almost physically ill.

When the knocking started, she straightened from her

desk in the back, assuming it was one of the stylists who'd forgotten her key. Instead the front door swung open to reveal two pairs of angry eyes glaring at her.

"How'd you do it?" Annabeth Sullivan asked, pushing past her into the salon without an invitation. Annabeth had been in the same high-school class as Julia, a girl Julia would have referred to as a "band geek" back in the day. She hadn't been kind, and Annabeth, who now managed the bank reviewing Julia's loan application, hadn't let her forget it. Annabeth's younger sister, Diane, followed her inside.

"Morning to you, ladies."

"He never goes on more than three dates." Annabeth held up three plump fingers. "Never."

"Can I see the ring?" Diane asked, her tone gentler.

Reluctantly, Julia held out her hand. "It's perfect," Diane gushed.

"Kind of small," Annabeth said, peering at it from the corner of one eye. "I figured you'd go for the gaudy flash."

Julia felt her temper flare. "You don't know me, then."

Annabeth took a step closer. "I know you, Julia Morgan. I know you had your minions stuff my locker with Twinkies the first day of freshman year. And made my life hell every day after that. I spent four years trying to stay off your radar and still you'd hunt me down."

The truth of the accusation made Julia cringe. "I'm sorry. I tried to make amends when I came back. I was awful and I'm truly sorry. I offered you free services for a year to try to repay a tiny portion of my debt."

"A year?" Diane turned to her sister. "You never told me that."

"Be quiet, Diane. That doesn't matter now. What I

want to know is how you cast your evil spell over Sam Callahan."

"I'm not a witch. No spells, no magic." She paused then added, "We fell in love. Simple enough. Is there something else you need?" She took a step toward the front door but Annabeth held up a hand.

"Nothing is simple with you. Sam is a good man. He went on three dates with Diane."

"Almost four," Diane added. "I thought I'd made it past the cutoff. But he got called to a fire and had to cancel our last dinner. After that, he told me he wanted to be just friends."

"So, how come you two are all of a sudden engaged when no one even knew you were dating?"

"Even Abby was surprised and she knows *everything* about Sam." Diane clamped a hand over her mouth as Annabeth leveled a scowl at her.

As Julia understood it, Abby Brighton had moved to Brevia to take care of her elderly grandfather. She was the police chief's secretary and dispatcher. She didn't know about Abby's relationship with Sam, but the way Annabeth was looking at her sister, there was more to the story.

"Plus, you're a little long in the tooth for Sam," Annabeth stated, getting back to the business at hand.

Her mom had just said she was no spring chicken and now this. Lucky thing she'd chucked her ego to the curb years ago. "I'm thirty-two, the same age as you, Annabeth. We're not quite over the hill."

Annabeth pulled a small notebook out of her purse. "That's old for Sam. He usually dates women at least four years younger than him."

"And how old is that?"

"Don't you know how old he is?" Diane asked.

Julia met Annabeth's shrewd gaze. Calculated error on her part. "Of course. What I don't understand is why you carry a notebook with Sam's dating stats in it."

Annabeth snapped the notebook shut. "I don't have his dating stats, just a few pertinent facts. He and Diane seemed closer than any of the other women he dated. I want my sister to be happy. She had a chance before you came into the picture."

Julia studied Diane and couldn't begin to picture the dainty woman and Sam as a couple. "Did Sam break your heart?"

Diane scrunched up her nose. "No," she admitted after a moment. "Don't get me wrong, he's supercute and such a gentleman. But he's a little um…big…for me."

Julia's mouth dropped open. "Big?"

"Not like that," Diane amended. "He's just…with the uniform, all those muscles and he's so tall. It's kind of intimidating."

"I know what you mean," Julia agreed, although Sam's size appealed to her. She was five-nine, so it took a lot of guy to make Julia feel petite, but Sam did it in a way that also made her feel safe.

"You have real feelings for him." Annabeth interrupted her musings.

"I… We're engaged. I'd better have real feelings."

"Frankly, I thought this was another one of your stunts to show up the other single women in town. Prove that you're still the leader of the pack and all that." She glanced at Diane. "I didn't want my sister to fall prey to you the way I did."

"I'm *not* the same person I was. I can apologize but you'll need to choose whether to forgive me. I don't blame you if the answer is no, but it's your decision. My priority is Charlie. I want to live a life that will make him proud. I don't intend to re-create the past. You're married now, right?"

The other woman nodded. "Five years to my college sweetheart. He's my best friend."

"Why is it so strange to believe that I might want that for myself? My parents had a great marriage and you probably remember my sister recently married the love of her life, who just happened to be *my* high-school sweetheart. They're happy and I want to be happy. Last time I checked, that wasn't a crime in this town."

Julia pointed a finger at Diane. "If your sister wants to find a man, she will without you hunting down potential suitors for her or tallying lists of how far ahead of other women she is in the dating pool. Sam is a real person, too. I don't think he intended to become such a hot topic of gossip. He's living his life the best way he can. We both are." She stopped for breath and noticed Annabeth and Diane staring at her, eyebrows raised.

She realized how much she'd revealed with her little tirade and tried to calm her panic. Maybe she didn't want to be known as the town's head mean girl anymore, but she had a reputation to protect. She made people think she didn't take things seriously so that they'd never notice when she got hurt. She plastered a smile on her face. "What? Was that a little too mama grizzly for you?"

Annabeth shook her head, looking dazed. "I didn't realize that's how you felt about things. Sam is lucky to have you."

"I'm not sure—"

"I'm sure."

The three women turned to see Sam standing in the doorway. Julia's face burned. "How much did you hear?"

"Enough to know that I agree with Annabeth. I'm damned lucky to have you."

Annabeth and Diane scooted toward the front door. "If you'll excuse us. We'll leave you two alone."

He didn't move. "Is this going to hit the gossip train or however it works?"

Diane shook her head. "We weren't the ones who started analyzing you. It was—"

Annabeth gave her sister a hard pinch on the arm. "It doesn't matter anymore. It's clear you're not the person everyone thought."

Sam eased to the side of the doorway. "I think that could be said for more than just me."

Annabeth threw a glance at Julia and nodded.

"Maybe you should spread that news around."

"I'll get on it, Chief." The two women hurried out of the salon, and Sam pulled the door shut behind them.

"I'm a real man?" he said, repeating Julia's earlier comment. "I'm glad you think so, Ms. Morgan."

Julia slumped into a chair, breathing as if she'd just finished a marathon run. Her eyes were bleak as they met his. "It's pointless, Sam. This is never going to work."

Chapter 5

Sam stared at Julia. Her blond hair curled around her shoulders and fell forward, covering one high cheekbone. His fingers itched to smooth it back from her face, to touch her skin and wipe the pain from those large gray eyes. She looked so alone sitting in the oversized stylist's chair.

Sam knew what it felt like to be alone. Hell, he'd courted solitude for most of his life. He'd learned early on only to depend on himself, because when he relied on other people for his happiness he got hurt. First when his mother died and his dad had almost lost it. Then, later, in the relationship that had ended with his fiancée cheating on him.

He'd come to believe that happiness was overrated. He wanted to work hard and make a difference—the only way he knew to chase the demons away for a little peace.

When he'd heard Julia defending his character, something tight in his gut unwound. He was used to making things happen and having people depend on him. He prided himself on not needing anyone. It bothered him to know that women were spreading rumors about him, but he would have soldiered through with his head held high. Hearing Julia take on those ladies had made him realize he liked not feeling totally alone.

Her declaration that they couldn't make it work made no sense. "Why the change of heart?" He moved closer to her. "You convinced Annabeth and Diane."

"How old are you?"

"Thirty-three."

"Why do you only date younger women?"

He stopped short. "I don't."

"Are you sure? I've heard you average women at least four years younger. I'm thirty-two. My birthday's in two months."

"I don't ask a woman about her age before we go out. If there's a connection, that's what I go on."

"You never asked me out."

"I asked you to marry me," he said, blowing out a frustrated breath. "Doesn't that count?"

She shook her head. "I mean when you first came to town. When you were making the rounds."

"I didn't make the rounds. Besides, you were pregnant."

"I haven't been pregnant for a while."

"Did you want me to ask you out?" The attraction he'd denied since the first time he saw her roared to life again.

She shook her head again. "I'm just curious, like most of the town is now. We've barely spoken to each other in the last two years."

"I thought the idea was that we were keeping the relationship under wraps."

"What's your favorite color?"

"Green," he answered automatically then held up a hand. "What's going on? I don't understand why you think this won't work. You made a believer of Annabeth Sullivan, the town's main gossip funnel."

Julia stood and glanced at her watch. "The girls will start coming in any minute. I don't know, Sam. This is complicated."

"Only if you make it complicated."

"What's my favorite food?"

"How the heck am I supposed to know?"

"If we were in love, you'd know."

Sam thought about his ex-fiancée and tried to conjure a memory of what she'd like to eat. "Salad?" he guessed.

Julia rolled her eyes. "Nobody's favorite food is salad. Mine is lobster bisque."

Sam tapped one finger on the side of his head. "Got it."

"There's more to it than that."

"Come to dinner tonight," he countered.

"Where?"

"My place. Five-thirty. I talked to my dad this morning. He didn't mention delving into my emotions once. Huge progress as far as I'm concerned. He can't wait to spend more time with you."

"That's a bad idea, and I have Charlie."

"The invitation is for both of you." He took her shoulders between his hands. "We're going to make this work, Julia. Bring your list of questions tonight—favorite color, food, movie, whatever."

"There's more to it than—"

"I know but it's going to work." As if by their own

accord, his fingers strayed to her hair and he sifted the golden strands between them. "For both of us."

At the sound of voices in the salon, Julia's back stiffened and her eyes widened a fraction. "You need to go."

"We're engaged," he reminded her. "We want people to see us together."

"Not here."

He wanted to question her but she looked so panicked, he decided to give her a break. "Dinner tonight," he repeated, and as three women emerged from the hallway behind the salon's main room, he bent forward and pressed his lips against hers.

Her sharp intake of breath made him smile. "Lasagna," he whispered against her mouth.

"What?" she said, her voice as dazed as he felt.

"My favorite food is lasagna."

She nodded and he kissed her again. "See you later, sweetheart," he said and pulled back, leaving Julia and the three stylists staring at him.

"Abby, how old are you?" Sam stepped out of his office into the lobby of the police station.

Abby Brighton, who'd started as the receptionist shortly after he'd been hired, looked up from her computer. "I'll be twenty-eight in the fall."

"That's young."

"Not really," she answered. "Maggie Betric is twenty-six and Suzanne over at the courthouse in Jefferson just turned twenty-five."

"Twenty-five?" Sam swallowed. He'd gone out to dinner with both women and had no idea they'd been that much younger than him. When did he become a small-town cradle robber? Jeez. He needed to watch himself.

"Julia's in her thirties, right?" Abby asked.

"Thirty-two."

"When's her birthday?"

"Uh…" Wait, he knew this. "It's in May."

Abby turned her chair around to face him. "I still can't believe I didn't know you two were dating."

"No one knew."

"But I know everything about you." She looked away. "Not everything, of course. But a lot. Because I make the schedule and we work so closely together."

He studied Abby another minute. She was cute, in a girl-next-door sort of way. Her short pixie cut framed a small face, her dark eyes as big as saucers. They'd worked together for almost two years now, and he supposed she did know him better than most people. But what did he know about her? What did he know about anyone, outside his dad and brother?

Sure, Sam had friends, a Friday-night poker game, fishing with the boys. He knew who was married and which guys were confirmed bachelors. Did knowing the kind of beer his buddies drank count as being close?

"Do you have a boyfriend, Abby?"

Her eyes widened farther. "Not at the moment."

"And your only family in town is your granddad?"

She nodded.

Okay, that was good. He knew something about the woman he saw every day at work. He looked around her brightly colored workspace. "I'm guessing your favorite color is yellow."

She smiled. "Yours is hunter green."

How did she know that?

"Does Julia make you happy?" she asked after a moment.

"Yes," he answered automatically. "Why?"

"I just wouldn't have pictured her as your type." Abby fidgeted with a paper clip. "She's beautiful and everything, but I always saw you with someone more…"

"More?"

"Someone nicer, I suppose."

"You don't think Julia's nice? Has she been unkind to you?"

Abby shook her head. "No, but I hear stories from when she was in high school. I'm in a book club with some ladies who knew her then."

"People change."

"You deserve someone who will take care of you."

"I'm a grown man, Abby. I can take care of myself."

"I know but you need—" She stopped midsentence when the phone rang. She answered and, after a moment, cupped her hand over the receiver. "Someone ran into a telephone pole out at the county line. No injuries but a live wire might be down."

Sam nodded and headed for the front door. "Call it in to the utility company. I'm on my way."

He drove toward the edge of town, grateful to get out and clear his head. He'd done more talking about himself and what he needed and felt in the past twenty-four hours than he had in the previous five years. His dad's fault, for sure.

This engagement was supposed to help Sam dodge his father's attempts to make him more in touch with his feelings. Hopefully, this dinner would smooth things over enough so life could return to normal. Other than the pretend engagement.

It wouldn't be as difficult as Julia thought to fool people. They'd hold hands, be seen around town together for a few PDAs and everyone would believe them. Kissing

Julia was one of the perks of this arrangement. He loved her moment of surprise each time he leaned in. Sam hadn't been with a woman for a long time, which must explain why her touch affected him so much.

He understood the importance of making this work. Tonight, they'd come to an understanding of how to get what they both wanted.

Julia lifted Charlie out of his car seat and turned to face the quaint house tucked onto one of the tree-lined streets near downtown Brevia.

"He even has a picket fence," she said to her son, who answered her with a hearty laugh and a slew of indecipherable words.

"My sentiments exactly." She kissed the top of Charlie's head.

"Do you need a hand?"

Joe Callahan stepped off the porch and headed toward her.

"I've got it, Mr. Callahan. Thank you."

He met her halfway up the walk. "Call me Joe. And you—" he held out his hands for Charlie "—can call me Papa."

"Pap-y," Charlie repeated in his singsong voice and leaned forward for Joe to scoop him up. Her son, the extrovert.

"You don't have to do that."

Joe was already swinging Charlie above his head, much to the boy's delight. "What a handsome fellow," he said. He smiled at Julia. "He favors his beautiful mother."

Julia couldn't help but return his grin. "Are you always this charming?"

Joe gave an easy laugh. "For decades I was a real

hard—" He lifted Charlie again. "I was hard-nosed. A walking grim reaper. Sam and his brother got the brunt of that. I've learned a lot since then."

"Wisdom you want to impart to your son?"

"If he'll let me." Joe tucked Charlie into the crook of his arm and the boy shoved his fist into his mouth, sucking contently. "You've already helped him start."

It was Julia's turn to laugh. "I don't have much wisdom to share with anyone."

Joe started toward the house. "Mothers have inherent wisdom. My late wife was the smartest, most insightful woman I've ever met."

"How old was Sam when she died?"

"Ten and Scott was seven. It was a dark period for our family."

"Was it a long illness?"

Joe turned and immediately Julia realized her mistake. "Sam hasn't told you about his mother?"

She shook her head, unable to hide her lack of knowledge. "It's difficult for him to speak about."

Joe sighed as if he understood. "That's my fault. After Lorraine passed, I was so overcome with grief that I shut down and made the boys do the same. Looking back, it was selfish and cowardly. They were kids and they needed me."

Julia patted his arm. "How did she die?"

"A car accident," he said quietly. Charlie rested his small head on Joe's shoulder as if sensing the older man needed comfort.

"How tragic. I'm so sorry for all of you."

"The tragic part was that it was my fault. I'd been on the force over ten years. I became obsessed with being the most dedicated cop Boston had ever seen. Like a bonehead, I took on the most dangerous assignments they'd give me—whatever I could do to prove that I was the baddest dude on the block. Lorraine couldn't handle the stress. She begged me to slow down. I wouldn't listen, brushed aside her worries and only focused on what I wanted."

He ran his hands through his hair, so much like Sam, then continued, "She'd started drinking at night—not so much that she was falling-down drunk, but enough to numb her. I was tuned out and didn't realize how bad it had gotten. I got home late one night and we fought. She went for a drive after the boys were in bed—to cool off. She wasn't even a half mile from the house when she ran the red light. She swerved to avoid another car. Wrapped her car around a telephone pole. She was gone instantly."

Julia sucked in a breath. The first time she'd met Sam had been when he'd found her after she'd hydroplaned on a wet road and gone over an embankment, her car slamming into a tree. She'd been pregnant at the time, and thinking the accident might have hurt her baby had been the scariest moment of her life. Sam had gotten her to the hospital and stayed with her until Lainey had arrived. She wondered if he'd thought about his mother during that time, or if it had just been another day on the job.

"How devastating for all of you." She leaned forward and wrapped her arms around Joe. Charlie squealed with delight then wriggled to be let down.

"Okay." She lifted him from Joe's arms and deposited him on the porch.

Joe swiped at his eyes. "I would have followed her in a minute. I could barely function and had two boys at home who needed me more than ever. Instead, I threw myself into the job like I was tempting fate. If they gave awards for stupidity and selfishness, I would have been a top candidate."

"Nothing can prepare you for something like that. I'm sure you did the best you could. Sam and his brother must know that."

Joe held open the screen door and Charlie headed into the house. "It should have been a wake-up call but it took me another twenty years to get my priorities straight. I want to make it right by Sam."

She looked into Joe Callahan's kind eyes and her stomach twisted. Julia didn't have much luck making things right by anyone, and if Joe knew the details of their arrangement, it would break his heart.

"Mama, come." Charlie peered around the doorway to the kitchen. Charlie. He was the reason she'd entered into this deal in the first place.

"Where's Sam?" She held out her hand to her son, who ran toward her to take it.

Joe smiled. "Grilling out back."

She scooped Charlie into her arms and followed Joe down the hall. She'd guess Sam's house had been built in the early 1900s, and he'd obviously renovated, drawing inspiration from the Craftsman tradition with hardwood floors throughout. In the open kitchen, beautiful maple cabinets hung on each wall. The colors were neutral but not boring, a mix of classic and modern traditions.

Joe led her through one of the French doors that opened to the back patio. It hadn't rained for a couple of days, and while it was cool, the evening air held the unmistakable scent of spring, with the elms and oaks surrounding the green yard beginning to bud.

Sam stood in front of a stainless-steel grill, enveloped in smoke. He turned and smiled at her and her chest caught again. He wore a dark T-shirt, faded jeans and flip-flops. Julia hadn't often seen him out of uniform, and while the casual outfit should have made him less intimidating, certain parts of her body responded differently.

"Ball," Charlie shouted and squirmed in her arms. When Julia put him down, he ran toward an oversized bouncy ball and several plastic trucks stacked near the wrought-iron table.

Sam closed the grill's lid and met her questioning gaze. "I thought he'd like some toys to play with over here."

She nodded, a little dumbfounded at the impact the small gesture had on her.

"Sammy said you two are mainly at your place."

"It's easier that way."

"Have you given any thought to where you'll live once you're married?"

"Here," Sam answered at the same time Julia said, "Not really."

Joe's brows furrowed, so she added, "My apartment is a rental, so I assumed we'd move in with Sam."

Sam came to her side and placed a quick kiss on her forehead. "We're going to make the spare bedroom into Charlie's room."

Julia coughed wildly.

"Can I get you a glass of water?" Sam asked.

"I'll grab it," Joe said and disappeared into the house.

Sam clapped her on the back. "Are you okay?"

"Not at all." She drew in a breath. "Charlie's room?"

"We're engaged, remember. It's going to seem strange enough that the kid barely knows me. I didn't have any of his stuff or toys in the house and my dad started asking questions."

At that moment, the bouncy ball knocked against Julia's leg.

"Ball, Mama. Ball." Charlie squealed with delight.

Sam handed Julia a pair of tongs. "Will you pull the steaks off the grill?" He picked up the ball and tucked it under his arm. "I'm going in for some male bonding."

Julia watched, fascinated as Sam walked over to Charlie and held out a hand. Without hesitation, Charlie took it and Sam led him into the yard to roll the ball back and forth.

The only man in Charlie's life was Ethan. Julia tried not to depend too much on him. Lainey, Ethan and Julia had a long history between them, and Julia didn't want to push the limits of their relationship.

Charlie did his best to mimic Sam's motions as he rolled and threw the ball, and Julia realized how important it was for her son to have a father figure.

"I knew he'd be great with kids," Joe said as he handed her a tall glass of water. "Scott is a wild one, but Sam…"

"Why do you think Sam never married?" Julia asked, tapping one finger against her lips. Annabeth's story about Sam's record as a three-dates-and-done serial dater came back to her.

"It's not for lack of trying," Joe answered candidly then amended. "But I can tell you're a better fit for him than Jenny."

Julia tried not to look startled. "Jenny?"

Joe studied her. "His ex-fiancée. He *did* tell you about her?"

"He was really hurt when it ended," she offered, not an outright lie but enough to cover her lack of knowledge. She and Sam had a lot they needed to get clear about each other if this charade was going to work.

Joe nodded. "Not that he would have told anyone. He bottled up his emotions just like I'd done when his mom passed. But Jenny's infidelity was a huge blow to him."

"I can understand why." Julia's mind reeled at this new information. Sam had been previously engaged and his fiancée had cheated on him. That might explain a little about his commitment issues.

"She wasn't a good match even before that. Sure, she was perfect on paper—a schoolteacher, sweet and popular with his friends, but she didn't get him. They were marrying what they thought they wanted without paying attention to what they needed."

Julia understood that line of thinking better than most. It was what had led her to believe her ex-boyfriend could make her happy. She'd thought she loved Jeff but realized what she loved was the image she'd had of him, not who he truly was. Was that what Sam had thought about his ex, as well, or had this Jenny been the love of his life? The thought gave Julia a sick feeling in the pit of her stomach.

Sam looked up from where he was currently chasing Charlie across the backyard. "How about those steaks, sweetie?"

"I'm on it," she called and headed for the grill.

Much to Joe's delight, Charlie insisted on sitting on Sam's lap during dinner. Sam looked vaguely uncomfortable as the toddler fed him bites of meat but dutifully ate each one.

In addition to the steak, Sam had roasted vegetables and made a salad. She'd brought a loaf of bread from the bakery next to the salon, along with a bottle of red wine. The dinner was surprisingly fun and Julia found herself relaxing. Joe did most of the talking, regaling her with stories, of his years with the force and more recently of the workshops he facilitated around the region.

"Someone needs a diaper change," she said as they finished the meal. At the look of horror on Sam's face, she laughed. "I'll take it from here."

"Good idea," he agreed.

"You'd better get used to stinky bottoms," his father chided.

Sam's eyes widened and Julia laughed again. "All in good time, Joe. For now, I'll take the poop duty."

Sam stood quickly and handed Charlie to her. "I'll clear the dishes." To her surprise, he placed a soft kiss on her mouth. Charlie giggled and Julia felt her world tilt the tiniest bit.

"Right," she said around a gulp of air. She met Joe's gaze as she turned for the house and he winked at her. Right. Sam was her fake fiancé. Of course he was going to kiss her sometimes. They'd discussed that it was all part of the act. It didn't mean anything.

At least, not to her.

Right.

She changed Charlie's diaper on the floor of Sam's living room. Unlike her cozy apartment filled with well-worn flea-market finds and hand-me-downs from her mother, the furnishings in this room appeared very new and hardly used.

A sleek leather couch faced an entertainment center with an enormous flat-screen television and several pieces of stereo equipment. He had a few books scattered on the shelves, mainly fly-fishing manuals and guide-books for the North Carolina mountains. A couple of pieces of abstract art hung on the walls. Unlike her family room, there wasn't a single framed photo of any of Sam's family or friends.

Julia loved the reminders of each stage in Charlie's life on display around her house. It was as though Sam didn't have a personal life. Maybe it was just a guy thing, she thought, but then remembered how Jeff had documented each of his research trips with photos spread around their condo in Columbus.

Maybe not.

She pulled on Charlie's sweatpants and watched as he scrambled to his feet and headed back toward the kitchen.

"Hey, little man, where are you headed in such a rush?"

Joe picked him up as Charlie answered, "Ou-side," and he planted a raspberry on the boy's belly, making him laugh out loud.

"I'll see you later, gator." Joe put Charlie on the ground and he made a beeline for the back of the house.

"It was nice to spend time with you." Julia gave the older man a quick hug.

"I hope it's the first of many dinners. I'd love to meet your family while I'm in town. Sammy said your mom is famous around here for the animal shelter she runs."

"It was a labor of love after my dad died." The thought of Joe Callahan and her mother getting together made her want to squirm. Keeping their respective families separate would make the summer much simpler. The complications of this arrangement were almost more than she could handle.

"I meant what I said at the restaurant," Joe told her. "Sam will protect you and Charlie. I don't know the details of your custody arrangement, but I believe that boy is better off with you than anyone else in the world."

Julia blinked back sudden tears. "Thank you. I better go track him down."

Joe nodded. "Good night, Julia. I'll see you soon."

The front door shut behind him, and Julia thought about Joe's last words. Charlie was better off with her. She had to believe that. He belonged to her and she to him. Nothing and no one was going to change that.

She turned for the kitchen just as Charlie's high-pitched scream came from the backyard.

Chapter 6

Julia raced onto the patio, following the sounds of her son's cries, her heart pounding in her chest.

Sam stood in the backyard, cradling Charlie against his chest with one arm. With his free hand he waved the tongs she'd used for the meat. A large gray dog hopped up and down in front of him.

"What happened?" Julia yelled as she sprinted down the back steps. "Is Charlie hurt?"

At the sound of his mother's voice, the boy lifted his tear-streaked face from Sam's shoulder. "Ball, Mama. No doggy." He pointed a slobbery finger at the Weimaraner running circles in the yard, the deflated bouncy ball clamped in his jaws.

His eyes never leaving the dog, Sam scooted closer to Julia. "Charlie's fine. Take him back to the house. I've never seen this animal before. He could be rabid."

Charlie shook his head. "No doggy," he repeated. "Charlie ball."

Julia looked from her son to Sam to the dog bounding and leaping, his stubby tail wagging, clearly relishing this impromptu game of keep-away. Rabid? Overenthusiastic and in need of some training. Not rabid.

Julia had grown up with a variety of animals underfoot. Her dad had been Brevia's vet for years, and the shelter her mother had built and run after his death attracted animals from all over the South. Her mom's ability to rehabilitate strays was legendary—Vera had even written a dog-behavior book that had become a bestseller a few years ago. Julia might not be the expert her mother was, but she had a fairly good sense for reading canine energy. And every inch of the Weimaraner was shouting "let's play."

"Sam, the dog isn't going to hurt you."

"It bared its teeth. It's a lunatic."

"You've never seen it before?" Julia moved slowly forward.

"No. I told you to get back on the porch. I don't want you or Charlie hurt."

She gave a quick whistle. The dog stopped and looked at her, its tail still wagging.

"Julia, you can't—"

"Drop it," she commanded, her finger pointed to the ground.

"Dop." Charlie mimicked her. "Charlie ball."

The dog waited a moment then lowered the lump of plastic to the ground.

"Sit."

The dog's bottom plopped to the ground.

She held out her palm. "Stay."

She took a step toward the dog. His bottom lifted but she gave a stern "No," and he sank back down.

"I'm sorry about your ball, sweetie," she told Charlie.

"Bad," he said with a whine.

"Not bad, but he needs someone to help him learn."

As she got nearer, the animal trembled with excitement.

"You shouldn't be that close."

"Do you have any rope?"

"I'm not leaving you out here. I'm serious. Back off from the dog."

"What is your problem? This dog isn't a threat."

"You don't know—"

As if sensing that her attention was divided, the dog stood and bounded the few feet toward her. The skin around its mouth drew back and wrinkled, exposing a row of shiny teeth.

"Get back, Julia. It's snarling." Sam lunged forward, but before he got the animal, the dog flopped at Julia's feet and flipped onto his back, writhing in apparent ecstasy as she bent to rub his belly.

Sam stopped in his tracks. "What the...?"

"He's a smiler."

"Dogs don't smile."

"Some do."

Charlie wriggled out of Sam's arms and, before either of them could stop him, headed for the dog. "Good doggy. No ball."

Julia put an arm around Charlie, holding him back, as Sam's breath hitched. "You shouldn't let him so near that thing."

She offered what she hoped was a reassuring smile. "My mom runs an animal shelter, remember? Charlie's been around dogs since he was born. I'm careful to supervise him and make sure he's safe." She tickled her fingers under the dog's ear and got a soft lick on her arm for the effort. "This boy is gorgeous."

"A good-looking animal can still be crazy."

Julia's shoulders stiffened. "What makes you think he's crazy?" Before he'd left for good, Jeff had said something similar to her. He'd told her she was beautiful but a nut job. He'd thrown in a dig about her intelligence as icing on the cake.

Her mother was the expert on stray animals, but Julia knew a thing or two about being damaged on the inside. Her gut told her this dog had a heart of gold.

"He snarled at me."

"He *smiled* at you," she insisted. "Pet him. He's a real sweetie."

"I don't like dogs," Sam said simply.

"I wouldn't have guessed it." She ran her hand along the length of the dog's side. "He's way underweight. No collar and he's dirty. I'd guess he's been on his own for a while now. You haven't seen him around?"

Sam shook his head. "A section of the fenced yard came loose in the storm a few nights ago. He must have smelled the grill and come in that way."

She straightened. "Would you take Charlie for a minute? I have a leash in the trunk of my car."

"You don't have a dog."

"Mom makes everyone keep an extra in case we come across a stray." The Weimaraner jumped to his feet and nudged at Julia's pants leg.

"Mama doggy," Charlie said as Julia shifted him into Sam's arms.

"No, honey, not mine. We'll take him to Grandma in the morning and she'll find a good home for him."

Charlie frowned. "Mama doggy."

Julia noticed Sam tense as the dog trotted over to sniff him. "Are you scared of dogs, Chief Callahan?"

"Wary, not scared." He held Charlie a little higher in his arms.

"If you say so." She headed up the steps toward the house and the dog followed.

"What if he runs away?"

"I have a feeling he'll stick close by. Weims are usually Velcro dogs."

"Are you going to keep him overnight?"

She nodded. "It won't be the first time. Mom says the strays have a knack for finding me. The scrappier they are, the harder I work to bring them in. I've rescued dogs from Dumpsters, highway ditches—"

"Stop!" Sam shook his head. "The thought of you luring in unknown dogs from who knows where makes my head pound."

"What can I tell you?" She laughed. "I have a soft spot for lost causes."

Sam met her gaze then, and for an instant she saw the kind of longing and vulnerability in his eyes she'd never imagined from a man as tough and strong as he seemed. "Lucky dogs," he whispered.

The hair on her arms stood on end and her mouth went dry. He blinked, closing off his feelings from her.

"Add this one to the lucky list," she said, her voice a little breathy. Quickly, she led the dog through the house, grabbing a piece of bread off the counter for good measure. But she didn't need it. The dog walked by her side, his early rambunctiousness tempered because he had her attention.

She pulled the leash out of her trunk and looped it over his head. He shook his head, as if he wasn't used to a collar. "Easy there, boy," Julia crooned and knelt to pet him. The dog nuzzled into her chest. "I bet you've had a rough time of it. If anyone can find you a good home, it's my mom."

She walked the dog back onto the porch, where she could hear the sound of the television coming through the open screen door.

"Is it okay if I bring him in the house?"

"As long as he doesn't lift his leg on the furniture," came the hushed reply.

She leveled a look at the dog, who cocked his head at her. "Keep it together," she told him, and his stubby tail wagged again.

"I should get Charlie home and to bed," she said as she walked into the family room then stopped short. Sam sat on the couch, Charlie nestled into the crook of his arm, their attention riveted to the television. An IndyCar race was on the big set, and Sam was quietly explaining the details of the scene to Charlie.

"Lubock thinks he's got this one in the bag. He's in the blue-and-yellow car out front."

"Blue," Charlie said, his fist popping out of his mouth to point to the screen.

"That's right, but watch out for Eckhard in the red and white. See where he's coming around the outside?"

Charlie nodded drowsily then snuggled in deeper.

"I thought you didn't like kids," Julia said quietly, as Charlie's eyes drifted shut.

Sam glanced at the boy then tucked a blanket from

the back of the couch around him. "I like kids. Everyone likes kids."

Julia scoffed. "Hardly. Most people like dogs. You don't."

"That's different."

She watched the pair for several seconds then added, "Charlie's father doesn't like kids."

Sam met her gaze. "His loss."

"You've never even said hello to Charlie before this week."

"He and I don't run in the same circles," he countered.

"You know what I mean."

Sam picked up the remote and hit the mute button. He knew what she meant. Ever since he'd found Julia after her car crashed, he'd avoided both her and her son. That moment had terrified him more than it should someone in his position. He didn't know whether it was the memory of losing his mother, or the strange way his body reacted to the woman sitting across from him. Or a combination of both. But when he'd lifted her out of that car and carried her to his cruiser, his instinct for danger had been on high alert.

Sam was used to saving people from mishaps. It was part of the job. But she'd looked at him as if she'd put all her faith in him. That had made it feel different. More real, and scary as hell. Charlie had been born that same day, and Sam had decided it was better for both of them if he stayed away. He had nothing to offer a single mom and her child. His heart had shut down a long time ago.

Holding Charlie in his arms, he felt something fierce and protective roar to life inside him. If he wasn't careful, he could easily fall for this boy and his mother. He had to keep his distance but still play the part. His dad had spent most of the evening fawning over Julia and her son, leaving Sam blessedly alone.

He wanted to keep up the charade long enough for his father to leave town satisfied. When the eventual breakup came, Sam was sure he'd have a better chance of convincing Joe how heartbroken he was over the phone than in person.

"We should go over a few things before you leave," he said, trying to make his tone all business but soft enough that he didn't wake Charlie.

Julia nodded. "I can take him from you first."

Sam shook his head and adjusted the blanket. "He's fine. Thanks for bringing him. You saw how happy it made my dad."

"He's going to be devastated when this doesn't work out."

Sam shrugged. "He'll get over it. You've given him hope that I'm not a total lost cause in the commitment department. That should hold him over for a while."

Julia adjusted in her chair as the dog settled at her feet with a contented sigh. Sam had heard a lot about Vera Morgan's exceptional skills with animals. It appeared the gift was genetic.

"He mentioned your ex-girlfriend."

Sam flinched. If he didn't have Charlie sleeping against him, he would have gotten up to pace the room. "Leave it to dear old dad to knock the skeleton from my closet."

"We're engaged. He assumed I already knew."

"And you thought knowing my favorite color was going to be a big deal."

"We need to understand the details about each other

if this is going to work. Otherwise, no one is going to believe we're legitimate."

"Why not?" he countered. "People run off to Vegas all the time. Maybe you fell so head over heels for me that you didn't care about the details."

"Highly unlikely. You're not that irresistible."

Her comeback made him smile, which he realized was her intention. It was strange that this woman he knew so little could read him so well. "I was engaged for six months. She cheated on me a month before the wedding."

"That's awful."

"I caught her with my brother."

Julia's jaw dropped. "Wow."

"That's an understatement."

"What happened? Do you still speak to your brother? Are they together? What kind of awful people would do that to someone they both loved?"

"The way Scott explained it, before I kicked him out of my house, was that she was bad news and he was saving me from making a mistake. The way Jenny spun it before she followed him out the door was that he'd seduced her." He expected to feel the familiar pain of betrayal but only emptiness washed over him. "They aren't together and weren't again as far as I know. Turns out he was right. I found out later it wasn't the first time she'd cheated. She'd also been with one of the guys on the squad. Made me look like a fool."

"She's the fool." Julia came to stand before him. She lifted Charlie from his arms and sat down, laying her son beside her on the soft leather. "And your brother?"

"Scott was in the army for several years. Now he works out of D.C. for the U.S. Marshals."

She squeezed his arm and the warmth of her hand relaxed him a little. "I'm not interested in his job. What about your relationship?"

"My dad had a health scare almost two years ago. I passed my brother in the hall at the hospital. That's the extent of it."

"Oh, Sam."

"We were never close. My dad didn't encourage family bonding."

"Still—"

"This isn't helping our arrangement." Sam took her hand in his. "How long have we been dating?"

"Four months," Julia answered automatically.

"Favorite color?"

"Blue."

"Where we going on a honeymoon?"

"A Disney cruise."

"You can't be serious."

"Because of Charlie."

He laughed. "Fine." Some of the tension eased out of his shoulders and he asked, "Big or small wedding?"

"Small, close friends and immediate family."

"Who are your close friends?"

Her eyes darted away and she took several beats to answer. "The girls from the salon, I guess. A few of them, anyway. My sister."

"What about your friends from high school?"

"I didn't really have friends. Followers was more like it, and most of them have outgrown me."

"Their loss," he said, using his earlier phrase, and was rewarded with a smile. "What about your ex-boyfriend? Do you still have feelings for him? Should I be jealous?"

"Of Jeff? No. We were over long before he left me."

An interesting way to phrase it. Sam couldn't help but ask, "Could I kick his butt?"

She smiled. "Absolutely."

"Good. When is your next court date?"

"Friday."

"Do you want me to come?"

She shook her head and Sam felt a surprising rush of disappointment. "I might be able to help."

"You already are."

"You can't believe the judge will award custody to Jeff and his family. Is he even going to be here?"

"I don't know. But I can't take any chances. Even if he gets joint custody, they could take Charlie from me for extended periods of time. I won't risk it. Jeff made it clear he didn't want to be a father, so I don't understand why he's letting this happen. He was never close to his family."

"Have you talked to him directly?"

"I left a message on his cell phone right after the letter came. I might have sounded hysterical. He hasn't returned my call."

"You're going to have to tell your family what's going on before it goes too much further."

She nodded. "I realized that tonight. If my mom finds out your dad knew before her… It's all too much. I'm finally starting to get my life on track, with the salon and Charlie. For the first time in as long as I can remember, my mother isn't looking at me with disappointment in her eyes. When she finds out…"

"Vera will want to help. This isn't your fault."

"It sure feels like it is." She sank back against the couch and scrubbed her hands across her face. Sam saw pain and fear etched in her features. It gnawed away at him until he couldn't stand it. Why was she so afraid of her mother's judgment? Why did she think so little of herself, to believe her son was at risk of being taken away? Maybe she'd made some mistakes in her past but Sam didn't know anyone who hadn't. She couldn't be punished forever.

He might not be willing to give his heart again, but he needed to give her some comfort. He wasn't great with words and knew that if he got sentimental, she'd only use her dry wit to turn it into a joke. Instead, he placed a soft kiss on the inside of her palm.

She tugged on her hand but he didn't let go. "You don't need to do that now," she whispered, her voice no more than a breath in the quiet. "There's no one watching."

One side of his mouth quirked. "It's a good thing, too, because what I want to do to you is best kept in private."

Her mouth formed a round *oh* and he lifted a finger to trace the soft flesh of her lips.

"Charlie."

"I know." He leaned closer. "You're safe tonight. Almost."

"We shouldn't…"

"I know," he repeated. "But I can't think of anything I want more."

"Me, too." She sat up and brought both of her hands to the sides of his face, cupping his jaw. "This isn't going to get complicated, right?"

"Other than planning a pretend wedding, a custody battle, my meddling father and a town filled with nosy neighbors? I think we can keep it fairly simple."

She smoothed her thumbs along his cheeks and her scent filled his head again. "I mean you and me. We're on the same page. It's all part of the show, the time spent together, pretending like we're in love. It ends when we both get what we want."

He agreed in theory, but at the moment all Sam wanted was her. He knew telling her that would make her more skittish than she already was. He didn't want this night to end quite yet, even if her sleeping son was going to keep the evening G-rated. So he answered, "That's the plan."

She nodded then licked her lips, and he suppressed a groan. "Then it won't matter if I do this..." She brought her mouth to his and they melted together. When her tongue mixed with his, he did groan. Or maybe Julia did. Her fingers wound through his hair and down his neck, pressing him closer, right where he wanted to be.

He deepened the kiss as his hands found their way underneath her blouse, his palms spread across the smooth skin on her back.

"Stop." Julia's breathing sounded ragged.

His hands stilled and he drew back enough to look into her big gray eyes, now hazy with desire.

A small smile played on the corners of her mouth. "I want to make sure we both stay in control. No getting carried away."

Like to his bedroom, Sam thought. All the wonderful, devilish, naked things he could do to her there ran through his brain. He wanted to know this woman—every inch of her—with a passion he hadn't thought himself capable of feeling.

He didn't answer, not sure his brain could manage a coherent sentence at the moment. They stared at each other and he wondered if Julia's heart was pounding as hard as his.

He heard Charlie snore softly and let his eyes drift closed for a few seconds. He counted to ten in his head, thought about the pile of work waiting in his office and tried like hell to rein in his desire and emotions.

He withdrew his hands, smoothed her shirt back down and forced a casual smile.

"My middle name is control, sweetheart."

She cocked her head. "That's a good point," she said and didn't sound at all as affected as Sam felt. "What *is* your middle name?"

He shook his head slightly. "Matthew."

"Mine's Christine," she told him, as if she had no memory of a minute earlier when she'd been kissing him as if her life depended on it. "I'm going to get Charlie home." She stood and picked up the sleeping boy. The Weimaraner jumped to attention and stayed close by her side.

Sam felt off balance at her switch in mood but didn't want to admit it. "I'll walk you to your car," he said, keeping the frustration out of his voice. This *was* a business arrangement, after all, passionate kissing aside. Maybe Julia had the right of it.

She nodded and grabbed the diaper bag, pushing it at Sam. "If you could carry that," she said, as if she didn't trust him with his hands free.

The night had cooled at least ten degrees and she shivered as she hurried down the front walk. "Do you want a jacket?" he asked, taking large strides to keep up with her.

"I'm fine."

While it might be true that Sam hadn't had any long-term relationships since moving to Brevia, and had stayed out of the dating pool totally for the past few months, his evenings never ended like this.

Usually he was the one who put the brakes on, sexually. More than once, he'd been invited back to a woman's house—or she'd asked to see his place—on the first date and gotten a clear signal that she'd been eager to take things to the next level. Sam was cautious and tried to not let an evening go there if he thought someone wanted more than he could give.

Never, until tonight, could he remember a woman literally running out of his house when he so badly wanted her to stay.

Julia opened the back door and placed Charlie in his car seat then gave the dog a little tug. The Weim jumped up without a sound, as if he knew enough not to wake the sleeping boy.

Turning, Julia held out her hand for the diaper bag.

"Are we good?" Sam asked.

"Yep," she said, again not meeting his gaze. "I'll talk to you in a few days."

A few days? They were engaged. He told himself it wouldn't look good to the town, but the truth was he couldn't wait a few days. Before he could respond, she'd scurried to the driver's side, climbing in with one last wave and "Thanks" thrown over her shoulder.

Sam was left standing alone at the curb, wondering what had gone so wrong so quickly. He headed back to the house, hoping a cold shower would help him make some sense of things.

Chapter 7

Julia swiped under her eyes and focused her attention on her mug of lukewarm coffee, unable to make eye contact with her mother or sister.

Lainey paced the length of Vera's office in the All Creatures Great and Small animal shelter. By contrast, their mother sat stock-still behind her desk.

"That's the whole story," Julia finished. "The judge ordered us into mediation and that meeting is tomorrow morning. I don't think it will do any good. I know what I want and Jeff's parents know what they want. If we can't come to an agreement with the mediator, there will be a final hearing where the judge makes a ruling."

"Is Jeff going to be there?" Vera asked, her tone both soft and razor-sharp.

"I guess so, but it will be better if he isn't, if it looks like it's his parents who want this." Her breath hitched.

"The latest document I got from their attorney asks for an every-other-year joint-custody arrangement. There's an opportunity for it to be amended if Charlie's well-being is in jeopardy with one of the parties."

"Every other year?" Lainey stopped pacing. "How can they think of taking him away from you for that long? You should have told us this as soon as you knew, Jules. Maybe we could have done something—"

"What, Lainey?" Julia snapped then sighed. "I'm sorry. I don't mean to take it out on you. But what could have been done? I hoped if I made it difficult for them, they might give up. The first letter said they wanted full custody and offered a hefty payment for the expenses I've already incurred in raising Charlie."

"They thought you'd sell them your son?" Lainey's voice was incredulous.

"That's one way of looking at it. The last Jeff knew, I'd gotten pregnant as a way to keep him. He could have told his parents I didn't really want to be a mother or wouldn't be able to handle it on my own."

"You're not on your own." Vera tapped one finger on the desk. "You have us. And Sam."

Conflicting emotions welled in Julia's chest again as she thought of Sam. He'd told her to talk to her mom and sister. She knew it was inevitable, so she'd called them both on the way home last night and asked them to meet her at the shelter before work. At the time, it had been a good way to distract herself from Sam and the way he made her feel.

He must have been baffled by her behavior after they'd kissed. Most women he knew could probably handle a simple kiss. Not Julia. Maybe it had been too long since she'd been in a man's arms. It had taken every ounce of her willpower not to beg him to take her to bed. His touch had rocked her to her core and she'd had to beat a quick retreat so she wouldn't do or say something she'd later regret.

When he'd proposed the pretend engagement, she'd had no idea how much her emotions would get in the way. She'd had no idea how it would affect her to see Sam cuddling Charlie against his broad chest. How much her body and heart would react to his arms around her. How quickly she'd come to depend on the comfort he gave her and how he made her feel strong by believing in her.

"I'm the one they're going after," she told her mom. "And Charlie." A sob escaped her lips and she clamped her hand over her mouth.

Lainey rushed to her side and Julia let herself be cradled in her sister's warm embrace. Silence descended over the trio. This was the time Julia would normally make a joke or sarcastic remark about her propensity to ruin her own life. But, right now, she was just struggling to not break down completely.

This was the reason she hadn't told her family. Their sympathy and the disappointment she felt from them brought back too many memories of the past and the feelings that went with it. Her LD and the shame that went with it had made her put up walls against everyone around her. She'd gotten used to getting by, keeping secrets, not letting on how bad things really were. It was a difficult pattern to break.

From the time she'd been younger, Julia had made an unintentional habit of disappointing the people she loved. She'd let other people's judgments guide the way she lived her life. The belief that she was lazy and stupid had stopped her from getting help so many times. It was easier not to open up to her family about her emotions. She was too afraid of being exposed as weak and lacking in their eyes.

Even when she'd shown up on her mother's doorstep, pregnant, broke and alone, she hadn't cried or offered long explanations or excuses. She just kept moving. Now she felt stuck in quicksand, as though nothing could save her.

Vera's palm slammed onto the desk. "We won't let this happen. Have you consulted Frank?"

Julia nodded. Frank Davis had been practicing law in Brevia for as long as she could remember and was a friend of her mother's. After Sam's suggestion that she see an attorney, she'd hired him to represent her. "He's helping with the case."

Vera nodded. "That's a good start. You need to talk to Jeff. To understand why he's doing this now when he had no previous interest in being a dad. Surely you'll be awarded sole custody. You're Charlie's mother and you do a wonderful job with him."

"I don't know, Mom. Jeff's family is arguing that they can give Charlie opportunities he'll never have with me."

"A child doesn't need anything more than a loving family. Let them set up a college trust if they're so concerned with opportunities."

"What do you want to see happen?" Lainey asked.

That question had kept Julia up many nights. "I'll support them having a relationship with Charlie. I'm sure as he gets older he'll have questions about his father's family. I want him to be surrounded by all the people who love him." She paused and took a breath. "I'm afraid he'll eventually choose them."

"He won't," Lainey said softly.

"You can't know that. But he needs to live with me now. Full-time. Swapping him back and forth is ludicrous."

"I'm going to the mediation," Vera announced.

Julia's stomach lurched. As much as she appreciated and needed her family's support, she was afraid it would only make her more nervous to have her mother with her. "That's not a good idea. I appreciate the offer but I need to handle this on my own."

Lainey squeezed her shoulder and asked, "Has Jeff contacted you directly or tried to see Charlie?"

Julia shook her head. "No. Neither have his parents, other than when I got messages about discussing the custody arrangement."

"When did that start?" Vera came around the side of the desk.

"About a month ago. I ignored them until the certified letter arrived last week."

"Ignoring your problems doesn't make them go away."

Funny, it had always worked for Julia in the past. She'd taken the easy way out of every difficult situation that came her way before Charlie. And thanks to the complexity of her difficulties processing both words and numbers, problems seemed to plague her. From bad rental agreements to unfair terms on a car loan, her inability to manage the details of her life took its toll in a variety of ways. Still, nothing had prepared her for this.

A knock at the door interrupted them.

"Come in," Vera said.

A member of the shelter staff entered, leading in a gray dog. Or more accurately, the gray dog led her. Upon seeing Julia, the animal pulled at the leash, his stubby tail wagging. His lips drew back to expose his teeth.

"That's quite a greeting," Lainey said with a laugh.

"Sam thought it was a snarl when the dog first came at him." Julia bent to pet him. The dog wiggled and tried to put his front paws on her chest. She body blocked him. "Down."

"What's the report?" Vera asked the young woman.

"We've done his blood work and tested him for heart-worm and parasites. Surprisingly, he got a clean bill of health."

"That's great." Julia felt relief wash over her. "Have you had any calls about a lost Weim?"

The young woman shook her head. "Not yet."

"We'll do a three-day hold before he moves onto the available-dog list." Vera dropped to her knees next to Julia. The dog lunged for her, teeth gleaming, but Vera held up a hand and gave a firm "No." The dog's rear end hit the carpet, although one corner of his mouth still curled.

Julia met her mother's gaze. "The smile's not good for him, is it?"

Vera shrugged. "It depends on the potential adopter, but a lot of people might think the same thing Sam did. We'll find a place for him. We always do."

Julia stroked the dog's silky ear. She'd planned on leaving the Weimaraner at the shelter this morning. "Can I foster him? Until the waiting period is over or someone shows interest. I'll work on basic training commands to help offset the shock of the smile."

Vera hesitated. "You've got a lot going on right now, honey. Weims aren't easy dogs. They can have separa-tion anxiety and get destructive."

Frustration crept across Julia's neck and shoulders. "You know being in a foster home is better for a dog's well-being." She couldn't believe her mother would insinuate the dog would be better in the shelter than with her.

"Of course," Vera agreed, as if she realized she'd crossed some imaginary line. "If you're willing to, it would help him immensely."

"Have they named him yet?" Julia knew the shelter staff named each animal that came in to make their care more personal.

The young woman shook her head.

"Call him Casper," Julia said.

"The friendly gray ghost?" Lainey asked, referring to the breed's well-known nickname.

Julia nodded. "It fits him and will give people a sense of his personality."

"Perfect," her mother said then asked the young woman, "They've done a temperament test?"

She nodded. "He's a big sweetie." The walkie-talkie clipped to her belt hissed. "I'll finish the paperwork with Julia as the foster." When Vera nodded, the woman smiled and walked out of the office.

"It's settled." Julia was going to make sure this dog found the perfect home. She straightened. "Charlie will be thrilled."

She turned to her mother. "I need to get Charlie from Ethan and drop him to the sitter before heading to the salon."

"I'll take him today," her mother said, in the same no-argument tone she'd used earlier.

"Really? I'm sure your schedule is packed after your trip."

"I'd love to."

Julia gave her mother a quick hug. "Thank you." She

turned to Lainey. "Both of you. It helps to know I'm not alone."

"You never have been," Vera told her.

"And never will be," Lainey added.

As she gave Charlie a bath later that night, Julia had to admit Sam had been right. Talking about the situation with Lainey and her mother had made her feel more hopeful. She might have flitted from job to job and through a number of cities during her twenties, but now she'd settled in Brevia. She was close to the point where she could make an offer to buy the salon, assuming this custody battle didn't wipe out her meager savings.

She wrapped Charlie in a fluffy towel, put on a fresh diaper and his pajamas, Casper at her side the whole time. She didn't mind the company. She'd taken him for a walk with Charlie in the stroller earlier, after the dog had spent the day with her in the salon.

A few of the clients had been shocked at his wide grin, but his affectionate nature had quickly won them over. It also made Julia feel more confident about his chances for adoption.

When the doorbell rang, Casper ran for it and began a steady bark. Carrying Charlie with her, she put a leash on the dog. A part of her hoped Sam was making another unexpected evening call.

Instead, Jeff Johnson stood on the other side of the door. Casper lunged for him but Julia held tight to the leash. She stumbled forward when the shock of seeing her ex-boyfriend combined with the dog's strength threw her off balance.

"Watch it," Jeff snapped as he righted her.

Casper smiled.

"What the...? Is that thing dangerous?" Jeff stepped back. "He looks rabid. You shouldn't have it near the baby. Are you crazy?"

"Casper, sit." Julia gave the command as she straightened. The dog sat, the skin around his mouth quivering. "Be careful, or I may give the attack command." She made her voice flip despite the flood of emotions roaring through her.

For a satisfying moment, Jeff looked as if he might make a run for it. Then his own lip curled. "Very funny."

"Good doggy." Charlie pointed at the canine.

"He talks," Jeff said, surprise clear.

"He does a lot of things," Julia answered, her eyes narrowed. "Not that you'd know or care since you beat a fast escape as soon as you found out I was pregnant."

Jeff flashed his most disarming smile, a little sheepish with his big chocolate eyes warm behind his square glasses. That exact smile had initially charmed her when he'd come in for a haircut at the salon where she'd worked in Columbus, Ohio.

For several months dating Jeff had been magical for her. He'd taken her to the theater and ballet, using his family's tickets. They'd gone to poetry readings and talks by famous authors on campus. Some of what she heard was difficult to process, and in a moment of vulnerability, she'd told Jeff about the extent of her learning disabilities. He'd been sympathetic and supportive, taking time over long evenings to read articles and stories to her, discussing them as if her opinion mattered. It was the first time in her life Julia felt valued for her intelligence, and she became committed to making their relationship work at any cost.

Soon she realized what a fool she'd been to think a

well-respected professor would be truly interested in someone like her. It was clear that Jeff liked how his friends reacted when he'd shown up at dinner parties with a leggy blonde on his arm. He'd also gotten a lot of use out of the way she'd bent over backward cooking and cleaning to his exacting standards when she'd moved in with him. If she couldn't be on his level intellectually, she'd fulfill the other roles of a doting girlfriend. She'd wanted to believe that a baby would make him see how good their life together could be. She'd been dead wrong. Once she wasn't useful to him, he'd thrown her off like yesterday's news.

"Come on, Julia," he said softly, his grin holding steady. "Don't act like you aren't glad to see me." She'd been fooled by that smile once and wasn't going to make the same mistake again.

She flashed a smile of her own. "I don't see anyone throwing a ticker-tape parade. You can turn right around. I've got no use for you here."

"I'm here to see my son," Jeff said, as any trace of charm vanished.

Charlie met his biological father's gaze then buried his face in Julia's shoulder, suddenly shy.

"Why now, Jeff?" She rubbed a hand against Charlie's back when he began to fidget. "Why all of this now?"

He sighed. "The custody request, you mean."

Jeff's IQ was in the genius range, but sometimes he could be purposefully obtuse. "Of course the custody request. Do you know the hell you and your parents have put me through? We've barely scratched the surface."

"Invite me in, Jules," he said, coaxing, "and we can talk about it. I have an offer that may make this whole mess go away."

It had felt different when Sam stood at her door waiting to be invited through. Her stomach had danced with awareness and her only doubt had been worrying about her heart's exhilarated reaction to him. Still, Julia relented. If she had a chance to make this better, she couldn't refuse it.

Jeff stepped into her apartment but froze when Casper greeted him by sticking his snout into Jeff's crotch. "Get away, you stupid mutt." Jeff kicked out his foot, hitting Casper in the ribs. The dog growled.

"Casper, no." She pulled him back to her side with the leash then leveled a look at Jeff. "Don't kick my dog."

"It was going for my balls. What do you expect?"

"I wouldn't worry too much. As I remember, your mother keeps them on her mantel."

Jeff gave a humorless laugh. "Always one for the quick retort. I miss that about you."

"Good doggy. Charlie doggy." The boy wiggled in her arms and Julia put him on the floor. His chubby finger pulled the leash from her hand and he led the dog toward the kitchen. "Doggy nice." Casper followed willingly.

"You trust that beast with him?"

"More than I trust you." Julia folded her arms across her chest. "For the record, there's nothing I miss about you."

Jeff's eyes narrowed. "He's still my son. Whether you like it or not, I deserve to be a part of his life. There's no judge in the world who will deny me access."

"I never wanted to deny you access. I called you after he was born, emailed pictures and never heard one word back. You haven't answered my question. Why now?"

His gaze shifted to the floor. "Change of heart."

"You need a heart for it to change. You made it clear

you never wanted to be a dad. What's the real story?" Before he could answer, Charlie led the dog back into the family room. He pulled a blanket off the couch and spread it on the floor. "Mama, doggy bed." She smiled as her son took a board book from the coffee table and sat on the blanket with Casper, making up words to an imaginary story.

Her gaze caught on Jeff, who yawned and looked around her apartment, obvious distaste written on his face for the kid-friendly decorating style. He didn't pay a bit of attention to his son. Since she'd opened the door, he'd barely looked at Charlie. It was the first time he'd laid eyes on his own flesh and blood. She realized he couldn't care less.

Unable to resist testing her theory, she said, "He's about to go to sleep. Do you want to read him a story? He loves books."

Jeff held up his palms as if she'd offered him a venomous snake. "No, thanks."

"I've got paperwork that says you want joint custody of my son. You act like you'd rather be dipped in boiling oil than have any interaction with him."

"I told you. I've got a proposition for you."

"What?"

"Marry me."

Julia stared at him, disbelief coursing through her. He couldn't have shocked her more if he'd offered her a million bucks. "Is that a joke? It's sick and wrong, but it must be a joke."

"I'm serious, Jules. You're right—I have no interest in being a father in any sense of the word. Ever. In fact—" he paused and ran his fingers through his hair "—I got a vasectomy."

"Excuse me?"

"After you, I was determined no woman would try to trap me again."

"It takes two. I'm sorry, Jeff, that I ever believed we could be a family. I know how wrong I was. But I don't understand why you've changed your mind now?"

"Are you kidding? I love my life. I've been on two research expeditions in the past year. I make my own schedule and can teach whatever classes I want. Why would I want to be tied down to a woman or a baby?"

"Then why are you suddenly proposing? Why the custody suit?"

Jeff had the grace to look embarrassed. "My parents found out about my surgery. It made them interested in our kid. You know I'm an only child. They expected me to marry and 'carry on the family line.'" He rolled his eyes. "Whatever. But my dad's company is a big funder of my grants. If he wants a grandchild, I need to give him one."

Julia's gaze strayed to Charlie, who was snuggled against Casper's back, sucking on his thumb. His eyes drifted closed. She felt a wave of nausea roll through her. "You need to *give* him one? And you think you're going to give him mine?"

Jeff shrugged. "Technically, he's *ours*. When my parents want something, they don't stop until they get it."

"How is anything you're saying good news for me? Why don't you get the hell out of my house and out of my son's life?"

"Not going to happen."

"When the judge finds out your plan…"

"No one is going to find out. I'm the father. You can't keep him from me."

"I want to keep him safe and protected."

"That's why you should marry me. Oh, I heard all about your engagement to the cop. He's not for you. I know you. You want someone who's going to make you look smart."

Julia sucked in a breath. "You have no idea what you're talking about."

"Does he know about your problem?"

When she didn't answer, Jeff smiled. "I thought so. I'm guessing you don't want him to. It hasn't come up in the court proceedings, either, but that can change. Here's my proposal. Marry me, move to Ohio. My parents' property is huge. They have a guesthouse where you can live with the boy. All of your expenses will be covered."

"Why would I agree to that, and what does it have to do with us being married?"

"A marriage will seem more legit to my parents' precious social circle. They'll get off my back with someone to shape and mold into their own image."

"Like they did you?"

"My parents are proud of me."

"I thought your father wanted you to give up the university and take over his business."

"Not going to happen."

"Instead, Charlie and I should spend our lives at their beck and call?"

"They'll keep fighting until they take him away from you. We all will."

Her temper about to blow, Julia yanked open the front door. "Get out, Jeff."

"On second thought, maybe I should read the kid a story. Get to know him before he comes to live with us."

"Get out!"

Jeff must have read something in her eyes that told him she would die before she let him touch her son tonight. He hesitated then turned for the door.

She slammed it behind him. The noise startled the dog and woke Charlie, who began to cry. She rushed over and cradled him in her arms.

"It's okay, sweetie. Mama's here." Tears streamed down her face as she hugged Charlie close. "No one's going to take you away from me. No one." She made the promise as much to herself as to him, wanting to believe the words were true.

Chapter 8

Julia stepped into the afternoon light and put on her sunglasses, more to hide the unshed tears welling in her eyes than for sun protection.

Frank Davis, her attorney, took her elbow to guide her down the steps of the county courthouse. They'd spent the past two hours in a heated session with Jeff, his parents and their lawyer. She couldn't believe how much information they'd dug up, from the details of her finances, including the business loan that had yet to be approved, to her credit history. Thanks to a loser boyfriend who'd stolen her bank-account information, her credit was spotty, at best.

They knew all of the dead-end jobs she'd had over the years, including those she'd been fired from or quit without notice, and had a detailed record of her habit of moving from city to city for short periods of time.

They'd brought in statements from one of her ex-boy-friends and a former employer stating she was flighty and irresponsible. Her old boss even said that she'd threatened to set fire to her hair salon. No one mentioned the woman had skimmed Julia's paycheck without her knowledge for over nine months after she'd discovered Julia's learning disabilities. Torching the place had been an idle threat, of course, but it hadn't sounded that way today.

"They made me seem crazy," she muttered.

Frank clucked softly. "It's all right, darlin'. A lot of mamas in the South are a bit touched. No one around here's gonna hold that against you." He checked his watch. "I got a tee time with some of the boys at one. Give me a call tomorrow and we'll plan our next move." He leaned in and planted a fatherly kiss on her cheek, then moved toward his vintage Cadillac parked at the curb.

Frank had known her since she'd been in diapers. He'd been one of her father's fraternity brothers in college. Not for the first time, she questioned the wisdom of hiring him to represent her. It was no secret Frank was close to retirement, and from what Julia could tell, he spent more time on the golf course and fishing with his friends than in his office or working on cases.

Lexi Preston might look like a pussycat, but she was an absolute shark. From her guilty expression every time they made eye contact, Julia knew Lexi was the one who'd researched her so thoroughly. Julia would have admired her skills if they hadn't been directed at her.

She glanced toward the courthouse entrance. Jeff and his parents could come out at any minute and she didn't want them to see her alone and on the verge of a break-down. She wished now that she'd let her mother or Lainey come with her today.

She turned to make her way to her car and came face-to-face with Sam.

"Hey," he said softly and drew the sunglasses off her nose, his eyes studying hers as if he could read what she was thinking. "How did things go today?"

"I told you not to come," she said on a shaky breath.

"I don't take direction well." He folded her glasses and pulled her into a tight embrace. "It's okay, honey. Whatever happened, we can make it better."

She tried to pull away but he didn't let her go. After a moment, she sagged against him, burying her face in the fabric of his uniform shirt.

As his palm drew circles on her back, her tears flowed freely. She gulped in ragged breaths. "So awful," she said around sobs. "They made me seem so awful."

"I don't believe that," he said against her ear. "Anyone who knows you knows you're a fantastic mother."

"What if they take him from me?"

"We're not going to let that happen. Not a snowball's chance."

Julia wiped her eyes. "They're going to come out any minute. Jeff can't see me like this."

"My truck's right here." Sam looped one arm around her shoulders, leading her away from the courthouse steps. He opened the passenger door of his truck then came around and climbed in himself. He started the engine but didn't make a move to drive off.

Julia kept her face covered with her hands and worked to control her breathing.

"Is that him?" Sam asked after a minute.

Julia peeked through her fingers as Jeff, his parents and the attorney walked out of the courthouse. Shading his eyes with one hand, Jeff scanned the area.

"He's looking for me so he can gloat." Julia sank down lower in the seat. "Jerk," she mumbled.

The group came down the steps.

"They're heading right for us."

"Sit up," Sam ordered, and she immediately straightened. "Smile and lean over to kiss me when they come by."

The urge to duck was huge, but Julia made her mouth turn up at the ends. "Here goes," she whispered as Jeff led the group closer, his father clapping him hard on the back. She waited until he noticed her through the windshield then leaned over and cupped Sam's jaw between her hands. She gave him a gentle kiss and pressed her forehead against his.

"That a girl," he told her. "Don't give him the satisfaction of seeing you upset."

"I can do this," she said, and Sam kissed her again.

"They've passed."

Julia stayed pressed against him for another moment before moving away. She leaned against the seat back in order to see out the side-view mirror. Jeff and his parents headed away, but Lexi trailed behind the group, looking over her shoulder every few steps.

"This isn't going to work."

"Yes, it is."

She shook her head. "I told you before, I made a lot of stupid decisions in my life. It's like they've uncovered every single one of them to use against me."

"Did you kill someone?"

Her head whipped toward him. "Of course not."

"Armed robbery?"

"No."

"Do you know how many people I meet in the course of my job who do bad things every day? Their kids are rarely taken away."

"Maybe they should be," she suggested, too unsettled to be comforted. "Maybe if they had people with buckets of money and tons of power going after them, they'd lose their babies."

He wrapped his fingers around hers. "You aren't going to lose Charlie. Stop thinking like that."

"You don't know, Sam. You weren't in that room."

"A mistake I don't intend to repeat. I should have been there with you. For you."

The tenderness in his voice touched a place deep within her: an intimate, open well of emotion she'd locked the lid to many years ago. She wanted to believe in him, to trust that he could protect her the way she'd never been willing to protect herself or even believed she deserved. The part of her who'd been hurt too many times in the past wanted to run.

She excelled at running away. She'd practically perfected it as an art.

That was what she'd been thinking in the courthouse. People disappeared all the time with no trace. She'd wanted to slip out of that room, gather up Charlie and whatever would fit in her trunk and drive away from the threat looming over her. She could cut hair anywhere. Why not start over in a place where no one knew her or her insecurities or all the ways she didn't measure up? She had friends around the country who'd help her if she asked.

The weight of trying to make a new life in a place that was as familiar to her as a worn blanket seemed too heavy. Of course trouble had followed her to Brevia. This was where it had started in the first place.

Sam's faith had made her feel as though things could

work out, the same way Charlie's birth had renewed her hope in herself and her desire to really try.

What was the use? This morning was a cold, harsh dose of reality and she didn't like it.

"Stop it," he said quietly. "Whatever's going through your mind right now, put it out. It's not going to do you or Charlie any good for you to give up."

Because she couldn't help it, she met his gaze again. "I'm scared, Sam." A miserable groan escaped her lips. "I'm terrified they're going to take my baby and I won't be able to stop them."

"We're going to stop them." He took her hand. "What did Frank say?"

"That all Southern women were crazy, so it wouldn't be an issue, and he needed to make his tee time and we'd talk tomorrow."

"Tell me what happened in there."

"I can't." She bit her lip again and tasted blood on her tongue. "I put my mistakes behind me. Or I thought I did. Their attorney knew things about my past I hadn't even told Jeff. They went after my character and I had nothing to offer in my defense. Nothing as bad as me killing someone, although the urge to wipe the smug smile off of Maria Johnson's face was almost overwhelming. They made me seem unstable and irresponsible. Two things I can't afford if I'm going to keep sole custody of Charlie."

"Then we'll come up with something."

"This isn't your problem, Sam."

"Hell, yes, it's my problem. You're my fiancée."

The lunacy of that statement actually made her laugh. "Your fake fiancée. Not the same thing."

"For the purposes of your custody case it is. You're not alone, Julia. We both get something out of this arrangement. My dad has talked about heading back home before the wedding. That's huge for me. Dinner was a big success. It's my turn to repay you."

Sam knew there was more to his interest in her case than wanting to repay her. Yes, his dad had backed off, but it was more than that. Sam cared about Julia and Charlie, about keeping them safe. No one should be able to make her feel this bad about herself. He also knew it was dangerous territory for him. He'd let his heart lead him before, with disastrous results.

His father might be the king of emotional diarrhea these days, but Sam remembered clearly the months after his mother's death. He'd fixed lunches for his little brother, made sure they both had baths at night and taken money out of his dad's wallet to buy groceries on his way home from school. He'd walked a mile out of his way once a week so no one at the local grocery would recognize him and be concerned. When he wasn't at work, his father had sat in the darkened living room, paging through photo albums, a glass of amber-colored liquid in his hand.

That was what loving someone too much could do to a man. Sam had learned early on he wasn't going to make that mistake. When he'd caught his brother, Scott, with his ex-fiancée, he'd been angry and embarrassed, but mainly numb.

When he'd broken off the engagement, Jenny had told him the entire situation was his fault. He'd been too cold and distant. She wanted to be with a man who could feel passion. She'd thought seeing her with someone else would awaken Sam's passion. Talk about crazy, and she wasn't even Southern.

He'd known he didn't have any more to give her or any woman. Even though his pattern of dating hadn't been deliberate, the look a woman sometimes got in her eye after a couple of dates scared him. The look said "I want something more." She wanted to talk about her feelings. Sam felt sick thinking about it.

As far as he was concerned, a pretend engagement suited him fine. He cared about Julia and he wanted to help her, but their arrangement was clear. He didn't have to give more of himself than he was able to, and she wasn't going to expect anything else.

"Jeff asked me to marry him," she said, breaking his reverie.

"During the mediation?" he asked, sure he must have heard her wrong.

She shook her head. "Last night. He came to my apartment."

Sam felt his blood pressure skyrocket. "You let him in? What were you thinking?" Especially since Sam had practically had to hold himself back from making the short drive to her apartment. He'd had a long day at work, and as he was pulling into his driveway, he'd realized how much he didn't want to be alone in his quiet house. He'd resisted the urge, telling himself that he shouldn't get too attached to Julia or her son. They had boundaries and he was a stickler for the rules. Now to find out that her creep of an ex-boyfriend had been there?

"He came crawling back." Sam kept his tone casual. Inside, his emotions were in turmoil. This was the guy she'd wanted to marry so badly. What if she still carried a torch for him? He'd obviously been an idiot to let her go once. If he came back now, trying to rekindle a romance and wanting to be a real family, would Julia consider taking him back? That thought hit Sam straight in the gut. "What did you say?"

She studied him for a moment. "He didn't quite come crawling. More like trumpeting his own horn. He told me the reason they're coming after Charlie is because his parents want an heir to the family business."

"They've got a son. Let him take over."

"Not his deal, and Jeff isn't going to have other children. He's made sure of that. Although it's crazy to think they could start grooming a mere toddler. No wonder Jeff has so many issues. If only I'd been smart enough to see it when we were together. You know what the strange part of this is? No one in Jeff's family has tried to get to know Charlie. It's like they want him on paper but they don't care about having a grandson. I want him to know their family if they have a real interest in him. But I saw how Jeff suffered from being a pawn in his parents' power games. I can't let the same thing happen to Charlie."

He held her hand, his brilliant blue eyes warm with emotion. "Your son needs you. He needs you to fight for him."

She nodded and wiped at her nose.

"What you need is a plan of defense. You flaked on some jobs. It happens."

"There's a reason," she mumbled, almost reluctantly.

"A reason that will explain it away?"

She shrugged and shook free from his hand, adjusting the vents to the air-conditioning as a way to keep her fingers occupied. "I have severe learning disabilities."

When he didn't respond she continued, "I've been keeping it a secret since I was a kid. It's a neurobiological disorder, both visual and auditory. Only my family and a few teachers knew, and I kept it from them for as long as I could. Everyone else assumed I was lazy or didn't care."

"Why would you hide that?"

"You have no idea what it's like, how much shame

and embarrassment is involved. To people who've never dealt with it, it seems cut-and-dried. It's not." Her hands clenched into fists as she struggled with her next words. "I'm a good mimic and my bad attitude served me well as a way to keep everyone from digging too much. I got by okay, but I can barely read. Numbers on a page are a puzzle."

"All those books on your shelf…"

"I'm nothing if not determined. I'll get through them someday. Right now, I'm working with a literacy specialist. They have a lot of methods that weren't available when I was in school. But it never gets easier. For years, I tried so hard in school but people thought I was a total slacker. Ditzy blonde cheerleader with no brain. A lot of the time that's how it felt. Once I was out on my own, I hid it as best I could. People can take advantage of me pretty easily when it comes to contracts or finances. And that's what happened. A number of times. It always seemed easier to just move on rather than to fight them."

"Every time someone got wind of it, you left."

She nodded. "It was cowardly but I don't want to be treated like I'm stupid. Although, looking back, I acted pretty dumb most of the time. Especially when it came to boyfriends. I trusted Jeff. He never let me forget it."

"That you had a learning disability?"

"That I'm just a pretty face. The blond hair and long legs. When I told him I was pregnant, he told me that once my looks faded I wouldn't have anything left to offer."

"He's a real piece of work." Sam couldn't believe how angry he was. At her idiot ex-boyfriend and all the others who took advantage of her. But also with Julia. Watching her, Sam could tell she believed the garbage people had fed her over the years. He threw the truck into gear, not wanting to lose his temper. "Where's your car?"

"Around the corner." She pointed then shifted in her seat. "Thanks for coming today, Sam. I was a mess after the mediation. You helped."

"I could have helped more if you'd let me be in there with you." He pulled out from the curb and turned onto the next street. Her car was parked a few spaces down.

"Maybe next time," she said quietly. She reached for the door handle but he took her arm.

"You have a lot more to offer than looks. Any guy who can't see that is either blind or an enormous jackass." He kept his gaze out the front window, afraid of giving away too much if he looked at her.

"Thanks."

He heard the catch in her voice and released her. After she'd shut the door, he rolled down the window. "The Mardi Gras Carnival is tonight. I'll pick you and Charlie up at five."

"I'm beat. I wasn't planning on going."

"I'll pick you up at five. You need to take your mind off this, and it's a good place for us to be seen together." Her chest rose and fell. "Fine. We'll be ready."

After she'd gotten into her car, Sam pulled away. Although the air was hot for mid-March, he shut the windows. Julia's scent hovered in the truck's cab. Sam wanted to keep it with him as long as he could.

He'd meant what he said about taking her mind off today. As police chief, he was obligated to make an appearance at town events, but he looked forward to tonight knowing he'd have Julia and Charlie with him.

Chapter 9

Julia dabbed on a bit of lip gloss just as the doorbell rang. She picked up Charlie, who was petting Casper through the wire crate.

"Let's go."

"'Bye, doggy."

Casper whined softly.

"We'll be back soon," Julia told him. The doorbell rang again. "Coming," she called.

She grabbed the diaper bag off the table and opened the front door, adjusting her short, flowing minidress as she did.

"We're ready."

"Sammy," Charlie said, bouncing up and down in her arms.

"Hey, bud." Sam held out his hands and Charlie dived forward.

Julia worried for a moment about Charlie bonding

so quickly with Sam. In a way it worked to their advantage, at least as their pretend engagement went. But she had concerns about Charlie's clear affection for Sam. She didn't want her son to be hurt once their time together ended.

"You don't have to take him."

"My pleasure." Sam looked her over from head to toe then whistled softly. "You look amazing."

Julia felt a blush creep up her cheeks. "You, too."

It was true. Tonight he wore a light polo shirt and dark blue jeans. His hair was still longer and her fingers pulsed as she thought about running them through the ends. He hadn't shaved, and the dusting of short whiskers along his jaw made him look wilder than he normally did as police chief.

It excited her more than she cared to admit. She hadn't been on a real date in over two years. This wasn't real, she reminded herself. This was showing off for the town, convincing people their relationship was genuine.

Not that being in this relationship had helped her earlier. She'd barely said two words in her own defense as the Johnsons' attorney had put forward more and more information about her deficiencies as a person and how they might be detrimental to raising her son.

The mediator, an older woman who was all business, hadn't said much, nodding as she took in everything and occasionally looking over her glasses to stare at Julia.

Sam was right. She needed to get her mind off the custody case. So what if this night wasn't a real date and Sam wasn't her real boyfriend? It wouldn't stop her from enjoying herself.

Because of Charlie's car seat, she drove. Once they were close to the high school, she could see the line of cars. Half the town was at the carnival. She knew Lainey and Ethan would be there along with her mother.

"Is your dad coming tonight?" she asked, a thought suddenly blasting across her mind.

Sam nodded. "I told him we'll meet him."

"My mom is, too."

Sam made a choking sound. "Okay, good. They can get to know each other. It'll be great."

"That's one word for it."

"Does your mom believe the engagement? I haven't seen her since she walked in on us."

"I think so." Julia slowed to turn into the lower parking lot. "It's not the first time she's seen me be impulsive."

Sam shook his head as she turned off the ignition. "You never give yourself a break."

"Why do I deserve one?" She paused then said, "It's fine. I'm repairing my reputation with my family. It's a long progress, but I'm getting there. What makes you ask about my mom?"

"I saw Ethan downtown yesterday and he gave me the third degree about my intentions toward you."

"Ethan?"

"His big-brother routine was going strong. Told me how special you are and that if I hurt you or Charlie I'd have him to answer to."

"I don't know why he'd care. He went through hell because of me, although it's ancient history now."

"There you go again with the self-flagellation. We're going to need to work on that."

"Whatever you say." She got out of the car and picked up Charlie from his car seat. As she turned, she took in her old high school. It looked the same as it had almost fifteen years ago.

She filled her lungs with the cool night air. This was her favorite time of year in the North Carolina mountains. It smelled fresh and clean, the scent of spring reminding her of new beginnings. Coming off of the cold, wet winter, the change of seasons gave her hope.

Just like Sam.

Julia knew hope was dangerous. She was a sucker for believing in things that would never come to pass. She'd been like that in high school, too—wanting to believe she'd be able to keep up. Or, at least, admit how deeply her problem ran.

For some reason, that never seemed an option. Sam could say what he wanted about her learning disabilities being beyond her control. She knew it was true. But by high school, when elementary-age kids read more clearly than she could, it felt like stupidity.

None of her teachers had understood what was going on in her head. She'd never truly opened up to anyone about how bad it was. It had been easier to act as though she didn't care, to limp through school with a lot of blustering attitude and paying smarter kids to write her papers.

Charlie tapped her on the cheek. "Hi, Mama."

She shook off the memories. Sam stood next to her, watching with his too-knowing eyes.

"I'm guessing you haven't been back here for a while?"

"Not since graduation." She adjusted Charlie and headed for the gymnasium entrance. "Remind me again why we're here."

Sam put his hand on the small of her back, the gentle touch oddly comforting. "The annual Kiwanis carnival not only celebrates Fat Tuesday but raises a lot of money each year for local kids. It's a great event for the town."

"Spoken like a true pillar of the community." She gave an involuntary shiver. "Which I'm not and never will be."

"You never know. Either way, I promise you'll have fun. Greasy food, games, dancing."

Since she'd been back, she hadn't attended any town events. It was one thing to reconnect with people she'd known within the relative safety of the salon. No one was going to rehash old resentments while she wielded scissors. Here she was out of her element and not confident about the reception she'd get from the girls she once knew. Especially since she'd taken Brevia's most eligible bachelor off the market.

A memory niggled at the back of her mind. "Didn't you do a kissing booth last year or something like that?"

Sam's confident stride faltered. "They auctioned off dates with a couple local guys."

She flashed him a smile. "How much did you go for, Chief?"

In the fading light, she saw a distinct trail of red creep up his neck. "I don't remember."

"Liar." She stood in one spot until he turned to look at her. "Tell me."

"A thousand," he mumbled.

"Dollars?" She gasped. "Who in the world paid that much money for you?" When he leveled a look at her, she added, "Not that I don't think you're worth it. But not a lot of people around here have that kind of cash."

"It was for a good cause" was his only answer.

Another thought struck. "Unless…it was Ida Garvey!"

He turned and she trotted to catch up with him, Charlie bouncing on her hip. "Let me take him." Sam slid his arms around Charlie and scooped him up.

"It was Ida, wasn't it? She's the only one around here rich enough to pay that amount."

He gave a reluctant nod. "I got the most money."

"What kind of date did you take her on?"

"Would you believe I escorted her to her fiftieth high-school reunion over in Asheville? She had me wait on her hand and foot. Kept calling me her 'boy toy' in front of her old friends." He shook his head. "I swear my butt had bruises from being pinched so often."

Julia laughed harder than she had in ages. "You really are a hero, you know?"

"It's not funny."

"Yes, it is." She looked at him and saw humor shining in his eyes, as well. Then she noticed they were at the gym entrance, light spilling out into the darkening night. She studied Sam for another moment, wondering if he'd told her that story to ease her nerves.

He really was a good guy, she thought. He should be with someone like him—a woman who was smart and sweet.

Someone nothing like her.

He smoothed the skin between her eyebrows. "Stop frowning," he said gently. "We're going to have fun."

He dropped his hand, intertwined his fingers with hers and led her into the gymnasium. He greeted the two women working the ticket counter, neither of whom Julia recognized. Sam made introductions, and both women gave her a genuine smile and shook her hand, offering congratulations on their engagement. She flashed her ring but noticed Sam stiffen when one of the ladies complimented him on it.

Charlie became suddenly shy and buried his face in

the crook of Sam's neck, something Julia would have loved to do, as well.

"Come on, buddy," Sam coaxed. "Let's find some cotton candy."

"I don't think so," Julia said. "He hasn't had dinner yet."

Charlie gave Sam a wide grin. "Can-ee."

"We'll get a hot dog first," Sam promised her and moved into the crowd.

"Kids can always count on their dad for a good time," one of the women said with a laugh.

"While Mom cleans up the sick stomach," the other added.

"He's not..." Julia began, wanting to explain that Sam wasn't her son's father. Then she realized they already knew that, although Sam was certainly acting like the doting dad.

"He's quite a catch." The blonder of the two women winked at her.

Julia's stomach flipped because she knew how right the woman's statement was. "I'd better stick with them," she said and hurried after the two, emotions already at war in her mind and heart.

"Julia!" Lainey's voice carried over the crowd, and a moment later, she was surrounded by her sister, Ethan and their mother. Lainey gave her a long hug. "Sam said today was rough. Are you feeling any better?"

"I knew I should have come with you." Vera shook her head. "I'd like to get ahold of that family and talk some sense into them."

"When did you see Sam?" The thought of Sam giving information about her to her family made her more than a little uncomfortable.

"I ran into him downtown," Lainey said. "What's the big deal?"

"He shouldn't have said anything."

"He's going to be your husband," Vera corrected. "He has a right to worry."

"We all do," Lainey echoed. "Jules, you've got to let us help you. You're not alone."

"Where's the little man?" Ethan asked, his internal radar about conflict between the three Morgan women practically glowing bright red through his T-shirt.

"Right here," Sam answered, balancing a huge cotton candy and a paper plate with hot-dog chunks and small pieces of watermelon on it.

Charlie reached for a piece of fruit and babbled a few nonsense words.

"You cut up the hot dog," Julia said, stunned.

Sam's forehead wrinkled. "I thought you were supposed to cut up round food when kids are little."

"You are." Julia felt ridiculous that something so minor had such an effect on her emotions. "I didn't realize you'd know it."

"Don't be silly." Vera reached for Charlie and snuggled him against her. "He's spent enough time around you and Charlie to realize that."

Julia saw Lainey studying her, a thoughtful expression on her face. "That's right. Isn't it, Jules?"

Julia nodded and stepped next to Sam, leaning up to kiss him on the cheek. "Of course. Thanks, hon."

Lainey's features relaxed and Julia blew out a quiet breath of relief.

"There's my favorite son and future daughter-in-law." So much for her short-lived relief. Julia heard Sam groan. She turned and was enveloped in one of Joe Callahan's bear hugs. He moved from her to Sam. "Look at you, Sammy. Surrounded by friends with the woman you love at your side." His meaty hands clasped either side of Sam's jaw. "I'm so proud of you, son. You're not a loner anymore. I thought my mistakes had cost you a chance at a real life. But you're making it happen."

"Dad, enough." Sam pulled Joe's hands away. "Not the time or the place."

"There's always time to say 'I love you.'"

Sam met Julia's gaze over his father's shoulders. His eyes screamed "help me," and as fascinating as everyone seemed to find the father-son interaction, she intervened.

"Joe, I'd like you to meet my family."

He turned, his smile a mile wide.

"This is my sister, Lainey, and her husband, Ethan Daniels."

Joe pumped their hands enthusiastically. "Pleasure to meet you both. I'm Joe Callahan."

"Are you in town for long, Mr. Callahan?" Lainey asked.

"As long as it takes," Joe said with a wink at Sam.

A muscle in Sam's jaw ticked and his eyes drifted shut as he muttered to himself. They flew open a moment later when Ethan added, "You, Sammy and I should do some fishing once the weather warms up."

"Don't call me Sammy."

"I'd love to."

Vera cleared her throat.

"Sorry. This is my mother, Vera Morgan. And you've met Charlie."

Joe's eyes widened as he looked at Vera. "Well, I certainly see where you two girls get your beauty. Ms. Morgan, you are a sight to behold."

Vera held out her hand like the Southern belle she'd once been. Joe bent over her fingers and kissed them lightly. "Why, Mr. Callahan," she said, her accent getting thicker with every syllable. "You are a silver-tongued devil, I believe."

"Shoot me now," Sam muttered.

Julia's eyes rolled. She was used to this routine with her mother. Vera had been a devoted wife to her late husband, but since his death, she'd reinvented herself not only as an animal-rescue expert but as a woman with a long list of admirers. Unlike Julia, her mother always made sure the men with whom she was acquainted treated her like a lady, fawning around her until Vera moved on to the next one in line.

"Here she goes," Lainey whispered, as Vera tucked her chin and fluttered her eyelashes. Charlie watched the two for a moment then reached for Sam.

"Can-ee," the boy demanded, and Joe took the cotton candy from Sam.

"Come here, Charlie," Joe said and lifted him from Vera's arms. At this rate, Charlie would be held by more people than the Stanley Cup.

"Why don't I take him," Julia suggested.

"Joe and I will take him to the carnival games," Vera said.

"That's right," Joe told them with a wink. "You young folks can head to the dance floor or grab a drink."

Before she could argue, Joe and Vera disappeared into the sea of people, Charlie waving over Joe's shoulder.

"I'm up for a beer." Ethan looked at Sam. "How about you, Sammy boy?"

"Don't go there," Sam warned.

"Stop—you're going to make me cry." Ethan laughed

until Lainey socked him in the gut. "Hey," he said on a cough.

"I thought Sam's dad was sweet." Lainey grinned at Sam. "He obviously loves you." Her gaze switched to Julia. "You and Charlie, too. Mom's going to eat him up with a spoon."

"A terrifying thought." Julia'd known this night was a bad idea.

"Come on," Lainey said to all three of them. "Let's get something to eat. They had a pasta booth in the corner."

Ethan wrapped one long arm around Lainey and kissed the top of her head. "Yeah, like a double date."

Julia couldn't help it—she burst out laughing. "This is going to be great. We'll be besties." Who would have thought that she'd be double-dating with her first boyfriend and her sister? It was too crazy to imagine.

She looked at Sam, expecting him to be laughing right along with her. Instead, his brows were drawn low over his vivid blue eyes.

"Fine by me." He took her hand to follow Lainey and Ethan toward the back of the gym.

"What's wrong?" she whispered, pulling him to slow down so they were out of hearing range. "Is it my mom and Joe? She's harmless, I promise. Her former admirers still adore her. Whatever happens, she won't hurt your dad."

Sam's arm was solid as a rock as his muscles tensed. "Does it seem strange to be so chummy with your ex-boyfriend?"

Julia thought about Jeff, then realized that was not who Sam meant. "Ethan's married to my sister. We've been over more than a decade. He's so much like my brother, I barely remember he's seen me naked."

Sam stopped on a dime, causing her to bump into the length of him. "Is that a joke?"

She wrinkled her nose. "I thought it was funny."

"It's not."

"Come on, Sam. You see how he looks at Lainey. He never once looked at me in that way. He's different with her, and I couldn't be happier. For both of them. It's old news, even around Brevia. That's an accomplishment, given how gossip takes on a life of its own in this town." She flashed him a sassy grin. "Chief Callahan, is it possible you're jealous?"

"I don't want to look like a fool. I've been down the road of public humiliation and the scenery sucks. Why would I be jealous? You said yourself Ethan's like your brother."

Julia studied him then placed a soft kiss on his mouth. "I'd never do something to make you look like a fool. Scout's honor."

"I can't imagine you as a Girl Scout." Sam forced his lips to curve into a smile, wondering at his odd reaction. He wasn't the jealous type, and he knew how happy Ethan and Lainey were together. "Let's find them." He took Julia's hand again.

A number of people waved or stopped to say hello as they made their way through the crowd. At first, Julia tensed at every new greeting. Eventually he felt her relax, but she never loosened her death grip on his hand. He wanted to protect her, he realized, and also to show her she could belong to this community again. The people of Brevia had welcomed him, and if Julia gave them a chance, he was sure they'd accept her.

They caught up with Ethan and Lainey and grabbed a table near the makeshift dance floor. The sisters bantered back and forth, making Sam wish for a better relationship with his own brother.

Even before Scott had cheated with Sam's fiancée, they hadn't been close. Sam had been the responsible brother, stoic and toeing the line, while Scott had been wild, always getting into trouble and constantly resenting his older brother's interference in his life.

"How are things around town these days?" Ethan asked as he set a second beer on the table next to Sam.

"Quiet for a change." Sam took another bite of pasta then swallowed hard as Julia tilted back her head to laugh at something Lainey said. The column of her neck was smooth and long. He ached to trail a line of kisses across her skin.

He pushed away the beer, realizing he was going to need his wits about him to remain in control tonight.

"Were you involved in the drug bust over in Tellet County a few nights back?"

Julia stopped midsentence as her eyes snapped to his. "What drug bust? Sounds dangerous. Why didn't I hear about a drug bust?"

Sam threw Ethan what he hoped was a *shut your mouth* look.

"Sorry, man," Ethan said quickly. "Hey, Lainey, let's hit the dance floor."

Lainey popped out of her chair. "Love to."

"Cowards," Julia muttered as she watched them go. She turned her angry gaze back to Sam. "You were saying?"

"A meth lab outside the county lines," he told her. It had been a long time since anyone had cared about what he was doing and whether it was dangerous or not. "It's been kept quiet so far because the sheriff thinks it's part of a bigger tristate operation. We want to see if we can flush out a couple of the bigger fish."

She tapped one finger on the table. "I don't like you being involved in something like that."

"It's my job, Julia."

"I need to know about these things. I bet Abby Brighton knew where you were during the drug bust."

"She's my secretary. Of course she knew."

"We're engaged."

"Is that so?"

To his great amusement, she squirmed in her chair. "As far as everyone around here thinks. I need to be kept informed."

"Why?"

"To know whether I should worry."

"One more reason I wouldn't be a good bet in a real relationship. Ask my ex. I don't like to report in. I don't like anyone worried about me." He blew out a frustrated breath. "My job is dangerous almost every day. I deal with it, but I don't expect you or anyone else to."

"No one's allowed to care about you?" Her eyes flashed, temper lighting them.

"I don't need anyone to care."

"The Lone Ranger rides again." Julia pushed away from the table. He grabbed her wrist so she couldn't escape.

"Why are you mad? This doesn't have anything to do with you. We have a business arrangement. That's what we both wanted. It's not going to help either of us to be emotionally involved with the other one's life."

"Some of us care, whether we want to or not."

Her eyes shone and his heart leaped in his chest. He pulled her tight against him, aware they were gathering stares from people standing nearby. "Thank you for caring. I'm not used to it, but it means a lot." He pressed his forehead to hers. "I'm sorry I'm bad at this. Even for pretend."

"You're not *so* bad," she whispered.

"Do you want to dance?"

"Do you?"

He grinned at her. "Hell, no. But I can make it work."

"Give me a minute. I need to catch up with my mom and Joe, make sure Charlie's okay."

He studied her. "If I didn't know better, I'd say you're avoiding me right now."

She shook her head. "I want to find Charlie."

"They headed back toward the game booths. I'm going to say hi to the mayor and I'll meet you over there."

The gym was full, and without Sam at her side, Julia got a little panicked by the crowd.

She moved toward the far end of the gymnasium where the carnival booths were set up, then veered off quickly when she saw two women from her high-school class standing together near one of the attractions. One was Annabeth Sullivan, whom Julia felt friendlier toward after their conversation at the salon. The other was Lucy Peterson, their graduating class's valedictorian. Julia had always been uncomfortable around her. She'd made it clear during high school that Lucy was persona non grata and knew the slightly chubby teen had suffered because of it.

Lucy had gotten her revenge, though. Because of her work in the school office and her access to the files, she'd found out about Julia's learning disabilities. She hadn't told anyone outright, but had spread the rumor that Julia had only graduated because she'd slept with one of her teachers and he'd fixed her grade.

She'd told Julia that if she denied it, Lucy would tell people the real reason she had so much trouble in school. Having a reputation as a slut hadn't been half as bad as the school knowing about her LD.

She ducked out a door and into the cool night air, walking toward the football field situated next to the main building. Two streetlights glowed in the darkness as her eyes scanned the shadowy length of the field.

She'd spent so much time here in high school. If she'd been queen of her class, this was her royal court. She'd felt confident on the field in her cheerleading uniform or on the sidelines cheering for Ethan. She'd hated falling back on her looks, but the insecure girl who had nothing else to offer had exploited her one gift as best she could.

Now she breathed in the cool night air and closed her eyes, remembering the familiar smells and sounds.

Her memories here were a long time gone. She was no longer a scared teenager. She had Charlie to protect. She'd made mistakes and was trying her damnedest to make amends for them. There was no way of moving forward without finally confronting her past, once and for all.

Chapter 10

She took another breath and headed toward the school, determined to hold her head high. She had as much right to return to her high school as anyone.

Once inside, she stopped at the girls' bathroom to sprinkle cold water on her face. When a stall opened and Lucy Peterson stepped out, Julia wondered if she'd actually conjured her.

"Hi, Lucy." The other woman's eyes widened in surprise.

Lucy hadn't changed much since high school. She was still short and full figured, her chest heaving as she adjusted the wire-rimmed glasses on her face.

"Hello, Julia. I didn't expect to see you here. I'm in town for the weekend for my parents' anniversary. Normally I wouldn't be caught dead back in this high school. I live in Chicago. I'm a doctor." Lucy paused for a breath. "I'm babbling."

"What kind of doctor?" Julia asked.

"Molecular biologist."

Julia nodded. Figured. Julia knew better than to compare herself to a genius like Lucy. "That's great."

The two women stared at each other for several long moments. At the same time they blurted, "I'm sorry."

Relief mixed with a healthy dose of confusion made Julia's shoulders sag. "I'm the one who should apologize. I know I was horrible in high school. You were on the top of my list. Not that it matters, but you should know I was jealous of you."

Lucy looked doubtful. "Of me? You were the homecoming queen, prom queen, head cheerleader, and you dated the football captain. I was nobody."

"You were smart."

"I shouldn't have spread that rumor about you." Lucy fiddled with the ring on her left finger. "You weren't a slut."

"There are worse things you could have said about me."

"You weren't stupid, either."

Julia made her voice light. "The grade record would beg to differ."

"I read your file," Lucy said slowly. "It was wrong, but I know you had significant learning disabilities, which means…"

"It means there's something wrong with my brain," Julia finished. "*Stupid* is a much clearer description of my basic problem."

"You must have been pretty clever to have hid it all those years. I'm guessing you still are."

"I cut hair for a living. It's not nuclear science. Or molecular biology."

"That's right. My mom told me you'd taken over the Hairhouse."

"I'm working on it. The loan still needs to go through."

"Are you going to keep the name?"

Julia relaxed a little as she smiled. "I don't think so. 'The Best Little Hairhouse in Brevia' is quite a mouthful."

Lucy returned the smile then pulled at the ends of her hair. "I'm in town until Tuesday. Could you fit me in?"

"You don't hate me?"

Lucy shook her head. "In high school, I thought I was the only one who was miserable. Once I got away from Brevia, I realized lots of kids had problems. We were all just too narcissistic to see it in each other. Some people can't let go of the past. I've moved on, Julia. I'm happy in Chicago. I have a great career and a fantastic husband. I don't even mind visiting my mom a couple times a year, although I avoid the old crowd. I know in my heart they can't hurt me because their opinions don't matter. I don't hate you. You probably did me a favor. You made me determined to escape. Now I can come back on my own terms."

"I'm glad for you, Lucy." Julia checked her mental calendar. She'd trained herself to keep her schedule in her head so she didn't have to rely on a planner or smartphone. "How about eleven on Monday?"

Lucy nodded. "Maybe we could grab lunch after. I may not care too much about certain ladies' opinions but I wouldn't mind seeing their faces if we showed up at Carl's."

"I'd love that."

"I'll see you Monday." With a quick, awkward hug, Lucy hurried out the door.

Julia studied herself in the hazy mirror above the row of bathroom sinks. She felt lighter than she had in years, the weight of her guilt over how she'd treated Lucy finally lifted. One past mistake vanquished, only a hundred more to go.

"She's right, you know." The door to one of the stalls swung open to reveal Lexi Preston.

Julia's shoulders went rigid again. "Eavesdrop much?" She took a step toward Lexi. "I don't suppose you're going to put that conversation on the official record? It didn't make me out to be the deadbeat you're trying to convince the court I am."

"I don't think you're a deadbeat," Lexi said, sounding almost contrite. "You're not stupid, either. But I have to do my job. The Johnsons—"

"They call the shots, right? You do the dirty work for them, digging up damaging information on me and probably countless other family enemies."

"It's not personal." Lexi's voice was a miserable whisper.

Julia felt a quick stab of sympathy before her temper began to boil over. She was always too gullible, wanting to believe people weren't as bad as they seemed. It led to her being taken advantage of on more than one occasion. Not this time, though.

She had to physically restrain herself from grabbing Lexi's crisp button-down and slamming the petite attorney into one of the metal stalls. "How can you say that? You're helping them take my son away from me. My son!" Tears flooded her eyes and she turned away, once again feeling helpless to stop the inevitable outcome.

"I don't want you to lose your son," Lexi said quietly. "If I had my way…" She paused then added, "Hiding who you are and the reasons you did things isn't going to help your case. You're not the one with the big secrets here."

Julia whirled around. "Are the Johnsons hiding something? Do you have information that could help me keep Charlie?"

Lexi shook her head. "I've said too much." She reached for the door. "You're a good mother, Julia. But you have to believe it."

Julia followed Lexi into the hall, but before she could catch up a loud crash from down the hall distracted her. She heard a round of shouts and her first thought was of Charlie.

Chaos reigned in the gymnasium as people pushed toward the exits. Julia stood on her tiptoes and scanned the crowd, spotting Joe Callahan with his arm around her mother near the bleachers. Vera held Charlie, who was contentedly spooning ice cream into his mouth, oblivious to the commotion.

Julia elbowed her way through the throng of people to Vera and Joe. "Charlie," she said on a breath, and her son launched himself at her.

"Banilla, Mama."

"I see, sweetie." She hugged him tight against her.

"Why is everyone rushing out of here?" She noticed that many older folks, like Joe and Vera, hung back.

"Big fight outside," someone passing by called. "Eddie Kelton caught his wife in the back of their minivan with his best friend."

"He's going to kill him," the man's companion said with a sick laugh. "Someone said Eddie's got a knife."

Julia grimaced. She'd gone to school with Eddie's older brother. "The Keltons are not a stable bunch," she murmured.

Joe patted her shoulder. "Don't worry, hon. Sam will handle it. I'd be out there but I don't want to leave your mom."

"Such a gentleman."

"Sam?" Julia's heart rate quickened. "Why is Sam out there?"

"Because he's the police chief." Vera spoke slowly, as if Julia were a small child.

"He's not on duty. Shouldn't they call a deputy?"

"Cops are never truly off duty," Joe said with a sigh. "But Sammy can take care of himself."

"Eddie Kelton has a knife." Julia practically jumped up and down with agitation. Her palms were sweating and clammy. Sam could take care of himself, but she couldn't stop her anxiety from spilling over. "This isn't part of the evening's entertainment. It's real life."

Joe nodded. "Being the wife of a law-enforcement officer isn't easy." He patted her shoulder again and she wanted to rip his wrist out of the socket. He pulled his hand away as if he could read her mind. "If it will make you feel better, I'll check on him. I may be rusty but I could handle a couple troublemakers in my day."

Vera gave a dreamy sigh. A muscle above Julia's eye began to twitch.

"I bet you were quite a sight," Vera practically purred.

"You know what would make me feel better? If I go and check on him." She sat Charlie on the bleachers. "Stay here with Grandma, okay, buddy?"

"Gramma," Charlie said around a mouthful.

"I'll escort you," Joe said in the same cop tone Julia'd heard Sam use. "If you're okay for a few minutes on your own?" he asked Vera.

"Be a hero," Vera answered, batting her lashes.

Julia thought about arguing but figured he could be useful. "Can you get me to the front?"

"Yes, ma'am."

He took her elbow and, true to his word, guided her through the groups spilling into the parking lot. Was it some kind of police Jedi mind trick that enabled cops to manage throngs of people?

She poked her head through the row of spectators to see Sam between two men, arms out, a finger pointed at each of them.

Eddie Kelton, his wife, Stacey, and a man Julia didn't recognize stood in the parking lot under the lights. The unknown man had his shirt on inside out and his jeans were half zipped. Julia assumed he was the man Stacey had been with. Another telltale sign was the black eye forming above his cheek.

Stacey stood to one side, weeping loudly into her hands.

"For the last time, Eddie, put the knife down." Sam looked as if he'd grown several inches since Julia had seen him minutes earlier. He was broad and strong, every muscle in his body on full alert. A surge of pride flashed through her, along with the nail-biting fear of seeing him in action.

Eddie Kelton couldn't have been more than five foot seven, a wiry strip of a man, aged beyond his years thanks to working in the sun on a local construction crew. His face sported a bloody nose, busted lip and a large scratch above his left eye. Julia gathered he'd been on the losing end of the fight until he'd brandished the six-inch blade jiggling between his fingers.

"That's my woman, Chief." Eddie's arm trembled. "My wife. He's supposed to be my best friend and he had my wife." Eddie's wild gaze switched to Stacey. "How could you do this to me? I loved you."

She let out a wretched sob. "You don't act like you love me. Always down at the bar after work or passed out on the couch." Her eyes darted around the crowd. "I found the adult movies on the computer. I want someone who wants me. Who pays attention to me. Who makes me feel like a woman and not just the housekeeper."

"I loved you," Eddie screamed.

"It was only—" the half-dressed man began.

"Shut up, Jon-o," Eddie and Stacey yelled at the same time.

Eddie slashed the air with his knife.

Sam held his ground.

Julia held her breath.

"Eddie, I know what you're feeling." Sam's voice was a soothing murmur.

"You don't know squat," Eddie spat out, dancing back and forth on the balls of his feet. "I'm going to cut off his junk here and now."

"Don't you threaten my junk," the other man yelled back. "If you were a real man—"

Sam's head whipped around. "Jon Dallas, shut your mouth or I'm going to arrest you for public indecency." He turned back to Eddie. "I do know. A few years ago I walked in on my brother and my fiancée getting busy on the kitchen table."

A collective gasp went up from the crowd and several heads turned toward Julia. "Not me," she whispered impatiently. "His ex."

Sam's gaze never left Eddie, so she had no idea if he realized she was there.

Eddie's bloodshot eyes brimmed with tears. "It gets

you right here," he said, thumping his chest with the hand not gripping the knife. "Like she reached in and cut out your heart."

Sam nodded. "You're not going to make anything better with the knife. Drop it and we'll talk about what's next."

"I'm sorry, Eddie." Stacey's voice was so filled with anguish Julia almost felt sorry for her. Except for the small matter that she'd been caught cheating on her husband. "I made a horrible mistake. It didn't mean anything."

"Hey—" Jon-o sputtered.

"I love you, Eddie." Stacey sobbed.

Eddie lowered the knife but Sam didn't relax. "Drop it and kick it to me," he ordered. "She loves you, Eddie."

"I love her, too." Eddie's voice was miserable. "But she cheated."

"We didn't even do it," Stacey called, and Julia wished the woman understood the concept of *too much information*. "He was drunk. Couldn't get it—"

Jon-o took an angry step toward her. "Shut your fat mouth, you liar. I was the best—"

For a second, Sam's attention switched to Jon-o and Stacey. In that instant, Eddie launched himself forward.

He lunged for Jon-o but Sam grabbed his arm. Julia screamed as Eddie stabbed wildly at Sam, who knocked the blade out of the man's hand then slammed him to the ground. Pete Butler, Sam's deputy, rushed forward and tossed Sam a pair of handcuffs before turning his attention to Jon-o, pushing him away from the action.

Stacey melted into a puddle on the ground. "Eddie, no," she whimpered. "Don't put handcuffs on my husband."

Sam got Eddie to his feet.

"Don't worry, honey." Stacey took a step forward. "I'll bail you out. I love you so much."

Tears ran down Eddie's face. "I love you, sugar-buns."

Stacey would have wrapped herself around her husband but Sam held up a hand. "Later, Stacey." Jon-o disappeared into the crowd and Sam yanked Eddie toward Pete. "Put him in the holding cell overnight. He can sober up."

Pete pointed to Sam's shoulder. Sam shook his head, so the deputy led Eddie toward the waiting squad car.

"We're done out here," Sam announced to the crowd. "Everyone head inside. There's a lot more money to be raised tonight."

After a quiet round of applause, people drifted toward the gymnasium. A couple of men approached Sam, slapping him on the back.

"I told you he'd handle it," Joe said proudly from Julia's side.

"You did." Julia felt rooted to the spot where she stood. Her body felt as though it weighed a thousand pounds. She couldn't explain what she'd felt when Eddie had rushed at Sam with the knife. She'd swear she'd aged ten years in those few seconds.

"Nice going, son," Joe called.

Sam looked up and his gaze met Julia's. He gave her a small smile and her whole body began to shake. She walked toward him and threw her arms around his neck, burying her face in his shirt collar. He smelled sweet, like leftover cotton candy, and felt so undeniably strong, she could have wept. She wouldn't cry. She wasn't that much of an emotional basket case, but she squeezed her eyes shut for good measure.

She willed the trembling to stop. It started to as he rubbed his palm against her back.

"Hey," he said into her hair. "Not that I'm complaining about you wrapped around me, but it's okay. It was nothing. Eddie was too drunk to do any real damage, even if he'd wanted to."

She didn't know how long he held her. She was vaguely aware of people milling about, of Joe watching from nearby. Sam didn't seem in any hurry to let her go. She needed the strength of his body around hers to reassure her that he was truly all right.

When she was finally in control enough to open her eyes, she was shocked to see blood staining his shirt near the shoulder. "You're hurt." Her voice came out a croak.

He shook his head. "The blade nicked me. It's a scratch. I'll stop by the hospital after we finish the paperwork to have it cleaned. Nothing more."

"He could have hurt you," she whispered, unable to take her eyes off his shoulder.

He tipped up her chin. His eyes were warm on hers, kind and understanding. "I'm okay. Nothing happened."

"It could have. Every day something *could* happen to you, Sam. Drug busts, drunken fights and who knows what else."

"I'm fine."

"I'm not. I can't stand knowing you're always at risk."

He looked over her shoulder to where Joe stood. When his eyes met hers again, they were cold and unreadable. He leaned in close to her ear. "Then it's a good thing this is a fake engagement. I'm not giving up my life for a woman."

Julia felt the air rush from her lungs. "I didn't say I wanted you to." She grabbed on to the front of his shirt as he moved to pull away. "I know this is fake. Sue me, but I was worried. Heaven forbid someone cares about you, Sam. Expects something from you. Maybe I shouldn't have—"

"Forget it." Sam kissed her cheek, but she knew it was because his father was still watching. "I have to go into the station and then to the hospital, so I'll be a while. Take Charlie home. We'll talk tomorrow."

"Don't do this," she whispered as he walked away, climbing into the police cruiser without looking back.

She knew this was fake. Because she'd never be stupid enough to fall in love with a man so irritating, annoying and unwilling to have a meaningful conversation about his feelings.

She turned to Joe. "At least he's okay. That's most important, right?"

"It's hard for him to be needed by someone," Joe said, taking her arm and leading her back toward the high school.

Julia snorted. "Ya think?"

Rotating his shoulder where the nurse had cleaned his wound, Sam stepped out of the E.R. into the darkness. His father's car wasn't in front, so he sat on the bench near the entrance to wait.

He scrubbed his palms against his face, wondering how he'd made such a colossal mess of a night that had started off so well. Julia had looked beautiful, as always, and they'd had fun with Charlie at the carnival. He'd even survived his dad and her mother meeting and almost felt okay about her relationship with Ethan.

Then he'd put his foot in his mouth in a thousand different ways when she'd been concerned about his job.

Hell, he couldn't name a cop's wife who didn't worry. He'd liked that she'd been worried, liked the feeling of being needed. It had also scared him and he'd pushed her away.

Like he pushed everyone away.

He was alone. Again. As always.

"Need a lift, Chief?"

He turned to see her standing a few feet away, the light from the hospital's entrance making her glow like an angel. Not that he knew whether angels glowed. He imagined they'd want to, if it meant they'd look like Julia Morgan.

"My dad's coming to get me. Where's Charlie?"

"He's having a sleepover with Grandma." She walked to the bench and sat next to him. "How's your shoulder?"

He shrugged, finding it difficult to concentrate with her thigh pressed against his leg. "Hurts worse after the nurse messed with it than when the knife grazed me."

She bit her lip when he said the word *knife*. "You're lucky it wasn't worse."

"I guess."

"Joe's not coming to get you."

"I may want to reconsider that ride."

"You may."

"Why are you here, Julia?"

She rocked back far enough to stuff her fingers under her legs. Lucky fingers. He'd give anything to trade places with her hands.

"Just because our engagement isn't real doesn't mean I can't worry about you. I'm human. I like you. Caring about friends is what people do."

"We're friends." He tried the word out in his mind and decided he liked it. Sam didn't have many real friends.

"I think so."

He couldn't resist asking, "With benefits?"

She continued to stare straight ahead but one side of her mouth kicked up. "That remains to be seen. You're not moving in the right direction with the bad 'tude earlier."

"Would it help if I said I was sorry?"

"Are you?"

With one finger, he traced a path down her arm, gently tugging on her wrist until she lifted her hand. He intertwined his fingers with hers. "Yes, I'm sorry. I'm sorry you were scared. I'm sorry I was a jerk."

"I know you don't owe me anything."

"I do owe you. So far, I'm the only one who's benefited from our arrangement. You wouldn't let me go to court with you. I made an enormous mess of trying to get your mind off the case and now you're here picking me up. What have I done to help you? Nothing."

"That's not true."

"It is. I want to help. I'm going to the final hearing with you."

"I—"

"No arguments."

She nodded. That was a start. "We can get people to submit affidavits on your behalf," he continued. "Character references for you. The girls from the salon will do it. I bet Ida Garvey would, too, now that her hair isn't bright pink. I want to hear you agree. I can help. You have to let me."

"My LD changes everything." She looked at him, her eyes fierce. He knew this moment meant something big.

"You have trouble reading," he said slowly. "And with

numbers. It caused a lot of problems but you told me you're working with a specialist."

"My brain doesn't work right." She made the statement with conviction, as if daring him to disagree.

"Is that the clinical diagnosis? Your brain doesn't work right? I don't think so, sweetie."

"Don't 'sweetie' me. I'm stupid, and Jeff and his family know it. My brain is broken. It takes me twice as long as it should to read a simple letter. Why do you think I bring paperwork home from the salon so often? I spend all night checking and rechecking my work so I don't make mistakes."

"Everyone makes mistakes."

"You don't understand. But Jeff does. He knows how badly I want this to stay a secret." She bolted up from the bench, pacing back and forth in front of him. "So much of what the attorney is talking about stems from my LD. I've hidden it for years and now they're using it against me."

"Why keep it a secret?"

"Because—" she dragged out the word on a ragged breath "—if the people around me knew how dumb I am, they could and would take advantage of me. In Brevia, I can hide it. If I really get into a bind, my mom or Lainey can help. I don't want the whole town talking about it."

Something struck a chord deep within Sam. He knew what it was like to put on a mask so people couldn't really see what was inside of you. He knew how it felt to be afraid you wouldn't measure up. But his demons were more easily buried than Julia's. The thought of how much time and energy she'd put into hiding this piece of herself made his heart ache.

She was smart, proud and brave. She'd spent years making everyone believe she didn't care, when the reality was that she cared more than she could admit. He could see it on her face, see the tension radiating through her body as she waited for him to judge her the way she'd been judging herself for years.

He stood and cupped her face between his hands. "You're not stupid."

She searched his eyes, as if willing the words to be true. "They're trying to use it against me, Sam. To prove that Charlie would be better off with them. Not only are they ready to lavish him with their version of lifestyles of the rich and famous, they're saying that if he has the same disorder…" Her voice caught and she bit her lip before continuing, "If I've given this to him, they have the resources to get him the best help."

"*You* are what's best for him." He used his thumb to wipe away a lone tear that trailed down her cheek then brought his lips to the spot, tasting the salt on her skin.

The automatic doors slid open and a hospital worker pushed a wheelchair into the night.

"Let's get out of here," Sam whispered.

Julia nodded, and he cradled her against him as they walked to her car.

"Let me drive," he said when she reached into her purse for the keys.

"You're the injured one." But when he took the keys from her hand, she didn't argue.

The streets were quiet. Julia didn't speak, but she held on to the hand he placed in her lap. He could imagine the thoughts running through her mind as she realized the secret she'd held close for so long was about to become public. She was wrung out emotionally, and he hated seeing it. All he wanted was to make her feel better, if only for a few moments.

He pulled into his driveway and turned off the ignition.

"I should go home," she said, releasing his fingers. "You need to rest."

Rest was the last thing on Sam's mind. He might not be a master with words but he knew he wasn't going to let her go tonight. If he couldn't tell her how amazing she was and have her believe it, he could damn well show her.

He came around to open her car door and draw her out, lacing his fingers with hers once again.

"I need to go," she repeated, her voice small.

Without a word, he led her up onto the porch and unlocked his front door. He turned and pulled her to him, slanting his mouth over hers. For a moment she froze, then she melted against him, the spark between them flaring into an incendiary fire.

He kissed her jaw and the creamy skin of her throat, whispering, "Stay with me."

She nodded as he nipped at her earlobe and, not letting her go, reached back to push open the door and drag them both through. He kicked it shut and tugged on the hem of her T-shirt.

"This. Off. Now."

"Bossy," she said breathlessly. Through his desire, he heard the confidence return to her tone and was so glad for it, he could have laughed out loud.

Just as suddenly, he couldn't make a sound as she pulled the soft cotton over her head and was left bathed in moonlight wearing only a lacy black bra and jeans slung low on her hips.

Sweet mercy.

He knew she was beautiful, but he'd been with beautiful women before. Watching her watch him, though, her eyes smoky and wanting, was almost his undoing.

He flicked one thin strap off her shoulder, then the other, not quite exposing her completely but giving him a view of more creamy flesh. He traced the line of fabric across the tops of her breasts and his body grew heavy at her intake of breath.

She wrapped her hand around his finger and lifted it to her mouth, kissing the tip softly. "You, now," she commanded, her voice husky.

Sam was happy to comply, and he threw his shirt onto the nearby couch. She stepped forward and, in one fluid motion, reached behind her to unhook her bra. It fell to the floor between them. Then she pressed herself against his chest and trailed her lips over his wounded shoulder.

"If it matters," he said, his voice hoarse, "that's not the part that hurts."

He felt her smile against him. "We'll get to that. All in good time, Chief. All in good time."

From Sam's point of view, that time was now. He bent his head and took her mouth, kissing her as he reached between them to unfasten her jeans. He dropped to his knees in front of her, kissing the curve of her belly. She smelled like sin and sunshine, and the mix made him dizzy with need.

"I want you, Julia Morgan." He lifted his head so he could look into her eyes. "I want you," he repeated. "All of you. Just the way you are."

Her lips parted, and he saw trust and vulnerability flash in her eyes. He wanted that, wanted all of this. For the first time in his life, he wanted to be a man someone could depend on for the long haul.

He wanted to be a real hero.

"I'm going to take care of you," he whispered.

She smiled at him and shimmied her hips so that her jeans slipped off them.

"What are you waiting for?" she asked, and he straightened, capturing her mouth again.

Sam broke the kiss long enough to lead her the few steps to the couch. He stripped off his jeans then eased his body over hers, relishing the feel of skin on skin. She fit perfectly under him, as he'd guessed she would.

He savored every touch, taking the time to explore her body with his fingers and mouth. Her answering passion filled him with a desire he'd never imagined before tonight. He finally made her his, entering her with an exquisite slowness before his need for her took over and they moved together in a perfect rhythm.

"You are amazing," he whispered as he held her gaze.

"You're not so bad yourself," she answered, but her eyes were cloudy with passion.

"I'm going to prove how very good I am." He smiled then nipped at the soft skin of her earlobe. "All night long."

Chapter 11

Wow.

Hours later, Julia's brain registered that one syllable.

"Wow," Sam murmured against her hair, clearly still trying to catch his breath.

She knew the feeling. She'd had good sex in her life—maybe even great a couple of times. This night had blown away her every expectation about what intimacy felt like when it was exactly right. She wanted to believe it was because she'd been on a long hiatus.

If she admitted the truth, Sam had been worth a two-year wait. Her body felt boneless, as if she never wanted to move from where she lay stretched across him, the short hair on his chest tickling her bare skin.

The unfamiliar feeling of contentment jolted her back into reality. Their relationship was precarious enough, sometimes hot and often cold enough to give her frostbite. He challenged her, irritated her and filled her with such incredible need, she wondered how she'd walk away when the business part of their arrangement was over.

That sobering thought in mind, she rolled off him. He automatically tucked the light duvet in around her. They'd made it to his bedroom.

Eventually.

After the couch in his living room. And the stairs. The stairs? She hadn't even known that was possible, let alone that it would be downright amazing.

It was still dark and she couldn't make out much more than the outlines of furniture around the room and the fact that his bed was enormous. It suited him.

She glanced at the glowing numbers of the digital clock on the nightstand next to the bed. He shifted, propping himself on one elbow and wrapping the other arm around her waist.

"Don't go."

She tilted her head away, his face in shadow from the moonlight slanting through the bedroom window. She couldn't see his eyes and hoped hers were hidden, as well.

How did he know she was getting ready to bolt? Julia had never been much of a cuddler. The emotional boundaries she put around herself often manifested in physical limits, as well.

She looked at the ceiling. Even if she couldn't see his eyes, she knew his gaze was intense. "As fun as this was…"

His soft chuckle rumbled in the quiet, making her insides tingle again. She'd done a lot of tingling tonight.

"Fun," he repeated.

"We've got chemistry."

He laughed again.

"This isn't funny." She didn't want to make more of this than it was. She'd start talking and end up embarrassing herself with romantic declarations about how much she liked—more than liked, if she admitted the truth—being with Sam, both in the bedroom and out of it. He was the first man she felt wanted her for her, not what she looked like or an image she portrayed. It was both liberating and frightening to reveal her true self to someone.

"*You're* funny." He kissed the tip of her nose and pulled her tighter against the length of him. "And smart." He kissed one cheek. "And sexy as hell." Then the other. "I want you to spend the night." His lips met hers.

She broke the kiss. "I think we've about wrapped things up here."

He traced the seam of her mouth with his tongue. "We've only gotten started."

Julia felt her resolve disappear. She knew it was a mistake but she couldn't make her body move an inch. "Are you sure?"

"I've never been more sure."

It had been ages since Julia'd wanted to be with someone as much as she did Sam. "I guess that would be okay."

"Okay?" He tickled her belly and she wriggled in response.

"More than okay."

"That's what I thought."

She expected him to kiss her again, but instead he snuggled in behind her, smoothing her hair across the pillow.

"Sleep," he told her.

"Oh. I thought you wanted to…"

"I do. Later."

Her spine stiffened. "I've never been much for spooning."

"I can tell." His finger drew circles along her back until she began to relax. "Why did you pick me up tonight?"

"I don't like pillow talk, either," she muttered, and he laughed again.

He didn't press her for more, just continued to trace patterns along her skin. The silence was companionable, the room still and soft in the night. She stretched her head against the pillow, relishing the feeling of being surrounded by Sam. His scent lingered in the sheets, the combination of outdoors and spice that continued to make her head spin.

"Okay," she said after a few minutes, "I kind of get why all those women were hung up on you."

"What women?"

She lightly jabbed her elbow into his stomach. "Your Three Strikes Sam fan club. You're pretty good at this stuff."

"Only with you."

"I don't believe that."

"No changing the subject. I was a jerk tonight. You gave me another chance. Thank you."

She took a deep breath. "I can use all the help I can get. There's no use hiding it."

"You shouldn't hide anything," he said softly.

"I saw Lexi Preston at the carnival."

"Your ex's attorney?"

"She was there checking up on me, I think. Lots of stories to be dished from my former frenemies." She gave a sad laugh. "Lexi thinks they wouldn't be so hard on me now if they'd known what I was dealing with back then."

"Maybe you wouldn't be so hard on yourself if you told the truth," Sam suggested.

"Could be," she said with a yawn. It had been a long day. A light shiver ran through her and he pulled her closer. "Good Lord, you're a furnace." She snuggled in closer. "My own personal space heater."

"Whatever you need me to be," Sam agreed.

That was the last thing Julia heard him say before she drifted off to sleep.

She woke a few hours later and they made love again in the hazy predawn light. His eyes never left hers as they moved together, and Julia knew this night changed what was between them, even if they both acted as though it didn't.

She'd wanted him since the first time she'd laid eyes on him, no matter how much she tried to deny it. Now that she knew how good it could be, she wasn't sure how she'd ever adjust back to real life. She had to, she reminded herself, even as she snuggled in closer to him. This night was a fringe benefit of their business arrangement, and if she let herself forget that, she knew she'd lose her heart along the way.

"You're finally ready to get back into action?"

Sam ripped open a sugar packet and dumped it into his coffee. "I haven't been sitting on a beach sipping fruity drinks for the past couple of years."

"You know what I mean."

He watched his brother shovel another bite of pancakes into his mouth. Scott always could eat like a horse. Not that Scott was a kid anymore. He was twenty-nine and a good two inches taller than Sam's six feet. They both had the Callahan blue eyes and linebacker build, but Scott had their mother's olive coloring and dark hair. Sometimes a look or gesture from Scott could bring back a memory of their mom so vividly it was as if she was still with them.

"I'm glad you called me." Scott downed the rest of his orange juice and signaled the waitress for another. "I felt real bad about what happened."

"About having sex with my fiancée?"

Scott flinched. "Pretty much. Although you have to know by now I wasn't the first."

Sam gave a curt nod. "I'm still not going to thank you, if that's what you're getting at."

"I'm not."

"I didn't come here to talk about Jenny or rehash the past."

"Dad called last week. He told me you're engaged again."

Sam looked out the window of the café into the sunny morning. He'd met Scott in a town halfway between Brevia and D.C., far enough away that he wouldn't see any familiar faces. It had been almost a week since the night of the carnival. He'd seen Julia and Charlie almost every day. Sometimes it was under the guise of making their relationship look real. He'd taken them to lunch and to a neighboring playground, stopped by the salon when he had a break during the day.

He was happiest when it was just the three of them. He'd pick up dinner after his shift, or she'd cook and they'd take the dog for a walk, and then he'd help get Charlie ready for bed. They agreed if he was going to be a presence at the mediation or future court dates, it would be smart for Charlie to feel comfortable with him.

Sam hadn't expected how much playing family would fill up the empty parts of him. He counted the hours each day until he could lift Charlie in his arms and even more the moments until he could pull Julia to him.

He took another drink of coffee then answered, "It's complicated. But I'm engaged."

Complicated might be the understatement of the century where Julia was concerned. She'd opened up to him and shared her deepest secret. She trusted him with her son, her dreams for the future, and it scared him to death. He steered their conversations away from the topic of his work, no matter how often she asked about details of his day.

After the scene at the carnival, he didn't want to see worry in her gaze or argue about the risks he took. It reminded him too much of his parents. Even so, he knew he was going to go through hell when their arrangement was finished. He'd called Scott last week and set up this meeting to talk about a new job away from Brevia, but now his purpose was twofold.

"I need some information on a family from Ohio, very prominent in the area. Dennis and Maria Johnson."

"What kind of information?" Scott asked.

"Whatever you've got. My fiancée, Julia, has a kid with their son and they're making waves with the current custody arrangement. They've got a lot of money and influence and are pulling out the stops to make her life hell. From my experience, people who want to throw their weight around like that have done it before. I'm guessing they have some skeletons from past skirmishes. I want to know what they are."

Scott nodded. "I've got a couple of friends up there. I'll make a call, see what I can find out." He stabbed another bite of pancake then pointed his fork at Sam. "This

Julia must be special. You always play by the rule book. It's not like you to fight dirty."

"I'm fighting to win. There's too much at stake not to."

"I'd like to meet her."

Sam felt his whole body tense. His voice lowered to a controlled growl. "Stay away from her, Scott. She isn't like Jenny."

Scott held up his hands, palms up. "I get it. I get it."

The waitress brought a second juice and refilled Sam's coffee. Scott winked at her and she practically tripped backing away from the table.

Sam wanted to roll his eyes. "I see you haven't changed. Still chasing tail all over the place?"

"Why mess with a system that works so damn well? I'm happy. The ladies are happy. All good. I wasn't cut out for commitment." He lifted one eyebrow. "Until I got Dad's call, I would have guessed you weren't, either."

"Dad thinks love makes the world go round."

"Dad's gone soft and it gives me the creeps."

"Amen to that."

"When you texted, you asked about openings at headquarters." Scott had worked for the U.S. Marshals Service since he'd gotten out of the army.

Sam took a drink of coffee. "You got anything?" It had been easy to imagine a future in Brevia when he'd only been the police chief, before it had started to really feel like home. Before Julia.

Scott nodded. "Maybe, but I don't get it. Why do you want to look at a new job if you're getting married? Being a cop is tough enough on a relationship. The Marshals Service would be the kiss of death. What we do doesn't compute with the minivan lifestyle."

"I told you, it's complicated."

"You're gonna run," Scott said, his voice quiet.

"I'm not running anywhere." Sam felt pressure build behind his eyes. Despite being younger, wild and reckless, Scott always had an uncanny ability to read Sam. It drove him nuts. "You said yourself the Callahans aren't meant for commitment. It may be a matter of time before she sees that. It'll be easier on us both if I'm not around for the fallout."

Scott nodded. "That's more like the brother I know and love. For a minute I thought Dad had brainwashed you with all his hug-it-out bull. Do you know he called my boss to see if he could do a seminar on using emotional intelligence in the field?"

"What's emotional intelligence?"

"Beats me," Scott said with a shrug. "But I'm sure as hell not interested in finding out. Did you fill out the paperwork I sent you?"

Sam slid an envelope across the table. "It's got my résumé with it."

"We'd be lucky to have you," Scott said solemnly. "I'd be honored to work together."

Sam's phone buzzed, alerting him that he had a voice-mail message. Coverage was spotty in this area, so he wasn't sure when the call had come in. He looked at his phone and saw six messages waiting.

"We did have some good times," he admitted as he punched the keypad to retrieve them. He wasn't on duty, so he couldn't imagine why anyone would need him so urgently.

"Here's to many more." Scott lifted his juice glass in a toast.

Sam listened to the first message and felt the blood

drain from his face. He stood, tossing a twenty on the table. "I need to go."

"Everything okay?" Scott asked, mopping up syrup with his last bite of pancake.

Sam was already out the door.

Chapter 12

Sam was about forty-five minutes from Brevia. He made it to the hospital in less than thirty.

"Charlie Morgan," he said to the woman at the front desk of the E.R., and she pointed to a room halfway down the hall. He stopped to catch his breath then pushed open the door.

A nurse stood talking to Julia as Vera held Charlie in her lap on the bed. A bright blue cast covered the boy's left wrist.

All three women looked up as Sam walked in. Julia stood so stiff he imagined she might crack in half if he touched her. The urge to ease some of her worry engulfed him.

"Sam," Charlie said, a little groggily, waving his casted arm.

"Hey, buddy." Sam came forward and bent down in front of the boy. "I like your new super arm."

Charlie giggled softly and reached out for Sam to hold him. Vera's eyes widened but she let Sam scoop him up. With Charlie in his arms, he turned to Julia.

"Are you okay?" he asked, wrapping his free arm around her shoulders.

She nodded but remained tense. "The nurse is giving me discharge papers. We've been here for over two hours." Her eyes searched his. "I couldn't reach you."

"I'm sorry," he said simply. "I was out of cell range."

She looked as if she wanted to say more but the nurse cleared her throat. "I've got instructions on bathing him with the cast," she said, holding out a slip of paper. "Take a look and let me know if you have questions."

Gingerly, Julia took the piece of paper. She stared at it, her forehead puckering as her mouth tightened into a thin, frustrated line.

Vera rose to stand beside him. Julia looked up and met his gaze, her eyes miserable. He tugged the paper from her fingers. "Why don't you go over what we need to do?" he said to the nurse. "Just to be on the safe side. We'll take the instructions home, too."

As the woman explained the procedure, Sam felt Vera squeeze his shoulder. "Thank you," she whispered then slipped out of the room.

When the nurse finished her explanation, Julia asked a couple of questions, and then the woman left them alone. Charlie's head drooped on Sam's shoulder and his eyes drifted shut.

"I can take him," Julia said, holding out her hands but keeping her gaze focused on her son.

"I've got him." Sam tipped her chin up so she had to look him in the eye. "I'm sorry, Jules. I'm sorry I wasn't here."

"You don't owe us anything." She picked up the diaper bag from the chair next to the bed. "I want to go home."

Sam followed her into the hall and toward the elevator. She didn't say a word until they were in the parking lot. "I shouldn't have called you. We're not your problem." She took Charlie and settled him in the car seat.

"I'm sorry," Sam said again. A warm breeze played with the ends of her hair. Spring was in full swing in the Smoky Mountains. He wondered how old Charlie needed to be to hold a tiny fishing rod. There were so many things he wanted to do with her and Charlie before their time together ended. Before she figured out she should have never depended on him in the first place. He couldn't stand the thought that today might be the first nail in his coffin. "I know you were scared. I wish I had been here earlier."

She jerked her head in response and he saw tears fill her eyes. "I put the toy car together—one of those ones a toddler pushes around." She swiped at her cheeks. "I swear I followed the directions, but when he knocked it against the kitchen table, it fell apart. Charlie went down over it and landed on his arm. His scream was the worst sound I've ever heard."

Sam wrapped his arms around her. "It was an accident. Not your fault."

She let him hold her but stayed ramrod straight, obviously trying to manage her fear and anxiety. "It *was* my fault. I'm sure I read the directions wrong and Charlie got hurt because of it. Because of me!"

She yanked away from him, pacing next to the car. "Maybe the Johnsons are doing the right thing." Her eyes searched his. "I felt like an idiot when the nurse gave me his discharge papers. Do you know how long it takes me to figure out the right dose of medicine for him? How many things I have to memorize and hope I don't mess up? He's still a baby, Sam. What's going to happen when he gets into school and needs help with his homework? When he wants me to read real books to him? He's going to know his mother is stupid."

"Stop it." Sam grabbed her wrists and pulled her to him, forcing her to look up at him. "Learning disabilities don't make you stupid."

"You don't know how people have looked at me my whole life. It will kill me if Charlie someday looks at me like that." She took a deep, shuddering breath and Sam felt the fight go out of her.

"He's not going to, Julia. He's going to see you like I do. Like your family does. Like a brave, intelligent, fearless woman who doesn't let anything hold her back."

"Really?" She gave him a sad smile. "Because I don't see anyone around here who fits your description." She shrugged out of his embrace and opened the door of her car. "I need to get him home. Thanks for coming, Sam."

"I'll meet you at your apartment."

"You don't need to—"

"I'm going to pick up dinner and a change of clothes and I'll be there within the hour. For once, don't argue with me. Please."

She nodded. "Nice touch with the *please*."

He watched her drive away then headed to his own car. He had to make Julia see how much she had to offer her son. That was the key to her winning the custody battle, no matter what crazy accusations her ex-boyfriend's family threw out. If he could make her believe in herself, he knew she was strong enough to overcome any odds.

She'd win and he'd get the hell out of her life. His heart

was lacking what it took to give her the life she deserved. He knew for certain that if she got too close to him, he'd only hurt her and Charlie. Just like he had today.

Sam was like a tin man, without a real heart. He might have been born with one but it had shriveled into nothing when his mother died. He couldn't risk loving and being hurt like that again.

Julia was standing over Charlie's crib when the doorbell rang. Casper growled softly from his place next to her.

"No bark," she whispered, amazed at how the dog seemed to know to keep quiet while Charlie was asleep.

She padded to the door.

"How's Charlie?" Sam asked when she opened it.

She nodded and stepped back. "Sleeping soundly."

Casper gave Sam a full-tooth grin and wagged his stubby tail. "No home for this guy yet?" Sam asked, reaching down to scratch behind the dog's ears. "You need to learn to keep your choppers hidden, buddy."

"I'm adopting him."

Sam's eyebrows rose. "Kind of a small place for a big dog."

"Charlie loves him." She didn't want to admit how much of her decision was based on her need to make something work, even if it was rescuing a stray animal. She took the carryout bag from his hand and turned for the kitchen.

Sam grabbed her around the waist and pulled her against him. "You've got a sharp tongue but a soft heart," he whispered against her ear.

"Wicked elbow, too," she said and jabbed him in the stomach.

He grunted a laugh and released her. "Why is it you don't want people to see how much you care?"

She busied herself pulling plates out of the cabinet. "I care about Charlie. That's enough for me."

"Ida Garvey told me you volunteered to do hair for the middle-school dance team's competition next month."

"Did you see those girls last year? It was updo à la light socket. I know Southerners love big hair but jeez." She set the table and took out the food. "Is this from Carl's?"

"Double burgers with cheese. Hope you approve."

"Perfect."

"I also heard you go to the retirement home once a week and do the ladies' hair."

She shrugged. "A lot of those gals were once customers at the Hairhouse, and their daughters and granddaughters still are. It's good for my business."

"It's because you care."

Why was Sam giving her the third degree on her volunteer hours? "You're making too much of it. I do things that benefit me. Ask anyone around here. I have a long history of being in it for myself."

"That's what you want people to believe."

"That *is* what they believe." She picked up a fry and pointed it at him, feeling her temper starting to rise. "What does it matter?"

He folded himself into the seat across from her. "I want you to understand you're not alone. You have a community here that would rally around you if you gave them a chance."

She took a bite of burger, her eyes narrowing. What the hell did Sam Callahan know about her part in this community? "Are you seriously giving me a lecture on letting people in, Mr. I-am-a-rock-I-am-an-island? You could take your own advice."

He frowned. "I'm a part of this community."

"No, you're not. You circle around the perimeter and insert yourself when someone needs a helping hand. No one really understands how much you give or the toll it takes on you. You're always 'on.' You're terrified of being alone with your empty soul, so you spend a little time with a woman. You get her to fall in love with you so you can hold on to the affection without having to offer any in return. People know what kind of cookies you like, so their single daughters can bake you a batch. But you're as closed off as I am in your own way."

He got up from the table so quickly she thought he was going to storm out. Instead, he grabbed two beers from her fridge, opened them and handed one to her. "We're quite a pair," he said softly, clinking the top of his bottle against hers. "Both so damned independent we'd rather fake an engagement than actually deal with real feelings."

"It's better that way," she answered and took a long drink.

"I used to think so," he said, and his eyes were so intense on hers she lost her breath for a moment. "Do you ever wonder what it would feel like to let someone in?"

She didn't need to because she already had, with him.

Oh, no. Where had that thought come from?

It was true. Without realizing it or intending to, Julia had let Sam not only into her life but into her heart, as well.

She was in love with him.

She stood, gripping the edge of the counter as if it was the only solid thing in her world. She'd called him today when Charlie had gotten hurt before she'd even called her mother. She loved him and she needed him. Julia didn't know which scared her more.

They had a deal, and she was pretty sure Sam was the type of guy who kept his word. He'd help her get through the custody battle as much as he could, but that didn't mean... It didn't mean what her heart wanted it to.

"I don't have room to let anyone in but Charlie," she said in the most casual tone she could muster. "There's not enough of me left for anyone else to hold on to. Everything I can give belongs to him."

"I never had that much to begin with," Sam said from the table.

When Julia felt as if she could turn around without revealing her true emotions, she smiled at him. "That's why we're a perfect match. Hollow to the core."

Sam tossed her a sexy smile. "I know a good way to fill the void."

She tried to ignore the flash of electricity that raced along her spine at the suggestion in his words. "It's been a long day."

He stood and she wrapped her arms around her waist. "Really long."

"It could be an even longer night if you play your cards right."

She couldn't help the grin that spread across her face. "The only game I play is Old Maid."

"I'll teach you."

"No, thanks."

He reached out his hand, palm up, but didn't touch her. "You want to be alone tonight? Say the word and I'll go. I'm not going to push you." One side of his mouth quirked. "No matter how much you want me to."

She shut her eyes, a war raging inside of her. Letting

him go was the smart thing to do, the best way to protect what little hold she still had on her heart.

"Tell me to go, Julia."

"Stay," she whispered and found herself enveloped in his arms, his mouth pressed hard on hers. Their tongues mingled and she let her hands slide up his back, underneath his shirt, reveling in the corded muscles that tightened at her touch.

"You feel like heaven," he said as he trailed kisses along her throat, her skin igniting hotter at every touch.

"Bedroom," she said on a ragged breath. "Now."

She gave a small squeak as he lifted her into his arms as if she weighed nothing. It felt good to be swept off her feet, even for the few moments he carried her down the hall.

She glanced at the door to Charlie's room. She hadn't had a man in her bed since she'd gotten pregnant with her son. It felt new and strange.

"It's going to be a challenge," Sam whispered.

"What?"

"Keeping you quiet with what I have planned."

"Oh." Her heart skipped a beat at the promise in his voice.

He laid her across the bed then followed her down, kissing her until her senses spun with desire.

"Too many clothes." She tugged on his shirt.

He stood, pulling the T-shirt over his head and shrugging out of his faded cargo shorts. Julia's breath caught again. His body was perfect, muscles rippling—actually rippling—as he bent forward and caught the waistband of her shorts with two fingers. She lifted herself to meet him as he undressed her, sliding his soft fingers across her skin.

She tried to speed their pace but Sam wouldn't have it, taking his time to explore every inch of her. He murmured endearments against her flesh, making it impossible for her to keep her emotions out of the equation.

When he finally entered her, Julia practically hummed with desire. They moved together, climbing to the highest peaks of ecstasy.

Later, as he held her, she tried to convince herself that it was only a physical connection, but her heart burned for him as much as her body did.

When she finally woke, light poured through the curtains. Julia glanced at the clock then bounded out of bed and across the hall. Charlie never slept past seven and it was already nine-thirty. Panic gripped her.

Her son's crib was empty. She heard voices in the kitchen and took a deep breath. Sam sat at the table next to Charlie's high chair, giving him spoonfuls of oatmeal.

Charlie waved his sippy cup when he saw her, squealing with delight. Casper trotted up, another big grin spread across his face.

Julia noticed the two paper coffee cups on the counter.

Sam followed her gaze. "We took the dog out to do his business and grabbed coffee and muffins. Charlie picked blueberry for you."

She dropped a kiss on Charlie's forehead. "How do you feel, sweet boy?" she asked, and he babbled a response to her. Her fingers brushed over the cast on his arm, but he didn't seem bothered by it. She sent up a silent prayer of thanks that he was okay.

She turned to Sam, who looked rumpled, sleepy and absolutely irresistible as he stirred the soupy oatmeal with a plastic spoon. "What time did he get up?"

"I heard him talking to himself around sunrise-thirty," he said with a smile.

Julia grimaced. "He's an early riser. You should have woken me."

"You were sleeping soundly. I figure you don't get too many mornings off, so…"

"Thanks." She leaned down to kiss him, and he pulled her between his thighs into a quick hug. "For everything. This morning and last night."

"More," Charlie yelled, and Sam shifted so he could give the boy another bite.

Julia stepped to the counter and took a long drink of coffee, and then she dug in the bag for a muffin.

This was too easy, she thought, as she watched Sam make faces at Charlie while he fed him, her son laughing and playing peekaboo with his cup. It felt too right. This was what she wanted, for Charlie and for herself. A family. This was what she'd never have with Sam. He'd made it clear to her that he didn't want a family. Now or ever. The thought was like a swift kick to her gut.

"I should get ready," she said, realizing her tone must have been too harsh when he glanced at her, a question in his eyes.

"I can stay while you shower," he offered.

She wanted to refuse. She knew she should push him out of her house and her life before it became harder to think of letting him go. But that would give too much away. Whether it was Old Maid or some other game, Julia did one thing well: playing her cards close to the vest.

"That would be great." She headed for the bathroom. By the time she was out, Sam had dressed, made her bed and cleaned up the kitchen. Charlie sat watching *Sesame*

Street, cuddled with Casper on the couch as Sam leaned against the back of it.

"When is the next meeting?"

She sighed. "Two days from now."

"I'll drive with you."

She nodded, unable to put into words what that meant to her.

"My dad left a message this morning. He wants to take us to dinner tonight."

"I can do that."

"Along with your mom."

"Uh-oh."

"You can say that again. If those two are plotting…"

"Do you think they suspect anything?"

He shook his head. "They want to talk about wedding plans."

Julia's stomach lurched. "That's bad."

Sam pushed away from the couch. "We'll make it work. We've come this far."

He brushed his lips against hers, a soft touch but it still made her stomach quiver. "Five-thirty. Do you want me to pick you up?"

"I'll have to get Charlie from the sitter's first. I'll meet you there."

He kissed her again. "Have a good day, Julia."

He made those five little words sound like a caress.

"You, too," she muttered and stepped back.

"I'll see you later, buddy." Sam bent and ruffled Charlie's hair, the gesture so natural Julia felt herself melt all over again.

Charlie's fist popped out of his mouth. "'Bye, Dada," he said, not taking his eyes from the television.

Sam straightened slowly.

"He didn't mean anything," Julia said with a forced laugh, not wanting to reveal how disconcerted she felt.

"I know," Sam said softly.

"He knows you're not his dad. He doesn't even understand what that word means. It's something he sees on TV. A word for men. It isn't—"

"Julia." He cut her off, his hand chopping through the air. "It's okay."

But it wasn't okay. Sam was spooked. She knew by the way he didn't turn to her again. He lifted his hand to wave, and with a stilted "See you later," he was gone.

Chapter 13

Sam was freaked out. He took another drink of his beer and glanced around the crowd at Carl's, reliving the pure terror he'd felt this morning.

In his career as a police officer, he'd had guns and knives pulled on him, dealt with drug dealers, prostitutes and an assortment of random losers. He didn't lose his cool or let his guard down. The danger and risk of the job never rattled him.

But one word from a toddler had shaken him to his core. Charlie'd called him Dada. Although Julia had tried to play it off, he knew that she was affected by it, too. He'd heard it in her tone. Not that he'd been able to do much talking, afraid his voice would crack under the weight of the conflicting emotions warring inside him.

Sam had never planned on being a father. Even when he'd been engaged to Jenny, neither of them had wanted kids. That was one of the things that had made him propose, even when he'd had the nagging sense something wasn't right in their relationship. It wasn't every day a guy found a woman who wasn't itching to have babies.

Sam liked kids, but he knew he didn't have what it took to be a decent father. He lacked the emotional depth to put someone else's needs before his own. He believed he was incapable of feeling something, much like his own father had been after his mother's death.

Charlie made him want to change, to be a better man.

He loved the feeling of that boy cuddled against him, his small head nestled in the crook of Sam's neck. He loved watching him follow the silly dog around and vice versa. He especially loved seeing Julia with Charlie, how happy it made her to be with her son.

He hadn't understood that bond when Charlie was a newborn. When he'd seen Julia with the small bundle after the boy's birth, Sam had run the other way. Part of him might have known instinctively how much he'd want to be a part of their world.

That was impossible. He could help her fight for her son, but he didn't have any more to give. He understood the look in her eyes when she'd thought he was in danger. He remembered the same fear in his mother's eyes each time the phone rang while his father was on duty. Her fear and worry had eventually turned into resentment.

He wouldn't give up who he was and he couldn't ask Julia to be a part of his life. He wouldn't risk what it could do to her. He knew Julia was stronger than his mother had ever been, but the life of cop's wife could wreck the strongest woman, no two ways about it.

He'd miss her like crazy, though. Already he could feel the loss of the two of them and he wasn't even gone.

"Okay, let's do this." Julia sat down at the table, her posture rigid. Her eyes darted around as if scoping escape routes. "They're not here yet?"

Sam shook his head. "Did you have a good day?" He reached across the table to take her hand but she snatched it away.

"No use for the small talk. Save it for the audience."

Despite the fact she'd never truly been his, Sam wished for the way it had been before this morning, when she'd been unguarded and happy to be with him. He glanced around at the crowded restaurant. "There's always an audience in Brevia. Where's Charlie?"

"His sitter had an appointment, so I had him at the salon this afternoon. Lainey is watching him tonight. I thought...it's simpler without him here. We should limit the amount of time he spends with you. So that he doesn't get too attached and all." Her eyes flashed, daring him to argue with her. She was in full mama-bear mode tonight. It made him want her all the more.

Sam's gut twisted at the thought of not spending time with Charlie. "He's an amazing boy, Julia."

"He's great," she agreed distractedly. Her fingers played with the napkin on the table.

He gave a short laugh. "I didn't realize how quiet my life was until you came along."

She glanced toward the front of the restaurant. "Where do you think they are? I want to get this over with."

"My dad and your mom are coming to discuss wedding plans. You look like you can't stand to be in the same room as me." He extended his ankle and pressed it against her shin. "Relax."

She snatched her leg away, her knee banging on the underside of the table. She grabbed the water glass before it tumbled over. "I can't relax," she said between clenched teeth. "This whole thing was a mistake. You're in our lives temporarily, and now Charlie is developing feelings for you. It has to end, Sam."

He swallowed the panic rising in his throat. "You don't mean tonight?"

"Why not?" she countered. "The sooner the better."

Hell, no, he screamed inside his head.

"I don't think that's prudent at this time, Julia," he told her, his voice calm and measured. "I don't want Charlie hurt, but our business arrangement is helping all of us in the long run. You're so close to a ruling, and my dad should be heading back to Boston within the week. Stick it out, Jules. I promise it'll be worth it."

"Business arrangement," she repeated softly. "You still consider this a business arrangement?"

Something in the way she looked at him made him uneasy, but she had to know what he meant. He was doing this for her benefit—at least that was what he tried to tell himself.

"We talked about it last night. You and I are built the same way, and it isn't for emotional connections. But you can't deny our chemistry, and Charlie is a great kid. We're friends and that doesn't have to change. I provide the stability you need. Don't throw it away now."

She bit down on her lip and studied him, as if trying to gain control of her emotions. "I can't believe..." she began, but she was cut off when Sam's dad came up behind her.

"Sorry we're late," he boomed, taking Julia's hand and placing a loud kiss on her fingers. "You're looking fantastic as usual, my dear. So good to see you again."

Vera's gaze traveled between the two of them. "Is everything okay?" she asked, studying Julia.

The color had drained from Julia's face. Her eyes had grown large and shadowed. Sam wished he could pull her aside and finish their conversation. He got the feeling he'd made a huge misstep.

"We're fine," Julia said, taking a sip of water. She stood and hugged Joe then her mother. "Just working out details. You know."

Sam watched her gaze travel up and down her mother. "Are you all right, Mom?" she asked slowly.

"Never better," Vera said, smoothing her blouse.

"Why is your shirt buttoned wrong?"

Sam looked at his father, who had the decency to turn a bright shade of pink. Joe and Vera broke into a fit of giggles. Sam didn't know Vera well, but she'd never struck him as much of a giggler.

"I'll head to the little girls' room and adjust this." She swatted Joe playfully on the arm as she passed. "You old devil."

"You've got to be kidding." Julia followed her mother toward the back of the restaurant.

Joe took the seat across from Sam and gave him a hearty pat on the back. "How's it going, Sammy? Wedding stress getting to your girl?"

Sam's temper flared. "Finding out her mother is having sex with you might be getting to her."

Joe looked genuinely confused. "Really? I thought you two would be happy for us." A grin spread across his face. "Who knows, maybe we'll beat you to the altar."

"You've known Vera about a minute, Dad. That's not funny."

"Who's joking?" Joe opened his arms, lifting them toward the ceiling. "Some things are destined to be."

Sam needed a bigger supply of aspirin if he was going to continue to spend time with his dad. He pushed his fingers through his hair and took a breath. "Dad, tell me you aren't serious. I swear I'll throw you in the cruiser and deposit you at the state line if you keep talking like this. If you have an itch you want to scratch with Vera, that's one thing. But marriage? No way."

"Let me tell you something." His father leaned forward. "I'm not a young man anymore, in case you haven't noticed. I spent a lot of years sad and lonely after your mother died. Vera knows what it's like to lose a spouse. She knows what it feels like to be alone and crave something more."

"Vera is hardly ever alone." Sam shook his head. "She dates, Dad. A lot."

"From what I understand, you dated a lot before Julia. Did it make you feel less lonely?"

Sam opened his mouth then snapped it shut again. His father was right. All the women he'd dated when he first got to Brevia had just been passing time. He'd never felt connected to any of them. He'd always been on his own.

Until Julia.

"I'm going to ask her to marry me," Joe said. "It was love at first sight, and I'm smart enough not to let her get away."

"Do you think she'll say yes? I'd hope to hell she's smart enough to know not to be swept off her feet."

"What's wrong with being swept away? But don't worry. We won't plan a wedding until after you and Julia are settled. Neither of us wants to take anything away from you kids."

"That's so reassuring," Sam ground out. He scrubbed his hand over his face. "You don't have to marry her. Date for a little while. Take your time. Why rush into anything?"

"Life is short. It can turn on a dime. I'm taking every opportunity for happiness I can get. Just like you and Julia."

Nothing like him and Julia, Sam thought. This was a disaster. His father's gushing romanticism made him look like an emotional robot.

He had to believe they were on the same page. She didn't want anything more from him than he was able to give.

Let his father rush blindly into marriage for love. It wasn't going to make him happy. If Joe hadn't learned that lesson from Sam's mother, Sam definitely had.

His plan was far more prudent. Enjoy each other but still protect his heart. It would be better for everyone in the long run.

The next day Julia cradled the phone between her cheek and shoulder as she sat in her office at the salon. She'd spent an hour staring blindly at the figures dancing before her on the computer and had made a call to an old friend to give herself a break.

"It's okay, Derek," she said with a sigh. "I'll figure it out."

"If those Southern belles get too much for you, I can always find a place for you in Phoenix. Everything's hotter out West, jewel-eyed Julia." Derek laughed at his own joke then said, "I've got to run, darlin'. My last appointment for the day just came in."

"Thanks, sweetie," Julia said, "I'll keep that offer in mind."

She hung up with Derek, a stylist she'd met years ago in Columbus. They'd both moved on from Ohio, but she still considered him one of her few true friends. For a brief moment she entertained the thought of taking Charlie and running away to Arizona. Not that it would solve her myriad of problems, but it sure seemed easier than facing everything head-on.

Julia drummed her fingers on the top of her desk, wishing she were out in the warm sun instead of stuck in the salon on such a gorgeous spring day. She needed to clear her head, and computer work wasn't cutting it.

What had started as a simple plan with Sam had gotten too complicated. She'd been stupid to think she could keep her heart out of the equation. If Julia were better at leading with her mind, she wouldn't have gotten into most of the trouble she'd had during her life. She wanted to be in control of her emotions. To be more like Sam, who could make every decision in his life based on rational thinking.

Not Julia. She was more a leap-first-then-look kind of person.

The only time that had worked in her favor was with Charlie. Now she'd even managed to mess up that.

Sam wanted to stay with her for the right reasons, at least on paper, but it felt wrong. His father and her mother were heading in that same direction on the express train. It had been torture to watch them last night at dinner, making googly eyes and barely able to keep their hands off each other.

She didn't realize it was possible to ache for a man's touch, but that was how she felt around Sam. Other than enough touching to make their fake arrangement seem real, they'd both kept their distance. Except when they were alone. In the bedroom, Sam was sweet and attentive and Julia had made the mistake of believing that meant something.

She pushed away from the desk and stalked toward the main salon. They were busy today, with every chair filled. She hoped to get the final approval on her business loan next week, needed to prove to herself and to the town and Jeff's family that she could stand on her own two feet.

Lizzy, the salon's longtime receptionist, stopped her in the doorway.

"Julia, could you take a look at this product order and make sure I didn't miss anything?" She shoved a piece of paper filled with numbers into Julia's hand.

Julia looked down as the figures on the page swam in front of her eyes. "Leave it on my desk. I'll check it over the weekend."

"I need to get it in before month end, which is today. It'll only take a minute. Please."

"I can't," Julia snapped with more force than she'd meant.

Lizzy took a quick step back and Julia noticed several customers and stylists glance her way. "Fine," she stammered. "But if we run out of anything, don't blame me." She turned away, ripping the paper from Julia's fingers.

"I'm sorry." Julia reached out to touch the woman's arm. "Lizzy, wait. I need to tell you something."

"That you're too dang important to be bothered by little details?"

Julia glanced around the crowded salon, her gaze landing on Lexi Preston, who watched her from where she sat with a head full of coloring foils. What was Jeff's attorney doing in her salon? Lexi blinked then raised one brow, as if in an odd challenge.

"I'm waiting," Lizzy muttered.

Fine. She was sick of hiding who she was, tired of working so hard to live up to her own unattainable expectations. She squared her shoulders and took a deep breath. "I have a learning disability."

"Come again?" A little of the anger went out of Lizzy's posture.

"I need time to look over the figures because I can't read them well."

"Since when?"

A hush had fallen over the salon and Julia realized everyone was waiting for her answer.

"Forever," she said, making her voice loud and clear. "I was officially diagnosed in third grade."

Lizzy looked confused. "I think I would have heard that before now. I was only a few years behind you in school."

Julia shrugged. "It wasn't public knowledge."

"Is that why you were always cutting class and getting kids to write your papers for you?"

Julia nodded. "I'm not proud of it. I was embarrassed and it made me feel stupid." She took a breath. "It still does. But I'm working on that. I hid behind a bad attitude and unkindness for a lot of years. I've changed. I don't want you to think I don't value what you're asking me to do. It just may take me longer to get it done." She swallowed down the lump of emotion crowding her throat. "That's my big secret."

Lizzy offered her a genuine smile. "My cousin was bulimic for most of her teenage years. She tried to hide that, too."

One of the customers tipped her head in Julia's direction. "My husband's addicted to internet porn."

"Oh." Julia didn't quite know how that related to her learning disability. "Well, I'll take these figures." She gently tugged the paper from Lizzy's hand. "I'll see if I can get through them this afternoon. If not, first thing Monday morning."

She looked around the salon one last time, her gaze catching again on Lexi's, and the lawyer gave her a surprisingly genuine smile. Head held high, Julia closed the door to her office. Once safely by herself, she leaned against it, bending her knees until she sank to the floor.

Her whole body trembled from the adrenaline rush that followed sharing her deepest, darkest secret with the ladies in the salon. Julia knew how the gossip mill worked in Brevia. Within hours, everyone to the county line and back would know about her learning disability.

The truth was that she no longer cared. Now that she'd talked about her disorder, its hold over her had loosened the tiniest bit. If people wanted to judge her or tried to take advantage of her, she'd deal with that. She realized she could handle a lot more when she used the truth to her advantage than when she tried to cover it up.

A little voice inside her head piped up, saying she might take that advice when it came to dealing with the custody case and Charlie's future. She quickly put it aside. Public humiliation she could risk—her son's fate she couldn't. Whether that meant keeping up the charade with Sam, or fighting tooth and nail with the Johnsons, Julia would do whatever she had to to keep Charlie safe.

Chapter 14

"The Callahan brothers ride again."

Sam slanted Scott a look. "Who are you supposed to be, Billy the Kid?"

Scott grinned. "It's about time you stopped hiding in this backwater town and did some real work."

"I'm police chief, idiot. That is real work."

"If you say so. But it's nothing like being a marshal. You're going to love it, Sam. You won't have time to think about anything else."

That was a plus, Sam thought. He'd gotten the job offer early this morning. Scott had shown up at the station soon after to offer his congratulations. Sam was on duty, so they had coffee and a breakfast burrito in the car as Sam went out on an early-morning call.

His father was going to hit the roof. Joe had taken Vera down to the coast for a couple of days, so at least

Sam would have time to formulate a plan before he had to explain what he was doing.

He had no idea what to say to Julia. He figured she'd understand. She'd tried to break it off last night. He knew their time together was at an end. After the custody ruling came through, she wouldn't need him anymore. Not that she ever really had. Despite her self-doubt, Julia was going to have a great life. He was the one who was hopeless.

Although he hadn't even thought himself capable of it, he felt his heart literally expanding every day with love for her and Charlie, but he couldn't make it work. He felt vulnerable, as if he was a moving target with no cover. He couldn't offer her anything more because he was too afraid of being hurt.

He'd spent most of yesterday working with Julia's attorney to file several affidavits on behalf of people around town attesting to Julia's character, her contributions to the local community and what they'd observed as far as her being a great mother was concerned. He knew she would never ask for help from anyone, let alone believe she deserved it. Once he'd explained what she was facing, people had come forward in droves to stand behind her.

He hoped that would be enough, would make up for what he wanted to tell her but couldn't find the guts to say. Instead, he was going to move on. Leave Brevia and cut his ties because that was easier than letting someone in.

"Before you go all bro-mance on me, you need to know I still think you're a jerk for what you did to me."

"You'll thank me eventually."

"I doubt that." Sam turned onto the long dirt road

that led to the house he'd received the call about earlier. Strange noises, the neighbor had said. Here on the outskirts of town, Sam knew the parties could go on all through the night. He figured someone hadn't known when to let it go.

He shifted the cruiser into Park and turned to his brother. "If we're going to work together, there need to be some ground rules. The first is you stay the hell out of my personal life. It's none of your business. Even if you think you've got my best interests at heart."

"What are you going to do about the fiancée when you leave town?" Scott asked.

"I'm going to do her a favor."

"That's cold, Sam. Even for you. And I thought I was the heartbreaker. You're giving me a run for my money in the love-'em-and-leave-'em department."

"Don't make it a bigger issue than it is, Scott. She's better off without me. It's not going to work out. I'm not what she needs, after all."

"I can see why she'd be what *you* need, though. Her legs must be a mile long."

The hair on the back of Sam's neck stood on end.

"When did you see Julia?"

Scott gave him a hesitant smile. "Probably shouldn't have mentioned that."

"When did you see her?" Sam repeated, his knuckles tightening around the steering wheel.

"I drove down to have lunch with Dad last week. I needed a trim, so I checked out her salon."

"And her," Sam said between clenched teeth.

"After what Dad told me about how in love you are and the way you skipped out of breakfast to go running to her, it had me worried. I wanted to see what could be so flippin' amazing about this woman to make you all whipped."

"I'm not whipped."

"I was worried," Scott continued. "I put my butt on the line to get you this job. It wouldn't look good for you to flake before you even started. I have to admit, she'd be a big temptation. Her kid was there, too. Cute, if you're into the whole family-man scene. But I know you, Sam. That isn't who you are. Never was."

"Stay away from Julia."

"It's not like that. I told you that what happened with Jenny, I did it for your own good. Granted, I could have found a better way to handle things but…"

"You slept with her."

"I'm sorry, Sam."

Scott's voice was quiet, sincere. It made Sam's teeth hurt, because he knew his brother was sorry. He also knew that, in a warped way, Scott had done him a favor. At that point in his life, Sam had been so determined to prove that he wasn't like his father, that he could have both a career and a personal life, he'd ignored all the warning signs about how wrong he and Jenny had been for each other. She would have left him eventually. He would have driven her away.

Now he knew better, and he wasn't going to risk it again. Not his heart or his pride. He thought Julia understood him, but it was for the best that their relationship ended. As much as he didn't want to admit it, he was falling for her. He was close to feeling something he'd never felt before in his life, and it scared the hell out of him. What if he did let her in and she realized there was nothing inside him to hold on to? His heart had stopped working right the day his mother had died and he didn't know how to fix it.

Sam glanced at his brother. "Do you think about what would have happened if Mom hadn't been in the accident?"

"I used to," Scott said, a muscle ticking in his jaw. "But she would have divorced him, and the end result on us would have been the same."

"Yeah." Sam nodded. "I think Dad discovered his emotional self about two decades too late to make any difference in my life."

"You need to get out of here. Once you're working for the Marshals, you won't have time for all this thinking about your life. I'm telling you—"

Whatever Scott was going to say next was cut off when a stream of shots rang out from the house. "Stay here," Sam yelled as he jumped out of the car.

"Not a chance," Scott said, right on his heels, his gun in hand. "Call me your backup."

Sam gave a brief nod. "You go around the side," he whispered and headed toward the front of the house.

Julia dropped her cell phone back into her purse and took a deep breath. "I didn't get the loan," she said to her sister, the words sounding hollow to her own ears.

Lainey reached out a hand. The Tellett County courthouse was crowded on a Tuesday morning, and they stood near the end of the hallway, in front of a window that looked out onto the street. Julia thought it odd that the people below went about their business so calmly as her life spun out of control.

"Why not? What did they say? Oh, Jules, there has to be another way."

Julia shook her head. "They don't think I'm a good investment. It's me, Lainey. Nothing is going to change that. Everyone in the salon yesterday heard me. I told Lizzy about my learning disabilities. Clearly, the bank doesn't think I'm the right person to own my own business." She tried to smile but couldn't make her mouth move that way. "I can't blame them."

"I can." Lainey's tone was severe. "It's the most outrageous thing I've ever heard."

"Annabeth Sullivan is a vice president at the bank. I thought we'd come to an understanding and she'd forgiven me. I guess she still wants revenge."

"How long are you going to have to pay for your past mistakes? You're not the same person you were in high school. You've changed and everyone who knows you can see that. You're a good person. It's about time people gave you credit for how much you've accomplished."

"I haven't accomplished anything. The salon was my chance to make something of my life, to become more than what anyone thought I could." She scrubbed her hands over her face. "There's a reason I kept the LD a secret for so many years. It's easier to talk my way out of people thinking I'm stupid than to deal with the truth."

Lainey sucked in a breath. "Don't say that. You'll find another way. Ethan and I—"

"No. I'm not taking charity from you and Ethan, or Mom for that matter. Some things weren't meant to be. I've had enough disappointment in my life to know that." She glanced down the hall and saw Frank Davis motioning to them. "The hearing is starting."

"I thought Sam was meeting you here."

Julia swallowed back the tears that clogged her throat. "Like I said, I'm used to disappointment."

"Don't be silly. He'll be here."

Julia gave her sister a small hug. "Whatever you say, Lain. Right now, wish me luck."

"You don't need luck. You're a wonderful mother and that's what's most important. I'll be here when you're finished. We'll have a celebratory lunch."

The elevator doors opened as Julia walked past and she paused, her chest tightening as she willed Sam to materialize. When an older woman walked out, Julia continued down the hall alone.

She took her seat across from Jeff, his parents and their attorney. A small smile played around the corners of Jeff's mother's mouth. Lexi Preston didn't make eye contact, her eyes glued to the stack of papers on the table. A pit of dread began to open in Julia's stomach.

She darted a glance toward her attorney, who appeared blissfully unaware. But Julia could feel the long tendrils of impending doom reaching for her. She'd been in their grip too many times before not to recognize it now.

"Frank, what's going on?"

He looked up, a big smile on his face. "Didn't Sam tell you? He got a bunch of folks to write testimonials about your character. Really good, too. All of them."

Sam did that. For her. Then why did the Johnson family look so smug?

"Where is Sam?" Frank asked. "I thought he was meeting us here."

"Me, too." Julia swallowed. "I don't know what's keeping him."

The judge came into the courtroom. "In light of the new information given to me by both parties, I'm going to need a few more days to render my decision."

"What new information did they give her?" Julia said in a frantic whisper.

"Your Honor," Frank said as he patted Julia's arm reassuringly, "we aren't aware of any new information brought forward by the other party."

The judge slowly removed her glasses and narrowed her eyes at him. "Mr. Davis, you do know about your client's recent professional setbacks."

Frank threw a glance at Julia. "I'm not sure—"

"I didn't get the loan," Julia said miserably.

"We've spoken to a reliable source that tells us Ms. Morgan is planning to move out of the area." Lexi's shoulders were stiff as she spoke. "A colleague of Ms. Morgan's, Derek Lamb, had a conversation with her last week in which she expressed interest in a job with him at his salon in Phoenix."

Julia knew Lexi had somehow gleaned that information, as well. "I wasn't serious. I was upset about…about a lot of things, and Derek is an old friend—"

"An old boyfriend," Lexi supplied.

Julia shook her head, panic threatening to overtake her. "Hardly. I don't have the right equipment."

Frank squeezed her arm. "Be quiet, Julia."

The judge pointed a finger at her. "Ms. Morgan, your petition for sole custody was based partially on the stability of your current circumstances. Your ties to the community and your family being close were something I took into account when looking at your request."

"Her ties to the community are highlighted in the affidavits I submitted." Frank's voice shook with frustration.

"There is also the matter of her engagement," Lexi said, reaching over to hand a piece of paper to Frank.

Blood roared in Julia's head. No one could have found

out her relationship with Sam wasn't real. They'd done everything right and she hadn't told a soul, not even Lainey.

Unless Sam...

She snatched the paper from Frank Davis's fingers and tried to decipher the words on the page, willing them to stop moving in front of her eyes. When they did, she felt the whole room start to spin.

"Were you aware," the judge asked, "that Sam Callahan has accepted a position with the U.S. Marshals Service in Washington, D.C.?"

Julia looked at the woman, unable to speak. Finally, she whispered, "No."

The woman's mouth tightened. "May I ask, Ms. Morgan, if you're still engaged to be married to Sam Callahan?"

Julia stared at the piece of paper in her hand, her vision blurring as angry tears filled her eyes. She blinked several times, refusing to cry in front of Jeff and his family. Refusing to cry over any man. "No, ma'am," she answered quietly. "I don't believe we are still engaged."

Frank sucked in a quick breath next to her. "In light of these new findings, I'd ask for a recess to regroup with my client."

"Yes, Mr. Davis, I think that would be a good idea. Our time is valuable, though, so please, no more wasting it. Get your facts straight and come back to me with a new proposal in one week."

"Judge Williams—" Lexi Preston's voice was clear and confident in the silence "—on behalf of my client, I'd like to request that you make your ruling today. The information that's come to light this morning is another example of Julia Morgan's inability to successfully manage her own life. It speaks directly to Jeff Johnson's concerns for his son and the reason he is here seeking joint custody."

Julia's gaze met Jeff's and he nodded slightly, as if to say "I told you so." Which, of course, he had. And she hadn't listened, convinced that this time events would work out in her favor. In large part because of Sam's confidence in her.

Sam, who'd encouraged her to go public with her learning disorder.

Sam, who'd promised to stay by her side until her custody arrangement was secure.

Sam, who'd betrayed her today.

Lexi cleared her throat. "I motion that you award sole physical custody of Charles David Morgan to Jeff Johnson."

The attorney's words registered in Julia's brain. They wanted to take Charlie from her. Completely.

She saw Jeff lean over and speak into Lexi's ear. The younger woman shook her head then glanced at Julia.

Julia felt the walls of the room close in around her. She looked at the judge's impassive face, trying to find some clue as to what the woman was thinking.

"Don't let this happen," she whispered to Frank. She needed to get back to Brevia, to wrap her arms around her son.

"We request you stay with your decision to rule next week," Frank said, his voice steady. "My client has been blindsided by some of these new developments. That in no way decreases her dedication as a parent or her love for her son."

To Julia's immense relief, the judge nodded. "We'll meet next Tuesday morning." She pointed a finger at

Frank Davis. "Before that, I expect you to submit a re-vised proposal for custody. Remember, we all want what's best for the child, not simply what's easiest for one of the parents."

What's best for Charlie, Julia wanted to scream, *is to stay with his mother.*

She'd come into this meeting so confident. How could things have gone to hell so quickly?

She pushed back from the table. "I need to get out of here," she told the attorney.

"Be in my office tomorrow morning, first thing." His frustration was clear as he watched her. "This was a clear-cut case," he mumbled. "What happened with Sam?"

She bit her lip. "I don't know." What she did know was that Sam had left her vulnerable to losing her son.

Julia would never forgive him.

Chapter 15

Sam ran his hands through his still-wet hair and straightened his shirt before knocking on Julia's door.

He'd stopped home for a quick shower after the mess this morning had finally settled down. An all-night party had turned into a domestic disturbance that led to a four-hour standoff. The homeowner, high on an assortment of illegal drugs, wouldn't let his girlfriend or her two kids out of the house. The situation had eventually ended with no injuries, for which Sam was thankful. But he'd been tied up in logistics and paperwork for most of the day.

He felt awful about missing the hearing and had called and texted Julia at least a half-dozen times with no answer. He'd then called Lainey, but she hadn't picked up, either. As mad as she'd be about him missing the meeting, the character affidavits he'd helped compile had to make up for it.

Sam couldn't wait to see the joy on Julia's face now that Charlie was safe. He wanted to hear how things went, take the two of them to dinner to celebrate her victory. Even if she didn't want to be with him anymore, he'd make her see how important it was to keep up appearances a little while longer. He told himself it was good for her reputation but knew he couldn't bear to let go of her quite yet.

Julia deserved all the happiness life could offer, and Sam wanted to have a hand in helping with that before they ended their relationship. The thought of leaving her and Charlie made his whole body go cold. But he knew it would be best for Julia and that was his priority now.

He knocked again, surprised when Lainey opened the door. Even more surprised at how angry she looked.

"You have a lot of nerve showing up here," she said through a hiss. "She doesn't want to see you. You've done enough damage already."

The confusion of not being able to get in touch with her turned to panic. "Where is she? What happened?"

Lainey went to shut the door in his face but he shoved one gym shoe into the doorway. Lainey kicked at his toe. "I mean it, Sam. You need to leave."

"I swear, Lainey," Sam ground out, "I'll push right through you if I have to but I'm going to see her. Now."

Casper came up behind Lainey, barking wildly. Sam could see the dog's teeth shining and wondered if the dog actually meant to bite him.

"Casper, quiet." The dog stopped barking but continued to growl low in his throat. Lainey studied Sam through the crack in the door. "I'd like to call the cops on you."

"I can give you the number."

She blew out a frustrated breath and opened the door. Sam went to push past. "Where is she?"

Lainey didn't move to let him by. "I'm warning you. She doesn't want to see you ever again. She's in bad shape."

He shook his head. "I don't understand. Everything was lined up. Didn't Frank Davis submit the affidavits? They were supposed to make everything better."

"Julia didn't mention any affidavits. What she did tell me, between sobs, is that you'd told her to go public with her learning disabilities. For whatever reason, Annabeth Sullivan convinced the bank that she was a bad investment for the loan."

Sam's breath caught. "No."

"The best part, " Lainey said and poked her finger into his chest, "the part that really made all the difference, was the little bombshell that you've taken a job with the U.S. Marshals Service."

Sam's whole body tensed. "How did they find out?"

"You don't deny it? How could you have done that to her?" Lainey turned on her heel and stalked several paces into the small apartment.

"No one was supposed to find out until after she got the custody ruling."

Lainey whirled back toward him, keeping her voice low. "And that makes it better? You were her fiancé. A stable father figure for Charlie."

"Did Julia—"

"Oh, yes." Lainey waved an angry hand toward him. "I know all about your *arrangement*. It's ridiculous."

"I didn't mean for it to be. I wanted to help."

"You've put her at risk, Sam. At real risk of losing custody of Charlie."

"Where is she?"

Lainey stared at him. "In the bedroom," she answered finally.

"I'm going to fix this." Sam tried for confidence but his voice cracked on the last word.

"I hope you can."

He walked past her, Casper at his heels. The dog no longer seemed to want to rip off his head. Julia, he imagined, was another matter.

"I can make this right," he muttered to the animal. "I have to."

He knocked softly on the door, but when there was no response, he opened it. The curtain was pulled back, the room bathed in early-evening sunlight. Julia sat on the bed, her knees curled up to her chin, arms hugging her legs tight against her.

Sam stepped into the room and the dog edged past him, silently hopping up on the bed and giving Julia's hand a gentle lick before curling into a ball at her side. Without acknowledging Sam, she reached out to stroke the dog's soft head.

"Jules?"

Her hand stilled. "Go away," she whispered, her voice awful.

"Julia, look at me." Sam took another step into the room.

"I said go away." She lifted her head, her eyes puffy from crying, tears dried on her cheeks. She looked as miserable as Sam felt. He waited for her to scream at him, to hurl insults and obscenities. He wanted her to let loose her temper but she only stared, her gaze filled with the pain of betrayal.

Knowing it was his betrayal that had caused her suffering almost killed him on the spot. "I'm sorry," he began but stopped when she scrambled back against the headboard. The dog jumped up and stood like a sentry in front of her.

"I could lose him." Her voice was dull and wooden, as if she was in a pit of despair so deep she couldn't even manage emotion.

"You won't lose him." Sam said the words with conviction, hoping they would be true.

"You don't know. You weren't there."

The accusation in her voice cut like a knife through his heart. "It was work, Jules. I meant to be there." He sat down on the edge of the bed gingerly, not wanting to spook her or the dog.

"You're leaving."

"I thought it was for the best," he lied. The best thing that ever happened to him was this woman, but he was too scared of being hurt to give her what she needed. "That when you didn't need me anymore, it would be easier for us both if I was gone."

"I needed you today and instead I found out from Jeff's lawyer that you were taking a new job. You made me look like a fool, Sam."

The truth of her words struck him to his core. She was right. He was supposed to be there for her and he'd let her down. In a big way. It was the reason he knew he was destined to be alone: the work always came first for him. He was the same as his dad had been. It had cost his mother her life and now it might cost Julia her future with Charlie. He had to make it better somehow. "What can I do?"

She shook her head. "Nothing. There's nothing anyone can do. I have one good thing in my life. Charlie was the one thing I did right. And I've ruined that, too."

"You haven't—"

"I trusted you, Sam." As much as the words hurt, her voice, still empty of emotion, was the worst. "My mistake. I should have learned by now I can't rely on anyone except myself." She gave a brittle laugh. "And I'm iffy at best."

"Where's Charlie?"

"He's with Ethan. I couldn't let him see me like this." She ran her fingers through her hair. "I'm going to pull it together. I have to. But I needed a little time."

"We can get through this."

"There's no *we*. There never really was. You proved that today."

"I didn't mean it to end like this." He reached out for her again and Casper growled like he meant it.

Julia went rigid. "Don't touch me. I never want to see you again. I don't know what's going to happen with the custody arrangement. But I'll find a way to keep my son. He's all that matters to me now."

Sam shook his head. "Don't say that," he whispered.

Her eyes blazed as she spoke. "I thought you were different. I wanted to depend on you. I wanted to love you. Hell, I was halfway there already. It's over. I don't care what you say to your father or anyone in town about why this is ending. Blame it on me."

"This isn't over and I'm not blaming anything on you. If you let me—"

"I did let you. I let you into my heart and into my son's life and you betrayed us." She took a shuddering breath. "We're over. Whatever I thought we had is done."

"You can't be serious."

"Please go, Sam. Please."

He stared at her as she turned to the dog, petting him

until he lay down again beside her. Sam wanted to grab her and pull her to him, hold on until she melted into him. This couldn't be the end.

He'd wanted to leave her happy, to do the right thing by her. Maybe he couldn't be the man she wanted but he'd been determined to see her through. To be the hero when it really mattered.

Now he was nothing more than the jerk who'd put her at risk of losing her son.

He stood slowly, his eyes never leaving her. He prayed she would look at him, give him some small glimmer of hope. When she didn't, he turned and walked from the room.

Lainey hung up the phone as he came down the hallway.

"How is she?"

He shook his head. "She should never have trusted me."

"But she did, Sam. What are you going to do now?"

He thought for a moment then answered the only way he could. "I'm going to do what I do best—disappoint someone I care about."

Lainey looked as if she'd expected him to give some white-knight answer. But Sam was only good at playing the hero when the stakes didn't matter to him personally. When his emotions were on the line, he had a knack for royally messing up everything around him.

He walked out the door and into the dark night knowing he'd just ruined his best opportunity at a happy ending in life.

The image of Julia so forlorn would haunt him for a long time. Her anger and hatred might be deserved, but it hurt the most to know that he couldn't take away the pain he'd caused her.

For that, he'd never forgive himself.

Julia pushed the stroller along the plush carpet of the retirement home until she got to the common room that also served as a makeshift salon for residents.

"Good morning, Julia."

"Hey, Charlie."

Several voices called out to greet them, and she was thankful the people here were unaware of her personal turmoil, unlike most of the town. Charlie waved as though he was in a parade, which made Julia smile a bit. Her first in several days. She took a small sip of her coffee then placed it in the cup holder attached to the stroller's handle. It had been a rough week.

She tried not to show her emotions in front of Charlie, so she had spent a few sleepless nights crying in the dark hours and worrying about her future. The days were just as difficult to get through, since everywhere she went someone had a comment on her recent struggles. To her surprise, most of what people said had been supportive. Old friends and other locals seemed to come out of the woodwork to offer her a word of encouragement or commiserate on her situation.

Even Val Dupree, the Hairhouse's owner, had called from Florida to tell Julia that she was still willing to work with her to find a way for Julia to buy the salon. Julia had thanked her, but at this point she was afraid it was too little, too late. The Johnsons had so much power and she wasn't sure there was anything she could do to keep her future with Charlie secure.

Nothing mattered except Charlie.

She hadn't seen or spoken to Sam, although a couple of ladies had come into the salon specifically to tell her how they'd given him an earful about his reprehensible behavior toward her. Apparently, being screwed over by a man made you an automatic member of a certain girls' club.

If it wasn't for her constant worry about Charlie, Julia might be happy right now. For the first time in as long as she could remember, she felt as if she was a true member of the Brevia community.

But everything else faded when she thought of her son and what she'd need to do to keep him with her.

Before moving forward with her plan, she had this one last loose end to tie up.

"Good morning, Mrs. Shilling," she said as she walked into the room.

"Well, hello, dear." A gray-haired woman, sitting at the games table with a deck of cards, lifted her head and smiled.

"Hi, Iris." Julia directed that greeting to the younger woman wiping down counters at the back of the room.

"Hey, Jules. Thanks for coming on such short notice." The younger woman waved at Charlie. "Hey there, Chuckie-boy. Do you want to check out the fish while your mommy helps Mrs. S.?"

Charlie bounced up and down in his seat. "Fishy," he squealed. "Charlie, fishy."

"Thanks, Iris." Julia picked up her coffee from the stroller and pushed the buggy toward Iris. She always brought Charlie when she came to Shady Acres. The residents and employees loved seeing him.

As Iris left with Charlie, Julia turned to the older woman. "Mrs. Shilling, where did you find the scissors?" She stepped forward and ran her fingers through the spiky tufts of hair on the top of the woman's head.

Mrs. Shilling placed her hand over Julia's and winked. "In the craft cabinet, dear. They forgot to lock it after our art class yesterday."

Julia opened her bag and pulled out a plastic apron, spray bottle, scissors and a comb. "What do you think if I clean it up a little? You've done a nice job here, but I can even up the sides a bit."

"I suppose," Mrs. Shilling answered with a shrug. "When I was a girl, I had the cutest haircut, just like Shirley Temple. I wanted to look that cute again." She met Julia's gaze, her hazy eyes filled with hope. "Can you make me look like Shirley Temple, dear?"

Julia patted Mrs. Shilling's soft, downy hair. "I'll do my best." She wrapped the apron around the woman's frail shoulders. "Next time, go easy with the scissors, Mrs. S. You're beautiful just the way you are."

She usually came to Shady Acres every other week to cut and shampoo the hair of a group of residents. But Iris had called her last night to say that Mrs. Shilling, one of her favorite ladies, had butchered her hair. Julia made time to come here before she needed to be at the salon.

She used the scissors to snip a few tendrils of hair as Mrs. Shilling hummed softly.

"Everything okay in here?"

Julia turned, shocked to see Ida Garvey walk into the room.

Mrs. Shilling's face lit up. "Ida, so nice to see you here this morning. This is my friend Julia. She's making me look like Shirley Temple." She glanced at Julia. "This is my daughter, Ida. She's a very good girl." Her voice lowered to a whisper. "She still wets the bed sometimes. Has nightmares, poor girl. I let her snuggle with me until she falls asleep."

Julia gave a small smile. "Nice to see you, Mrs. Garvey."

The older woman shook her head. "I haven't wet the bed since I was seven years old. The Alzheimer's has affected my mother's memory of time."

"I figured as much. I won't be long here."

"They called to tell me she'd cut her own hair again."

"If she ever wants a part-time job, we could use her skills at the Hairhouse." Julia continued trimming the woman's fluffy hair.

"She can't do any worse than some of those girls you've got working there."

"Play nice, Mrs. Garvey. I've got the scissors."

One side of Ida's mouth quirked. "She talks about you a lot."

Julia glanced up. "Really? Me?"

"In fact, I have a suspicion she might have done this just to get you out here again."

Mrs. Shilling pointed a bony finger at her daughter. "Children are supposed to be seen and not heard, young lady."

"I'm almost seventy, Mom."

"Still holds true," the woman said with a humph. "Besides, she's going to make me look like Shirley Temple. Or maybe Carole Lombard."

Julia smiled, something about this woman's affection lifting her spirits the tiniest bit. She was grateful for every lift she could get right now. "I was thinking Katharine Hepburn, circa *Adam's Rib*. Gorgeous but spunky."

"I'll take spunky," Mrs. Shilling agreed and settled back into her chair.

"I heard about your recent troubles," Ida said, her gaze assessing. "What are you going to do about the salon?"

"My loan wasn't approved. What else can I do? I'm not sure if I'm going to be in town for much longer, actually." She squeezed Mrs. Shilling's shoulder. "I'll miss you when I go."

The woman heaved a sigh. "All the good ones move on." She gave a watery smile to her daughter. "Except Ida. She's my best girl. Always has been."

Julia's chest fluttered at the love in the older woman's gaze when she looked at her daughter. She suddenly saw crotchety Ida Garvey in a new light. Julia knew she'd look at Charlie like that one day. She'd do anything to keep him by her side so she'd have that chance. Nothing was more important to her.

Ida gave her mother an indulgent smile, and then with her customary bluntness she asked Julia, "How did the bank deal get messed up?"

Julia pulled in a deep breath and paused in her cutting. "They didn't think I was a good investment, I guess." She paused, squaring her shoulders, and then said, "As you've probably heard, my learning disabilities are severe. Not exactly the type of applicant you'd trust to run a business, even a small local salon. Too bad, though. I had big plans."

Mrs. Shilling clapped her hands. "She told me all about it, Ida. Getting rid of that horrid name. She's going to offer spa services. I want to bathe in a big tub of mud!"

"Is that so?" Mrs. Garvey asked, looking between her mother and Julia.

Julia gave a small laugh, embarrassed now that she'd confided so much in the older woman. "My idea was to make it a destination for people traveling in the area and the go-to place for a day of pampering for women around the region. There's really nothing like that unless you head over to Asheville or down to the coast."

Ida nodded. "Tell me about it. I've put most of the miles on my car driving back and forth for a monthly facial."

Julia felt color rise to her cheeks, embarrassed she'd shared her dream now that it wasn't going to come true. "That's probably more information than you wanted for a simple question." She used a comb to fluff Mrs. Shilling's white hair. "There you are, beautiful." She handed her a small mirror. "Katharine Hepburn, eat your heart out."

The woman smiled as she looked in the mirror then at her daughter. "Do you love it, Ida?"

"I do," she agreed.

Julia removed the apron and took a broom from the supply closet in the corner. "I'll have one of the girls come out to do your hair when I'm gone." She began to sweep up the hair from around the chair.

"Ida, give her some money," Mrs. Shilling ordered.

Mrs. Garvey pulled her wallet from her purse.

Julia shook her head. "I don't charge for my time here."

Ida took out a business card and handed it to Julia. "This is the firm that handles my financial portfolio. The president's contact information is there."

Julia took the card. "Oh." She knew Ida Garvey's late husband had left her a sizable inheritance.

"If you decide you want to stay in the area and are still interested in investors for your business, call him. I see the need for the type of spa you're describing. I assume you have a business plan our loan team could review?"

Julia nodded, dumbfounded by the offer.

"Good. I don't want to pressure you. I don't know why

the bank here didn't approve your loan, but I'd guess it had something to do with Annabeth. That girl isn't the sharpest knife in the drawer. But I certainly hope it wasn't because of your learning disorder. It doesn't make you a bad bet for a loan."

"Thank you for saying that."

Mrs. Shilling reached out and took Julia's hand. "Ida is rich," she said in a loud whisper. "She takes good care of me."

"You're very lucky," Julia told the woman, feeling a tiny flicker of hope that her own luck had taken a turn for the better.

Chapter 16

Sam hit the mute button on the television and jumped off the couch, throwing on an old T-shirt in the process.

His heart soared at the thought that Julia could be the person insistently knocking on his front door.

He groaned as he opened it to reveal his father and brother standing side by side on his front porch. "Not now, boys," he said and went to swing the door shut again.

His dad pushed it open and knocked him hard in the chest. "What the—" Sam muttered as he stumbled back into the house.

"That's what I'd like to know." Joe's voice was hard as he stalked past Sam. Gone was the gentle emotion of his recent visit and in its place the tough, take-no-prisoners Boston cop had returned. Sam wanted to be grateful but knew what it was like to be on the receiving end of his father's temper. His own fuse felt too short to deal with that right now.

He glanced at his brother, who shrugged and stepped into the house, closing the door behind him.

"What the hell were you thinking?" Joe bellowed, slamming his palm against the wall. "You took advantage of that girl. You used her to deceive me and now you've deserted her. That's not how I raised you. I've never been so angry and disappointed in all my years."

Angry and disappointed? Even in the midst of a full-blown tirade, Joe was talking about how he felt. Sam had damn near had enough of it.

"This is your fault," Sam countered. "If you had left me alone, none of this would have happened." He squared his shoulders, warming up to the subject, needing a place to vent his own anger. "You came in here, emotional guns a-blazin', and wanted me to turn into somebody I'm not. It's never going to happen, Dad. I'm never going to be some heart-on-my-sleeve kind of guy, spouting out my feelings and crying at sappy chick flicks." He pointed a finger at his father. "You raised me to ignore my emotions. It's what you made Scott and me into after Mom died. I can't change. The mess I made of things with Julia is proof of that."

"You faked an engagement," his father interrupted, hands on hips, matching Sam's anger.

"It was wrong. I know that now. The alternative was you following me around waiting for unicorns and rainbows to come spewing out of my mouth. It ain't going to happen. Ever. Julia and I had a business arrangement and I messed it up. If I could go back and change things, I would."

"No, you wouldn't."

Sam and his father both turned as Scott spoke for the first time.

"You don't know anything about me or what I would do," Sam spat out. "Neither of you do."

"I know you," Scott countered. "I know that girl got too close. She got under your skin, and I bet it scared the hell out of you. It sure would have me. With her big eyes, long legs and cute baby. She made you feel things and the Callahans don't like to feel." He nodded toward Joe. "Another gift from you, Dad. I don't know what she wanted or expected from you, but it's a good thing you ended it when you did. We don't do love. We're not built that way."

How could his brother be so right and so wrong at the same time? Being with Julia and Charlie had scared him. But it was because he realized he did love her even though he'd tried to ignore, then bury, his emotions. He'd fallen hard and fast, and it had made him want things that could never be.

She wanted someone to be a father to Charlie. Sam's paternal relationship was so dysfunctional it was almost laughable. How could he be a decent father with the role model he'd had in Joe?

What if he tried and failed with Julia? He was capable of love, but not in the way a woman like Julia deserved.

Suddenly Joe fell back onto the couch, clutching at his chest.

"Dad!" Both Sam and Scott were at his side in a second.

"What is it, Dad?" Sam asked.

"It's his heart, you idiot."

Joe's eyes drifted closed, and Sam moved his head and legs so he was lying flat across the cushions. "Call 911," he ordered his brother.

Scott pulled his cell phone from his back pocket, but

Joe's eyes flew open and he reached out a hand. "No, I don't need medical attention."

"The hell you don't," Sam said on a hiss. "Make the call, Scott."

"My heart hurts," Joe said, his voice trembling, "because of the pain I've caused the two of you." He lifted himself to his elbows and looked from Sam to Scott. "My sons, I've failed you and I'll never forgive myself for it." He covered his eyes with one hand as sobs racked his shoulders.

"Of all the…" Sam grumbled and sank to one arm of the sofa.

Scott threw his cell phone on the coffee table and stalked to the front window, grumbling under his breath.

"Scoot over, old man." Sam sank down on the couch next to him. "You just about gave *me* a heart attack there."

"I need a drink." Scott's voice was tense.

"Make it three," Sam told him. "There's a bottle of Scotch in the cabinet next to the stove."

Joe still sat motionless, other than an occasional moan. Sam's headache spread until his entire body hurt. "Dad, pull it together. It's going to be okay."

"Do you believe that?" Joe asked finally, wiping his damp cheeks. "Do you feel like you're going to be all right without her?"

No. Sam knew his life was going to be dark and dim, that he could spend years chasing the adrenaline rush that came with his career and nothing would compare with the excitement of having Charlie call him Dada. He felt as though he could be a hero to hundreds of nameless people, and it would pale in comparison to coaxing a real smile out of Julia.

"What choice do I have?"

"You always have a choice. That's what I didn't realize until recently. I had a choice to let your mother's death practically kill me, too, or to keep living. I didn't do a very good job of making my life count until recently. But I'm learning from the mistakes I made and doing my damnedest to make them better. You have a real chance for love with Julia. Take it."

"What do I have to offer her?" Sam asked quietly, finally getting to the real heart of the matter. His own fear. "She deserves so much more."

"I know you think that, son. But if there's even a glimmer of hope, you've got to try. Hell, you've got to try even if there isn't. Because what you have to offer is everything you are. It may not feel like it's enough but that's for her to decide. If you never put it out there, you'll spend your whole life feeling empty and alone. Trust me, that's no way to live."

What if Sam opened himself up to try? He may not feel as if he had enough to offer, but he was certain he'd work harder than any other man alive to make her happy. He wanted to see Charlie grow up, to be there for every T-ball game and skinned knee. He wanted to watch Julia hold their babies and grow old with her and everything that came between.

She was everything he'd ever wanted but was too scared to believe he deserved. He nodded as resolve built deep within him. "I've got to talk to her."

"You'd better get moving, then. She's got a head start on you."

Scott walked back into the room, balancing three glasses of whiskey. "Turn on ESPN and let's drown your sorrows."

Sam ignored his brother. "What do you mean 'head start'?" he asked his father. "Where did she go?"

"According to Vera, Julia took Charlie and headed to Ohio this morning. They caught a flight out of Charlotte. She told her mother she had some kind of a plan and needed to talk to the ex-boyfriend before the final ruling."

Sam's head spun. All he could think of was that Jeff had offered to marry Julia—some sort of business deal where Julia would come to Ohio to raise Charlie near the grandparents and they'd pay all the living expenses. Not a real relationship, but it was no better than what Sam had offered. And it would end the custody battle once and for all.

How could he have been stupid enough to let her go? What if she wouldn't take him back? What if she figured Charlie's father was a better deal?

Sam had to stop her. He loved her with his heart and soul. His life would be incomplete without Julia and Charlie in it, and he'd fight as long and as hard as he could to win them back.

He jumped off the couch and grabbed his keys and wallet from the side table. "I've got to go," he yelled to his father. "Lock up behind you."

Scott grabbed his arm as he strode past. "Don't do this. No woman is worth running after like you're some cow-eyed schoolboy."

"You're wrong," Sam answered, shrugging him off. "Julia is everything to me. Someday I hope you'll find a woman who makes you want to risk your heart. You deserve that. We both do. Dad's right. He messed up after Mom died, but we don't have to repeat his mistakes. I've got a chance to make it work and you'd better believe I'm going to take it."

"What if it's too late?"

"I've got to try."

Scott shook his head, disgust obvious in his angry gaze. "You have to be in D.C. tomorrow at eight o'clock sharp. You're going to make it, right?"

"I sure as hell hope not."

Scott cursed under his breath. "Idiot," he mumbled and drained his glass of Scotch.

"Sam."

Sam turned to his father. "I'm going to make it work, Dad. You know how relentless we Callahans can be."

"Good luck, son." Joe smiled at him. "I'm proud of you."

Scott snorted and picked up a second drink. "You go turn in your man card. I'm getting drunk."

Sam wanted to shake his brother, to open his eyes the way Sam's had been, but he didn't have time. His only priority right now was Julia and getting to her before she made a deal with Jeff Johnson.

"Sam?"

He turned to his father, who threw a small, velvet box in his direction. Sam caught it in one hand. "Is this...?" His voice trailed off as emotion overtook him.

"I had it sent down from Boston. Your mother would want you to have it."

He nodded. "Thanks, Dad," he said on a hoarse whisper then sprinted out the door.

"You've got a lot of nerve coming into my home un-invited." Maria Johnson looked down her nose at Julia. "Watch your child," she barked suddenly. "That's an antique Tiffany vase."

Julia leaned forward to pick up Charlie, who had toddled over to a wooden table and reached up to rub his tiny fingers on a glass vase perched on top.

"Hi, Mama," he said. His gaze went to Maria, who scowled at him, causing him to bury his face in Julia's neck.

Julia looked around the formal sitting room where a housekeeper had led her. It was cold, sterile and, like the rest of the house, totally inappropriate for an energetic boy. Even now she heard Maria *tsk* softly when she noticed the fingerprints Charlie had left around the bottom of the vase.

She'd asked for Jeff, but he was on his way back from a round of golf with his father. Unwilling to be distracted from her mission, or maybe afraid she'd lose her nerve, Julia had insisted on being let into the enormous house. She'd known Jeff's family had money when they'd dated, but the *Dynasty*-sized home gave her a much better perspective on how rich the Johnsons really were. They clearly had unlimited resources at their disposal to get what they wanted.

Which brought her back to the matter at hand.

"I still can't believe you have the nerve to try to take my son from me," she said with a dry smile. "I guess that makes us even."

"Your case is crumbling, and you lied about your relationship status. It's only a matter of time until they take him from you. It will be better in the end. We can give him so much more than you could ever dream of. Look at Jeffrey."

"Speaking of *Jeffrey,* he asked me to marry him."

Maria didn't speak but the anger in her eyes said it all. Her face remained as smooth as marble, her expression typically blank, thanks to one too many cosmetic procedures. "Why would he do that? We don't need you to raise the child properly."

"Maybe giving a kid every material thing they want doesn't cut it. Your son is a loser, truth be told."

"How dare you! He's a respected professor with—"

"Funny, I thought that, too, when I first met him. Turns out, Jeff is a bit of a joke around campus. He does his research expeditions, conveniently funded by your husband's corporation, but little else." Julia sat Charlie on the floor and gave him several plastic toys from the diaper bag to keep him occupied. She dug through her bag for a stack of papers. "I have written documentation from the university about the sexual-misconduct charges filed against Jeff by four different undergraduates. Apparently, when he was teaching, it took a bit of extra work to get an A from Professor Johnson." Julia didn't mention that three of the incidents had happened during the time she'd been dating Jeff.

Maria tried to narrow her eyes, but they only moved a fraction. "How did you get those?"

Julia wasn't going to say where because she honestly didn't know. She hadn't even known until this moment whether the information she'd been given was real or fake. She'd been desperate, racking her brain for a way to make the custody battle go away, even wondering if she actually should accept Jeff's horrible proposal for Charlie's sake.

Then, two days ago, a package had arrived for her at the salon, containing the information about Jeff and other sordid details regarding the Johnsons.

At that moment, Jeff and his father walked into the room.

"What's she doing here?" Dennis Johnson said through his teeth.

"Julia, have you finally realized my offer's the best you're going to get?" Jeff gave her a wink and a sneer. To think she'd once found him attractive. She'd been such a fool. Charlie threw the set of plastic keys then went to retrieve them. Both men looked at him as though he was some sort of flesh-eating alien. There was no way she was going to let this family get their hands on her son for one minute, no matter what she had to do to prevent it.

"Jeffrey, be quiet." This from Maria. "Thanks to your on-campus dalliances, Ms. Morgan thinks she has some hold over us."

Jeff's voice turned petulant. "Mom, I didn't—"

"Sit down, son." Maria's voice took on a dictator-like quality and Jeff's mouth clamped shut. "You were groomed for so much more. We gave you everything." She pointed to the damask-covered couch. "Sit down and let your father and I fix this problem like we have all your others. You've messed up things for the last time. We've got another chance with your son. I won't let you get in the way."

A sick pit grew in Julia's stomach as Jeff's shoulders slumped and he threw himself onto the couch. She'd known he didn't get along with his parents and now she understood why. She wondered how many of his problems were thanks to being raised by Mommy Dearest's twin sister.

Julia might have problems, but she knew she'd always put Charlie's best interests first in her life. Which was why she straightened her shoulders and said, "Jeff's not the only one in the family who has trouble keeping his parts in his pants." She waved a few more papers toward Dennis. "Like father, like son, from what I've discovered."

Dennis swallowed visibly as Maria sucked in a harsh breath. "How do you know that? No one has that information. I paid good money to make sure of it."

"Not enough, apparently." Julia picked up Charlie, who was grabbing at her legs. "Now let's talk—"

The door to the sitting room opened and Sam burst through, followed closely by the Johnsons' housekeeper.

"I'm sorry, ma'am," the older woman said, gasping. "He barged right past me."

Sam stood in the entry for a moment, looking every bit the bull in a china shop. Oh, how she loved him, even now. Every part of him. Julia's heart seemed to stop for a second. Charlie squirmed in her arms at the sight of Sam, squealing with delight. Julia hated that her body had the exact same reaction.

"The fake fiancé?" Jeff drawled from the couch. "Really, Julia? This is a bit of a production, even for you."

Sam pointed at Jeff. "Shut your mouth, pretty boy, or I'll come over and do it for you."

"What are you doing here, Sam?" Julia asked, her voice hoarse with emotion. She didn't want to need him. She didn't want to need anyone but was so relieved to not be fighting this battle alone, she could barely hold it together.

He looked at her and she knew he saw it, saw everything about her. He knew she had a tough exterior but was soft and scared at the core. And she knew it was okay to be vulnerable around him, that he wouldn't judge her or use her weakness to his advantage. Even with all that had happened between them, she ached to trust him. To lean on him and use his strength as her own.

"I'm here because at your side is where I belong. Forever."

"Don't bother," Maria said with a sniff. "There's no audience. The judge isn't here. No use pretending now, Chief Callahan. It's too late."

"That's where you're wrong." Sam took a step forward. "At least I hope you're wrong. Is it too late, Jules?"

"For what?"

"For me to be the man you want and need me to be." He walked toward her then bent to his knee. "For this." He pulled a small box out of his pocket and opened it, a diamond flanked by two emeralds twinkling up at her.

Julia and Maria gasped at the same time.

"It was my mother's ring. I want you to have it." He smiled at her hopefully. "I want all of it, Julia. You and Charlie and me. I love you. I want to spend the rest of my life proving how much. Proving I can be the man you deserve."

"What about the U.S. Marshals job?"

"I called today and said I wouldn't be joining them. The Brevia town council has renewed my contract for another three years. I'm there for keeps, and I want it to be with you. We're going to make this work. I'll be at your side fighting for Charlie, for our family, as long and as hard as it takes. Just don't give up on me, Julia."

Confined to her arms long enough, Charlie practically dived forward toward Sam, who wrapped his arms around him. "Hey, buddy. I've missed you."

He took the box from Sam's hand. "Here, Mama." Perched on Sam's knee, Charlie held the ring up to Julia.

She held out her hand, and the two men she loved most in the world slipped the ring onto her finger. "I love you, Sam. Always have. You had me at the car wreck two years ago."

He straightened and wrapped both her and Charlie

in a tight hug then kissed her softly, using the pad of his thumb to wipe away the tears that flowed down her cheeks.

"This doesn't change anything," Maria hissed. "We've got all the time and money in the world."

"But don't forget the information I still have. I don't want to use it but I will, Mrs. Johnson. I'll do anything to keep my son safe."

"That won't be necessary." Jeff stood, looking as thoughtful and serious as Julia could ever remember.

"Jeffrey, stay out of this."

"Not this time, Mother." He took a step toward Julia and Sam. "I don't want to be a father. I never did. But I can tell you that my son deserves better than what I had growing up."

"You had everything," Dennis argued, his face turning bright red.

"He deserves a family who loves and cherishes him." Jeff's gaze never left Julia. "Have your attorney draw up the paperwork for me to relinquish custody and send it to my office at the university. I'll sign whatever you want me to."

"No!" his mother screeched.

Julia felt a lump form in her throat as Sam placed a calming hand on her back. "Thank you, Jeff. You won't regret it."

One side of his mouth kicked up. "When it comes to funding my next research trip, I may. But I'll take that risk. Good luck, Julia." And with that, he walked from the room, followed quickly by his parents, screaming at him the entire way.

"Too 'oud," Charlie said, covering his ears with his chubby hands.

Sam's arm was strong around her shoulders. "Let's take our son home," he whispered against her ear. "We've got a wedding to plan."

* * * * *

From the time she was ten years old and read *Anne of Green Gables* and *Little Women*, **Lee McKenzie** knew she wanted to be a writer, just like Anne and Jo. In the intervening years, she has written everything from advertising copy to an honors thesis in paleontology, but becoming a four-time Golden Heart® Award finalist and a Harlequin author are among her proudest accomplishments. Lee and her artist/teacher husband live on an island along Canada's west coast, and she loves to spend time with two of her best friends—her grown-up children.

Books by Lee McKenzie

Harlequin Heartwarming

The Parent Trap
To Catch a Wife
His Best Friend's Wife

Harlequin American Romance

The Man for Maggie
With This Ring
Firefighter Daddy
The Wedding Bargain
The Christmas Secret
The Daddy Project
Daddy, Unexpectedly

Visit the Author Profile page
at Harlequin.com for more titles.

THE DADDY PROJECT

Lee McKenzie

For Mom and Dad, with love

* * *

Acknowledgments

Thank you Geoff W. for an excellent idea

Chapter 1

Kristi Callahan rang the doorbell of her dream home. A sprawling 1960s rancher with two fireplaces, a breeze-way separating the house from the two-car garage, and enough West Coast flair to appeal to potential buyers searching for their own dream home in one of Seattle's family-friendliest neighborhoods. And it was just her luck to be on the wrong side of the door.

This house was well beyond the reach of a single mom raising a teenage daughter on a single mom's income, but that didn't stop her imagination from playing with the idea of actually living in a house like this someday. And since she'd been hired to get this one staged for the real estate market, she would at least get to put her personal stamp on the place before returning to reality. Her modest two-bedroom town house was no dream home, but it was hers. Or it would be hers in twenty-three and a half years.

The other reality was that by the time she and her team at Ready Set Sold were finished here, this client would get top dollar, even in today's less-than-stellar market, putting this house even further out of her reach.

Speaking of clients, she had an appointment and she was only five minutes late. Okay, eight, but surely Mr. and Mrs. McTavish hadn't given up on her and gone out. There was a big silver-colored SUV and two pink plastic tricycles parked in the driveway but that didn't necessarily mean anyone was home.

She dug her phone out of the side pocket of her bag. No messages, no missed calls. Taking care not to get tripped up by a tattered teddy bear missing half its stuffing and three small yellow rubber boots strewn across the wide front step, she rang the bell again, and waited. A moment later her patience was rewarded with footsteps, lots of them. Two identical faces with earnest blue eyes and blond Cindy Brady pigtails appeared in the glass sidelight next to the door. One had her thumb in her mouth; the other's pigtails were oddly askew. No doubt these were the tricycle riders. And then they were dwarfed by a huge dog whose head appeared above theirs, a panting, drooling Saint Bernard.

"Is your mommy home?" Kristi asked, loud enough so they could hear.

Their pigtails shook from side to side.

The dog pressed its moist nose against the glass.

Hmm. The children stared at her but made no attempt to summon a grown-up. Surely they hadn't been left here on their own with only a dog to look out for them. A dog that let loose a strand of drool that now slithered down one of the blond pigtails.

Gross. Kristi quickly looked away and reached for the

doorbell yet again, pulling her hand back when another set of footsteps, heavier ones, approached from the other side of the door.

The man who opened it was wearing faded blue jeans, a gray T-shirt with what appeared to be a complicated chemical equation in green lettering stretching across his chest, and the annoyed expression of someone who wasn't expecting anyone.

"Can I help you?" he asked.

Darn. Did she have the wrong day? No. She had checked her calendar and this appointment had definitely been scheduled for Wednesday. And it was Wednesday, wasn't it?

The man at the door gave her a wary look and held up his hands, both clad in dirt-caked gardening gloves. "If you're selling something, I'm not interested."

"No." She shook her head emphatically, trying to ignore his mucky gloves and struggling not to be distracted by the intensity of his eyes. Cool blue eyes that a girl could practically swim in. "I'm not selling anything."

"Who's she, Daddy?" the girl with the crooked pigtails asked before Kristi could continue.

"My name's Kristi." She smiled down at the adorable little girls, then extended her hand to their father. "Kristi Callahan. I have a two o'clock appointment to meet with the owners. The McTavishes?" Maybe she had the wrong address. "I'm the interior decorator with Ready Set Sold. You hired my company to stage your home and set up the real estate listing."

His expression went from accusatory to apologetic and he slapped a hand to his forehead—apparently forgetting about the gloves as he remembered the appointment— and applied a grimy streak to his brow.

She stared at it, contemplated the protocol with strangers who had spinach in their teeth, toilet paper stuck to a shoe, dirt on their faces, and decided there wasn't one.

He must have realized what she was looking at because he gave his forehead a hasty swipe with his forearm. The streak blurred to a smudge.

Kristi fought off a smile and lowered her gaze to the two little girls, who now flanked the man, each with an arm wound around a kneecap. The one was still sucking her thumb.

"Right. I'm Nate McTavish." He held out his hand, jerked it back and pulled off the glove. His handshake was confident, firm but not too firm. His skin was warm and, given the state of his gardening gloves, surprisingly dirt-free. "Your company was recommended by a colleague of mine. I plan to sell but the house needs some work and I wouldn't know where to start."

"I see." She noted that he said "I" rather than "we," and the little girls had already indicated their mother wasn't here. The hand that might give a clue to his marital status was still inside a gardening glove. *Not that it's any of your business,* she reminded herself, and tried to ease her hand out of his.

He quickly let go.

She dug a business card out of her bag and handed it to him, wishing her partner Claire had come instead. She always knew how to handle awkward situations.

"If this is a bad time—"

"No, not at all. I've been working in my greenhouse this afternoon and I lost track of the time."

In a way it was good that he hadn't been expecting her. She didn't have to apologize for being late.

"As I said, I'm the company's interior decorator. I help

our clients get organized prior to listing their homes, assist with any decluttering or downsizing that might be needed. We'll work together to create a design plan to suit your home and your budget. Samantha Elliott, one of my partners, is a carpenter and she'll take care of any repairs or remodeling that has to be done. My other partner, Claire DeAngelo, is a real estate agent," she added, striving to sound polished and professional. "She handles the appraisal, the listing, arranges the open house, that sort of thing."

"This sounds like exactly what I need. I don't have much time for these kinds of things."

Kristi's initial uncertainty faded, but she forced herself to take a breath and slow the flow of information. "We take care of everything. I'm here today to take a look around and get an idea of what needs to be done and we'll take it from there. Um…will your wife be joining us?"

His earlier wariness was back, and if anything it was intensified. "No. She's…" He glanced down at his children and gently eased the thumb out of his daughter's mouth. "My wife passed away two years ago."

"Oh, I'm sorry. If there's anything I can—" *Stop. You don't offer to help a complete stranger.* "I'm so sorry."

"Thank you." Except he didn't sound grateful. He sounded as though he wished people would stop asking where his wife was, and stop offering clichéd condolences when they found out.

The little girl with the crooked pigtails tugged on his hand. "What's she doing here, Daddy?"

The other child had already recaptured her thumb.

"She's going to help us sell the house."

"Why?"

"Because we're going to move into a new one."

"Why?"

Kristi was reminded of her own daughter at this age, when the answer to every question generated another, especially when the answer was *because.* Creating a distraction had been the only way to make the questions stop.

"What are your names?" she asked.

"I'm Molly. She's Martha. We're sisters."

"Nice to meet you, Molly and Martha. How old are you?"

"Four." Molly appeared to be the pair's designated spokesperson.

Martha held up the four fingers of her free hand, apparently happy to let her sister do the talking.

They were adorable. They were also a poignant reminder of how much she loved children, how she'd never really got past the disappointment of not having more of her own. The panting dog nudged her elbow with its moist nose, making her laugh. She rubbed the top of its head in response.

"You should come in." Nate reached for the dog's collar and backed away from the door, taking the girls and the dog with him. "Sorry, I shouldn't have kept you standing out there."

"Thank you." She'd begun to wonder when that would occur to him. She stepped into the foyer and tripped over the fourth yellow rubber boot.

Stupid high-heeled shoes. She'd put them on, thinking they made her look more professional, and instead they turned her into a klutz.

Nate grabbed her elbow and held on till she'd regained her footing. She looked up and connected with his intense blue-eyed gaze, and for a second or two, or ten, she couldn't draw a breath. He was gorgeous.

When the clock started ticking again, he abruptly let her go, as though he'd read her thoughts, maybe even had similar ones of his own, and then with one foot he slid the boot out of her path. The dog snapped it up by the heel and gave it a shake, sending a spatter of drool across the floor.

Kristi shuddered.

"Girls, remember what we talked about? You need to put your things in the closet."

"That's Martha's," Molly said. "Mine are outside."

Martha tugged the boot out of the dog's mouth, tossed it onto the pile of things in the bottom of the closet and tried unsuccessfully to close the bifold door. She was remarkably adept at doing things with one hand.

"Sorry about the mess," Nate said. "If I had remembered you were coming, I would have tidied up."

Kristi couldn't tell if the closet door wouldn't close because the pile of clothing and footwear was in the way or if a hinge was broken, or both. She made a mental note to have Sam take a look at it, and added storage baskets to the list already forming in her head. She lived with a teenage girl and a dog so she knew a thing or two about clutter. At least the slate tile floor was clean, which, given the amount of traffic generated by two small children and one large dog, was a good sign. This man must be a decent housekeeper, or maybe he had a cleaning service. Either option scored him some points. The children looked well cared for, too, and in the grand scheme of things they were most important.

All this made Nate McTavish pretty much the opposite of the deadbeat dads in her life. That, along with his offhand charm and those heart-stopping eyes, should elevate her opinion of him. Instead the combination set off a loud clamor of mental alarm bells.

Get over yourself. Quiver-inducing blue eyes aside, she was here to do a job, not strike up an unwelcome relationship with a client.

"Not a problem. That's why I'm here." And if the rest of the house was anything like the foyer, she had her work cut out for her.

"Where would you like to start?" he asked.

"Is this the living room?" she asked, pointing to a pair of mullioned glass doors. With the frosted glass, they looked more like Japanese rice paper than traditional French doors.

He hesitated, then reluctantly pushed them open. "It is. We almost never use it so I keep the doors closed."

Kristi surveyed the interior. The curtains were closed and the room was dark and cool. The vaulted cedar-plank ceiling was draped with yellow-and-mauve crepe paper and clusters of matching balloons. Several balloons appeared to have come loose and were now on the floor, looking a little deflated.

"We had the girls' birthday party here last week and I didn't get around to taking down the decorations. I'll be sure to do that tonight."

Martha clung to her father's hand but Molly scampered into the room and attempted a balloon toss. The massive dog lumbered in behind her. The yellow blob of a balloon slithered to the floor so the child stomped on it instead. When it didn't pop, she lost interest and rejoined her father and sister. The dog nudged it with its nose, picked it up and gave it a chomp. Still no pop, so

Lee McKenzie 243

the Saint dropped the slobbery mass in the middle of the sisal area rug.

The room was furnished with comfortable-looking furniture and there was an abundance of books and newspapers, a few kids' toys and dog toys, and sofa cushions that needed straightening.

Kristi took her camera out of her bag and looped the strap around her neck. "If it's okay with you, I'd like to photograph each room. When I get back to my place... my office—" He didn't need to know she did most of her work out of the back of her minivan and at one end of her kitchen table. "The photographs help me create a design plan and draw up a budget."

"Fine with me. Are you okay to look around on your own? I still have some work to do outside." He pulled his gardening gloves back on.

"You go ahead," she said. "I'll look through the house and we can talk when I'm done."

"And I will tidy up in here tonight," he assured her again.

The week-old remnants of the party seemed to embarrass him. Kristi didn't see them as a problem, quite the opposite. At least there had been a party, and that was definitely to his credit. She couldn't remember the last time Jenna's dad had even called to wish their daughter a happy birthday. Gifts? Not even a consideration.

"Molly. Martha. Let's go. You can play outside while I work."

"Daddy, why is she taking pictures?"

"She needs to know what the house looks like."

He took Molly's hand and coaxed her out of the room along with her sister, who needed no urging at all. The dog seemed content to amble along after them.

"Why?"

"Because."

"Because why?"

"Because she just does."

To say Nate McTavish was overwhelmed by single-parenthood would be the understatement of the century, but what he lacked in technique, he made up for with patience. In spades.

As he walked away, she smiled at the green lettering on the back of his T-shirt. Go Green With Photosynthesis. At least now the equation on the front made sense, and confirmed her guess that he probably was a gardener. Her gaze dropped a little lower. There was a lot to be said for a flattering pair of jeans, but these particular jeans were simply magic. She quickly looked away. *You have a job to do, and* that *is not it.*

Since her ex, Derek the Deadbeat, had left twelve years ago, she had been on a number of casual dates, mostly with men her family and friends had set her up with, but she had guarded against anything that would distract her from becoming a self-sufficient single mom and career woman.

Everything about this man was distracting. The hair that could use a trim but suited him anyway, his being oblivious to the streak of dirt on his forehead, and oh… those eyes. She never felt awkward with new clients, but if she'd had to go through every room in the house with him, knowing those eyes watched every move she made, she would not have been able to focus. Especially after the moment they'd had when she tripped over the little yellow boot. And it hadn't just been *her* moment. He'd felt it, too. She was sure of it.

With him out of the room if not entirely out of her

mind, she pulled open the heavy drapes and imagined the clutter away. The rich wood of the floors and beamed ceiling created a warm contrast to the polished river rock of the open-hearth fireplace. She would start staging in this room, she decided. The fireplace was the focal point of the room, and it would create the perfect jumping-off point for the casual West Coast decor she would carry throughout the house. She didn't even need to see the other rooms to know she could make it work.

She raised her camera, snapped a photo of the fireplace and then systematically documented the rest of the room.

Her BlackBerry buzzed before she had a chance to move on. It was her mother. She could either take the call now or wade through a half dozen messages later on. Kristi adored her mom, but in the history of motherhood, Gwen Callahan's persistence in checking up on her daughter was unmatched.

"Hi, Mom. What's up?"

"Hello, dear. I hope I'm not interrupting anything."

"Actually, I'm in the middle of a job."

"Oh. Well then, this'll just take a minute."

I suppose there's a first time for everything. "What would you like?"

"I was just talking to my old friend, Cathie Halverson. You remember her, don't you? They lived across the street when you were in high school, then they moved to Spokane."

"Ye-e-e-e-s." Kristi already knew where this was going.

"Her son Bernard has just moved back to Seattle. I'm sure you remember him."

All too well. Bernie Halverson had asked her to a

school dance when she was fifteen. She went because it was the first time anyone had ever asked her out and she hadn't had the sense to say no. The date had been a disaster. They'd had nothing to talk about, and his idea of slow-dancing was synonymous with groping. He had reeked of cheap cologne, and the next day she'd had to wash her favorite sweater three times to get the smell out of it. But the worst part had definitely been the kiss.

"Sure," she said. "I sort of remember him."

"He doesn't know that many people in Seattle," Gwen said. "So I was thinking we could invite him to Aunt Wanda and Uncle Ted's Fourth of July barbecue. Doesn't that sound like a good idea?"

To Bernie Halverson, it might. For a split second she considered telling her mother he'd been the first boy to stick his tongue in her mouth, she hadn't liked it one bit and if he was still single after all these years it's because he was still a letch.

She couldn't tell her mother that. Gwen Callahan did not like to discuss "intimacies," as she so delicately referred to them. But then straight out of the blue, Kristi had a better idea.

"I don't think so, Mom. I've actually just met someone." It wasn't a lie, really. She had just met *someone.* Nate McTavish. So it was only the teeniest of lies. Just a fib, really. "It's nothing serious or anything but I don't think we should give Bernie… Bernard…the wrong idea."

It took her mother five full seconds to respond. "You're seeing someone? When did this happen? Why haven't you said anything? Has Jenna met him? Are the two of you—"

"Mom, stop. It's recent, very recent, and like I said,

it hasn't turned into anything serious. And no, Jenna hasn't met him so I'd appreciate it if you didn't say anything to her."

"What's his name? What does he do?"

"Oh. Nate. His name's Nate and he's a… He works in landscaping." And in a blink the fib turned into a terrible lie that she would, without question, live to regret.

"Well, this is certainly a surprise. Where did you meet him?"

"Through work." That part was true. "And I'm at work right now, Mom, so I really can't talk."

"I'll call you tonight so we can make plans. You'll have to invite him to Wanda's barbecue so we can all meet him. So Jenna can meet him. Or you can give me his number and I'll invite him."

And there came the part where she would live to regret this…right on schedule. "No! No. Thanks, Mom. I'll talk to him about it. I'm not sure if he's free, though. I think maybe he mentioned something about having plans with his family." *Stop. Talking.* The hole she was digging would soon be so deep, she'd never climb out of it. "I have to go, Mom. I'm working with a new client this afternoon. I'll talk to you later."

"I'll call you tonight," Gwen said again.

Kristi couldn't tell if there was a subtle threat in her mother's parting words, or if the guilt she was feeling had skewed her perception. Most likely a little of both.

Over the years her mother and Aunt Wanda had tried to set her up with more eligible men than she could count. She'd managed to avoid going out with most of them, but occasionally they'd caught her off guard, like the times they had invited someone like Bernie Halverson to a family event. Not one of those men had come close to look-

ing like Nate McTavish. Not that looks were everything,
but there hadn't been any chemistry with any of them,
either. Shaking hands with Nate had left her insides bub-
bling like a beaker over a Bunsen burner.

Even his T-shirt has chemistry written all over it.

She rolled her eyes at that thought. She had no business getting all dreamy-eyed schoolgirl over her new client. She had a job to do.

From somewhere in the house, a phone rang. She
counted six rings before it stopped, unanswered.

She quickly scrolled through her photographs of the
living room. Satisfied she had everything she needed
for now, she crossed the room, opened a second set of
frosted glass doors and walked into the dining room.
Another unused space, judging by the cool temperature
and drifts of gift wrap and empty toy packaging littering
the floor. There were more yellow-and-mauve streamers and dejected-looking balloons, but everything else
about the dining room was neat as a pin. It was spacious, with plenty of room to maneuver around a table
that would comfortably seat ten. The furniture was a
little too flea-market-finds-meet-grandma's-attic to really suit the house, but some of it was solid and in good
condition. She always liked to keep her budget as low as
possible, so she would make it work.

From the moment she'd driven up, she'd loved this
house, but now she felt a little sad for it, having its beautiful rooms closed up and uninhabited. This house deserved to be lived in by someone who would love it at
least as much as she did.

At the back of the dining room was a third pair of
opaque glass doors, closed like the others. She pulled
them open, stepped into a spacious and *very* messy

kitchen, tripped over the dog's water bowl and sent a small tidal wave gushing across the tile floor.

"Oh, for heaven's sake. Who puts a bowl of water in front of a closed door?" Apparently a frazzled single dad did. She had no idea where to look for a mop and she couldn't leave this huge puddle on the kitchen floor. So much for working through the house on her own. Now she had to find that distractingly sexy and very single dad and ask him for help.

Chapter 2

Nate herded the girls and the dog through the family room.

"Why can't we stay with the lady?" Molly asked.

"Because I have work to do."

"We can stay with her."

"She has work to do, too," he said, sliding the patio door open.

"Taking pictures?"

"Yes." And he was happy to leave her on her own. It was one thing to stand with her in the living room, or almost any other room, while she made notes and took photographs. But eventually they would get to his bedroom, and the idea of going in there with her had brought on a mild state of panic.

"She has a pretty purse," Molly said.

"Does she?" He shut the patio door behind them. He had only noticed her bag was huge. And stuffed full.

"It has cupcakes on it."

"Does it?"

Martha pulled her thumb out of her mouth. "I yike cupcakes."

"I know you *like* cupcakes. Why don't you two go in the playhouse and have a look at the new dress-up clothes Aunt Britt dropped off this morning." He'd asked Britt to bring them out here because the girls' bedroom already looked like Toys "R" Us had tangled with a tornado. "Maybe she brought you some purses."

His sister, a self-proclaimed clotheshorse, frequently cleared out her closet to make room for new things and bestowed the items she no longer wanted on her nieces. The girls loved it, but their bedroom, the family room and now the playhouse overflowed with toys and Britt's cast-offs.

"Come on, Martha. Let's see what she brung us." Molly snagged the dog by the collar and tugged. "You, too, Gemmy."

At the entrance to the playhouse, she let go of the Saint's collar and skipped inside. Martha straggled in behind her, and Gemmy sprawled across the doorway, head resting on her paws.

After they were settled, Nate turned his attention to the rows of potted asters in his makeshift greenhouse and tried not to think about the beautiful woman with the ginormous cupcake purse who was discovering that he was not the world's greatest housekeeper. How had he not remembered to put a reminder about this meeting in his calendar? If he had, he would have spent last evening tidying up instead of going over the final draft of his current research paper.

He measured the height of a plant and recorded the data in the spreadsheet on his laptop.

Kristi Callahan was stunning in a wholesome girl-next-door sort of way, with a lively swing to her blond ponytail and an engaging flash in her gray-green eyes. More green than gray. She smelled good, too.

His cell phone rang. After three rings, he tracked it to the end of the workbench, where it was hiding beneath a spare pair of gloves. His in-laws' phone number was displayed on the screen. What now?

"Hello, Alice. How are you?"

"Nate, I was getting worried. I called the house but no one answered."

Nate sighed. He and the kids could have been out for the afternoon or even just at the supermarket, and he refused to check in with her every time they left the house.

"Sorry, Alice. I didn't hear it ringing. I'm out in the greenhouse."

"Where are the girls?"

He resented the accusatory tone. Where did she think they were? "They're in the playhouse. Gemmy and I are keeping an eye on them."

"That's good. You know if you're busy, you can drop them off here anytime. Fred and I are always happy to see them."

There were lots of things he'd like to say, but only one of them was polite. "Thank you. I appreciate that."

"Did that person from the real estate company show up?"

Now they were getting to the real reason for her call. At least she'd called and not shown up unannounced as she often did. He never should have told her he was going to sell the house, especially since her constant interference was one of his reasons for wanting to move. He didn't like the idea of being too far from the university, but his next house would be a lot farther than fourteen blocks from Alice and Fred's.

"She's taking a look at the house right now."

"And you're out in the greenhouse?"

"I wanted to keep Gemmy and the girls out of her way, so I brought them outside. Besides, she's just deciding what needs to be done." He didn't have to be around for that.

"You should have asked us to help instead of spending good money to have someone else do this."

Nate closed his eyes and, for several seconds, indulged in the idea of applying for a faculty position at another university. One on the other side of the country. Or maybe in a different country.

"There's a house for sale down the street from us," Alice said. "It would be perfect for you and the girls, and they're having an open house on the weekend. You should come by and have a look."

"That sounds...interesting." Nate picked up a garden trowel and imagined stabbing himself in the head with it. Alice had lost her only child, he reminded himself, but that didn't make it easy for him to rationalize her interference. After Heather died, Alice had transferred all of her attention to her granddaughters. Understandable, and he appreciated everything she did for them. Mostly. But she had always made it clear that she considered him to be partly responsible for Heather's death. He'd managed to heap a fair amount of blame on himself and he didn't need her adding to it. She was Molly and Martha's grandmother and he had to be civil, but no way was he buying a house within walking distance of the world's most meddlesome mother-in-law. He set the trowel on his workbench.

"While I have you on the phone," Alice continued. "Remember that children's beauty pageant we discussed?"

His insides coiled into a knot. There had been no discussion. Only her saying he should enter the girls, and him saying no. "Yes, I remember."

"You might not like the idea, but you should look at their website before you make up your mind. It will be so good for them."

Good for them? They were four years old.

"Especially Martha," she said. "These sorts of things build confidence and that will help her to stop sucking her thumb."

"I've been busy, Alice."

"The application deadline is only a couple of weeks away."

He contemplated the trowel again. "Right. I'll take a look." Or not. There was no way *his* daughters would be paraded around like a pair of miniature beauty queens, not to mention having to compete with one another. No way in hell.

"Speaking of the girls," he said, not wanting to leave her with another opening. "I need to check on them. Thanks for calling, Alice. I'll talk to you later."

He set his phone on the table and stared at it, picturing it impaled by the garden trowel. Instead he measured the next plant and updated the spreadsheet while he shoved the conversation with Alice to the back of his mind. He had more important, and appealing, things to think about. Like the woman currently inside his home.

He could kick himself for forgetting she was coming

here this afternoon. A colleague at the university had recommended Ready Set Sold, so he had called them from his office and scrawled the appointment on a notepad, which by now was buried on his desk beneath everything else he'd been working on—the syllabus for the summer school course he was teaching next month, a draft of a research paper he was coauthoring with a colleague and the latest edition of the *American Journal of Botany*. He really needed to be better organized, but he could scarcely remember a time when his life wasn't out of control.

In the months after his wife died, he had welcomed the help and support he'd received. Even relied on it. Over time, his family had backed off, but not Heather's. They meant well, at least that's what he wanted to believe, but their good intentions frequently overstepped the boundaries. Without coming right out and saying it, Alice often implied that he should be doing a better job of raising her granddaughters, of keeping the house tidier, of being two parents instead of just one.

She insisted Molly and Martha were old enough to look after their own things, and part of him acknowledged that might be true, but he couldn't bring himself to make them do it. They had already lost their mother, so it didn't seem right that they be stuck with an overbearing father who made them earn their keep. Alice was also of the opinion that Martha was too old to be sucking her thumb, and she was now pressuring him to put an end to that by entering her in a beauty pageant of all things.

Heather would have known exactly how to handle her mother and their daughters. Why didn't he? He was a bright guy with a PhD and a career as a scientist. When it came to family, he felt hopelessly in over his head, and he was also smart enough to know that reflected his own upbringing. His mother had kept house and raised him and his sister. His father had been the family's sole breadwinner and his fallback approach to child rearing had always been "go ask your mother." Over the years Nate had learned a lot of things from his dad, but parenting skills weren't among them.

These days Nate rarely thought about the weeks and months after Heather died, leaving him with a pair of toddlers and a fledgling career as a professor of botany at the University of Washington. When he did reflect on those dark days, they were blurred by grief, and even a little guilt. His two-year-old daughters had needed his undivided attention, 24/7, and that had kept him going. The university had even granted him a semester's leave. Many people, including his family and Heather's, thought he should have taken more time off but he had wanted to get his life back to normal.

Now, two years later, he was probably as adept at juggling his family and his professional life as he would ever be, and it felt as though the ship had sailed on establishing boundaries for his in-laws. Selling the house and moving to another neighborhood might not be the best solution, but right now it felt like his only one. And it was better to do it now. The girls wouldn't stay little forever. They'd be starting school next year, and this would get easier. It had to.

He knew the future would bring different demands, not fewer, but a smaller house would be more manageable, and a fresh start might make it easier to lay down some new ground rules. But first he had to sell this house, and he was definitely smart enough to know he needed professional help with that. Heather had planned to decorate right after they bought the place, but she was already pregnant, and then she got sick. The girls were born six weeks early, and then she got even sicker. Curtains and cushions had never been on his list of priorities, and they had dropped off Heather's. Once he'd made the decision to sell the house, Ready Set Sold seemed like the perfect solution. Alice might think "home staging" was a waste of money and phony as hell, but Kristi Callahan seemed like the real deal. Even her blond hair looked natural. Nice curves, great legs—

"Nate?"

He dropped his calipers.

"I'm sorry," Kristi said. "I didn't mean to startle you."

"Oh. No, you didn't." Like hell she didn't. His imagination had been on the verge of conducting a closer examination of those legs. He hoped his red face didn't give that away. "I'm just clumsy," he lied.

Her laugh sounded completely genuine. "Clumsy is my middle name. I'm afraid I spilled your dog's water bowl. It was in front of the door between the dining room and the kitchen, and I can't find anything to clean it up."

He bent down to pick up the calipers, came face-to-knee with the hem of her skirt and jolted himself back to the upright position. "Don't worry about it. I'll come in and mop it up."

"So, this is your greenhouse," she said, looking around. "It's not what I expected."

"It's technically not a greenhouse. It was built as a pergola and the previous owners converted it into a pool house by adding the change room at the back. We don't use the swimming pool." He gestured at the bright blue cover. "So I closed this in with heavy-gauge plastic and use it as a greenhouse instead."

"I see."

He could tell she didn't, but at least she hadn't called it an eyesore like his mother-in-law had.

"You have a lot of plants," she said. "Is this what you do for a living?"

He surveyed the rows of asters. "I teach botany at Washington U. I'm collecting data for a senior undergraduate course I'll be teaching this fall."

"So, you're a university professor." She was still looking at the plants as though she wasn't quite sure what to make of them.

"Yes, and I also do research." Oh, geez. As if she would care.

"What are you researching?" she asked, probably because she felt she had to say something.

"The poor reproductive barriers in species of angiosperms."

"Really?" She looked puzzled. "I didn't think plants had sperm."

Nate laughed. "I said *angio*sperms. That's the botanical term for flowering plants. You're right that plants don't have sperm. At least not in the strictest sense of the word."

Her cheeks flared pink. Her comment had been innocent enough and he wished he had let it go.

"I thought you might be a gardener," she said.

Now it was his turn to be puzzled.

"You were wearing garden gloves when you answered the door and your T-shirt—" She glanced at his chest and away again. "So…"

He liked that she was still blushing.

"It's the equation for photosynthesis," he said. "I got this at a conference I attended last year."

"I thought so. I mean, that's what it says on the back. So, about the mop…" She hiked her thumb toward the house. "I need to clean up the water I spilled and finish looking through the other rooms."

He also liked that she was outwardly more flustered than he felt on the inside. "I'll clean it up. It's my fault for leaving Gemmy's bowl in front of the door."

He set the calipers beside the next plant he needed to measure, saved the spreadsheet and closed his laptop. "Molly? Martha? I'm going inside for a couple of minutes."

"We're playing school," Molly yelled back. "An' I'm the teacher."

"Good for you. I'll be right back. Gemmy, stay," he said, giving the dog the palm-out signal for "stay." She rolled onto her side with her back firmly pressed against the playhouse door and her eyelids slowly slid shut. She wasn't going anywhere and neither were the girls.

"I take it Gemmy is a girl," Kristi said as they circled the pool together and walked toward the house.

"She is. It's short for Hegemone."

"That's an unusual name. I've never heard it before."

"Hegemone is the Greek goddess of plants. The botany connection seemed like a good idea when I got her. Then the girls came along and they couldn't pronounce it so they shortened it to Gemmy. She also responds to Gem. And Milk-Bone treats."

"My dog's name is Hercules. That's a Greek god, too. I think."

"Roman, actually. Borrowed from the Greek Heracles, son of Zeus. He was half mortal and half god."

"Oh. We thought he was the god of strength or something."

She wasn't wearing a wedding ring so he'd assumed she was single. The "we" implied otherwise.

"He was, among other things," Nate said. He resisted the urge to elaborate. She probably already thought he was a complete nerd. No point sounding like a walking encyclopedia and removing any doubt. "What kind of dog is Hercules?"

"A Yorkshire terrier."

He laughed. "Good name. Does he live up to it?"

He slid the patio door open for her and waited for her to go inside.

"Only in that he has me and my daughter completely wrapped around one of his tiny little paws."

"But not your husband?"

She met his gaze head-on. "I don't have a husband."

"I see." He had wanted it to sound like an innocent question. It was anything but, and they both knew it. For a few seconds they stared awkwardly at one another, then she looked away.

"So… I'll just grab the mop."

He left her waiting in the family room and sidestepped the massive puddle on the kitchen floor. He looked in several places before he located the mop in the mudroom and the bucket in the garage.

In the kitchen, Kristi stood at the end of the peninsula that separated the kitchen from the eating area. She had set her enormous cupcake bag on the counter next to her and was looking at the monitor of the camera in her hands. The bag was a light purple color and printed with wildly colorful cupcakes, which the girls had gushed over. It was also large and completely stuffed. He'd heard all the jokes about the contents of a woman's handbag, but this was over-the-top. How much stuff did one woman need to carry around with her?

"You have a great house," she said, without looking up from the camera.

"Thanks." *You have great legs,* he thought as he quickly looked down and up again, past the purple skirt and short, matching jacket with the big black buttons, relieved she wasn't watching him.

He set the bucket on the floor, and Kristi reached for the mop.

He shook his head. "I'll look after it. It was my fault anyway. I keep the door closed, so I put the water there because it was out of the way."

As he ran the mop over the floor, he kept a surreptitious eye on Kristi. She wasn't paying any attention to him. Instead something on the fridge door had caught her attention. The latest strip of pictures of him and the girls from the photo booth at the mall.

"Cute photographs," she said.

"Thanks. We started taking them when their—" *When their mother was dying.* Daily visits to the hospital had become too much of a strain for her and too stressful for the girls, so he'd started taking the photographs to her instead. He couldn't tell that to a stranger. "We started taking them a couple of years ago. It's sort of become a tradition."

"I think it's lovely," she said.

He worked the mop across the floor, keeping what seemed like a safe distance from her. Safe, that is, until his gaze sought out the shapely curve of her calves, the slender ankles....

The mop handle connected with something.

He whipped around in time to see her enormous cupcake bag slide off the counter, but he was too slow to catch it. Like a slice of buttered toast, it flipped and hit the floor upside down, and then there was no need to wonder what was in the bag because its contents were strewn across the damp kitchen floor. "Dammit."

Kristi set her camera on the counter, laughed and knelt at the same time he did, the tip of her blond ponytail brushing the side of his face as she tossed it over her shoulder. She smelled like springtime and lilacs.

She started cramming her possessions back into the bag.

He gathered as many things as he could and handed them to her. A notebook, several pens, an empty Tic Tac box, a hairbrush, two tampons and...oh, geez...a condom? The warmth of a flush crept up his neck, but he was sure his red face was no match for hers. She held the bag open and he dropped everything inside, avoiding eye contact.

"Thanks." She stuffed a bunch of receipts and a wallet into the bag. "I think we got everything."

He stood up, and she stood up, wobbling a little on account of her heels. He grasped her arm to steady her, reminded of how she'd nearly tripped on Martha's boot. She smiled up at him, and when he looked into the depths of her green eyes he felt like a cliff diver plunging headfirst into an unfamiliar sea.

"So..." she said, then stopped as though she wasn't sure what else to say. A lot of her sentences started that way.

"I should get back outside. The girls are out there, and I still have work to do."

"Me, too." She flung the overstuffed bag over her shoulder. "Inside, not outside. It won't take me long to finish up, then I was thinking I could just let myself out. Would it be okay if I come back tomorrow? In the morning, maybe, say around nine, if you're not too busy. That'll give me a chance to look through the photos I've taken, talk to my partners." She stopped, drew a long breath.

She was embarrassed, probably in a hurry to get out of here, and it was his fault. If he'd been paying attention to what he was doing instead of admiring her legs, he wouldn't have knocked her bag off the counter. And then, if he'd been paying attention, he would have left the little plastic packet for her to pick up and pretended not to see it.

Now the stupid condom had become the elephant in the room—

The bad analogy practically had him groaning out loud.

"Tomorrow morning's good," he said. "Nine o'clock. I was planning to work at home anyway."

"Great. I'll put together a proposal tonight and we can discuss it then."

She reached for her camera, and as she got close he backed away, sensing it was a bad idea to get *too* close to a woman who smelled like a cross between an English country garden and a Hollywood starlet's boudoir. Not that he knew anything about the latter, but he was a man after all, and he did have an imagination. She must have been thinking the same thing…about getting too close…because she hastily backed away, too.

"Thanks. And, um, I'm sorry about the water, and for taking you away from your work. I'm usually not *this* clumsy."

He didn't believe her. In spite of her polished appearance she seemed to have a knack for running into things, tripping over them. Oddly, it made her even more captivating. He had no business being captivated, though. She might not have a husband, but the condom in her bag meant she was involved with someone. And if she wasn't…well, he didn't want to know what it meant.

"Is there anything else I can tell you about the house?" he asked, not knowing what else to say.

"I don't think so. I'll just take a quick look at the bedrooms and let myself out. I assume they're down the hallway off the foyer."

He nodded.

She whirled around and once again his nose filled with her heavenly scent.

She crossed the family room like it was a runway, the flippy hem of her skirt flirting with her knees and the heels of her shoes making a crisp, sharp sound against the hardwood. Just before she left the room, she smiled at him over her shoulder, as if to say she knew perfectly well why he was still standing there.

"See you in the morning." And then she was gone.

You're wasting your time, he told himself. *She's not your type.*

Did he even have a type? He'd thought it was Heather. She had been every bit as attractive as this woman was, just in a more down-to-earth, practical way. No swirly skirts and purple cupcake bags for her. Heather had been studiously working toward a doctorate in psychology when they'd started dating. They hadn't talked about marriage, but it was the obvious thing to do after they'd found out they were expecting.

The pregnancy had taken a heavy toll on Heather's health, but then the girls arrived and they seemed like such a gift, such a natural extension of their lives that neither of them had given much thought to any scenario other than Heather getting better. She hadn't.

He'd been left with a lot of questions. Would she have married him under any other circumstances? Would he have married her? Those were questions with no answers, only regrets. Would she still be alive if not for the pregnancy? Of course she would. It took two people to make a baby and the rational scientific part of his brain knew that. The part that housed his conscience was another matter. It ate at him with a relentless appetite.

As for the beautiful woman who had just disappeared down the hallway, the one who might be walking into his bedroom at that precise moment, he had questions. Truth was he shouldn't have any, but that wouldn't prevent him from looking forward to seeing her tomorrow morning and maybe getting the answers to some of them.

Chapter 3

The next morning Kristi yawned and poured herself a cup of tea, then settled in at the kitchen table with her laptop. She had stayed up far too late last night, going over the photographs of Nate McTavish's house and drafting a design plan. She was not a morning person at the best of times, and agreeing to meet him at nine o'clock had been a bad idea. Now she had just over an hour to review her proposal, check her email and make the twenty-minute drive to the university district.

Hercules nosed her ankle. He sat on his haunches and cocked his head when she smiled down at him.

"Hey, Herc. Do you want to sit with me?"

He danced on his hind legs, tail wagging, and she swept him onto her lap. From beneath shaggy brows, his black-button eyes sparkled up at her.

"Sit and be good or I'll put you down."

He settled in, and Kristi opened her email.

She wrapped one hand around her teacup and breathed in the heady jasmine-scented steam rising from it. After a quick scan of her in-box, she clicked on a message from her business partner Claire DeAngelo.

Thanks for sharing your photographs and design plan for the McTavish house. Love your ideas! Knowing you, the place will be organized in no time. Let's see what Sam says about the renos you've suggested. The "greenhouse" definitely has to go, but the professor looks like a keeper. C.
PS: remember our 10:30 conference call.

The message ended with the emoticon for a wink.

Very funny, Kristi thought. She had wanted Sam to see the pergola–pool house structure that Nate had converted into a greenhouse, but she shouldn't have sent a picture with him in it.

She opened a folder on her desktop and clicked to open the photograph.

Turning the structure back into a pool house wouldn't take much work, so there was really no justifying the amount of time she'd spent studying the photo last night. Claire was right. He looked ridiculously good. If anyone had asked her to imagine what a botany professor looked like, her imagination would have conjured up the exact opposite of this tall, fit-without-being-totally-ripped man with gorgeous eyes and a killer smile.

She quickly clicked to close the image and opened Sam's email next.

I agree with Claire. Great house. Great ideas. Definitely looking forward to meeting your Professor Hottie. S.

    Sam's email ended with two winks.

    Oh, for heaven's sake. Their comments were all in good fun, but Kristi rolled her eyes as she read them. She had given some sketchy background information on their new client when she'd sent the photographs and the proposal to her partners late last night. Sketchy details were all she knew. He was a single dad and a widower who found that one big house and two small girls were more than he could juggle with his demanding career.

    Claire, recently separated and almost certainly headed for divorce court, had declared she was off the market. Besides, Nate wasn't her type. Her ex was an investment broker with a taste for money and a penchant for keeping up appearances. Kristi had never liked him, had always thought Claire could do better, but her friend was totally type A when it came to organizing her life. Nate's disorganization would drive her crazy.

    Sam and the love of her life, recently married at a quiet ceremony with a small gathering of family and close friends, wouldn't give another man a second glance, no matter how hot he happened to be. Kristi had been thrilled to share maid of honor duties with Claire, and they couldn't be happier that their business partner was happily settled with her husband AJ and their young son, Will.

    Claire's and Sam's teasing was strictly for Kristi's benefit. That they had picked up on her immediate attraction to this man was a testament to how well they knew one another. They also knew she was determined to maintain control of her life, at least until her daughter was grown-up and off to college, and that meant not having a man in it.

Her deadbeat dad had abandoned her and her mother after he'd lost his job, remortgaged their home and gambled everything away. And then she'd made the same mistake her mother had. Let herself be swept off her feet by a guy who was all talk and no substance. Got pregnant right out of high school. Married the guy because of course that was the right thing to do, and learned too late that he couldn't hold down a job, didn't know how to be a husband much less a dad and had no interest in learning.

Now her mission in life was to set an example for her daughter and break the cycle so Jenna didn't make the same mistake. Setting a good example meant not getting involved with a man, any man, but especially not another deadbeat, until Jenna was past the age of being impressionable.

Anyone could see that Nate McTavish was smart, decent, easy on the eyes and about as far from deadbeat as any man could be, but he was still a man. He had a lot going on in his life, including grieving the loss of his wife. Kristi would be the first to admit she had enough baggage of her own. To heck with taking on anyone else's.

Once more she scrolled through all the photographs she'd taken, from the living room and dining room with their festive party streamers to the cluttered kitchen where a board game on the table was still surrounded by lunch dishes that hadn't been cleared away.

One photo captured the refrigerator and a cluttered counter. Like hundreds of other homes, the front of the fridge was plastered with notes, calendars, kids' artwork. It was the photo booth strip that leaped out at her, though.

She enlarged the photograph and leaned closer to the screen for a better look. Four images of Nate and his girls, snapped in rapid succession, laughing and grinning and making silly faces at the camera. Her chest went tight, the way it had when she'd first seen the pictures yesterday. There had been more strips on a tackboard in the girls' bedroom, one on Nate's dresser in the master bedroom and several on the desk in his home office. None of them, at least none that she'd seen, had included the wife and mother this family had lost, but together they created a poignant record of Nate's daughters as they grew up. Altogether she'd noticed eight or ten of the strips scattered throughout the house, and she felt sure she would encounter more as she drilled down through the layers of clutter.

Organizing a client's personal mementos fell well outside the kind of work she usually did, but the mother in her wanted to do something special with those photographs. She wished she had started a tradition like that when Jenna was little. Suggesting it now would yield one of her daughter's signature eye rolls and a "Mo-om, that's so lame."

Speaking of Jenna…

Kristi glanced at the clock. Darn. In a futile attempt to keep herself on track, she kept it set five minutes fast. Even deducting those precious minutes, they were running late and it was almost time for her daughter to leave for school.

She scooted Hercules off her lap and drained her teacup as she shut down her laptop and stuffed it into her bag along with the rest of her things. On her way through the kitchen she deposited her cup in the sink and hauled her bag to the bench by the front door. Now to find her keys.

"Jenna?" she called up the stairs as she scanned the

surface of the small console table inside the front door. "Are you ready?"

"Almost. Do you know where my iPod is?" Jenna shouted back.

Kristi put her search for her missing keys on pause. *Exactly where you left it,* she thought. *Ditto for my keys.*

"Haven't seen it, sweetie." And she didn't have time to look. Her daughter could survive for one day without Justin and Selena. She, on the other hand, couldn't get her day started until she found her keys.

She should have taken less time going through photos, less time checking email and a lot less time fussing with her hair and makeup. Then she had put on her blue sneakers, realized they were scuffed and grimy from clearing out a previous client's garage and changed to the pink ones. But her blue T-shirt didn't go, so she changed to a white one, decided against it and dashed downstairs to retrieve a pink shirt from the dryer. Then she'd let herself get distracted and had folded the rest of the laundry and put it away.

How she managed to stay on task in a client's home while being so disorganized in her own was a constant source of frustration for her…and an endless source of amusement for Sam and Claire. And now, because of it, she was going to be late.

Back in the kitchen she picked up a dish towel to see if her keys were hiding beneath it. They weren't. This was rapidly turning into one of those mornings when nothing went the way she wanted it to. She quickly folded the towel, hung it on the handle of the oven door, moved on to the dining room table. No keys on the half she used as her office. The other end was Jenna's homework space, and the two halves met in the middle in a muddle of personal items, assorted junk mail and a pair of hurricane candle lanterns, placed there to create a little ambience after their last cleaning session.

No sense looking there. Had she put the keys in her bag? Claire, the poster girl for organized efficiency, had suggested attaching a lanyard to the strap of her handbag and clipping her keys to that when she wasn't using them. An excellent suggestion and it had worked like a charm, until she'd switched purses and didn't transfer the orange lanyard because it didn't match the purple bag. *Note to self. Buy a lanyard to match every bag.*

She retrieved her bag from the front hall and set it on the kitchen counter. Wallet, makeup bag, lint roller, dog leash, but no keys. She shoved those items aside and dumped the rest onto the counter. The loose contents included a handful of spare change, two Milk-Bone treats, the tube of lipstick she'd hunted for earlier that morning…and one condom.

She picked it up and stared at it, recalling in excruciating detail Nate McTavish's embarrassment when he'd realized what he had in his hand. She had been every bit as mortified. Did he think she was one of those women who was always ready for a little action? Ugh. Nothing could be further from the truth. She avoided as many blind dates as possible, and the only action she saw when she did date was never more than an awkward good-night kiss. No condom needed.

Yesterday she had been even more embarrassed when Nate told her about his research. Something about poor reproductive barriers in flowering plants. She still didn't completely understand what he'd been talking about, even though she'd tried to look it up on the internet last night. He might as well have been talking Greek.

"For sure he was talking geek," she said, smiling at her own cleverness.

Fourteen years ago she had learned the hard way that at least one brand of condom had provided a very poor barrier to reproduction. Thank goodness she hadn't revealed that yesterday. Bad enough she'd blurted out some nonsense about sperm. What had she been thinking? His laugh had been a few registers lower than his speaking voice, deep and sexy with a flash of perfect white teeth. He might be a geek, but he was a darned sexy one.

Jenna thundered down the stairs. "Mom? Are you *sure* you haven't seen it?"

Kristi shoved the small plastic packet into her bag and hastily put everything else back on top of it. "Have I seen what?"

"My *iPod*."

Right. "No, I haven't."

"Well, crap."

"Excuse me?"

"'Crap' isn't swearing, Mom." Jenna dropped her backpack by the front door and glanced around the living room.

Kristi didn't have time to argue. "Do you remember what you were doing the last time you used it?"

"No. If I did…" Jenna was halfway across the room when she stopped. "Sleeping! I fell asleep listening to Katy Perry." She whirled around and dashed for the stairs. "I'll bet it's still in my bed. Thanks, Mom!"

"You're welcome." Now if only the same strategy would work for her. She had come home from work yesterday afternoon, brought in a handful of mail, picked up the paper…aha, that was it. She must've left her keys on the coffee table where she'd deposited everything else.

Sure enough, there they were, under the newspaper. Jenna had flipped it open to check the movie listings, not wanting to wait until Kristi had finished uploading photographs to her laptop so she could check them online. Being a typical teenager, she had used the inconvenience as an opportunity to bemoan the fact that she was stuck with her mother's retired cell phone instead of the iPhone she so desperately needed.

A car horn sounded in front of the town house and Jenna raced back down the stairs. "That's my car pool. Gotta go."

"I'll be home early," Kristi said, as much a warning to her daughter that she shouldn't bring boys home after school. One boy in particular. That strategy would work until next week when school let out for the summer. Then she wasn't sure how she would do her job and chaperone a teenager who was too old for a babysitter but too young to be left on her own all day.

"See ya later, Mom!"

"We're having pasta for dinner. If you could make a—" Her request that Jenna make a salad to go with it was cut off by the slam of the front door. She could leave her a note, but Jenna would say she didn't see it. Better to send her a text message. Teenagers *never* let a text go unread, and her daughter was no exception.

Kristi opened the door to their backyard patio and shooed Hercules outside. "Go on. Do your business, then I have to get out of here."

While he was outside, she checked her bag to be sure she had everything she needed for the day, then glanced at her watch. She hadn't packed a lunch, but if she left now she would only be a few minutes late. Ten minutes, max. She'd have to take a break at lunchtime and run out to grab a bite to eat, and that would waste more time. She opened the fridge and scooped up a couple of bottles of water, an apple and the makings of a cheese sandwich. Now she could work through lunch to make up for not being on time. She took out a plastic container filled with the cupcakes she had baked on the weekend. She hated to see them go to waste, and Nate and his daughters might like them.

"Come on, Herc." She picked him up when he scampered inside, gave him a scratch behind the ears and set him in his bed. "Keep an eye on Jenna when she gets home. I have to dash."

Worrying about being late was likely a waste of time, though. Nate McTavish didn't seem like the kind of guy who paid any attention to the clock. He probably wouldn't even notice that she was running a little behind.

Nate poured himself a second cup of coffee and settled at the breakfast bar with his laptop. Behind him, Gemmy was sprawled on the family room floor, and Molly and Martha lay between her front legs and her back legs, using her ample girth as a pillow while they watched a daddy-approved program on television.

While he kept an eye on the clock, anticipating the ring of the doorbell, he opened the file containing the first draft of a research paper he was coauthoring with a colleague.

Kristi had said she would be here at nine, and it was now two minutes past. *Actually, she said* around *nine, and it's not like it matters*. He would be here all day.

The doorbell startled him, even though he'd been expecting it. "I'll be right back," he said to the girls.

He hotfooted it to the front door and opened it to find his mother-in-law standing there.

"Alice. This is a…surprise." And yet another affirmation of why he needed to move.

As always her dark clothing reminded him of a military uniform, and the pinched lines around her mouth made him think she needed to smile once in a while.

"These are the pageant applications. I wasn't sure if you would get around to looking at the website before the deadline." She handed a large envelope to him. "I know how busy you are." Her tone implied otherwise.

He didn't want to get into it with her now, with the girls practically in the next room and Kristi due to arrive any minute. Now he really hoped she got held up somewhere and wouldn't arrive until Alice was gone. "You didn't have to go out of your way. I would have—"

"The girls' photographs are in there with the application forms," Alice said, cutting him off, saving him having to lie to her. "We had them taken the last time Molly and Martha spent the weekend. The applications have to include full-length poses and head shots. We know how busy you are, so we took care of it."

Head shots? He resisted the urge to tear open the envelope.

"I can't stay," she said. "I'm on my way to have my hair done."

Her dark silver coif was as smooth as a helmet, not a hair out of place.

He waved the envelope at her. "I'll take a look at this." *No, you won't, and you shouldn't be letting her think you will*. He needed to put an end to this insanely inappropriate plan to enter his daughters in a beauty pageant.

"Heather would have been okay with this." And without waiting for him to reply, she strode down the sidewalk in her no-nonsense shoes, got into her gray sedan and drove away without a backward glance.

He didn't give a damn what Alice said. Heather would not have been okay with this. What he didn't understand was why this was suddenly so important to Heather's mother.

"Who was that, Daddy?" Molly asked when he returned to the family room.

He slipped the envelope underneath his laptop, glad the girls hadn't heard their grandmother at the door, and even more grateful she hadn't asked to see them.

"Just a courier, sweetie. Dropping off some papers for me to look at."

He sat on a stool and scrolled back to the top of the document and read the introduction for the third time. So much for his plan to get some work done before Kristi arrived.

Who was he kidding? Between Alice's unexpected visit and Kristi's impending arrival, he couldn't concentrate anyway. Last night, after the girls were in bed, he'd spent an hour and a half taking down streamers, cleaning bathrooms and trying to catch up on laundry. Then he'd spent another hour looking at online real estate listings for smaller homes that were still close to the university and the girls' day care, yet a safe distance from his in-laws. His findings weren't impressive. For the first time since deciding to sell this place, he'd had some truly genuine misgivings, but Alice's unexpected visit this morning strengthened his resolve.

The doorbell pealed…this time it had to be Kristi… and on his way to answer it, he reminded himself to play it cool.

"Good morning," she said. In cropped black pants and a pink T-shirt and sneakers, she could be dressed for yoga class. She looked completely different from the woman who had breezed in here yesterday, taken up residence in pretty much every waking thought and occupied at least one of his dreams last night.

Wow. "Good morning." He stood there, realized he was staring at her and hoped he hadn't said "wow" out loud.

"I would have been here sooner, but I waited until my daughter left for school, and then I couldn't find my keys...." She hitched the purple cupcake bag higher on her shoulder. "Sorry. I should have called."

"That's okay. I'm used to students who show up late for class." *Moron.* How was that playing it cool? Had he forgotten how to have a normal conversation with a woman?

She seemed to find him amusing. "Well, I hope I don't lose marks."

She said it with just enough sass to put him in his place, but not so much that he minded.

"Come in," he said, stepping aside for her. This home staging thing was a complete mystery to him but he was more than willing to learn. It would be like being a student again, and he had a pretty good idea he was going to like his teacher.

Kristi walked with Nate through the house, noting that the living room doors were open, the streamers were gone and he had even attempted to tame the kitchen clutter. Molly and Martha were sprawled with the dog in the middle of the family room floor, watching a children's show she didn't recognize. Something new in the years since Jenna was little.

"Good morning, girls. What are you watching?"

Molly angled her head and looked up at her. *"The Cat in the Hat."*

Martha tugged her thumb out of her mouth. *"Knows a Lot About That."* Back went the thumb.

Kristi looked to Nate for an explanation.

"The Cat in the Hat Knows a Lot About That! It's a kids' science show."

Of course it was. This family was all about science. Nate's T-shirt this morning read Evolution of a Botanist and had a series of silhouettes, starting with a chimpanzee, progressing through various human forms, and arriving at a man with a plant pot under one arm. She wondered how many botany T-shirts were among the items of clothing she'd seen lying around his bedroom. She hadn't dared look too closely, but her money was on lots.

The kitchen countertops were still home to more items than potential buyers needed to see, but he'd made a valiant attempt to clear them. She was impressed.

"Coffee?" he asked.

"No, thanks. I've already had tea."

She pulled a file folder and her laptop out of her bag, and carefully set the bag on the floor out of the way. She was not risking a repeat of yesterday's disaster.

She took the stool next to his at the breakfast bar and slid the folder toward him.

"This is my proposal," she said. "I've tried to keep it simple and straightforward. Mostly painting and bringing in some fabrics to freshen things up. I would also like to give you some solutions to help you keep things organized."

She watched him open the folder and scan the contents, hoping he wasn't overly offended by her inference that his home was, well, disorganized.

"Outside, we'll want to uncover the pool, have it cleaned and filled. It's one of the main selling features of the house. And...ah...it would be a good idea to turn the pergola back into a pool house."

Since he was currently using it for his work at the university, she hesitated to suggest that the plants had to go because she wasn't sure how he would react. She still didn't really understand exactly what it was that he did. Last night she had found his page on the university's website, which included a description of his research interests and a list of papers he'd published recently. She'd hardly understood a word of it. Who knew plants were so complicated? Or that a man who could pass for a film star would find them so interesting?

"No problem," he said, surprising her. "Can you give me a week?"

"Of course. There's lots to do inside."

He closed the folder. "This isn't as bad as I expected. Where do we start?"

"I've listed the rooms in the order I'd like to work on them." She had decided to tackle the rooms that were in the worst shape first. "My plan is to begin with your daughters' bedroom and your office."

"That's fine with me. Is there anything I can do?"

"Yes. If there are items in your office that can be filed or put in storage, that will help at lot. Those are decisions I can't make for you."

"Makes sense."

Relieved that he seemed willing to go along with her suggestions, she pressed on. "This morning I'll get going on the girls' bedroom. I'll bring in some bins they can use to help sort their things."

Nate seemed unsure. "I'm not sure how that'll go over."

Did he think four-year-olds couldn't take ownership of their own messes? she wondered. Or that it was a parent's job to do everything for them?

That could explain why he was so overwhelmed. Or maybe he was overwhelmed and didn't even realize it.

"Let's see how it goes," she said. "I have a couple of tricks up my sleeve."

"Daddy, can we watch something else now?" Molly called from the next room.

"Maybe later. Kristi would like you and Martha to show her your bedroom."

She and Nate slid off their stools and joined the girls in the family room. The TV was already off and both girls were on their feet.

"Come on," Molly said.

Martha took her hand and tugged.

Kristi grabbed her bag and let them lead her down the hallway with Nate following, somewhat reluctantly if she had to guess.

Once inside the room, each girl climbed onto her unmade bed, Kristi sat on an upholstered ottoman, and Nate hovered in the doorway.

"First I'd like to talk about your favorite things," Kristi said.

"Barbie!" Molly said.

Martha shook her head. "Barney!"

Okay, no theme there. "What about colors? What's your favorite?"

"Purple!" they said in unison.

Okay, she could work with that.

"I like purple, too." She pulled a binder and her paint palette out of her bag and fanned the chips to show them. "Is there another color you both like?"

"Blue."

"Red."

Purple, red and blue. Not going to happen. She slid a sample of soft, pale apple green from the palette. "What about this? If we paint your walls pale green, we can use your favorite color as an accent for things like bedding and curtains."

"I yike purple and green," Martha said.

"Me, too."

"I wonder what your dad thinks," Kristi said, glancing at Nate, who was leaning against the door frame.

"Doesn't green clash with purple?"

Kristi flipped the pages in her binder and showed him the color wheel. "They're on opposite sides of the wheel, so they're actually complementary colors." She ran her finger in a line across the page. "Think of a plant that has purple flowers and green leaves."

He leaned in for a closer look. "Okay, that makes sense."

She congratulated herself on the plant analogy. "I suggest a very light shade for the walls, and then we can put together some accessories the girls will enjoy now and that they can take with them. Before we can start painting, we'll need to move all your stuff into the guest room," she said to the girls. "Would you like to help with that?"

Molly bounced on her bed. "Yup. We're good helpers."

Martha stuck her thumb in her mouth and shook her head.

"Why not?" Kristi asked.

"She likes sleeping here," Molly said.

"Martha, is that true?"

The little girl nodded.

Kristi looked to Nate for help.

"I have an idea," he said. "How about we turn this into a little holiday? I'll set up the tent in the family room, and you can sleep in there till your room is ready. It'll be like a camping trip."

Martha's eyes lit up and she gave her head a vigorous nod.

Molly jumped off the bed. "Sleeping bags! Can we have hot dogs? And marshmallows?"

"Sure we can."

Martha leaned close to Kristi and pulled her thumb out of her mouth again. "You, too?" she asked.

Kristi didn't know if she was being invited for hot dogs or the whole camping holiday.

"Thank you for asking me," she said, avoiding looking at Nate. "But I have to go home and have dinner with my daughter."

"She can come."

"How old is she?" Molly sounded as though she was looking for a new playmate.

"She's fourteen. A lot older than you and Martha. She likes hot dogs, though." Camping not so much. "Are you ready to get started?"

Nate stepped into the room. "If we're having hot dogs, we'll have to make a trip to the market. Do you mind if we leave you on your own for a while?"

"I want to stay," Molly said.

Martha's head bobbed in agreement. "I don't yike the market."

"If you don't like the market, I could sure use some help here." Kristi wondered what Nate would think of that. "They'll be fine with me if you'd like to go on your own."

"Are you sure?"

"Of course." She loved kids and these two were adorable. Besides, she had a hunch they would be more willing to cooperate with her cleanup plan if their dad wasn't here.

"Girls, are you okay to stay with Kristi?"

"Yes!" they chorused.

The telephone rang, interrupting their conversation. "I'd better take that," he said.

"While you're still here, I'll bring in the bins I use for sorting."

Kristi followed Nate as far as the foyer. From there he went into the kitchen to get the phone and she let herself out the front door.

Several minutes later she returned with as many plastic bins as she could carry. She set them on the floor inside the front door and went in search of Nate. She hoped he would agree to pare down some of the toys, especially the stuffed animals, but she hadn't wanted to ask in front of the girls.

The dog, still doing a bear-rug imitation, gave her a lazy blink. Nate stood by the patio doors in the family room, his back to her, phone to his ear.

"Mom, I'm sure your friend's daughter is very nice," she heard him say. "And I'd be happy to meet her some other time, but it's Britt's birthday so this should be about her."

He paused to listen to his mother's reply.

Kristi cringed. His mother was obviously trying to set him up with someone, and it was just as clear that he didn't want to be set up. Poor guy. She could relate. Yesterday's call from her mother still echoed in her head, and remembering the story she'd made up brought on a fresh wave of guilt. And she shouldn't be listening to Nate try to wriggle out of a similar situation. This was way too personal.

"Here's the thing," he said. "I'm sort of seeing someone."

Okay, you really need to get out of here, Kristi told herself. But curiosity kept her rooted in the doorway.

"Oh. Ah, her name is Kristi. She's—" He turned around and stopped talking.

Their gazes locked and held.

He ran a hand through his hair. "Mom, I'll call you back. I have to check on the kids." He ended the call without waiting for a response.

The room was suddenly warm and much smaller.

"Oh, God. I am so sorry. I didn't mean for you to hear that." He spiked his hair again. "It's just that my family has this thing about introducing me to women. I was trying to figure a way out of it this time, but I shouldn't have mentioned you."

"A blind date?" Kristi laughed. She couldn't help herself. "Trust me, you do not have to apologize. My family does the same thing to me all the time."

"Really? So…you're not seeing anyone?"

"No, I'm not." Although she was surprised he asked. "A fact that makes my mother a little crazy. Yesterday she called about my aunt's Fourth of July barbecue. She was going to invite this guy who used to live across the street when I was in high school."

"How did you handle it?"

Should she tell him? If she did, it might make him less uncomfortable. "I did the same thing you just did."

His eyes narrowed.

"I told her I'd met someone, and your name kind of slipped out."

There was no humor in his laugh. "So your family thinks you're taking me to your aunt's barbecue."

"I guess so. I'll have to come up with some excuse why you won't be there but—"

"And my mother will expect you to be at the cocktail party she's throwing for my sister's birthday."

She didn't respond, but then he didn't really seem to be talking to her anyway.

"This could work. You come to my sister's birthday party. I go to your aunt's barbecue." He sounded calm and rational, as though he was laying out the steps in a lab experiment. "What do you think?"

She was pretty sure he didn't want to know what she was thinking. "I don't know. I used to lie to my mother about some of the guys I was dating, but I've never lied about someone I'm *not* dating."

He shrugged. "So you'd rather spend an afternoon at a family picnic with the guy who lived across the street?"

God, no. "I'd rather go by myself."

"That's how I feel about my sister's birthday party. But unless I come up with an alternate plan, I'm going to be paired with my mother's bridge partner's daughter."

"So I heard." And she would suffer the same fate if she didn't make plans of her own.

"What is it with families?"

"They mean well," she said. "At least mine does. My mom was a single parent, too, and it was hard for her. I think she always wished she'd find someone but never did, and now she's shifted that focus onto me."

"My family wants to find a new mother for Molly and Martha." His voice was thick with resentment. "They seem to think I'm in over my head."

"Oh, I'm sure they don't. Your girls are great. They're happy. Anyone can see they're well cared for."

"Thank you." The tension around his eyes softened.

"You're welcome."

"So, how about it? You come to my sister's birthday party, I'll go to your family barbecue, and we'll call it even."

Say no. "Sure," she said instead.

He offered his hand to seal the deal. "It's a date."

She shook it. "A fake date."

"Make that two fake dates." He smiled and her insides turned to Jell-O.

Chapter 4

Kristi tugged her hand out of Nate's and hiked a thumb over one shoulder. "I'll just go and start sorting."

"Sure, good idea. And I'll run out to the market but, ah, first I have to make a call."

Kristi made her escape, collected her things from the foyer and headed down the hallway to the children's bedroom.

He was going to call his mother. There'd be no turning back after that. What were they thinking? What was *she* thinking? Her mother and Aunt Wanda would be happy, but how was she going to explain this to Jenna? Only time would tell if this fake-date idea was brilliant or ill-conceived.

The giggling emanating from Molly and Martha's room was like music to Kristi's ears. Such sweet kids. Each girl was wearing dress-up clothes over their pajamas. Molly's black spaghetti-strap cocktail dress bunched on the floor around her. Martha had a messenger bag slung crosswise over her shoulder and a floppy-brimmed hat all but covered her eyes. Scattered around them were toys and clothes and the largest collection of stuffed animals Kristi had ever seen.

After agreeing to the fake dates, she had completely forgotten that she'd gone into the kitchen to ask Nate about the toys. For now she and the girls would sort them and make decisions later. She looked around for a place to set up the bins and ended up having to clear a space near the door.

"How would you girls like to play a little game?"

"I'm going to a party," Molly said. She twirled, got one foot tangled in the hem of the black dress and collapsed onto a pile of what appeared to be even more dress-up clothes.

Martha giggled. "I'm going on a safari to look for dinosaurs."

"You both look very cute," Kristi said. "Do you like playing dress-up?"

"Yup!" Molly straightened out her dress and bounced to her feet.

"Aunt Britt gave us these clothes," Martha said.

Kristi separated the three bins, set them side by side and took another look around the room. "I need helpers who are good at sorting things."

Martha took off the hat and tossed it in the air. "I can do that. Daddy got us a card game that's all about sorting." The hat landed on one of the beds.

"That sounds like fun." An image of Nate and his daughters playing a card game had Kristi thinking how the world could use more dads like him.

"What are we going to sort?" Molly asked, attempting another twirl, this time successful.

"Let's start with all the clothes on the floor. Do you think you can put your everyday clothes into a red bin and dress-up clothes into the blue one?"

"Yup." Martha pulled the messenger bag over her head and tossed it in the blue bin. "See?"

"Good job."

"I can sort, too." Molly slithered out of the black dress and added it to the blue bin.

"What's going in the yellow bin?" Martha asked.

"Well, let's see…" Kristi pretended to give the question some thought. "I guess some of the stuffed animals could go in there for now. What do you think?"

Molly scooped two teddy bears and a toy killer whale off her bed and dumped them into the yellow bin. Martha followed with a frog, a rabbit and another teddy bear.

"Our grandmas gave us these," Molly said.

"Except for Winnie the Pooh and Curious George. Aunt Britt gave them to us on our birthday."

Kristi recalled the party streamers that Nate must've taken down last night. "Did you have a cake with candles to blow out?"

Both girls shook their heads.

"We had cupcakes!" Martha said.

"Daddy bought them at the store."

"I yike cupcakes better than cake."

Their excitement made Kristi smile. "Me, too."

"Is that why you have them on your purse?"

"It is." She liked that they had noticed her bag. She had found the fabric on sale and had sewn the bag herself. As for birthdays, she made a mental note to suggest to Nate that he ask his family to consider clutter-free gifts, like admission to the Seattle Aquarium or the Children's Museum. It hadn't been easy, but even Kristi's mom had gradually been retrained to give movie passes and iTunes gift cards instead of items Jenna didn't need.

Kristi picked up a purple T-shirt and a pair of jeans. "Who do these belong to?" she asked.

"Me!" Martha reached for them.

"Why are they on the floor?" Kristi asked.

The child shrugged. "There's no room in my dresser."

"Are you sure?" Kristi opened a drawer in one of the matching dressers. Sure enough, it was crammed full.

"Those clothes don't fit us," Molly said.

It took Kristi three tries to get the drawer closed again. No wonder the kids didn't use it. "All right, then. You can put your clothes in the bins for now." Later she would talk to Nate and figure out what to do with the things the girls had outgrown.

Would Nate be open to getting rid of the dressers and building some cubbies for storing the girls' clothes? A couple of months ago Sam had built a modular system for clients who had then taken them to their new home.

"Can you girls keep sorting while I take a look at your dad's office across the hall?"

"Yup."

"We can."

"Good. Maybe there'll even be a prize for the winner." She'd learned long ago that bribery was never a parent's best tactic, but in this case she wasn't the mom. She was just a desperate decorator who wanted all this stuff picked up in the least amount of time.

"What do we win?"

"Well…it just so happens that I brought cupcakes with

me. You can each have one at lunchtime, as long as it's okay with your dad."

"Goodie!"

"We yike cupcakes!"

Kristi laughed. "It's a deal, then. I'll come back in a while and see how you're doing."

With the twins engaged in a sorting game, she moved across the hall to the bedroom Nate used as an office. She paused in the doorway, thought of him working here, grading his students' papers, researching the projects she'd read about last night while letting herself indulge in a little daydream about what it would be like to be with a guy like him. Smart, hot, sexy. And now she was about to find out. Not *with him* with him, but spending time with him. A flash of panic caused a flutter in her chest. Fake dating a man she was already attracted to could get complicated.

"Only if you let it." Which she wouldn't. She didn't dare. Besides, she could always change her mind, back out. She knew what that would mean, though. Her high school memory of fending off Bernie Halverson's unwelcome advances flickered through her mind. She wasn't risking a repeat of that. And Nate didn't want a relationship any more than she did, which made this a perfect arrangement. The opposite of complicated.

His office was another story. At one time it must have been a boy's bedroom because two of the walls were papered with sports motifs, the other two were painted bright blue, and the ceiling fixture was a basketball pendant, and a decidedly hideous one at that. How could he work in here?

His large oak desk wasn't old enough to be an antique, but it had that vibe about it. It had been shoved into one corner, and the surface was covered with neat stacks of paper and books, with a clear space in the middle that was about the right size to accommodate the laptop she'd seen on the kitchen peninsula when she arrived a while ago. The floor-to-ceiling shelves that spanned one wall were every bit as crammed as the desk, but like the desk, the books and papers were arranged in neat rows and stacks.

She quickly perused the books on one shelf. Botanical research, plant physiology, forest ecosystems. Molecular phylogenetics, whatever that was. Nate McTavish was one really smart guy, and she couldn't even understand the titles of the books he read. It was a good thing their fake dates would be restricted to family events with plenty of other people around to keep the conversation moving. If they went on an actual date, just the two of them, they would never find anything to talk about.

Here in his office she saw the same kind of organization she'd noticed in the greenhouse yesterday. He had a ton of stuff but she was willing to bet he had a system, that he knew exactly where to look if he needed something. If she had to describe her idea of what a scientist's brain looked like, this would be it. Lots and lots of neat compartments overflowing with information but at the same time never quite full.

She knew better than to try to organize this room, although it would be nice if Nate would agree to reduce some of the sheer volume of it, maybe store the things he didn't need in boxes. Until the house was sold, she would like to create a better sense of space here. Would Nate be as eager to tackle his office as the two little girls chattering in their room across the hall? Maybe he liked cupcakes, too. That made her smile.

She would also swing the desk around and away from

the wall to give it the importance it deserved, and so he didn't sit with his back to the door. She wouldn't tell him its present position was bad feng shui—he'd probably think that was totally unscientific—but when she was finished in here, she knew he'd find it a more productive place to work.

She pulled her notebook out of her bag. At the top of a clean page she jotted "Nate's Office" and started a list. She was still making notes when her BlackBerry buzzed a few minutes later. The Ready Set Sold office number appeared on the screen. Their morning conference call. Claire was right on time, as always. This would give her and Sam a chance to discuss her ideas for Nate's place. As for other developments with this client, well, she might hold off talking about those.

After Nate was sure that Kristi was down the hall and out of earshot, he dialed his mother's number before he lost his nerve. While it rang, he let himself out through the patio doors and walked to his greenhouse, where there was no chance of being overheard. His mother would be full of questions and in case he needed to get creative, he'd rather Kristi not have a chance to eavesdrop.

"Hi, Mom," he said when she answered. "Sorry I had to cut you off."

"No problem. Are the girls okay?"

"Oh, yeah. They were just…ah…being a little too quiet so I thought I'd better check on them."

"Of course. So, about Friday night. Your father and I are throwing a little cocktail party to celebrate Britt's thirtieth. I wanted to give you enough notice so you can find a sitter for the girls. And of course now we're hoping your *friend* can join us."

He drew a deep breath and took the plunge. "I just talked to her and she's free. So yes, we'll be there."

"Wonderful. You said her name is Kristi? We can't wait to meet her. I'm glad we talked before I invited Evelyn's daughter."

So was he. "So, about the party. Do I…*we*…do we need to bring a gift?" He hated shopping for anything, groceries included, but he could always grab some flowers on his way there.

"It would be a brave man who showed up empty-handed at Britt's birthday party."

Flowers it is.

"We're also having a family brunch on Sunday and of course you'll bring the girls for that. Kristi, too."

The fake date tally rose to three. And he would have to take another gift, and it couldn't be flowers. "We'll be there."

Would Kristi agree to go? He hoped so. He had no more interest in meeting Evelyn's daughter than he'd had any of the other daughters, sisters and second cousins twice removed of his mother's friends. In the past six months she and his sister had introduced him to a string of women deemed to be suitable wife-and-mother material. Apparently they discussed his sorry existence with everyone they knew. He shuddered to think how those conversations played out, but he could well imagine they'd read like an ad on an online dating site.

Desperate widower seeks equally desperate single woman. Must love kids and dogs.

Not anymore. He and Kristi had an arrangement that was both mutually beneficial and blissfully uncomplicated.

"I should go, Mom. I'll see you on Friday."

"Tell Kristi we're looking forward to meeting her."

"She's looking forward to meeting you and Dad, too," he added because he knew that's what she wanted to hear.

"See you on Friday. And Nate, we're so glad you're seeing someone. All any of us want is for you to be happy."

Leaving him alone would make him happy. Taking Kristi to his sister's birthday party would feel a lot like being under a microscope, but it couldn't be as bad as any of the blind dates he had agreed to. Like the one he'd met for coffee and an awkward conversation after work last month. Or the woman he and the girls had met at the park one Saturday afternoon when the babysitter backed out at the last moment. That woman had made a valiant effort to find his daughters engaging, and failed dismally.

Back in the kitchen, he dropped the phone into its cradle and scrawled the time and dates of his sister's two birthday parties on the magnetic calendar on the fridge door. Before he left for the market he should do a little tidying up in the kitchen. He stowed the girls' breakfast dishes and his coffee mug in the dishwasher and wiped down the counter. He closed his laptop and lifted it up, uncovering the pageant information Alice had dropped off. Kristi's arrival and his mother's phone call had pushed all this nonsense out of his mind. He set his computer down, picked up the envelope and removed the contents. Fanning through the pages, he saw there were application forms, which Alice had conveniently completed, waivers that required his signature, a bio for each girl, and pages of information about the venue and answers to frequently asked questions. Alice had clipped a note to the sheets describing the contestants' talent, pointing out that if the girls were taking ballet or piano lessons, they could also enter this part of the pageant. The head shots were at the bottom of the stack.

Nate set the application package on the counter and stared at the photographs. Molly and Martha stared back. Instead of their usual pigtails, which were the only way he knew to manage their flyaway blond curls, they each had a poufy updo with flower barrettes that matched clothes he'd never seen before. He took a closer look. Was that makeup? Had Alice actually put makeup on his kids, got them dolled up and taken them to a photographer? How did he not know about this? He remembered them saying they'd had pictures taken, but he assumed Alice and Fred had done them. Dammit, what was this woman thinking? This crossed a line.

He stuffed everything back in the envelope, fighting the urge to toss it in the fireplace with a match and a can of kerosene. That would be the easy way to resolve this. What he needed to do, what he should have done long ago, was sit down with Alice and Fred and remind them who called the shots here. He did. He was Molly and Martha's father, he made the decisions and they needed to back off. Way the hell off.

He tucked the laptop and the envelope under his arm and strode through the house. For now he would put this stuff away and deal with his in-laws when he cooled off a little and wouldn't say anything he'd regret. Then he would find Kristi and break the news that two fakes had turned into three, an idea that was sounding better by the minute.

"Good morning, Claire." Kristi settled into Nate's creaky old desk chair with her BlackBerry in her hand and her notebook on her lap.

"Hi, Kristi. Sam's on the line, too."

"Hey, Sam. How's it going?"

"Good. I'm finishing up at the Baxter house this morning."

"That's the place that needed the faux wood paneling stripped out of the living room?"

"That's the one. And I'm happy to say the drywall underneath was in good shape, except for the nail holes. It's been patched and primed, and I'm painting it this morning."

"Big job." Claire, who claimed she didn't know one end of a hammer from the other, was always impressed by Sam's work.

"The paneling was a lot easier to take down than wallpaper," Sam said.

Kristi took that as an opportunity to shift the conversation to Nate's place. "I was just thinking about you and wallpaper. I need some stripped from one of the bedrooms here in the McTavish house."

Sam groaned.

"Just two walls."

"That's it?"

"That's it. I promise."

"You're sure you can't make it work?"

"Not a chance, and when you see it, I think you'll agree." The juxtaposition of the sports motifs with Nate's old desk and scholarly-looking books was laughable. "It was a boy's bedroom at one time, but the current owner uses it as an office."

"Speaking of the owner…" Claire said.

Here we go. "What about him?"

"He's very photogenic," Sam said.

Kristi doodled in the margin of her notebook. "He is, isn't he?"

Sam, usually so serious, was laughing. "You've photographed a lot of homes, but I've never seen you take pictures of the owners. Last night you sent three of this guy."

"And we thank you for it." Even Claire thought it was funny.

"I sent photographs of the house—he just happened to be in them." That wasn't exactly true, not even a little bit, especially considering how much time she'd spent looking at them.

Should she tell them about the latest development? She had more or less decided not to, but if she didn't tell someone, she was going to explode.

"He seems nice," she said, keeping her voice low. "He invited me to a party on Friday night."

Several long seconds ticked by before Sam or Claire said anything, and then they were both talking at once.

"That was fast."

"You already have a date with him?"

"How did that happen?"

"Are you sure this is a good idea, hon?"

No, she wasn't sure of anything, including her spur-of-the-moment decision to tell Sam and Claire. "It's not a date," she said. "Not a real one."

"If it's not a 'real' date, what kind of date is it?" Sam asked.

"It's sort of a fake date." Except it had sounded okay when she'd said it in her head. Out loud it sounded ridiculous. She could hardly blame them for laughing. "It's really just one of those crazy coincidences. You know what my mother's like. She wanted to set me up with a date for my aunt's Fourth of July barbecue, and Nate's family tried to arrange a date for him to take to his sister's birthday party. So we're going together. We're not interested in *dating* dating, so this is a perfect arrangement. Neither of us has to suffer another blind date, and our families back off with their matchmaking."

"So you're going on two fake dates, and both will be spent with your families?"

"Our families are the reason we're doing this. If we went out, just the two of us, then it would be a real date. That's not going to happen."

"Isn't this going to get complicated?" The ever-practical Claire never took risks.

To Kristi, being at her aunt's barbecue with Bernie Halverson was complicated. Especially if he tried to kiss her. Just the idea of it made Kristi shudder. Nate wasn't likely to kiss a woman he wasn't dating, and she probably wouldn't mind if he did.

"What are you going to tell Jenna?"

She'd been wondering the same thing. She still had to set an example for her daughter, after all. "I'll downplay the whole thing, make sure she understands we're just friends."

"I hope you have fun," Claire said. "You deserve it. I'm sorry if I didn't sound supportive at first, but you caught me by surprise."

"And we don't want to see you get hurt," Sam said. "I'm sure it's nice to meet another single parent, though. You both already have a lot in common."

"Not really. For one thing he's smart, and I mean *really* smart."

"And hot," Sam said.

Claire laughed. "Hot and smart. Two more things he has in common with our Kristi."

"I wish. He's not just average, everyday smart. He's university-professor smart. He studies all kinds of scientific things about plants and hybrids. You should see the books he reads. I don't even know what some of the titles mean. And then there are Greek gods, Roman gods. He's a walking encyclopedia."

"What do Greek and Roman gods have to do with hybridized plants?" Claire asked.

"Nothing. We were talking about our dogs' names."

"S-o-o-o…" Sam drew out the word for effect. "Let's get this straight. He's single, he's smart, he's hot, he obviously must love dogs, but all you want is a fake date."

"I said yes to the date because there are no strings attached. You know me well enough to realize there's no way I'll take a chance on another deadbeat."

Kristi heard the groans and knew rolling eyes accompanied them.

Claire spoke first. "Sweetie, you said it yourself. He's smart. And last time I checked, university professor is not exactly a deadbeat occupation."

"And he's hot," Sam said.

"You know what I mean."

"We do," Claire said. "You're a wonderful mom, an amazing woman—"

"Who deserves to have a hot guy in her life," Sam said.

"Enough! The two of you sound like my mother." Except that her mother had yet to come up with anyone who qualified as hot. "I should get back to work. I'll see you at our next meeting. Nine o'clock, right?"

"That's right," Claire said. "At the usual place."

"It's in my calendar. I'll see you both then." Kristi tucked her BlackBerry into her bag and tried to refocus on the lists she'd been working on before taking the call.

What was the point? She closed the book and shoved it in her bag. She needed to check on Molly and Martha anyway. It was her job to keep an eye on them till their father was back from the market.

Nate parked his SUV in the driveway, got out and carried two bags of groceries through the breezeway and the side door that led to the mudroom and kitchen. A couple of hours ago he'd congratulated himself on having his personal life firmly back in his control, but all the way to the market and back he'd pondered the newsflash that, according to Kristi, he was a *deadbeat*.

Seriously? He'd wanted to let her know that his mother was throwing two parties this weekend instead of just one. He didn't want to talk about it in front of the girls, so he'd planned to invite her to join him in the kitchen.

Molly and Martha's chatter had drifted past the door, which was slightly ajar. Luckily they hadn't seen him. He had heard Kristi's voice, too, but she hadn't been in the girls' room. She was in his office across the hall, sitting there in his chair with her back to the door and her phone to her ear.

She said something about no strings attached, and then she'd said, "You know me well enough to realize there's no way I'll take a chance on another deadbeat."

She had paused, listening to what the other person had to say. He had hightailed it back to the kitchen, not wanting to hear any more.

Kristi had agreed to go out with him because there were no strings attached. Fair enough. They were both on the same page. But did she really think he was a deadbeat? Had he completely misinterpreted all the signs?

As he put the groceries away he debated what to do.

He supposed he should let Kristi and the girls know he was back, but he was in no hurry to face her. Instead he poured himself a cup of coffee and stared out the kitchen window. He still had to break the news that there were two parties this weekend instead of one, and by now his mother would have told Britt he was bringing a date. Hell, she'd probably sent out a press release.

Maybe you're looking at this from the wrong perspective, he told himself. Kristi had agreed to pose as his date at his sister's birthday party if he would reciprocate and attend her aunt's barbecue. No strings attached. That's what she'd said; that's what they both wanted. If going together to these functions meant no blind dates, no unexpected setups with strangers, did it really matter what she thought of him? Not one bit, he decided. She wasn't perfect, either. Not that he'd seen any major flaws yet, but she was bound to have at least one.

"Daddy, come see our room."

He swung around, expecting to see Molly. Instead he got an eyeful of Kristi, holding Martha's hand on one side and Molly's on the other. They were all smiling at him.

He mustered a smile in return and set his coffee cup on the counter. "Let's take a look."

He joined them, avoiding eye contact with Kristi. Both girls seemed content to hold her hands, so he was left to follow them down the hall. They stopped outside the bedroom door, Molly and Martha grinning impishly. He humored them by being the first to go inside, prepared to feign surprise, and being thoroughly taken aback when he saw what they had accomplished.

"Wow. Great job, girls." And he meant it. Except for the furniture and Kristi's big, brightly colored plastic bins, the floor that had been obscured by his daughters' belongings was now clear.

"We had a race," Martha said, her eyes like miniature saucers, as though even she couldn't quite believe what they'd done.

"We put dress-up clothes in the blue boxes and our clothes in the red boxes," Molly said.

"And stuffies in the yellow boxes," Martha tried unsuccessfully to push the overflow of stuffed animals beneath the rim. "Just like Kristi told us."

"Who won the race?" he asked.

"We both did. Kristi said."

He finally allowed himself to make eye contact with the woman who had accomplished more in half an hour, by simply turning work into a game, than he could have managed in a whole week of cajoling. "Thank you."

Her smile, so genuine, made it hard to believe she was the same woman who had called him a deadbeat earlier that morning.

"You're welcome. They're good workers. I might have to hire them as my assistants." She tweaked their pigtails, and they both giggled. "And now they each get a cupcake at lunchtime, as long as that's okay with you. I have some out in my van."

"Sure. I got everything I need to make hot dogs, too." And since she had offered dessert, it would be rude not to include her. "You're welcome to join us."

"Yay! Hot dogs!"

"Yay! Cupcakes!"

"We found our coloring books." Molly pointed to their little table. "I'm going to color."

"Me, too." Martha settled onto one of the chairs.

"I'd like to talk to your dad about his office," Kristi said.

The girls, already intent on choosing crayons, didn't respond.

She slipped out of the room and he followed her across the hall.

"That's pretty amazing," he said. "What you got them to do in there."

"I think they had fun." She consulted several lists on a page in her notebook. "I have some suggestions to help you streamline the things in their room, but first I'd like to go over my ideas for your office."

He would like to go over her idea that he was a deadbeat, but bringing it up now didn't feel right, and he wasn't ready to hear what she had to say anyway. Instead he listened as she outlined her plan, and then indicated the bundle of flattened boxes that he could assemble and use to sort and store papers. She showed him the paint color she had in mind, and he agreed it would be an improvement over the blue. He had never liked it anyway. And he was fine to get rid of the wallpaper.

She pulled a small pocket knife from her bag—was there anything she didn't have in there? he wondered—and cut the strap on the bundle of boxes. "We might as well assemble these while we talk."

That was fine with him. He watched her turn one of the neatly folded pieces into a box with a lid, and followed her lead.

"If you're okay with the colors, I'll order the paint this afternoon. For the master bedroom, I'd like to use a similar green but a few shades darker. It'll be a little more dramatic. The off-white in the fourth bedroom is nice and neutral so I'll leave it and bring in some green accessories to tie everything together."

"It all sounds good."

"I have a meeting with my business partners first thing tomorrow morning. After that our carpenter will drop by and measure for the new bookshelves in here. I have some ideas for organizing your daughters' room, too."

Between them they had assembled five boxes and she was still folding.

"I was also wondering how you feel about putting some of their things in storage. After the house is listed and being shown, I think it'll be easier for you…and them…if there's less stuff for you to manage."

He had only thought of moving as a way to get distance from his in-laws, but now he could see that streamlining their belongings would really streamline their lives. Across the hall, Molly and Martha sat happily coloring at a table that had always been buried beneath clutter. How had he let that happen?

"Putting things in storage is a good idea. My sister keeps giving them dress-up clothes, and some of their own clothes are getting too small. And every time they see their grandparents, we add two more stuffed animals to the zoo."

She smiled. "Could you ask them to hold off on that for now? At least until you've moved?"

"Of course." He should have asked them to stop a long time ago.

"For things that don't fit anymore, I know a great consignment store that takes good-quality children's clothes, and I can also arrange to donate things to charity."

"You don't mind doing that?" He wished he could stay annoyed with her, but she was so patient, and so helpful, and she smelled so damned good.

"I don't mind at all. It's actually part of my job."

"Well, I still appreciate it." And in spite of what she

thought of him, he was glad she was willing to go to his sister's party weekend. "I talked to my mother again, and there's one minor change in plans."

"Oh? What's that?"

"There's a family brunch on Sunday. I hope you don't mind going to that, too. I didn't know how to say no."

Instead of being annoyed, she laughed. "If they're anything like my family, saying no isn't easy."

"So you don't mind?"

She added another box to the pile. "Is your mom a good cook?"

"She's a great cook."

"Then I don't mind at all." Instead of looking at him, she pulled a black marker from her bag and handed it to him. "This should be enough boxes to get you started, and you can use this to label them. I also brought in a blue bin for recycling. I'll let you get started while I go order the paint. And then, if you'd like, I'll help you make lunch."

"I'd like that." She was being so nice. Had he misunderstood what she'd said on the phone? Did it matter? She had also said "no strings attached." No matter how nice she was and how great she smelled, she was absolutely right, and he'd better not let himself forget it.

Chapter 5

After dinner on Friday, Nate cleaned up the kitchen, got the girls ready for bed and settled down at the kitchen counter with his computer. After putting in a full day working on his house, Kristi had gone home with a promise to be back in two hours. Those two hours were nearly up, and they felt more like four. Under normal circumstances he would have picked her up. He hadn't been able to find a sitter, though, so she had volunteered her teenage daughter. It made sense that she would drop Jenna off and they would leave from here.

From where he sat, he could see Molly and Martha in their pajamas, curled up with Gemmy in front of the TV in the family room. It wasn't a show they normally watched, but it seemed harmless enough.

He leaped to his feet when the doorbell pealed. The girls jumped up, too, Gemmy heaved herself onto all fours, and they followed him to the front door.

Kristi, all smiles, was worth the wait. He had pictured her wearing a little black dress but realized he would have been disappointed if she had. Her green cocktail dress was almost a perfect match for her eyes. With a fitted waist, a modest halter-style neckline and a skirt that flared softly to her knees, she looked a lot curvier than she did in yoga pants and a T-shirt. She'd let her hair down and he liked it. A lot.

Beside her stood a younger version of her. Jenna was wearing black leggings or tights or whatever kids called them, and over them she had on a pair of tattered denim cutoffs with the bottoms rolled up. Her baggy black-and-white-striped pullover had long sleeves and frayed cuffs with thumb holes cut in them. Her hair was shaggier and a few shades lighter than her mother's, and her eye makeup a lot thicker and darker. He knew nothing about fashion trends, but grunge came to mind. Kristi had said she was fourteen, and he supposed this was what he had to look forward to in ten years.

"Hi, Nate. Hi, girls. This is my daughter, Jenna. Jenna, this is Nate and his daughters."

"I'm Molly. She's Martha."

Nate tried to ease Martha's thumb out of her mouth so she could speak for herself. She was having none of it.

"Hi," Jenna said. She even had her mother's smile. "It must be cool being twins. I always wanted a sister."

"I'm the oldest," Molly said.

Martha nodded, clinging to his leg with one arm.

"This is Gemmy. She's our dog."

Martha released her thumb long enough to say, "I want a kitten."

Jenna scratched Gemmy's head. "She's huge. I brought

my dog, too." She shot Nate a quick look. "My mom said it was okay."

He nodded.

"Would you like to meet him?" she asked his daughters.

"Where is he?" Molly asked.

"He's in here," Kristi said, patting what could pass for a woman's handbag. "Thanks for letting us bring him. He's okay at home during the daytime when I'm at work and Jenna's at school, but he doesn't like to be left alone at night."

"No problem. Gemmy's good with other dogs."

Jenna closed the door, and Kristi set the bag on the floor and unzipped it. A small, shaggy head emerged, followed by what just might be the scrawniest excuse for a dog Nate had ever seen. And it was wearing clothes. He fought a brief battle with his arching eyebrows, and lost.

Martha let go of his leg and crouched on the floor. "Look, Gemmy. A puppy."

The poor little thing started to shiver.

Jenna knelt next to Martha and picked up the little dog. "He's not a puppy. This is as big as he'll get."

"He's wearing a sweater," Molly said.

"It's a polo shirt," Jenna said.

"I yike him." Martha gently stroked the top of his head. "Daddy, can we get a dog yike this?"

"You just said you want a kitten." Not that he had any intention of getting one. Or another dog for that matter, not even a rat-size one.

"Daddy, can we get clothes for Gemmy?" Molly asked.

"Dogs don't—" He cut himself off before he blurted out that dogs don't need clothes. "Dogs like Gemmy have lots of fur to keep them warm. If she needs a shirt, I guess she can wear one of mine."

The twins giggled.

Gemmy, who had been staring at the newcomer as though not sure what to make of him, took a step closer, lowered her snout and gave him a sniff. Nate grabbed a towel off the closet doorknob and wiped the drool from her jowls.

Kristi watched the dogs' tentative nose-to-nose greeting, then smiled up at him. "It'll take Hercules a while to get used to a new dog and different surroundings. Jenna can keep him in the carrier."

The Yorkie let out a single sharp bark.

Gemmy's ears perked up and she backed away. Nate laughed at the Saint's reaction to the yipping, quivering Yorkie, who didn't amount to much more than a large dust bunny. He grasped her collar and tugged.

"Come on in," he said to Jenna. "I'll show you where everything is and give you a rundown of the girls' routine."

They all trooped into the family room.

"You have a tent in here," Jenna said to the twins. "Cool."

"That's where we sleep."

"'Cause your mom took everything out of our room."

Kristi tweaked their pigtails. "Just until it's painted. Then you can move back in."

"Green," the girls chorused.

Molly held up the flap. "Come in and see. We got sleeping bags."

"And pillows and teddy bears."

"You can sleep here, too, if you want."

Jenna thanked them and admired the interior of the tent, agreeing that it looked very cozy.

With the girls and Gemmy settled in the family room and Kristi chatting with them about Hercules and asking about the television show they were watching, he showed Jenna the list of numbers he'd made for her. His cell phone, his parents' home phone number, Britt's cell number. He had briefly considered adding his in-laws, but decided not to. Not that he anticipated an emergency, but if something came up, he didn't want to explain why he hadn't asked them to look after the girls, and why he had a date with his interior decorator.

Jenna pulled a cell phone from her pocket. "I'll put the numbers in here. I have my mom's, too."

He watched Kristi's daughter carefully program the contacts into her phone. "There," she said. "If anything comes up, I just have to push a button."

Kristi got up off the sofa and joined them. "Ready to go?"

Jenna studied him like an amoeba under a microscope, then shifted her examination to her mother. "This is so weird."

"What is?"

"You...going on a date."

"It's not a date," he and Kristi said in perfect unison, their gazes locking briefly before they both looked away.

Jenna rolled her eyes. "Yeah, I know. You're just friends. Yada, yada. And it only took you an hour to get ready."

Kristi flushed. He understood why she'd be embarrassed, but it was an hour well spent. Kristi looked beautiful with her glossy blond hair curling in loose waves around her shoulders, the stunning green dress hugging her body and showing off those amazing legs. Until now he hadn't noticed her shoes, strappy white heels that matched the small white handbag she was carrying and the shawl draped over her arm. He was glad she hadn't changed perfumes. This one was so her, and he liked it.

His family would approve of her, too, as long as they didn't find out they were being duped. He needed to make sure that didn't happen, but for tonight, he was actually looking forward to being in the company of a woman—a very beautiful woman—who was no more interested in being in a relationship than he was. He could even overlook the fact that she thought he was a deadbeat.

"Where are you going, Daddy?"

"To your aunt Britt's b—" Geez, he'd almost blurted out *birthday party.* He'd never hear the end of it.

Jenna saved him. "They're going to some boring grown-up thing." She held up a bag. "I brought a DVD for us to watch—*The Parent Trap*—it's about twins. And some books I thought you might like, and some micro-wave popcorn. I hope that's okay?"

Molly grabbed for the bag and even Martha let go of her thumb. "We yike popcorn!"

"Popcorn is fine," he said. "Just be sure to brush your teeth before bed, okay?"

Molly climbed onto a stool at the counter, chattering nonstop while Jenna pressed buttons on the microwave. Martha curled up on the sofa with Hercules, who had re-treated into his carrier.

"Good night." He planted a kiss on top of Molly's head.

"G'night, Daddy. We're making the popcorn right now so we can eat it as soon as the movie starts."

"Good idea." He lowered himself to the sofa and gave one of Martha's pigtails a gentle tug. "Good night."

She was peering through the mesh window of the pet carrier. "Can we get a dog yike Herca— Herca—"

"Hercules." It was good to see Martha with both hands occupied and her thumb out of her mouth for a change.

"Except I wanna girl dog with a purple dress."

Oh, geez. "I have to go, sweetie. Kristi and I don't want to be late. We'll talk about this later, okay?"

They did not need another dog. Or more laundry. "Good night, girls. Have fun and be good for Jenna," he said. "For tonight, it's okay for them to stay up till the movie's over." They'd most likely be asleep before then anyway.

"Yay!" the twins chimed.

"Have fun on your 'this-is-not-a-date' date." She gave her mother a saucy little wink.

"Teenagers," Kristi said, walking with him to the front door. "See what you have to look forward to?"

"Times two." He hadn't spent any time around teenage girls since he'd been a teenager, and that didn't count. "She seems very grown-up. How old did you say she is?"

"Fourteen. Most days. She still has moments when she acts like a ten-year-old but the rest of the time she's fourteen going on twenty-one."

He reached for the doorknob and hesitated, glancing back to the family room for one last look.

"She's great with little kids. You don't have anything to worry about."

"Good to know." He picked up a bouquet of flowers off the table in the foyer. "For my sister," he explained.

"Ooo, those are pretty. Do you think I should have brought something for her?"

"Not at all. These will be from both of us."

He held the door open for her, followed her out and locked up behind them.

"If you like, we can take my van."

"I thought we'd take my old Beetle. I don't get to drive it very often because it doesn't have anchors for the girls' car seats, but it could use a run. Do you mind?"

"Not at all. Jenna was really excited when she saw it in your driveway. She said it's the kind of car she wants to buy when she's old enough to get her license. I didn't want to burst her bubble by telling her there's no way we can afford another car."

He opened the passenger door for her. "It's a nice night. We can even put the top down if you don't mind a little wind in your hair."

"Ordinarily I would say top down for sure, but since we're going to a party and I'll be meeting your family, I should probably arrive looking presentable."

"Good point." He circled to the driver's side and got in, thinking it would take more than a little breeze to ruin her appearance.

"It is a cute car. How long have you had it?"

He started the engine. "Since I graduated from high school. My aunt bought a new car, couldn't get much for this in a trade-in, so she passed it on to me."

"That was lucky."

He backed out of the driveway. "I didn't think so at the time. I had my eye on a Pontiac Firebird."

Kristi gave him a long look. "I'm having a hard time picturing a university professor and a dad driving a car like that."

"I did mention that I had just graduated from high

school, didn't I? I wasn't looking for safe or sensible or economical."

"Let me guess. You thought a Firebird would be a chick magnet."

"Yeah, well, in the head of a teenage boy, it doesn't sound so tacky."

"Oh, I know how it is for teenage boys."

It was his turn to look at her. "You know someone who has one?"

She looked away. "I did. Jenna's dad."

Okay. He hadn't thought about it until now, but Kristi couldn't be much over thirty and her daughter was fourteen. That meant she was just a teenager herself when she became a parent. For some reason, that got him thinking about the condom she'd had in her bag the day they met. He shouldn't put condoms and Kristi into the same thought. Still, he gave the little white purse on her lap a quick glance, and for one fleeting moment he wondered what was in it.

Nate's parents lived in a stately two-story brick house, built in the forties, Kristi guessed, on a spacious lot with a sweeping front drive. The lawn was immaculate, the shrubs sculpted and the flower beds carefully tended.

"What a lovely home," she said as Nate pulled up and parked. "And such a gorgeous garden."

"All thanks to my mother. She's the green thumb in the family."

"So that's where you get your interest in plants?"

"I'm afraid not. I started university with the idea of becoming a veterinarian, but the botany component of one of my biology courses changed all of that. I'm interested in the science of plants, though. That doesn't necessarily translate to the garden."

Considering the state of Nate's yard, that explained a lot.

"Wait here," Nate said. He stepped out of the car and quickly came around to open her door. He took the flowers she was holding and extended a hand to help her out.

She didn't mind opening doors for herself, but it was nice to be given some special treatment every now and then. Even nicer that he was such a gentleman, and that he seemed to do these little things without thinking about them.

She teetered slightly when her heels hit the pavement, making her regret she'd opted for these shoes instead of the flats. Nate held her hand till she regained her balance, then she looked into his eyes and nearly lost her composure.

"Ready?" he asked.

Not even a little bit.

He held her hand all the way up to the front door, probably in case someone was watching from inside, she told herself. With that thought, her nerves nearly got the best of her. She was going to meet his family, a family who thought she and Nate were dating, maybe even believed there was more to their relationship than that.

"I just have one question before we go in," she said.

"What's that?"

"How well do your parents think we know each other?"

He grinned down at her. "I don't know. Whatever they think, they didn't hear it from me."

"I didn't mean *that*. I just wondered if you told them how long we've been seeing each other. *Supposedly* seeing each other."

"I didn't say."

"What if someone asks? What if they want to know how we met?" She hadn't thought of that until now. "What do we tell them?"

"Why don't we go with the truth? I hired your company to sell my house, the two of us hit it off. Easier to keep our stories straight that way."

He was right, of course. No sense making this more complicated than it needed to be. "That's a good idea."

He squeezed her hand. "My mother actually throws a pretty good party. Let's just relax and enjoy ourselves." And then he opened the front door without ringing the bell and led her inside.

The entryway was small but elegantly decorated with a mosaic tile floor, a walnut console table and an antique mirror flanked by wall sconces. Kristi hardly had a chance to take in her surroundings before a petite brunette in a formfitting, retro-inspired red wiggle dress threw her arms around Nate's neck. It was a stunning dress, one Kristi was sure she could never afford, but definitely something she could replicate on her sewing machine.

"You're here! Oh, are these flowers for me? They're beautiful!"

Nate hugged her back and relinquished the flowers. "Happy birthday, sis. I hope you weren't expecting anything extravagant."

"From you?" she asked, laughing. "Never. Hi, you must be Kristi. I'm Nate's sister, Britt. The birthday girl. Happy to finally meet you. I've heard *so* much about you."

Kristi shot Nate a look. "You have?"

He took her hand, squeezed it again reassuringly. "Don't listen to her. She's just messing with me."

"I am," she said, a hint of mischief in her blue eyes. "He's been keeping us in the dark about you. That's brothers for you, but now that you're here I can't wait to get to know you. Come on, I'll introduce you to our parents." She passed the flowers back to Nate. "Be a sweetie and take these into the kitchen for me? And get Kristi something to drink. What would you like? A martini? Cosmopolitan? Wine? There's also mineral water if you prefer something nonalcoholic."

Feeling a little breathless just listening to her, Kristi glanced over her shoulder at Nate as his sister hurried her toward the sound of conversation and laughter in the living room. "A glass of white wine would be nice."

"I'll catch up with you." He disappeared, leaving Kristi to fend for herself.

"Mom!" Britt was waving across the sea of people who filled the living room. "Nate and Kristi are here."

They wound their way between groups of people and met in the middle of the room.

"Mom, this is Nate's girlfriend. Kristi, my mom, Helen McTavish."

Kristi extended her hand and found herself in a warm embrace instead.

"Hello, dear. We've been looking forward to meeting you." Helen McTavish had passed along her short stature to her daughter, and her captivating smile and blue, blue eyes to both of her children. She wore an expensive-looking navy pantsuit with a coral blouse that complemented her coloring. "What a beautiful dress you're wearing. That color is perfect for you."

"Oh, thank you."

"I love it, too," Britt said. "Where did you get it?"

"I made it myself, actually."

"You sewed that?" Britt eyed her dress with renewed interest. "Okay, now I am seriously impressed, and more than a little jealous."

Hoping this was a sign she was making a good impression, Kristi decided not to tell them she'd whipped it up last night after going through her closet and deciding none of her options were quite right for this occasion.

The doorbell chimed. "I'll get that," Britt said. "Be right back."

"You're very talented," Helen said. "That son of mine has excellent taste."

Flustered by the attention, Kristi decided it was time to change the subject. "I was admiring your front garden when we arrived. Nate tells me you're an avid gardener."

"How sweet of you to notice."

Before she could respond, Nate appeared at her side with a glass in each hand. He gave her the white wine she'd requested, then slid that hand around her waist as casually as if he'd done it a dozen times. Then he touched the rim of his beer glass to her wine goblet.

"I see you've met my mother."

Helen offered her cheek and he bent down and gave it a kiss.

"You look beautiful, Mom."

"Thank you, dear. Kristi was telling me how much she likes our front yard." Helen was still beaming. "Are you a gardener, too?" she asked.

"I try to grow a few things in planters on my patio, but I'm afraid I don't know much about plants."

"That's okay. Neither does Nate." She laughed at her own joke.

"Very funny, Mom." But Nate was laughing, too. "Did Kristi mention that I showed her my greenhouse?" He pulled her even closer as he said it and she went willingly, taking a nervous sip of her drink as she did.

Helen wagged a finger at him. "You be careful, young man. I wasn't born yesterday and I know a smart aleck when I see one."

"Yes, ma'am."

"Kristi said she sewed this dress herself," Helen said. "You told me she was beautiful but you didn't mention she was so talented, as well."

"What was I thinking?"

Kristi couldn't bring herself to look at him, and she was pretty sure he would avoid eye contact anyway.

Britt rejoined them. "So, how did the two of you meet?" she asked. "I don't think you mentioned that, either."

He smiled down at her then with an I-told-you-so sparkle in his eyes. "Remember I told you I hired a real estate company to help me sell the house?"

"Yes, although I'm still surprised you want to sell," Britt said. "I've always thought that was a perfect house for you and…you and the girls."

"Kristi is one of the owners of that company," Nate responded without missing a beat.

"Are you now?" Helen studied her with even more interest. "So you're a real estate agent?"

"No, I'm an interior decorator. One of my business partners is a Realtor, though, and the other is a carpenter. Our company is called Ready Set Sold. We help our clients renovate and stage their homes before they go on the market."

"I'm impressed. And since you're helping Nate get the house ready to sell, I take it you've already met my two darling granddaughters and that behemoth of a dog of theirs."

"I have. The girls are adorable." They were, and in just a few short days she had grown far more attached to them than common sense dictated. "And Gemmy is…" She had no idea what a behemoth was, but she guessed it was large. "Gemmy is the biggest dog I've ever met, especially compared to mine, who happens to be one of the smallest you'll ever see."

"So you love dogs and you're good with children. You're artistic and entrepreneurial. No wonder Nate is so taken with you."

He looked down at her, and during those few brief seconds while their gazes locked, all of this… Nate's affection, Britt's admiration, Helen's approval…it didn't just feel real. She wanted it to be real.

"Britt, why don't you and Nate go out to the backyard and see if you can find your father? And make sure Ned Grainger from next door didn't give him one of those horrible cigars. Kristi, you come with me. There are some people I'd like you to meet. And I'll tell you about the time Nate nearly blew up the basement. He decided he wanted to be an inventor."

"I was nine," Nate said as his sister dragged him away.

"Well done, brother," Kristi heard her say.

She tucked her clutch firmly under her arm, tightened her grip on the stem of her wineglass and let Nate's mother lead her into the fray. This was going much better than she ever could have expected, and she realized she could easily get used to this. *Don't,* she reminded herself. A lot of real relationships didn't last. Fake ones didn't stand a chance.

Three hours later, Kristi was in the kitchen, washing stemware by hand. The 1940s charm of the McTavish home had been maintained everywhere but the kitchen, which was a model of modern efficiency and a joy to work in.

Helen cleared counters, stowed leftover hors d'oeuvres and unopened bottles of sparkling water in the refrigerator and loaded the dishwasher while Nate and his father went through the house, gathering glasses, plates and crumpled napkins.

The evening had flown by, and in a way Kristi wished the party wasn't over. Helen had introduced her to numerous people as "my son's girlfriend, the owner of Ready Set Sold." She had handed out a surprising number of business cards—even Claire would have been impressed—and she had made contact with a woman who did upholstery and draperies. Kristi would be calling her on Monday to get more information about her rates and availability. The evening had been overwhelming and invigorating. She had not expected Nate's family to welcome her into their home and their lives with such genuine warmth, and she felt guilty as hell.

At one point during the evening, Nate's mother had shown her through the house, including a tour of the back garden. Everything Nate had told her about his mother's green thumb was true. The back garden was a private oasis, filled with flowering shrubs and fruit trees, bird feeders and an old cast-iron birdbath. In the back corner a tire swing hung from the branch of a big old chestnut tree. Nate's father had put it there when Nate and his sister were kids, and Molly and Martha loved to play on it now. On Sunday she would get to see that firsthand because she and Nate were bringing the twins and Jenna here for Britt's birthday brunch.

"I think this is it," Nate said, setting an overloaded tray on the counter next to the sink.

"Where's your father?" Helen asked.

"He's having a nightcap out on the terrace."

"No cigars, I hope."

"No cigars," Nate said.

"Why don't you go join him?" Helen dumped soap in the dishwasher, closed the door and turned it on. "Kristi and I can finish up in here."

"No nightcaps for me. I have to drive home."

Kristi felt his hand slide beneath her hair, the light stroke of his thumb across the nape of her neck. *This is for his mother's benefit,* she reminded herself. *Not yours.* But that didn't lessen the sensations that shimmered along her spine.

"I think we're ready to call it a night," he said.

More shivers.

"Nate told me that your daughter is looking after Molly and Martha."

Kristi eased away from his touch and dried her hands on a kitchen towel. "She is. And we should really get home...back to Nate's, I mean...and see how they're doing."

Helen smiled. "Thank you for your help in here. I'll see you both on Sunday. It'll be good to see the girls, and I'm looking forward to meeting your daughter, too."

Kristi hadn't mentioned the brunch to Jenna yet. She

had told her daughter that she and Nate were just friends, and that this evening was strictly casual. She wasn't sure she believed it herself, and she knew for sure Jenna wouldn't believe they were just friends if Nate was as attentive on Sunday as he had been tonight. So much for not being complicated.

Chapter 6

The evening had gone well, Nate thought as he took the on-ramp to the I-5, geared down and merged into the northbound lane. Kristi had been quiet since they'd left his parents' place, though, and he wondered what she was thinking. Her silence made him a little uneasy, although he couldn't exactly say why.

Best way to find out what she's thinking is probably to ask. Even though he might not like the answer. "I hope you had an okay time tonight."

"I had fun," she said. "Your family's great. Your mother introduced me to lots of people, and I even made some business contacts."

Okay. She'd enjoyed herself, hit it off with his mother. All good. So why did he detect a "but"?

"But I'm not sure this was such a good idea."

And there it was. "Really? Why is that?"

He'd had reservations about tonight, but being with her had felt natural. So natural, he'd found himself wishing this was real. And since his mother and sister seemed genuinely taken with her, he was confident they would stop trying to fix him up with every single woman they encountered. "You really had that bad a time?"

"Oh, no. I enjoyed myself. It's been ages since I've gone out for something that wasn't related to my job or my daughter's school. I'm just worried that we've given your family the wrong idea."

"I hope we did." That had been the whole point.

"Your mother invited me to have lunch with her next week. Did she tell you?"

"No, she didn't." And he had not anticipated anything like that. "What did you say?"

"That I have a busy week lined up and I would have to check my calendar."

He relaxed a little. "Okay. So you'll tell her you're busy. That shouldn't be a problem."

"Will your mother settle for that and not keep asking?"

If his mother truly wanted to have lunch with Kristi, there wasn't an ice cube's hope in hell that she would let this drop. "We'll figure something out," he said. "Maybe I'll talk to her."

"Then you'd better talk to your sister, too, because she invited me to go shopping with her. She wants to re-decorate the master suite in her condo, and now that you and I are together…her words, not mine…she's going to take advantage of having a 'decorator in the family.'" To drive the point home, Kristi added air quotes to the end of her sentence.

Well, hell. What could be a sticky situation with his mother just got more complicated. Helen McTavish might be deterred, hell's snowball aside, but Britt? Not a chance. She never took no for an answer.

"Britt can be persuasive but she had no right to ask you for free advice. I hope you didn't agree."

"She did say that if I ever need legal counsel—"

"Seriously?" He and Britt would definitely be having words over this. "Did she tell you she's a criminal defence lawyer?"

Kristi laughed at that. "Yes, but she said her firm handles other things—contracts, wills, real estate—and she'd be happy to set me up with another lawyer."

He gripped the steering wheel and stared at the taillights ahead of him. He had not seen any of this coming, although knowing his family as he did, he should have anticipated it. Now the solution to one problem had snowballed into a bigger one.

"Did I mention that Jenna has also been invited for brunch on Sunday?"

"No. My mother didn't say anything. What did you tell her?"

"I couldn't think of an excuse why she couldn't be there so I said I'd bring her. I'm afraid the invitation caught me off guard."

He signaled for the next exit. "Do you think Jenna will mind?"

"I don't think so. I'm worried about giving her the wrong impression, though. She already thinks tonight was a date, and your family is convinced this is the real thing."

He appreciated why she didn't want to deceive her daughter. Molly and Martha were too young to understand the concept of dating, but Jenna knew the score. Kristi couldn't very well tell her this was an elaborate ruse to make their families stop setting them up with blind dates.

"If you would rather not go on Sunday, just say the word. I can tell my mother that you had a family thing come up and you couldn't get out of it." His mother and Britt would be disappointed. So would he.

Being with Kristi tonight had been a lot more enjoyable than he'd expected, and convincing everyone that they were really dating had been a lot easier. Putting his arm around her, touching her hair from time to time—it all felt perfectly natural.

"I don't think lying to them is a good idea," she said. "No more than we already are."

"You're sure?"

"I am. And since I didn't think to get anything for your sister, I'll tell her the shopping trip is her birthday present."

"Thanks. I owe you."

She laughed. "You might regret that. You haven't met my family yet."

He glanced sideways and caught her smile, but he couldn't tell if she was joking or not.

"Do you mind if I ask you something?" Kristi said.

"Ask away."

"You told me your wife died. She must have been pretty young. What happened?"

To his surprise, he didn't mind talking about it. He did want some context, though. "Let me guess. My sister said it's been two years and about time I finally dived back into the dating pool. And my mother said that after two years, it would be good for Molly and Martha to have a female role model in their lives."

"You took the words right out of their mouths," Kristi said.

"Heather was diabetic, had been since childhood, and she'd had a kidney removed before we met. Her doctor warned that a pregnancy would be hard on her health. We should have been more careful. I mean, we *were* careful, but nothing's ever one hundred percent."

"Tell me about it. The last thing I expected to be at eighteen was a mother. We thought we were being careful—at least *I* thought we were being careful."

He gave her a quick side glance, recalling her earlier reference to Jenna's father's car. "Do you have any regrets?"

"Not now. There was a time when I wished my daughter didn't have a deadbeat for a dad. I know there are times she feels as though she's missing out, like when her friends' fathers are driving the car pool or running kids to the mall, but most of the time she's fine with not having him around."

Deadbeat. He'd heard her use that term once before, to describe him. Let it slide, he decided.

"But you were telling me about your wife," Kristi reminded him.

"Right. The pregnancy was a lot harder on her than anyone expected. By the time we found out we were having twins, it was too late...not that she would have done anything anyway. She really wanted children and thought it would be better to have them while she was young and still reasonably healthy.

"When it became obvious just how big a toll the pregnancy was taking, she was put on bed rest, and then the girls were delivered eight weeks early."

"Oh, Nate. That must have been hard."

"The girls were pretty tiny so they spent a couple of months in the neonatal unit. They were healthy and they were being well cared for, so we focused on getting Heather better. Only that didn't happen."

Kristi didn't respond, so he kept talking as he negotiated the familiar streets of his neighborhood.

"She only had the one kidney and it was failing. She started dialysis, and the doctors put her on a wait list for a transplant."

"That's awful. So many people don't understand how important it is to be an organ donor."

"Everyone in my family learned that pretty quickly. We all volunteered to be tested, but her mother was the only match. The girls were just a year old when Heather had the surgery. Everything looked good for the first few months, then her body rejected the new kidney. The doctors did everything they could but they couldn't save her."

He pulled into the driveway and turned off the engine.

Kristi put a hand on his arm. "Thank you for telling me. I had no idea. Your poor daughters…"

He covered her hand with his, not wanting to lose the connection. For the first time since those dark days, he thought about opening up, telling Kristi how devastated Heather's mother had been, how she considered her loss to be paramount to everyone else's, and that she now seemed to believe her sacrifice granted her some degree of ownership of his family. Could he say those things to Kristi? Should he? Or was he simply reacting to a pleasant evening in the company of a beautiful woman?

"Most of the time Heather was too sick to be with Molly and Martha, and they were too young to remember her." He stopped himself from saying more. Spilling his guts was not the way to keep this thing with Kristi casual and uncomplicated.

"I guess that would make it easier," she said. "But it's also sad they never knew their mother, that they never had a chance to make memories with her."

He'd never thought of it that way, and honestly, he didn't want to dwell on it now. And aside from a desire to change the subject, there was something he wanted to know, too. "Now do you mind if I ask you a question?"

"Not at all."

"I heard you talking on the phone the other day. I wasn't trying to eavesdrop, but you were in my office, and when I went to tell you we were on for tonight, you were telling someone you'd agreed to this date because there are no strings attached, and that you weren't taking a chance on another deadbeat."

She covered her face with her hands. "You heard that? Oh, Nate. I'm so sorry."

"So you do think I'm a—"

"No!" She dropped her hands and met his gaze head-on. "I wasn't talking about you. I was talking about men in general. My dad was a deadbeat, and then I did the same thing my mother did and married one. I have this lousy track record and I want something else for my daughter."

He felt bad for putting her on the spot. She was obviously embarrassed, but he was glad he asked. "Good to know," he said. "That I'm not a deadbeat, I mean. Not that the other men in your life are. Were." *You can stop talking anytime now.*

She touched his hand again and he liked it even better the second time around. "I'm so sorry you thought I was talking about you. No one could think that. You're raising two little kids on your own...you have an amazing career."

"And I'm a terrible housekeeper, I second-guess every parenting decision I make and I can't get my four-year-old to stop sucking her thumb." He'd never said those things out loud to anyone, and he hoped they didn't sound as pathetic to her as they did to him

"Kids don't come with a how-to manual. We have to follow our instincts and not be afraid to ask for help or advice when we need it. Jenna used to suck her thumb, too. I asked our pediatrician about it, and he told me it was perfectly normal and that kids grow out of it. And you know what? He was right. I can't remember when she stopped, but it feels like forever ago."

"Thanks. I needed to hear that." Would Alice back off if he mentioned the pediatrician?

Everything he'd ever attempted had come easily. Academia was second nature. He'd sailed through graduate school with high marks and scholarships. He got the first faculty position he applied for. He'd never failed at anything except marriage and parenthood. Talking to Kristi about it made him feel as though he was doing an okay job after all.

He was glad she had asked about Heather, and he was damn glad he'd asked about what she'd said on the phone. Now he was done talking. He and Kristi were sitting angled in their seats, facing one another, her hand still on his. He touched her arm, her skin soft and smooth beneath his fingers. It wasn't enough. He followed the warmth till his hand found the curve of her neck beneath the soft weight of her hair, and when he leaned closer, she did the same. The move caused his hand to slide a little higher, his thumb now resting on the smoothness of her cheek.

She didn't say anything, didn't need to because her

eyes told him everything he wanted to know. If he kissed her right now, she would let him. Would it be a mistake to end a fake date with a real kiss? Of course it would. Did he care? Hell no.

The kiss, at first too tentative to be considered intimate, quickly turned into an exploration, an intoxicating mix of taste and touch. Her luscious scent rushed through him, and then she wound her arms around his neck as though they belonged there. A first kiss had a steep learning curve. He wanted this one to be perfect, and it was. He wanted it not to end, but it did.

"Wow." The single word floated past her lips and brushed over his.

"You took the word right out of my mouth."

The coach lanterns on the front of the garage cast enough light that he could see her smile.

"No regrets, I hope."

She shook her head. "None."

"We should go in."

"We should." Neither of them moved. Instead she nestled her head against his shoulder, and he wished the narrow space separating them wasn't taken up by the e-brake and stick shift. He wanted to touch her in places he shouldn't, and he wanted her to do the same for him.

If he'd been capable of using his head, he might have helped her out of the car and put an end to this fake date. But he wasn't thinking, at least not with his head. He kissed her again, a longer, deeper kiss that shut down the rest of his brain cells.

"I don't suppose there's any chance you still have that condom in your purse."

She pulled away. "Seriously? A couple of kisses and you think, you think—?"

Shit. He wanted to smack his head on the steering wheel. "Sorry. I think it's safe to say I wasn't thinking."

"But you think that because I'm a single mom, and because I had a condom in my bag that I'm…what? Easy?"

"I did *not* think that." Not completely. They'd just met, he hadn't known anything about her and he had sort of wondered. "I figured you were seeing someone."

"Well, I'm not."

"I know that now. And I think we agree that I'm an idiot?" A complete idiot who hadn't been with a woman in a very long time.

"Agreed. And for the record, I had a perfectly good reason for having that condom in my bag. And no, I don't have it with me now."

"You don't owe me an explanation—"

"Well, you're getting one. I signed up for a parenting class on how to have 'the talk' with kids."

"The talk?"

"The facts of life, the birds and bees…sex, birth control, abstinence."

Ah, *that* talk.

"My daughter is fourteen—she's getting interested in boys." She sighed as she said it. "Even worse, boys are interested in her. Mostly I want to talk to her about *not* getting involved with boys, not *that* way. She's way too young. But I also want her to know how to be safe, how to protect herself. How not to make the same mistakes I made."

"They have classes for that?"

"They do. I'm afraid I'm not a very good student, though. Jenna and I still haven't had the talk, which is why I was still carrying the stupid condom around with me."

Apparently the serotonin was wearing off and his brain was starting to function again. He wanted to ask how the condom factored into *the talk* but didn't dare ask. And then he experienced a mild sense of panic at the thought of someday having to have *the talk* with Molly and Martha. Luckily he had ten years to figure out how to handle that.

"Don't they tell kids about stuff like this in school?" One could always hope.

"They teach the biology of how it all works, but it's up to parents to help their kids make the decisions that are best for them."

Okay, that made sense, although it didn't make him any more confident about someday having to have this conversation with his own daughters. Maybe it would be easier if he'd had sons instead. No, it wouldn't. Not if his father was any kind of example. There had been no father-son talk. His dad had left his and Britt's upbringing to their mother, who'd been a stay-at-home mom and a great one at that. There'd been plenty of talk about treating girls well, being polite, being a gentleman. Looking back, he was damn sure his mother's between-the-lines message had been to avoid all situations that called for condoms.

"So in this parenting class, they give you all the information you need to have this conversation with your teenager?"

"Yes. They gave us pamphlets to help us talk to our kids about preventing STDs, unplanned pregnancies. The only problem is…" She paused, looked down at her hands now folded primly in her lap. "I haven't figured out how to initiate the conversation, and I'm not looking forward to demonstrating how to use a condom."

Surprise didn't come close to describing his reaction. *"Demonstrate?"*

"With a banana."

Laughter was not an appropriate adult response, but he couldn't help himself. "I thought stuff like that only happened on TV."

"I wish." She was laughing, too. "Now you know why I had a condom in my bag. And that I'm not as great a mom as I'd like to be."

"Don't." He held a finger to her lips. "You're smart, beautiful, and I can tell that you're a wonderful mom. You know exactly what you need to do with your daughter, and I envy that." He pulled his hand away and gave her a light, lingering kiss.

"Speaking of parents and kids, we should go inside and see how ours are doing."

She was right. He'd rather be alone with her, wanted to kiss her again, but he'd already moved too fast.

"The house is still standing…there were no frantic phone calls. Everything must have gone well."

"They're fine," Kristi said, looking a little sheepish. "I called Jenna earlier, from the powder room."

And there it was, proof that she was a better parent than he was, or at least a more conscientious one. It hadn't even occurred to him to call. Fake dates aside, it was good that Kristi had come into his life. He had a lot to learn. Kristi closed the front door of the town house, flipped the dead bolt home and let Hercules out of his carrier.

"You're awfully quiet," Jenna said.

"I'm tired." It was true. Who knew a fake date followed by a very real good-night kiss could crowd her thoughts and sap her energy? "It's been a busy week and

I'm not used to being out this late." She pulled off her shoes and set them on the hall bench with her handbag. She was ready to turn in.

"Lots of nights you're up way later than this, sewing or working on one of your designs." Jenna scooped the dog into her arms and carried him into the kitchen. "And we could have been home half an hour ago if you guys hadn't been making out in the driveway."

"Jenna! Where did you get an idea like that?"

"I heard Nate's car pull into the driveway…you can hear one of those Beetles coming a mile away…but it was twenty minutes before you came inside."

Damn. It hadn't occurred to either of them that Jenna might hear the car. So much for setting a good example. "We were talking."

She followed her daughter into the kitchen in time to catch her rolling her eyes.

"It wasn't a date and we weren't…" *Yes, it was. And yes, you were.*

"He seems nice." Jenna got a bottle of water out of the fridge and unscrewed the cap.

"He is nice. And we're invited to have Sunday brunch with his family," Kristi said, hoping to change the subject.

"Cool."

"You don't mind?"

"Not if you don't mind me tagging along on one of your dates." Jenna grinned as she took a sip of water.

There was no point persisting with an argument she couldn't win. "Do you have plans tomorrow?"

"Studying for one more final. Math." She wrinkled her nose. "And then Abbie and I want to go to the mall in the afternoon. Can you drop me off? Her mom said she'll bring me home?"

These days Jenna and her best friend were spending a lot of time with two boys named Matt and Jordan. According to the parenting class, there was safety in numbers. Did four hormonal teenagers constitute sufficient numbers to ensure safety?

"Will it just be you and Abbie?"

"Don't know. Probably."

"I need to work for a couple of hours tomorrow. I suggested that Nate buy a new sofa for his family room—"

"Good idea. The one he has now is pretty gross. The cushions are all squishy, and the material on one of the arms is nearly worn off."

"He said Gemmy chewed on it when she was a puppy. Which is why he's agreed to buy a new one. It'll really spruce up the family room, and he can take it to their new house."

Jenna absently stroked the top of Hercules's head. "It's weird that he'd want to sell it. Did you know there's a pool in the backyard? I would kill to live in a house like that."

That makes two of us, Kristi thought, although she would never let Jenna think she was anything but completely content with their town house. "Will you stay with the girls for a couple of hours in the morning? Sam will be there, too. She's going to start painting."

"I guess. What about the mall?"

It seemed like a fair exchange. "You help out in the morning and I'll drive you to the mall in the afternoon."

"It's a deal. Can I take my study notes to Nate's?"

"Can you study and keep an eye on the girls at the same time?"

"No problem. They're pretty cute kids and they keep each other entertained."

Molly and Martha had completely different personalities, but they were very close. That was probably normal for twins, but it might also have something to do with growing up without a mom. Kristi's chest tightened, as it had when Nate told her how his wife died. So sad.

"They are pretty adorable." Kristi stifled a yawn. "I think I'll turn in." She would take her laptop with her and go over her notes for tomorrow to make sure she had everything she needed.

"I'm going to see what's on TV."

"Don't be up too late. I'd like to get an early start in the morning."

Upstairs, she slipped out of the green dress that had been such a hit with Nate's mother and sister, and pulled on an old T-shirt and a pair of boxers. After she removed her makeup and brushed out her hair, she climbed into bed, turned on her computer and opened the file for Nate's house. She absently scrolled through her lists and photographs, but her thoughts were elsewhere.

The kiss had been an unexpected but welcome end to their this-is-not-a-date date, and if any other man had asked if she had a condom, she'd be heading for the hills by now. Instead he had opened the door to a conversation about parenting that they might not have had otherwise. She was glad he'd talked to her. He had everything going for him—intelligence, incredible good looks, confidence—and yet when it came to raising his kids, by his own admission, he second-guessed every decision. Even worse, she suspected he had some residual guilt over his wife's death. The mother-in-law who had donated a kidney and lost her daughter anyway might have something to do with that.

Kristi thought back to her brief marriage to Jenna's father. Derek hadn't taken responsibility for anything, not even the condom that, looking back, he had most likely been carrying around in his wallet for months. No wonder the stupid thing hadn't worked. Did he ever feel guilty for bringing Jenna into the world and then bailing on her and her mother? If he did, he sure never let on. They hadn't heard from him since he'd called the day after Christmas. He wasn't working—no surprise there— so he had no money for gifts, although judging by his slurred words and the raucous racket in the background, there was money for partying. Not wanting to listen to his usual string of flimsy excuses, she had handed the phone over to Jenna.

Their conversation had been short and, as was always the case, Jenna didn't want to talk about it afterward. Kristi prided herself on having a good relationship with her daughter. She worked hard to maintain it and it broke her heart that in this one area, perhaps the one that mattered most, Jenna refused to open up. Kristi had always been careful not to say anything negative about him, in spite of the fact that Derek really was a deadbeat.

The opposite of Nate in pretty well every way possible. Thankfully he'd called her on the deadbeat reference because she would hate for him to believe that's what she thought of him. When it came to measuring a man's character, Nate and Derek were at opposite ends of the yardstick.

She turned off her laptop, set it on the nightstand and snuggled in between the sheets. Until tonight, she would have told herself that Nate McTavish's parenting skills were none of her business. That kiss had changed everything.

No, not *everything*. She was a single mom, determined as ever to set an example for her teenage daughter. A single mom who didn't need a man in her life. But she could still help Nate see that he was doing a great job as a single dad. And if that involved another kiss, or two, so be it.

Chapter 7

Sam's old utility truck was parked in front of Nate's house when Kristi and Jenna arrived the next morning.

"Cool," Jenna said as they pulled up behind it. "Do you think she brought her little boy with her?"

"No, he's at home with his father, or maybe the nanny. Won't you have your hands full with the twins?"

"I guess. He's about their age, though. I bet they'd get along great."

True. But Sam would be working, so the twins and the two dogs would be plenty of responsibility for Jenna, especially if she planned to study, too.

"Can you carry Hercules in with you? I'll get my bag out of the back."

Inside, Sam's toolboxes and the wallpaper steamer lined one side of the foyer. In the family room the TV was on, the tent flap was open and the sofa bed had been unfolded. Nate had said he would sleep there, closer to the girls. Gemmy was sprawled on the bed. Nate and the girls were nowhere to be seen, but Molly's and Martha's voices drifted in through the open patio door. They were in their playhouse, Kristi guessed, and Nate would be in his greenhouse.

Jenna set the pet carrier on the sofa bed and unzipped it. "Here we are, Herc. Come on out and see your girlfriend."

The huge dog sat up, making the springs sag. Hercules popped his head out and Gemmy's ears perked forward.

"It's kind of cute that they get along so well," Jenna said.

That was true. Last night Kristi and Nate had come home and been amused to find the dogs curled up together in Gemmy's bed, a snarl of tattered blankets in the corner of the family room.

"Would you go out and let Nate and the girls know we're here? I need to talk to Sam about today's work plan."

"Will do." Jenna dumped her math books on the bed next to Hercules's carrier, gave each dog a treat and headed outside.

Kristi found Sam in the girls' bedroom, kneeling on the floor, unscrewing the covers of the electrical outlets and dumping them in a small plastic bucket.

"Good morning. You're an early bird."

Sam checked her watch and grinned. "And you're not."

"Very funny. I said we'd be here by nine, and we almost made it."

"So, I met your professor. Seems like a nice guy."

Here we go. "He is." Best to ignore the reference to him being hers.

"How was your date last night?"

"It wasn't a date."

"Right." Sam stood up and shoved the screwdriver in her back pocket. "How was your fake date?"

Kristi closed the door behind her. She did not want anyone eavesdropping on this conversation. Not Nate, and especially not Jenna. "It was good—his family's great. He…"

"What?"

"He kissed me." She'd planned to keep that to herself, but it popped out like the cork from a shaken bottle of champagne.

"Ha! I knew it."

"You knew what?"

"That it was a real date." Sam picked up a putty knife and opened a pail of patching compound. "How was it?"

"The date?"

"The kiss, silly."

Magical. Heart-stopping. Best kiss ever. "It was nice."

Sam was grinning again. "Just 'nice'? That's too bad. I'd have guessed that a man who looks like he does could soften up a girl's bones without any effort at all."

"Okay, it was nicer than nice. By a factor of ten, at least. But it was unexpected. I mean, we agreed this was strictly a matter of convenience, no strings attached."

"Sounds simple, but we both know chemistry doesn't work that way. The attraction between two people doesn't have a whole lot to do with logic. Actually, it kind of defies it."

True. Sam herself was living proof of that. Last winter she had reconnected with AJ Harris, a man from her past, the man who had fathered her son, Will. They were now married and happily ensconced, with Sam's mother and Will's nanny, in the house that Ready Set Sold had been hired to renovate when AJ considered selling it.

Kristi was thrilled for Sam. She'd had a hard life, and if anyone deserved to have her happily-ever-after, she did. It's what every woman wanted and it's what Kristi promised herself she could have, *after* she finished raising her daughter.

"Have you talked to Claire this morning?" Kristi asked.

"No, have you?"

"No. She's been super busy with new clients looking for properties. She hasn't seen this place yet. After she saw the photographs, she decided to hold off on an appraisal until we have most of the work done."

"Good idea. Along with being the busiest woman on the planet, she's also been getting a lot of grief from her ex. She said he keeps calling and bugging her about stuff."

"That guy is such a jerk. I hope he's not trying to get back together with her."

"No, thank God. He wants her to sell their condo."

"He probably needs the money."

"And Claire doesn't. She says she isn't ready to sell it, and when she is, it'll be on her terms."

"He should have taken all of that into account before he hooked up with his new girlfriend." The guy was a two-timing weasel and Kristi had absolutely no sympathy for him.

"She'll work it out. I've been hoping she'll meet someone and put this behind her."

"She might if she wasn't so busy."

Sam pulled out a couple of picture hangers with the claw end of her hammer and troweled some plaster over the holes. "We're all busy. I used to think that working and taking care of my mom was all I could manage. Now I have a home, a husband and a son, and yes, I'm busy. Never been busier, actually, but I've never been happier, either. Claire deserves to have that."

Kristi couldn't agree more. "We all do."

"Now that you're dating Nate, maybe you will."

And we're back to that. "Clever, but I don't see it happening."

"What about the kiss?"

"It was just a kiss."

"It was so *not* just a kiss. You said so yourself. Maybe you should give this thing a chance. Give him a chance."

Now that Sam was happily ensconced in a beautiful home with the love of her life, she wanted the same for everyone else. Sure, Kristi wanted what Sam had, someday, but for now she was happy with her life as it was.

"The kiss just happened, caught us off guard. We're both on the same page about this being a way to make our families stop matchmaking."

Sam was paying close attention to patching the walls but she wasn't hiding her amusement. "And if you say it out loud often enough, it's bound to be true."

They could go around and around this issue all day, and Sam would still think this thing with Kristi and Nate was something it wasn't. "I should see if Nate's ready to leave. Jenna's watching the girls, and both dogs are here, too."

"No problem. Tell her to give me a shout if she needs a hand with anything. And have fun."

"There'll be no fun. This is strictly business."

Sam opened the door and gave her a playful shove into the hallway. "Get going, and whatever you do, don't have any fun."

* * *

Nate couldn't remember the last time he'd been in a furniture store. He completely agreed that a new sofa would spruce up the current family room as well as the next home he and the girls moved to, and almost anything would be an improvement over the one he had now. It was a hand-me-down from Heather's parents, hauled out of their basement and into the family room after he and Heather got married and bought the house. Like everything else, the plan had been to buy a new one after they were settled and the babies were born, but like all the other plans, it had been put on hold temporarily, and then permanently. Until now.

This morning he was grateful to have Kristi with him because gazing across what appeared to be an acre of furniture was overwhelming. She wanted to bring him here because it was her favorite place for good-quality affordable furniture designed for everyday living. She breezed through the store with confidence and style, and he was content to trail behind, taking in her scent and admiring those dynamite legs. She was wearing lower heels than that first day she'd come to the house, but he still liked the way they emphasized the smooth curves and slender ankles.

She stopped unexpectedly and swung around to check the price tag attached to the arm of a brown sectional, and he almost ran into her. Instinctively he reached out, put his hand on her waist. She smiled up at him, green eyes sparkling, lips within easy kissing distance.

"What do you think?" she asked. She was talking about the sofa.

He was thinking about something else. "It looks good."

She took a seat and patted the cushion next to her. "Give it a try."

He sat, bounced a couple of times. "Comfy. I'll take it."

"You can't buy the first sofa you see."

"Why not?"

"Because there might be something better." She ran a hand over the sofa. "Nice fabric, though. It'll stand up to a lot of wear and tear."

"I like brown. It won't show the dirt, or the dog hair."

That made her laugh.

"You have no idea how much I hate housework. It's a lot to juggle…the girls, my job, the house."

"I know what you mean."

Of course she did. She was single-handedly raising a teenager who he suspected, having met Jenna, could be a real handful.

"This will probably sound sexist," he said. "But women are always better at this."

"Not always. Hardly ever, actually. You're doing a—"

"You look like a happy couple." A salesman in a gray suit stood in front of them. "Anything I can do to help?"

Damn the interruption. He and Kristi were in the store to buy furniture, but he liked hearing her say he didn't stink at being a single dad as badly as everyone else seemed to think he did. If she said it a few more times, he might even start to believe her.

He stood, held out a hand to help Kristi, amused to see that the "happy couple" remark had her blushing.

"We're here to buy a new couch for the family room," Nate said. It was too complicated to explain that they weren't a couple. "This is the first one we've looked at."

"My name's Walt." The guy pulled a card from his

pocket and handed it to Nate. "Let me know if you have any questions."

"Thanks," Kristi said. "We'd like to keep browsing."

"Sure thing. I'll just let you know that this particular model happens to be on sale, and it's available in several colors." Walt handed her a set of fabric swatches. "You folks take a look around and let me know if I can be of any assistance."

Nate wondered if this one was a sofa bed. Not that he needed a pullout in the family room, but sitting on it with Kristi had him thinking about beds.

"We'll do that." With a hand on Kristi's back, he guided her away, hoping Walt wouldn't follow them.

Twenty minutes and half a dozen couches later, they were back at the brown sectional.

"So you still think this is the one?" Kristi asked.

Walt, who had been hovering the whole time, closed in. "Looks like you folks have made a decision."

"I think we have."

"Well then, why don't you follow me over to the sales desk and we'll get this taken care of."

They crossed the showroom floor behind Walt. To Nate's surprise, this furniture shopping expedition had been painless, with the exception of Walt's dismal attempt to schmooze. It helped that Kristi seemed to understand Nate's taste better than he did.

The sectional he'd settled on was everything she'd said it would be, affordable and versatile. Walt keyed the sale into his computer, assured them there was one in the warehouse and promised it would be delivered on Tuesday.

"Why don't we take a look at children's bedroom furniture while we're here?" Kristi asked after they parted company with Walt. "I'm not suggesting you need to buy any, but I like the way their displays are set up. They're like actual bedrooms and might give us some ideas."

"Sure." Since she didn't expect him to make any more decisions or purchases, he was happy to agree. Plus it extended their time together…and what could he say? He enjoyed spending time with her.

What she'd said about the children's furniture displays was bang on. He could easily see any of them working for Molly and Martha if it weren't for all their clothes and toys.

"Have you decided what to do with all of those stuffed animals?" she asked.

He had not. "I wish their grandparents would stop giving them to us, but I hate to ask the girls to get rid of the ones they already have."

Kristi pulled her camera out of her bag. "Let me show you something."

She turned it on, scrolled through some photos, then handed it to him. On the monitor was a picture of Martha sitting on her bed, smiling happily, surrounded by her stuffies. Kristi clicked to the next photograph, a similar one of Molly.

"Because we were moving everything out of their room, I asked each of them to pick their three favorites. Molly quickly chose three. Martha really only had one—"

"The purple dinosaur," Nate said.

"Barney." Kristi grinned. "She finally chose two more, and then we bagged up the rest and hauled them into the spare room. I took the photographs because I thought that if you and the girls agreed to donate those stuffed animals to charity, I would have these photographs framed for them. That way they would have a permanent reminder of them but without the clutter."

He liked that idea. A lot. What he didn't like was the guilt that threatened as he wondered what Alice would think.

Kristi must have read his mind. "I know you're worried about what your mother-in-law might say, but the toys belong to the girls now and the ultimate decision about what to do with them is really yours, and theirs."

Taking a stand sounded so sensible, so easy when she said it, but she didn't know the half of it. Dealing with the toys would be much simpler than the beauty pageant. In fact, maybe the toys would be a good practice run.

"The photographs are a great idea, but I don't know if the girls will agree to get rid of all the toys."

Kristi's smile suggested she knew better. "Why don't we try this? After the room is painted and we move the girls back in, we'll leave the stuffies in the bags in the spare room. All the too-small clothing and dress-up clothes will be pared down, and I guarantee they'll love the room without the clutter because they'll have space to play, and when they look for something they'll be able to find it."

Everything she said made sense, but would she be there when he told Alice to stop buying toys and Britt to stop bringing dress-up clothes?

She seemed to read his mind.

"If it helps, I'll back you up when you tell them." Her grin had a mischievous little twist to it. "Since everyone already believe we're dating, I don't think that's too much of a stretch."

He wanted to kiss her, right there in the middle of the furniture store. "It's a deal," he said instead. He felt a little as though he was taking the coward's way out, but when it came to his mother-in-law, that worked for him.

"What do you think of these storage solutions?" Kristi asked.

The display room had a closet outfitted with cubbies, bars for hanging clothes and upper shelves filled with large baskets. It looked perfect, and pretty much the opposite of what the girls had now.

"I like it. How much will something like this cost?"

"The components are sold separately, and they can really add up. I've already discussed this with Sam, and she can build something very similar for a fraction of the price. I'll pick up some dollar-store baskets to go in the cubbies, and the girls can use those for everyday things. The larger baskets overhead can store out-of-season clothes."

The house would be so well organized, he might not want to sell. "We won't want to leave them behind."

"You won't have to. Sam will build everything in sections so they're easy to move and can be adapted to any closet."

"I've never met a female handyman…person…handywoman."

"She's an amazing carpenter, but I don't think there's anything she can't do. Painting, installing light fixtures, fixing leaking taps—Sam does it all, and with so much attention to detail. Our clients are always really happy with her work."

The same could be said for Kristi. He should probably tell her that, and he wasn't sure why he didn't. "Good to know" was all he could manage.

"Claire is pretty incredible, too, and super busy. She's

going to swing by sometime next week to take a look at your place. You'll meet her then."

Claire was the real estate agent, the one who was going to appraise the house and get it on the market, and then there'd be no turning back. For the first time in what felt like forever, the weight he'd been shouldering was starting to lighten. Maybe he really could make a comfortable home for himself and the girls. With Kristi's help, that is. He hadn't quite figured out how to do this on his own, but maybe someday.

Kristi was glad to see Sam's truck was still parked in front of the house when they returned from shopping. After they'd left the furniture store Nate had insisted on taking her out for lunch, and although she should have said no, she'd said yes. She'd called Jenna to make sure she had everything under control, and Sam to let her know she'd be back a little later than expected.

They'd gone to a casual deli-style cafeteria close to the university and not far from his place. They ate made-to-order sandwiches while they talked about her plans for the house…so it had really been a working lunch. Then they'd shared a brownie with whipped cream for dessert. One brownie and two forks felt more like a date, but wasn't.

Nate was easy to talk to, and more relaxed than he'd been since she'd started working for him. Sitting in the café with her, he wasn't a man struggling to keep house, decipher the needs of two little girls, meet his family's demands. He didn't even have to be a university professor, although she suspected that's the role he was most comfortable in. And by the time lunch was over, she was more intrigued by Nate McTavish than ever, and far more than common sense dictated.

Now, back at his place, she reminded herself that she had a job to do.

"What are your plans for the afternoon?" Nate asked.

She ran through her mental checklist. "We should empty your office so Sam can strip the wallpaper. Will you have time to help with that?"

"Already done. I finished it last night."

"Wow. I'm impressed. I'd like to tackle the foyer closet this afternoon, and Sam and I will do a walk-through before she leaves so she can make a list of the other things that need to be done."

"Let me know what I can do to help."

"Oh, believe me. We will."

They sat a moment longer without saying anything, listening to the Saturday sounds of the neighborhood. A lawn mower, someone hammering, boys shooting hoops in a driveway down the block. Last night they'd sat like this in the dark and he had kissed her. Today they were out in the open for all the neighbors to see. Neither of them was ready for that kind of PDA, as Jenna liked to call it.

"We should go in," she said. This time she didn't wait for him to come around and open her door.

The house was quiet when they went inside. Almost too quiet. The family room-turned-campground was still a chaotic mess of camping gear.

Nate looked inside the tent and laughed. "Take a peek."

Gemmy, sprawled on her side on top of Molly's and Martha's sleeping bags, filled the entire space. Hercules was curled up under her chin. Both were sound asleep.

Kristi pulled out her camera and snapped a photograph of them. "This has to be the cutest thing ever."

The patio doors were open and voices drifted in from the backyard.

"The kids must be out in the playhouse," Nate said. "I'll go check on them."

"I'll come with you and let Jenna know I'm back. She needs a ride to the mall to meet her friend."

They walked together across the patio and found the three girls crowded into the playhouse. The twins each wore a dress that flowed to the floor. Molly's was bright shimmery turquoise and Martha's was a lavender sequined number. A sash fashioned from a scarf was draped diagonally across the top of each girl's dress.

Jenna had combed out their pigtails and given each girl a unique hairdo. The contents of her makeup bag were strewn across the top of a little table. Molly's vivid aqua eye shadow and bright pink blush coordinated with her dress, and Martha's purple-rimmed eyes matched hers.

"Daddy!" Molly twirled and curtsied. "Look at us! Jenna did our makeup."

Kristi had to press her lips together to keep from laughing out loud. They looked a little outlandish and absolutely adorable. "You guys look so sweet. Jenna did a great job of—"

One glance at Nate wiped the smile off Kristi's face. He was not impressed. He was angry. Really angry.

"Molly. Martha. Get out of those clothes and in the house, now."

"Daddy, we're playing," Martha said. "Me an' Molly are beauty queens."

"In the house," he repeated. "I want you to go in the bathroom and scrub that makeup off your faces. Now."

Molly struck a defiant pose. "I don't want to."

"Now." He backed away from the playhouse door and waited, indicating he wasn't taking no for an answer.

Jenna hastily swept her makeup into the case and zipped it up. "Go on, girls. You need to do what your dad says."

Martha wriggled out of her dress.

"Why do we got to go in?" Molly asked.

"Because I said so."

Because? Kristi cringed.

Molly wasn't giving up that easily. "We're still playing."

What to do? Kristi wondered. Step in or stay out of it? If she sided with the girls, Nate would think she was interfering. If she sided with him, Jenna would think she'd done something wrong. That made staying out of the argument the best plan. The kids were just having some harmless fun and she didn't understand why Nate was making it such a big deal, but she'd be wise to let things slide and try talking to him about it when they were alone.

"You can find another game to play *after* you're cleaned up."

Jenna rolled her eyes.

Kristi gave her daughter a reassuring smile and a warning look that said, *Let this one go.* The last thing they needed was for Jenna to tell Nate that this was a load of crap.

Molly stomped barefoot out of the playhouse. "I want to play dress-up with Jenna. She's cool."

Kristi didn't know what Nate thought of her daughter, but she'd bet *cool* wasn't on the list.

Jenna gathered up her things and followed Molly, bending down to fit through the door. Kristi put a reassuring arm around her shoulder. "Let me handle this," she whispered.

Nate held out his hands to his daughters. Martha took one, but Molly pulled away and grabbed Kristi's instead. They trooped inside, a sullen-faced Jenna bringing up the rear. Nate hustled both girls, Molly still protesting loudly, down the hallway to the main bathroom.

"I'll go wait in the van." Jenna grabbed her math books off the counter and stormed out the front door, leaving Kristi standing alone in the middle of the family room with only the sound of Gemmy snoring inside the tent.

What the hell had just happened? She couldn't even guess, but there'd be no point trying to talk to Nate until he'd calmed down. For now she didn't want to keep Jenna waiting, but she had to let Sam know she was back, and that she was leaving again to run Jenna to the mall.

She tapped lightly on the twins' bedroom door and let herself in.

"You're back," Sam said, pulling her earphones out of her ears. "What's up?"

Kristi closed the door behind her and filled Sam in on the dress-up fiasco. "Nate has them in the bathroom now, scrubbing off their makeup."

"Huh. That's kind of over-the-top, but he must have his reasons."

"I'm sure he does, but he didn't have to freak out. Poor Jenna's sulking out in the van. I'll have to smooth things over because we're having brunch with Nate's family tomorrow."

"I'm sure it'll be fine," Sam said. "How was lunch?"

"Good. Really nice, actually. And then we got here and everything went south." Kristi looked around the room. "You're putting on primer already? At this rate we'll easily get the job wrapped up in a week or so, maybe less."

"That's the beauty of fast-drying patching compound." Sam set her paint roller on the edge of the tray and perched on the end of a sawhorse. "You might be finished with the house in a week, but I have a feeling you and Nate will be seeing each other after that."

Half an hour ago as they'd bumped forks over a brownie, Kristi would have agreed. He was the sexiest, smartest man she'd ever met. He was grounded, interested in all sorts of things, and contrary to her idea of a stereotypical professor, he had a great sense of humor. About some things, anyway.

"I wouldn't count on it. He's really angry, and so is Jenna."

Sam popped the lid off a Tupperware container and took out a carrot stick. "Want one?" she asked.

"No, thanks."

Sam crunched the carrot. "I can see you're into this guy—this wouldn't bother you if you weren't—but don't make it into a big deal, because it isn't."

"I just met him," Kristi reminded her. "What if this is how he reacts all the time? I can't handle that."

"And you shouldn't. All you need to do right now is relax and get to know him. If he turns out to be a jerk… or a deadbeat," Sam said with a wink, "then don't see him anymore."

Sam was right. Kristi had never let herself get crazy over a man, not since her divorce. What was different this time? She wasn't ready to examine that question too closely. "When did you get so smart?" she asked instead.

"When I let the man I love tear down my fortress. I thought I was protecting myself, but I was really just hiding, making excuses for not living my life. He saved me. I'm guessing you and Nate can do that for each other. If you'll let him, that is."

Kristi hugged her. "I'm so happy for you. It's a real-life fairy tale, and if anyone deserves a happy ending, it's you."

"So do you, hon. You and Jenna. Don't be too quick to slam the door this time."

Kristi's BlackBerry buzzed. It was a text message from her daughter. Can we go now?

"That's Jenna."

"I'll hold down the fortress till you get back," Sam said, giving her a sly wink. "Just don't slam that door on your way out."

"Subtle as always. I'll be back in an hour."

Chapter 8

The mall parking lot was busier than usual for a Saturday afternoon. People must be getting ready for summer vacation, Kristi thought as she scanned the row ahead for a parking spot.

Jenna's cell phone buzzed. "It's a text from Abbie. She's meeting me at the main entrance. You can drop me off there."

"Is she already here?" Kristi asked. "If not, I'll wait with you till she arrives."

"Mom! You're treating me like a baby. I can be on my own for two minutes."

"What if something happens and she doesn't show up? I don't want you hanging around the mall on your own, and I don't want to have to come back for you. Sam and I have a lot to do this afternoon."

"How much longer do you have to work there?"

"Another week or so. Why?"

"'Cause he's a jerk. No way am I babysitting for him again."

Kristi let the remark about Nate slide. "He pays you, and I thought you liked the girls."

"Yeah, they're cute. But Nate totally flipped out about me putting makeup on them. What's that all about? It's not like I got them tattoos or had their ears pierced."

He had overreacted, no question about that. "I'm sure this is just a misunderstanding," Kristi said, even though she didn't really believe it. "I'll talk to him when I get back, smooth things over."

"Whatever." Jenna's phone buzzed again. "It's Abbie. There she is, right over there."

Kristi pulled into a loading zone and waved to her daughter's friend. "Her mom's picking you up, right?"

Jenna was already out of the van. "Yup."

"What time?"

"Four-thirty." The door slammed.

"I'll be home by five," Kristi yelled.

Jenna's wave didn't indicate whether or not she'd heard.

Kristi scanned the shoppers streaming past Abbie. There was no sign of the two boys they'd been hanging out with, but that didn't mean they weren't waiting inside or planning to show up later.

"She's a good kid," Kristi said out loud. She did a quick shoulder check before pulling away. She could trust Jenna to make good decisions, but they still needed to have that talk. "And you need to do it soon."

She would talk to Nate, too. She couldn't understand his being annoyed about the makeup. After all, he was fine with the dress-up clothes. Something about

the makeup had set him off, and she wanted to find out
why. Partly because she wanted to get to know him better, especially if they were going to keep up this charade
of dating but not dating, but mostly because of the way
he'd treated Jenna. She was just a kid, after all. She'd
meant no harm, and caused none as far as Kristi was concerned. Nate owed Jenna an apology, and Kristi didn't
mind telling him.

"That's better," Nate said to the girls after their faces
were clean and their hair brushed and put back into lit-
tle-girl pigtails. As usual, Molly's were a little lopsided
because she wouldn't sit still.

Martha was still pouting. "We were playing. We
weren't being bad."

"I know, sweetie. But I don't want you wearing
makeup."

"Why?" Molly asked. "Grandma Alice put makeup
on us and you didn't get mad."

Oh, yes, he had. And now it was also clear that Alice
had filled their heads with this pageant nonsense, otherwise they wouldn't be dressing up as "beauty queens." He
should have called her the day she'd dropped off the head
shots and told her no. Instead he'd used the house reno-
vation as an excuse to put off the confrontation, and now
he'd made an ass of himself in front of Kristi and Jenna.

"Why can't we wear makeup?" Molly asked again.

"Because you're too young."

"It's just pretend," Martha said. Was it his imagination, or had she become more talkative, even a little more
assertive since Kristi had come into their lives? Right
way he'd noticed that Kristi wouldn't let Molly do her
sister's talking for her. Something he should have insisted

on long ago, even though it meant having two headstrong little girls questioning his decisions.

"I know you were just playing, but you don't need makeup for that. You can use your imaginations."

"We had makeup at Halloween."

"That's different."

"Why?"

"Because it just is." He took both girls by the hand and walked them down the hallway to the family room. "How would you like to watch a movie? We still have the DVD about rain-forest animals we borrowed from the library."

"Are you going to watch with us?" Martha asked.

He supposed he could, at least until Kristi got back. Then he'd need to take her aside and apologize. He flipped open the plastic case and slid the disc into the player. "I'll get it started for you. Then if Sam doesn't need me to help with anything, I'll come back and watch."

"Sam has a lot of tools," Martha said. "I'm going to be a carpenter when I grow up."

"You are?" Not if he had anything to say about it. His daughters were going to college, not trade school, and definitely not beauty school, but that conversation could wait. He recalled, with a certain degree of distaste, what Kristi'd said last night about needing to have "the sex talk" with her daughter. At least talking about education and careers would be a lot easier.

Molly bounced onto the sofa next to her sister. "I'm going to be like Jenna and wear makeup and be pretty and get a cell phone and a boyfriend."

Martha's pigtails bounced in agreement.

And we're back where we started, Nate thought. How did parents get their young daughters to understand tha what was inside their heads had far more value than what was on the outside? Did they have classes for that?

He picked up the remote and pressed Play. "How do you know Jenna has a boyfriend?"

"'Cause he wrote something on her phone."

"And she said it was from her boyfriend?" he asked, hoping he sounded casual.

"Nope. She just said it was from a boy."

"His name's Matt."

"But pretty girls like Jenna get boyfriends." Seriously? When had Molly become an expert on teen dating?

"Look at Herc and Gemmy." Martha pointed at the dogs sleeping in the tent. "He's her boyfriend."

Nate had to smile at that. If there was ever an unlikely pair, these two dogs were it. They'd really hit it off, but he still couldn't believe his four-year-olds were talking about boyfriends.

"The program's starting," he said. "Can you hear it okay or do you want me to turn it up?"

"Up." Molly reached for the remote. "I can do it."

Of course she could. He handed it to her. "I'll be down the hall if you need me."

The girls were already engrossed in the opening segment of a pair of orangutans picking nits from one another's fur. Too late now to worry about whether the film would demonstrate how primates made babies. He could already hear the questions. *Daddy, why...* And as usual, he wouldn't know how to answer.

Sam was in the girls' room rolling primer on the walls, and it looked as though she was almost finished.

"Nice work," he said. She'd only started this morning and the room looked better already.

"I have a system," she said, without taking her eyes off the paint roller. "We like to get in and out with minimal disruption so our clients can sell their homes and get on with their lives."

Now that Kristi was "in," he was in no hurry to have her out, although after his earlier outburst, she'd likely want the opposite. He hated to think about how badly he'd behaved, and he had to apologize as soon as she came back.

"Is there anything you'd like me to do?"

"It'd be great if you could give me a hand moving the bookshelves out of your office." Sam stepped back from the wall and surveyed her work. Apparently satisfied, she wrapped her paint roller in a plastic bag and set it on the tarp-covered floor. "I'll clean this later."

She picked up a clipboard and checked an item off her list. "Kristi asked me to talk to you about new shelving. Something with a lower profile instead of the floor-to-ceiling, wall-to-wall unit you have in here now."

"I've had this since I was a student. It was cheap and it served its purpose, but I won't miss it." Especially since, now that it was empty, it looked like something that belonged in a student's dorm room. "I'm not sure what I'll do with it but I'll put it in the garage for now."

"I can help you move it out there, and I'll bet Kristi can sell it for you."

"Really?" Someone would pay good money for this?

"She lists items on a couple of online sites. You'd be surprised what people will buy if it's priced right."

He didn't think there was anything Kristi could do that would surprise him. Without talking they dismantled the shelving unit and stacked the parts in the hallway, but he finally felt the need to break the silence. "How did you get into this kind of work?"

"From a woodworking elective I took in high school. There was just me and my mom in those days and she wasn't well enough to work, so there was no money for me to go to college. My teacher told me about an apprenticeship program, which meant I could learn on the job and have an income. I love what I do, so it was definitely the best option for me."

He had done his homework before he hired Ready Set Sold. The portfolio on their website confirmed that Sam was also extremely good at what she did. So was Kristi, and no doubt the third partner was every bit as accomplished.

"One of my girls just said she'd like to be a carpenter when she grows up." He wanted what was best for his girls and as far as he was concerned, that was college. But after what Sam said about her career choice, maybe he needed to revise his assumptions about what having "the best" meant. "Martha's impressed that you have so many tools."

Sam laughed. "Kids do love tools. My son is three and a half, a little younger than your girls, I think, and he can't get enough of them."

"What's his name?"

"William. We call him Will."

"It must be hard, doing the work you do plus running a business and raising a child at the same time."

"I don't think any parent has an easy job, but I'm one of the lucky ones. My husband's a writer, so he mostly works at home, and we have a live-in nanny who takes care of the whole family."

After Heather died he considered hiring a nanny or

a housekeeper, and in the end he'd ruled it out because
he hadn't wanted anyone else around. Relying on Alice
and Fred to help with the girls when they were babies
had been a mistake, but now that the girls were older he
liked having them at the university's day care. And he
was content to look after the house himself, even though
he wasn't doing the greatest job. And then Kristi breezed
in, and overnight all that had changed.

"It must be nice to have a creative outlet like this,"
he said.

"Kristi's the creative one in the business. She can walk
into a home and immediately come up with a design that
suits the client and still has broad appeal for prospective buyers. She tells me what she wants and I make it
happen."

"She does have a good eye for detail." At the furniture store, he had liked everything she'd shown him. In
fact she knew what would work for him and his family
far better than he did.

"Kristi's also done a wonderful job of raising a child
on her own," Sam said. "And Jenna's a great kid. She
looks after Will sometimes when our nanny has a day
off. He adores her."

Okay, he could be dense at times but he knew where
this conversation was going.

"I can see that," he said. Molly and Martha were already crazy about Kristi and her daughter. And unless he
admitted he'd screwed up, Sam would continue to sing
their praises. "I overreacted to something this afternoon.
I owe them an apology."

Sam used her hammer to knock the last stubborn shelf
out of place, stuck it back in her tool belt and handed the
board to him. "If you don't mind taking these shelves out

to the garage, I'll get started on this wallpaper." Judging by her satisfied smile, he'd said everything she wanted to hear and the conversation was over.

Nate's garage door was open and Kristi could see him inside when she returned from the mall. There was no sign of the girls or Sam. A good thing, because it would give them a chance to talk in private.

She walked in, and his grim smile suggested he wanted to talk to her, too. "Hi."

"Hi," she said. "Are those the bookshelves from your office?"

"They are. I thought I'd store them here till I figure out what to do with them. Sam helped me take them apart and now she's inside pulling down the wallpaper."

And probably grumbling about it, knowing Sam. "What are the girls doing?"

"Watching a DVD."

"Good. I was hoping we'd have a chance to talk."

"Me, too." He separated a couple of white plastic lawn chairs and offered her one. They sat facing each other, sandwiched between his SUV and the workbench that ran the length of one wall.

"I'm really sorry about the way I reacted to Jenna putting makeup on the girls. She didn't do anything wrong, and I was completely out of line. I hope you'll tell her that."

"Thank you, I will. But I think you should speak to her yourself."

"I will. Tomorrow before we go to my family's place." *If she'll agree to go.* "I'll be sure to tell her that when get home."

"Thanks. If there's anything I can do to make it up to her…"

Poor guy. He really did feel badly about what had happened. "Well, she's been begging me to buy her an iPhone," she said, hoping to lighten his mood.

His eyebrows went up a notch.

Kristi laughed. "That was supposed to be a joke."

That got her a smile, and he seemed to relax a little. "It would serve me right if it wasn't."

"Jenna's feathers were a little ruffled but she'll get over it. If you don't mind me asking, and feel free to tell me to mind my own business if you do, what made you so angry? The girls have loads of dress-up clothes. I understand why parents don't want little girls wearing makeup, but they were just playing and it washes off."

He ran a hand through his hair, the way he did when he was carefully choosing his words. She resisted the urge to smooth it out for him. "It's kind of a long story," he said.

"I have time."

"I told you about Heather's mother, how she did everything she could to save Heather's life."

A knot formed in Kristi's stomach as she wondered where this was going.

"Losing Heather was hard on everyone, but for Alice…" He sighed. "She didn't cope well. She blamed me. Still does, I think."

"What? Why? That's crazy."

"Not to her. If it wasn't for the pregnancy, Heather would still be alive. And since I'm the one who got her pregnant, I'm the one who caused her death."

"Oh, Nate. I understand that grief hits people hard but you said your wife had already lost one kidney. Anything could have happened."

"Yeah, well, Alice doesn't see it that way."

"How is she with Molly and Martha? Surely she doesn't take it out on them."

"Oh, no. Pretty much the opposite. She dotes on them and she's constantly buying toys and clothes."

Hence the overabundance of things in the girls' bedroom.

"Her latest thing is wanting to enter them in a children's beauty pageant."

So that was it. The girls had been pretending to be beauty queens, and the disgust in his voice told her exactly what he thought of pageants. "And I gather that's not what you want?"

"They're four years old. What do they need with a beauty pageant?" He looked at her as though he couldn't believe she had asked. "Would you have put your daughter in one? Did you?"

"No, of course not. I agree with you. Lots of parents think it's the right thing to do for their kids, though."

"Alice isn't the parent here. She has no business pushing this on us."

"Did you tell her that?"

"I told her I didn't think it was a good idea."

Not a good idea? Clearly it was the worst idea Nate had ever heard. Kristi understood why he was reluctant to stand up to the woman, but he had to do it.

She covered his hands with hers. "Again, this is none of my business, but your mother-in-law sounds like the kind of woman who doesn't like to take no for an answer. So if you don't tell her no, she sure isn't going to hear it."

"You're right, of course. I've been hoping that if I let it slide, we would miss the entry deadline and then it wouldn't be an issue."

He was a smart man, so he couldn't possibly believe that. And it was kind of sweet that he didn't want to offend the girls' grandmother, even though Kristi had a hunch he mostly wanted to avoid a confrontation. "If she doesn't get her way with this, is she likely to back off? If she really believes the pageant is a good idea, she'll just try again next year."

He turned his hands over and curled his fingers around hers. "You're right. She will, and if it's not the pageant, she'll come up with something else."

"So you're going to talk to her?"

He gave a reluctant nod. "I'm not looking forward to it but you're right. I don't have a choice."

"Can I offer one more suggestion?" She didn't want to seem like yet another person who was meddling in his life, but he could do with a little encouragement.

"Of course."

"Don't let this just be about the pageant. Make it about your family—you and your daughters. Your mother-in-law needs to know that you're open to her suggestions, but in the end, you're the one who makes the decisions about what's best for them."

She held her breath, not sure how he would react. For a few seconds he didn't, then he squeezed her hands and gave her a smile that heated up her insides. "I don't suppose you'd like to talk to her," he said with a shallow laugh.

She laughed, too. "No way. I'm scared of her, and I haven't even met her."

Nate slid his hands up her arms, making her shiver a little. "That makes two of us. But I will do it."

They sat, knee to knee, gazes locked. His hand stopped at her shoulders, and he pulled her closer as h leaned in. His kiss was easy and light, unexpected and welcome.

"Thank you." The words against her lips were as soft as a whisper.

"You're welcome."

"I should go in and check on the girls."

"And I should get back to work."

Neither of them wanted to break the connection, though.

"It's too bad this thing we've got going on here isn't real," he said. "We'd make a great team."

She should be hearing alarm bells right now, but instead her heart was doing cartwheels in her chest. She wasn't looking for a team, she was used to doing things for herself. So where were those damn bells, and why weren't they ringing?

Chapter 9

On Sunday morning, Nate put Gemmy in the backyard, strapped the girls into their car seats in the backseat of the SUV and drove to Kristi's place. To his relief, she had accepted his apology and agreed to keep their "date" to his sister's birthday brunch. Now he just needed to apologize to Jenna and they'd be good.

Kristi's town house complex was well cared for and located in a good neighborhood. He easily found her unit and pulled into the space next to her minivan.

"Girls, I want you to stay buckled up and wait in the car, okay? I'll ring the bell and let Kristi know we're here, then I'll come back and wait with you.

"No!" the girls chorused from the backseat.

"I want to see Jenna's room!"

"I want to play with Herc!"

"There's no time to play with Hercules this morning

You can play with him next time Kristi brings him to our place." He got out and closed the door on any further protest.

Kristi's front entrance was flanked by a pair of cedar planters filled with petunias that badly needed deadheading. He stuck a finger in the soil. And water. The painted metal Home Sweet Home sign on the front door was either old, or made to look old. Either way, it was a nice touch.

He pressed the button for the bell and Hercules started to bark. The yipping grew louder, and Nate could hear Kristi shushing the dog. She was all smiles when she opened the door, the overexcited little dog wriggling in her arms.

"Hi," he said.

"Hi. We're running a little behind, but we're almost ready."

He'd been half expecting that. "Anything I can do to help?"

"Can you take your sister's gift and this box of cupcakes out to your car?" She indicated the items sitting on the bench inside the narrow entryway. "Jenna?" she called upstairs. "Nate's here. Are you ready to go?"

"Yeah, yeah, yeah. I'll be down in a second," she yelled back, but didn't sound convincing.

"I'll get this little guy settled in his crate and be right back."

"No problem." Nate stepped inside, picked up the items on the bench and took a hasty look around. The three wicker baskets lined up under the bench had name tags on them, one for each resident, including the dog.

Given what Kristi did for a living, he had expected her home to be ultraorganized, but the living room looked lived in. The white furniture was cozy and inviting. Everything else in the room, from the accent cushions to the prints on the walls, was splashed with color—pink and red and orange. The overall effect was bright and fresh and feminine, and it was Kristi to a tee.

Listen to you, he thought as he carried the gift and the cake box outside and stowed them securely in the back of his SUV. *You've turned into a regular Martha Stewart.*

His daughters' excited voices filled the car. "Jenna!"

Kristi's daughter stood in the doorway, wearing a pair of narrow-legged black jeans, a baggy white T-shirt with an indistinguishable black print on the front and a sullen expression. The long red scarf looped several times around her neck matched the red canvas runners on her feet. Her hair hung in two loose braids, and he'd swear she had on even more eye makeup than ever. She was not happy, and a guy didn't need to be a rocket scientist to figure out he was the source of her displeasure.

So much for Kristi saying she would talk to her and smooth things over. Or maybe there *had* been talking, just no smoothing. And right now, holding the car door open for the reluctant daughter of the woman he was fake dating, he didn't care for either scenario.

"I hope you don't mind riding in the back with the twins," he said.

She shrugged and got in without making eye contact, then bestowed a bright smile on the girls. "Aw, look at you guys. I love your outfits."

They had insisted on wearing the fussy, frilly dresses Alice and Fred had given them for their birthday.

"No fair!" Martha said. "I want Jenna beside me."

"No! She's aside me." At least Molly left off her trademark nya-nya-nya-nya-nya.

"You can trade places on the way home," Jenna said. "That way I get to sit beside both of you."

"That's a good idea," Nate said.

Jenna ignored him and shut the door, not quite firmly enough for him to say she slammed it but darned close.

He should have apologized to her yesterday but she'd stormed out, and then by the time he'd cooled off, she was gone. Now she wasn't going to make this easy for him, and who could blame her?

He was debating whether to go back inside or wait for Kristi by the car when she hurried out of the house and locked the door behind her.

God, she looked good. Her navy pants, cropped just below the knee, kept those great gams in full view. Her white top and bright yellow jacket were neither too casual nor overly dressy. Perfect for a family brunch.

"How was Jenna?" she asked, keeping her voice low.

"Not happy."

"I'm sorry about that. I'll talk to her again."

So, she had tried.

"I'll talk to her." At least he would try. "I need to apologize, and that's not something you can do for me."

Kristi looked unconvinced. "I'm sorry I kept you waiting. I was working on something for your girls' bedroom and lost track of time."

"No problem." She was worth the wait. He opened the door for her, appreciating the graceful way she slid in.

He was lucky that things were okay between him and Kristi. Now he had to come up with a plan to win Jenna over.

At his parents' place, Britt met them at the front door and chaos reigned for several minutes. She gushed over everyone's gifts, declaring "oh, you shouldn't have" without being even a little bit convincing. Molly and Martha, excited to demonstrate the swirliness of their party dresses and shamelessly encouraged by their aunt, twirled until they fell into a giggling heap.

Kristi introduced Jenna, who was still giving him the cold shoulder but instantly warmed to his sister's compliment on her T-shirt. Turns out the baggy garment with the indiscernible print on the front was, in fact, the work of a hip young Seattle designer, and everybody who was anybody either had one or wanted to have one.

"I'll take these into the kitchen," he said, carefully balancing the large plastic box filled with Kristi's cupcakes.

"I can take them," Kristi said.

"No, you stay here with my sister and the girls." He followed the scent of coffee and bacon and his mother's amazing pastry into the kitchen, deciding he'd go back out after introductions, birthday greetings, dress twirling and gushy compliments about everyone's fashion sense dropped from earsplittingly loud to something a little more conversational.

"Nathan, sorry I didn't meet you and Kristi at the door. I was whipping cream and I didn't want to leave it."

"No problem, Mom." He set the box on the counter and kissed her cheek. "You look wonderful."

"Thank you. What's in the container?"

"Kristi's cupcakes. They are really good."

"You've already sampled her cupcakes?"

He studied her face, expecting a sassy smile to accompany that remark. Instead, she opened the container. "Wow. These are really something."

"I know. She brought some for the girls, sort of a

reward for clearing out their bedroom, and they loved them."

His mother covered a tray of deviled eggs with plastic wrap and slid it into the fridge. "She runs a business, sews her own clothes, decorates cakes…she sounds like a keeper."

"Mom…please." He didn't want to go there.

"I'm just saying…"

"I know you are, but don't start. Not today, okay?"

"Is something wrong?" Her concern was genuine, and it touched him.

"Everything's fine. Her daughter and I had a little run-in yesterday, and she's not very happy with me right now." He wasn't looking for sympathy or advice, he just wanted to explain the situation up front. Nothing got past his mother, and Jenna's frosty demeanor was not subtle so she wouldn't miss it.

"Blended families require a big adjustment. They take work," she said. "And patience." She rinsed a mixing spoon and put it in the dishwasher. "Can you get me a clean towel, please?"

He pulled one from a drawer and passed it to her. Blended families? Geez, where did that come from? This wasn't even a real date, but then she didn't know that.

"We just met. Talking about families is a little premature." Raising a pair of four-year-olds was hard enough. He wasn't ready for a teenager.

"Don't worry," she said, filling the coffeepot with cold water. "I would never say anything in front of Kristi and her daughter, but I have a good feeling about this. All I'm saying is that it's going to take work." She measured ground coffee into the basket.

Time to change the subject, he decided. If Kristi or,

heaven forbid, Jenna were to walk into the kitchen right now, he didn't want them to overhear this conversation. Ditto for his sister. His mother might not say anything to Kristi, but Britt wasn't known for her restraint.

"Would you like some help?" he asked.

"Since it's such a beautiful day, I thought I would serve brunch in the sunroom. The table's already set, but you can start carrying the salads out there."

"You made more than one salad?"

"I made four."

"Four salads?"

"That's right. I always make potato salad for your father—it's his favorite. I made a green salad for Britt because it's swimsuit season and she's watching her weight. And it is her birthday, after all. There's also the macaroni salad that Molly and Martha like so much, the one with ham in it. I wasn't sure if Kristi and Jenna would care for any of those, so I whipped up a fruit salad, as well."

Nate opened the fridge. The four huge salads seemed like way too much for eight people, but he kept that thought to himself. "What's in the oven?" he asked, setting the bowls on the counter.

"Quiches. Your father has to watch his cholesterol, but since it's a special occasion, I promised I'd make quiche lorraines for him."

For most of his life Nate had taken his parents' easy, comfortable relationship for granted. It was only in the past few years that he'd realized they worked at it, not because they had to but because they wanted to, and after all these years they were still very much in love.

"The salad servers are in the second drawer, next to the stove," his mother said. "I also made tomato and basil quiches, in case Kristi and her daughter are vegetarian."

He peeked through the oven door as he opened the drawer. Four quiches. Enough food to feed a small army, as usual. He peeled plastic wrap off the salad bowls, stuck a serving spoon into each and carried two of them into the sunroom.

The table was set with white china and crisp-looking green linens, a centerpiece of freshly cut flowers from his mother's garden and his grandmother's silver candelabras, which had been polished till they sparkled. He knew his mother well enough to realize she'd set the table last night, but he was also certain she'd been up since before dawn to make sure Britt had a special day.

He set the salads on the sideboard and met Kristi on his way back to the kitchen. She was carrying the other two salads.

"Your mother said you were out here."

He took one of the bowls from her, liking the feel of her hand against his as she let it go.

"Thanks," she said after the transfer was made. "Where should I put the fruit salad?"

"Over there with the others."

"Wow. That's a lot of salads."

"This is just the beginning," he said. "There's also a tray of deviled eggs and umpteen quiches. Then there'll be a birthday cake, and I'm sure dessert won't stop there because my mother was whipping cream when we arrived." So much for his father's arteries.

She laughed at that. "Oh, my goodness. Maybe I shouldn't have brought the cupcakes."

"Mom was impressed that you made them." He touched the small of her back on their return to the kitchen, and he leaned in to whisper, "She says you're a keeper."

Kristi stopped walking. "She said that?"

"She did." Although, after asking his mother not to say anything to Kristi, he had no idea why he was telling her.

"Well, I'm flattered. What did you say?"

"Oh, don't worry. I downplayed it as much as I could. Reminded her that we'd just met and we're taking things slow."

A flirty little smile tugged at the corners of her mouth. "Right. Good answer."

She was thinking about their Friday-night kiss. And their Saturday-afternoon kiss. That was a lot of kissing for two people who'd just met and were going slow.

"I don't want her to get the wrong idea," he said. "We don't want to go down that road." That was such a contradiction, given that he was pretty far down the wrong road himself.

"But we don't want her to get the *right* idea, either."

"The right idea?"

She leaned close, and her whisper caressed his ear. "That we're not really dating at all."

For a few seconds he was only aware of his physical reaction to her warm breath against his skin.

"All right, you two. Get a room."

He'd been so caught up with Kristi, he hadn't seen Britt walking toward them with the deviled eggs. Had she heard what Kristi said? Judging by her approving grin, she had not.

Kristi pulled away, her face flushed.

"God, you guys are cute." Britt winked as she breezed by. "Kristi, my mom dug out her cupcake stand for you."

"She has a cupcake stand?"

"Actually, she has two. Crate & Barrel has nothing on our mother. Right, Nate?"

What could he say? He didn't want to talk about cup-cakes or their mother's extremely well-equipped home. He wanted everyone to go away. He wanted Kristi to whisper something, anything, in his ear again. It didn't even have to be real words.

"Right," he said instead. "Come on. I'll give you a hand."

Kristi let him guide her down the hallway and into his mother's kitchen.

You can do this, he told himself. *You're a smart guy.* He would get through this phoney date, he would figure out a way to get Jenna on his side and he would ask Kristi out on an actual date. No kids, no dogs, no family. Just the two of them, for real.

The brunch was elegantly simple, very much like Na-te's mother, Kristi thought. Her family's events tended to be a little more freewheeling and raucous, which now had her second-guessing the wisdom of inviting him to Aunt Wanda and Uncle Ted's next weekend. The Fourth of July festivities would take place in their backyard and every year it was the same, with Uncle Ted presiding over the barbecue and her cousin Bart in charge of keeping the cooler stocked with soft drinks and beer. Aunt Wanda would provide a mountain of sweet, buttered corn on the cob, Kristi's mom would bring coleslaw and Kristi would bake a double batch of her grandmother's cupcakes, a family favorite that only she had ever learned to make.

It was always fun, but very different from brunch with Nate's family. His parents sat at either end of the table. His mother had seated Jenna between the twins, and across from them Nate sat between Kristi and Britt.

This arrangement put Nate and Jenna directly across

the table from one another, and by the middle of the meal her daughter had yet to look directly at him. On the one hand, Kristi didn't blame her for being annoyed with Nate. On the other, her standoffishness was becoming tiresome. Nate was sorry he'd overreacted, and last night Kristi had pleaded his case. Jenna was having none of it, which, hormonal teenager aside, was out of character for her.

Kristi couldn't tell if anyone else noticed her frostiness. And to her daughter's credit, she good-naturedly helped Molly and Martha unfold their napkins and even cut their quiches into manageable bite-size pieces. She politely answered Helen's and Roger's questions about her friends and her favorite subjects at school, and she was clearly captivated by Britt's vivaciousness. On the one occasion that Nate had addressed a comment directly to her, she had pretended not to hear and he had wisely let it go.

"Would anyone like more salad or quiche before I clear the table for dessert?" Helen asked.

Kristi quickly slid her chair back from the table. "Let me help."

"Certainly not. You sit and chat with Britt. Pour yourself another mimosa if you'd like."

"I'd like one," Britt said. "It's not every day a girl turns thirty, and I'm not driving." She filled her champagne flute and reached for Kristi's.

"Just half a glass, please."

Britt poured a generous half. "Nate? More for you?"

"I'll pass, thanks. I am driving."

Helen nodded approvingly. "Good plan. Besides, I thought I would ask you and Jenna to give me a hand clearing away the dishes so I can serve dessert."

"Birthday cake!" Molly shouted.

"Candles!"

Nate shushed them. "Martha, Molly. Inside voices, please."

Kristi connected with Jenna's wary look and gave her an encouraging smile, wondering as she did if Helen's request was as innocent as it sounded.

Jenna got up and flipped her scarf over her shoulder. "What would you like me to do?"

"I'll clear the table if you and Nate will take the salad bowls into the kitchen. He'll show you where I keep the containers for leftovers."

Nate leaned close and gave Kristi's shoulder a gentle squeeze as he got up from the table. "Wish me luck." Fortunately no one else could hear over the girls' clamoring to help.

"I can carry stuff," Martha said.

Molly's fork clattered onto her plate. "Me, too."

"Thank you, but I have a special job for the two of you," their grandmother said.

"What?" they chorused. "What?"

"See that basket of presents over there by the door? How would the two of you like to carry them over to the table and put them next to your aunt Britt? Then she can open them right after we have cake."

While Britt checked her iPhone for messages and Roger stepped outside to stretch his legs and "make room for dessert," Kristi sipped her mimosa and watched Helen slowly and carefully stack the plates. She appeared to be taking her time so she could monitor her granddaughters as they ferried Britt's gifts from the basket to the table, but Kristi wasn't buying it. She had a pretty good hunch that Helen knew something was amiss between Nate and

Jenna, and she'd intentionally sent them to the kitchen so they could work out their differences.

Would they, or would Helen's plan make matters worse?

Kristi kept an ear tuned to the hallway that led to the kitchen, but heard nothing. How long did it take to pack up a couple of salads?

"Good job, girls. You're both such great helpers, and I really like how you made sure the cards and gifts stayed together. Thank you."

Helen bent and put an arm around each child. Martha rested her head against her grandmother's thigh and popped her thumb in her mouth, but Molly only stayed for a second before bouncing back around the table and leaning next to her aunt.

"Aunt Britt?"

"Yes, Molly?"

"Do you need help opening your presents?"

"I definitely will. Any chance you and Martha would be interested?"

"Yes!"

Martha continued to cling to her grandmother, but she nodded vigorously.

Helen smoothed the little girl's hair and helped her back into her chair, then slowly gathered up the cutlery.

She's definitely killing time, Kristi thought.

Finally Helen picked up the dishes. "I'll take these into the kitchen and see how Nate and Jenna are getting along."

And there it was. She had picked up on Jenna's resentment, or maybe Nate had said something to her, and she was giving them a chance to work out their differences. Kristi hoped her plan didn't backfire.

* * *

Nate knew why his mother had sent him and Jenna into the kitchen together. He had deliberately not told her why Jenna was angry with him, but his mother was one astute woman. And because she thought he and Kristi were embarking on a serious relationship, she was taking it upon herself to fix things. Now it was up to him to find the right thing to say to Jenna so he didn't make matters worse.

He found four empty containers in the pantry and set them on the counter.

"Here you go. We can put the leftovers in these."

She didn't say anything as she scooped macaroni salad from the bowl into the plastic container. She didn't have to. The thump of the spoon against plastic spoke volumes.

"Jenna, I'm sorry about yesterday. I overreacted—"

Thump, thump, thump.

"Okay. I was completely out of line. I was…well, let's face it… I acted like an ass, and I'm sorry."

That worked. He could tell she wanted to smile but wasn't giving in to the urge.

"My mom wouldn't be happy to hear you swearing."

"I'm sure she wouldn't. I'll apologize to her, too."

For the first time that day, she made direct eye contact. "I didn't do anything wrong. Even my mom said so."

"She's right. After you went to the mall with your friends, she told me she would talk to you." Apparently that conversation had not gone well.

Jenna crossed her arms. "Your kids wanted to play dress-up and I thought it would be fun for them to do makeup, too. We were just playing. There's nothing wrong with that."

From her perspective, he could see that was true.

From his, with a mother-in-law who wanted to primp his daughters into a pair of pageant princesses, it had been a red flag. But that had nothing to do with Jenna, and he'd had no business losing his temper with her.

"You're right. There was nothing wrong with it. It's just that fathers…" As soon as the words were out, he realized that talking about fathers with a rebellious girl who didn't have one was venturing into dangerous territory. "Fathers can be clueless when it comes to stuff like this."

She seemed to relax a little.

"Even though Molly and Martha want to grow up and try new things, I guess I want them to stay the way they are." He thought about telling her that if his girls were as great as she was when they were her age, he'd consider himself lucky. But that was a dumb idea. Jenna was way too smart to be won over by sugarcoated compliments.

"What I'm saying is that this is my problem, not yours. I had no right to take it out on you, and I'm sorry."

She unfolded her arms and went back to work on the salad. He wasn't sure if they were okay or not, but he hoped this was her way of letting him know they were.

"My mom hardly ever goes on dates."

He hadn't expected the conversation to turn on a dime, and he was totally unprepared for this new revelation. Telling her that he and her mother technically weren't dating would be the wrong thing to say, but what was the right thing? He had absolutely no idea.

"Is that so?" The question sounded lame but it was the best he could do.

"She wants everyone to think it's on account of my dad ditching us when I was little, but it's mostly because she wants to set an example for me."

Those were almost the exact words Kristi herself had

used when she had explained the deadbeat reference. Did she realize that her daughter knew what was motivating her? Somehow he didn't think she did.

"Do you and your mom talk about those things?"

"Not really, but I hear stuff and see stuff."

Good to know. "How do you feel about her not dating?" He asked because he genuinely wanted to know. He just wished he could have found a way to do it without sounding like a psychologist on a TV talk show.

Jenna shrugged. "I don't know. I just want her to be happy, I guess."

"Do you think she is?"

She faced him again. "Yeah, I do. She's a pretty cool mom…"

How many teenagers would admit to thinking something like that?

But Jenna wasn't finished. "And I'd be really pissed if anybody did anything to hurt her."

Bingo. Now they were getting somewhere. She resented his misdirected anger over the makeup fiasco—and who could blame her?—but her real resentment ran a lot deeper.

A few minutes ago their conversation had been well outside his comfort zone. This new twist had him scrambling. What was the right thing to say here? To hell with the right thing—he couldn't think of *anything* to say.

He remembered one time back in his senior year in high school, he had gone to a girl's home to pick her up, and her father had outlined the consequences for any boy who did anything to his daughter. It hadn't even been a date, as he recalled. They were going to a chemistry study group. Then there had been numerous lectures from his own father. Not "the talk" in the sense that Kristi had referred to the other night, but more of a "be a gentle-man" kind of thing. He'd managed to wait till he was al-most finished grad school before getting his girlfriend pregnant, and by then he knew well enough what doing the right thing meant.

That's not what Jenna meant, though. Or he hoped it wasn't. She would be "pissed" if someone hurt her mom in the emotional sense. She was also enjoying being in control of the situation, having turned the tables on him, and she was waiting for him to respond.

"Ah..." He hated to think what shade of red his face had turned. "I would never...not intentionally...ever do anything to hurt your mother."

Not what she wanted to hear, apparently.

What else could he say? He and Kristi had a business relationship, and together they'd hatched this plan to be each other's plus-one as a way to avoid the awkward setups their families kept arranging for them. This was supposed to be simple, straightforward, easy. How had it become so complicated, so fast?

It became complicated when he kissed her, which was right around the time he'd figured out that he'd like their arrangement to be more than a matter of convenience. That much he could acknowledge, even to Jenna, because it was true. And if she repeated it to Kristi, which he strongly suspected she would, it would sound as though he was covering up the fake dating scenario by making it sound real.

"Your mom and I are just getting to know each other, and right now neither of us has a clue where this is headed or how the future's going to look. We're taking it slow." Kristi had laughed when he'd said that earlier. Lucky for him, Jenna seemed to accept it at face value.

"Good." She went to work on the last salad bowl—no thumping this time—while he stowed the other containers in the fridge.

For another couple of minutes they worked in comfortable silence while she rinsed the bowls and he loaded them in the dishwasher.

On their way back to the sunroom they passed his mother, carrying a stack of plates and cutlery.

"Everything okay?" she asked.

"Everything's fine," he said. "Do you need a hand with anything else?"

"You go join the others, and let your father know he should come in for dessert. Jenna, would you mind helping me? You can bring in your mom's cupcakes."

Kristi gave him a questioning look when he joined her at the table.

"Everything okay?" It was the same question his mother had asked, right down to the subtext.

He seated himself and reached for Kristi's hand beneath the table, glad that for the moment Molly and Martha were outside with their grandfather and Britt was occupied with her phone.

"Better than okay."

Her smile was probably meant to convey *thank you*. What he saw was a mouth he desperately wanted to kiss, a face he wanted to look at over and over again and a woman who deserved so much more than a fake relationship.

Chapter 10

Every Monday morning Kristi met Sam and Claire at Ready Set Sold's downtown office, dropped off the past week's receipts and other paperwork, and then the three of them held their weekly business meeting over coffee at a café down the block. This morning, in spite of her best intentions, she was running a little late. Sam and Claire were already at the coffee shop, and Marlie, their office manager, was talking into her headset, her long acrylic nails clacking on her keyboard.

Today the nails were purple with silver glitter to match her purple skirt and complement a snug-fitting cream-colored sweater that was lavishly bedazzled with rhinestones. Her hair was big, as were her other assets, including the engagement ring on her left hand. Her boyfriend, Thomas, had proposed last winter but appeared to be in no hurry to set a date.

"Good morning, angel," she said when she was off the phone. "The other two have already gone for coffee." Her nickname, Marlie, was short for Marline. She referred to her three employers as "Marlie's angels," and they loved her for it.

"I know. Claire just sent me a text message." Kristi pulled a manila envelope out of her bag. "These are my receipts. I'm afraid I didn't have time to sort them for you."

"Did you write the clients' names on them?"

"These are all for the Anderson house. I finished there last week, so this should be it for that project."

Marlie reached for the envelope. "Hand them over. I'll sort them."

"You will?" Kristi blew her a kiss. "You're my favorite office manager in the whole world."

"I understand you've taken on an interesting new client." Her emphasis on the word *interesting* told Kristi that Sam or Claire, possibly both, had told her about Nate. She knew her partners well enough to know they wouldn't tell Marlie the whole story.

Kristi decided to play along. "Very interesting. Of all the houses I've worked on, this is definitely my favorite so far."

"And the owner?"

Ditto. "He's…"

"Sam says he's a real catch."

Kristi laughed. "Okay, Sam did *not* say that." Sam never said things like that.

"You're right, but she didn't have to. Besides, Claire showed me his picture." The phone rang, and Marlie clicked a button on her headset. "Ready Set Sold. How may I help you?"

Kristi took advantage of the distraction and slipped into the tiny office she shared with her two partners. Shortly after they opened the business, they'd found space on the second floor of an old building near Pioneer Square. The small reception area was Marlie's domain. It led to an even smaller office that Kristi technically shared with her two business partners. Kristi tended to work at home and out of her minivan because it meant she could spend more time with Jenna, and Sam ran the construction end of the business out of the ancient delivery truck she had converted into a mobile workshop.

Claire used the office more than either of them, especially to meet with clients, and the space was organized accordingly. The glass-topped desk with dark espresso-colored legs had been Kristi's idea because it made the small room feel more open. The surface, completely free of fingerprints and clutter, was all Claire's doing.

On the back wall above a narrow credenza were three framed photographs that showcased some of their recent projects. Kristi changed them every month, and next week she'd be adding new ones. Right now the display consisted of a cedar deck Sam had recently refurbished on the back of a home overlooking Lake Union, a one-and-a-half-story Tudor in Montlake with Claire's Sold sign in the front yard and a before-and-after montage of a handyman's workbench that Kristi had organized.

Her phone buzzed. Another text message from Claire, wondering when she would join them. She grabbed her bag and waved at Marlie as she retraced her steps through the front office, texting a hasty I'm on my way!

The house felt quiet, almost too quiet. Nate set his laptop on the peninsula and turned it on. Half an hour ago his mother had picked up the girls and they were spending the day at the zoo and having dinner at their favorite fast-food restaurant. They wouldn't be home until bedtime.

Kristi had a meeting with her business partners this morning, and then she was going shopping for "storage solutions" that would help him keep the house organized. He probably could have found a reason to go with her, but as much as he enjoyed spending time with her, he didn't care for shopping. Her business partner, Sam, would arrive midmorning to finish painting. She had also made arrangements for someone to give him an estimate on putting a fence around the swimming pool. He walked to the patio doors and gazed out at the yard where Gemmy lay sprawled in the sun.

He and Heather had loved the idea of having a pool, spending time out there with the girls. It had been one of the deciding factors when they bought the house, right after they got married, but they had never used it. By the time they moved in, Heather's health was deteriorating. After the girls were born, he could barely keep his head above water in the figurative sense. With the demands of his family and launching his career at the university, there had been no time for relaxation. By the next summer Heather was very sick, and with two toddlers, the pool had been nothing more than a safety hazard. He'd had it drained and the cover installed, and it had been like that ever since.

For the past two years, fixing up the pool had been relegated to the list of things it would be nice to do...someday. For now, he had two little girls who depended on him for everything. Three meals a day, clean clothes, bedtime stories. Everything he had to do to live up to his promise to Heather, to love the girls enough for both of them. In between he prepared lectures, graded papers, carried out research projects and sat on faculty committees.

Give your head a shake, man. He had a rare day to himself and he had work to do. He shouldn't be dredging up the past. After being in a holding pattern for the past two years, his life was changing. And all because of Kristi. He was disappointed she wouldn't be here today. If she was, he might have an easier time settling down to work. Or he'd be completely distracted.

He turned away from the window, switched on his computer and forced himself to take a seat. One thing was certain. Kristi's being here couldn't be any more distracting than her not being here. He opened the document containing the paper he was working on and stared at the screen. He was so relieved when the phone rang that he grabbed it and answered without checking the call display.

"Nate, it's Alice. I've been expecting you to call."

He knew that, and in spite of the talk he'd had with Kristi on the weekend, he had been reluctant to contact Alice.

"Sorry. It's been pretty hectic around here, with all the renovations going on, and I had some family things this weekend."

"I see."

"We celebrated my sister's thirtieth birthday." The last thing he needed was for Alice to feel snubbed.

"That's nice," she said, without sounding as though she meant it. "I'm calling to see if you've filled out those entry forms yet."

"Not yet. Like I said, we've been busy."

"The entry deadline is next week. We don't have much time."

"I've been meaning to talk to you about that. I appreci-ate you thinking of the girls, but I've decided not to enter them. It's just not right for us." He stopped talking before he added that there was no way in hell his daughters were being paraded around in public like a pair of little divas.

There was a long silence. "I wish you'd said something sooner. I had those head shots taken. Their dresses have been picked out."

He held the phone away from his ear and stared at it for a few seconds. *No one asked you to do any of those things.* "I'm sorry you went to all that effort. Next time something comes up, I won't take so long to make a de-cision."

"Fine." Her tone implied she was anything but. "What are the girls doing this morning? Can I talk to them?"

"Sorry, Alice. They're not here. My parents picked them up half an hour ago. They're spending the day at the zoo."

"Oh. All right, then." As usual, she didn't mind let-ting him know she was disappointed.

"We'll call you before bedtime so they can say good-night."

"That gives me and Fred something to look forward to."

If Fred had ever had an opinion about anything, the poor man had given up expressing it years ago. Now he wouldn't dare look forward to something unless his wife told him to.

"Great. We'll talk to you then."

He set the phone on the counter, then let out a whoop and punched the air. He'd done it! Kristi would be so proud of him. He'd stood up to Alice, said no to the pag-eant, and it had been way easier than he ever would have imagined. Why hadn't he done this a long time ago? He knew the answer.

Half an hour after saying goodbye to Heather for the last time, he'd stood in the hospital corridor with Alice and Fred. He had probably been exhausted, no doubt worried as hell about how his future as a single father would unfold, but all he remembered about that day was the overwhelming numbness.

And then there was Alice, in his face, her emotions raw and roiling on the surface.

"How could you do this to her? My daughter would still be alive if it weren't for those babies."

Those babies—his two innocent darling girls, the loves of his and Heather's lives—were with his family. Unbeknownst to them, their lives had changed forever, and now they had a grandmother who resented their very existence. And since their existence was his doing, she resented him, too. He had a vague recollection of Fred hovering silently in the background, saying nothing as always. He'd had little more than disdain for his father-in-law in those early days after Heather died. Now he sympathized with the man.

Heather had been their only child, and when she was diagnosed with type 1 diabetes at age seven, keeping her healthy had become Alice's sole purpose in life. Not long after he and Heather met, she had described how her mother had become overprotective, constantly worrying and monitoring her blood sugar, preventing her from doing many of the things kids did—having dinner at a friend's house, going to sleepovers, even playing sports. Heather had been strong-willed and determined, and she had rebelled. To some degree, her rebellion led to complications, and by the time she was in her late teens she'd had a kidney removed.

Having a baby would be risky—she'd known that—and when they did find out the twins were on the way, Alice had wanted the pregnancy terminated. Heather dug in her heels and insisted on going through with it, and Nate had been caught in the middle, not knowing whose side to be on, not wanting to have to choose.

Although they hadn't planned to have a family—hell, they hadn't even planned to get married at that point—he'd always assumed he'd have one someday. A career, a wife, a house, a couple of kids, a dog…that's what he'd grown up expecting to have.

He'd felt trapped and guilty and that guilt had been compounded by his mother-in-law after Heather's death. But then a month after the funeral she'd rung his doorbell and insinuated herself back into Nate's and his daughters' lives. There had been no explanation, no apology, and she'd been around ever since, lavishing the girls with expensive gifts and sending him on a guilt trip every chance she got.

Today, after two years, he'd finally put a stop to it. He couldn't wait to tell Kristi. He sat down at his computer, but instead he was thinking about all the ways he'd like to thank her.

Kristi dashed into the coffee shop and joined Sam and Claire at their usual table in the back corner. "Sorry I'm late."

"You're always late," Sam said. She was dressed in her usual blue jeans and work shirt, and her coffee cup was already half-empty.

"Funny. I meant later than usual. I can't seem to get—"

"Organized?" Claire asked. Her navy jacket over a crisp white blouse suggested she'd be showing properties to prospective buyers that morning.

"Also funny. I was going to say focused."

Sam and Claire exchanged a look.

"Don't start," Kristi said. "This has nothing to do with Nate." They wouldn't believe her, and why should they when she couldn't even convince herself?

"We'll talk about that later." Claire ran a finger across her iPad screen and perused her list. "Let's get started."

When they'd first formed their partnership, they had established one simple rule for their meetings. Business first, then, if there was time, they could chat about personal stuff.

"Thanks for ordering a pot of tea for me." Kristi pulled out her wallet and laptop, handed Claire a pair of ones to cover the purchase and turned on her computer.

Claire tucked the money into her handbag. "So, we have a couple of projects wrapping up. Where are we with those?"

"New gutters and downspouts installed on the Anderson house," Sam said. "The perimeter drains have been cleaned out, too, so the moisture problems in the basement have been addressed."

"Let's hope so," Kristi said. "That was one of the worst basements I've seen in ages."

"But you should see it now," Sam said to Claire. "This woman worked her magic, convinced the Andersons to replace the carpet with laminate, painted the dark blue walls a nice off-white. You'd never know it was the same place."

"You did most of the work," Kristi reminded her. And as usual she'd done an amazing job.

"You hauled the junk out of there and got rid of it." Sam gave a mock shudder. "All those boxes of musty old magazines. Gross."

Claire shuddered for real. "You both amaze me. I meet with the Anderson family tomorrow. Now that the estate has been settled, we can move forward with the listing." She made some quick notes.

Twenty minutes later brought them to the McTavish house. Kristi's dream home. Nate's place.

Claire looked to Sam first. "What's left for you to do?"

Sam slid her empty coffee cup aside and tapped a pencil against the list on her clipboard. "I primed the office and the kids' bedroom walls on Saturday…while Kristi was out shopping." She winked at Claire.

"I saw that," Kristi said.

They both smiled.

"Got started on the closet organizers and bookcases on Saturday afternoon."

"How does AJ feel about you working so much?" Claire asked.

"I'm building them in my workshop at home and Will was out there with me, so he didn't seem to mind at all." Sam grinned. "Besides, he had a deadline for an article for a business magazine, so he was working, too."

"You have no idea how jealous I am." Claire was the most traditional of the three of them. She longed for a husband, a home in the suburbs with a white picket fence and a family, and in that order. So far she had a soon-to-be ex-husband, an ultramodern penthouse in a downtown condominium and a biological clock that, according to her, ticked so loud it kept her awake at night.

"Don't be jealous," Sam said. "Your time will come when the right guy comes along."

"Like he has for Kristi." Claire gave her hand a warm squeeze. "I'm jealous of you, too. But before we talk about you, we need to wrap up here. What else needs to be done on the McTavish house?"

Kristi opened the file. "Inside, after Sam's finished painting, I'm pretty much down to decluttering and cleaning. That'll take another week or so. Oh, and I'm making curtains for the girls' bedroom—"

Sam and Claire exchanged another look.

"Don't start, you two. I looked for ready-mades online and couldn't find anything, and I can make them for a lot less anyway."

"I think it's very sweet of you," Claire said.

Kristi pressed on. "The exterior of the house is fine but the backyard needs a fair bit of work."

"What about the swimming pool?" Claire asked. "That's one of the main selling features of the house, especially since it's going on the market in the summertime.

"I'm already on it," Sam said. "It was a safety concern with two small children in the home, so it's been empty and kept covered for several years. I discussed the options with Nate when I was there on Saturday, and he's decided to go with glass rails around the pool."

Kristi could picture it perfectly. Molly and Martha in water wings, paddling in the shallow end of the pool. Jenna and her friends hanging out at the other end. She and Nate keeping an eye on all of them from their matching loungers. One big happy...

"Kristi?" Claire's voice snapped her out of the daydream.

"What?"

"We lost you for a minute. I'm wondering how this affects your timeline."

"I was a bit concerned about the pool, especially since the pergola needs work, too. But Sam has a solution."

Sam beamed. "As luck would have it, one of our neighbors owns a company that installs all kinds of railings. Interior, exterior, glass, steel, custom designs, you name it. He and his wife had a baby girl a couple of months ago. Someone in their family gave them a beautiful oak crib and they wanted to add a canopy to it. I had some oak boards left over from the Mill's house we worked on last winter, so I built one for them. They're great neighbors, and since it was basically built from scrap material, I didn't charge them for it. They said if I ever need anything..."

"Perfect," Claire said. "I love it when these things happen."

Kristi patted Sam's hand. "Me, too. Sam's neighbor is meeting her at the house later this morning to give us a quote, and he's said he'll make this a top priority."

"He's a lot like me," Sam said. "He hangs on to everything that's left after an install, and he's pretty sure he has enough material on hand."

Even though Sam had married into money, she was still careful with it. And if she thought something could be used in the future, she didn't throw it away. Ready Set Sold leased a storage locker, and Kristi had lost count of the number of times Sam had dug out something she'd tucked away, saving them a lot of time, and often saving their clients a lot of money.

"That leaves the pergola," Kristi said. "By Wednesday, Nate will be finished collecting data from all those plants and Sam can get started in there. Once they're gone and the plastic cover has been removed, it just needs a coat of stain."

"And then it's a wrap?" Claire asked.

Kristi nodded. They prided themselves on being fast and efficient, but she wasn't ready for this to end.

Claire turned off her iPad and tucked it in her bag. "All right. Now we can get to the good stuff. I want all the details, starting with your first date."

Kristi had a hard time knowing where to begin. Even though she would trust these two women with her life, and even though she knew anything she said went into the vault, she wasn't sure how much to tell them.

Sam leaned on her elbows and grinned. "This could take a while. They've had three dates already."

"We've had *two* dates, and there's not much to tell. Both were with his family, and the second one included our kids. Besides, they're not real dates."

"Ah, but the first 'it's-not-a-real-date' date ended with a kiss." Sensible, practical Claire actually looked a little dreamy eyed.

Kristi's face got warm. Even days later, thinking about that first kiss left her a little breathless.

"The kiss shouldn't have happened," she said. "Seriously, it took us both by surprise. But I wasn't prepared for how easy it is to talk to him."

"Why wouldn't it be?"

"I don't know. For one thing, he's smart."

"So you're saying smart people make lousy conversationalists?" Sam laughed as she said it.

"No, of course not. But he's not your average intelligent guy. He's really smart. He's a university professor, a scientist. He's had stuff published. I saw some of his articles when we were clearing out his office and I couldn't even understand the titles. He's even a member of Mensa." Underneath a pile of books in his office, she'd found a framed certificate with "We're proud of you! Love, Mom & Dad" written on the matte.

"Wow," Claire said.

"Impressive. But doesn't that make him even more interesting?" Sam asked.

"It should, except I'm not smart enough to know what he's talking about."

"Excuse me?" Claire took exception to that. "Don't you dare sell yourself short. You are one of the smartest women I know. Not to mention creative, compassionate and gorgeous. I would kill to have your figure."

"There's nothing wrong with the figure you have," Sam said. "The world would be a boring place if we all looked the same, and if we all had exactly the same interests and ability. Look at us. We're totally different people but we work well together and we're good friends."

True. But as much as Kristi was attracted to Nate and enjoyed being with him, one thing was still niggling at her. Sam had witnessed the scene he'd made over the makeup incident.

"Fine, yes, everything you say is true. But there's still a lot I don't know about him, and I'd be irresponsible if I rushed into anything. Sam, you saw him on Saturday, how angry he got after Jenna put makeup on the twins after they got all dolled up in dress-up clothes."

"Yes, that did seem a little over-the-top."

"Is he still mad?" Claire asked.

"No. He apologized to me on Saturday, and he seemed to smooth things over with Jenna on Sunday." She decided not to mention the children's pageant because she was sure Nate wouldn't want anyone to know about it.

"Dads can be awfully protective when it comes to their daughters," Claire said.

Sam shrugged. "I wouldn't know."

"Neither would I," Kristi said. And maybe that was part of the problem. Nate was so completely different from the fathers she had known. Maybe the good ones were, as Claire suggested, overprotective. "I've known this man for less than a week, and I have more than myself to think about here. Everything I do, every decision I make, it all affects Jenna, too. For me to make the right decisions, I need to take things slow."

"For sure." Claire put an arm around her shoulders and gave a gentle squeeze. "We're not telling you to rush into anything. But I'd hate to see you miss out on a good thing because you're too afraid to take a chance on this guy."

"I do that sometimes, don't I?"

Claire laughed. "Sometimes? Every man you've dated since we've known you has had some major flaw."

Sam laughed, too, and Kristi joined them. "What can I say? My mother and my aunt Wanda introduced me to them. Apparently the world is full of Bernie Halversons."

"Who's Bernie Halverson?" Sam asked.

"The guy who'd be going with me to my aunt and uncle's Fourth of July barbecue if Nate and I hadn't come up with the fake date arrangement."

Claire checked her watch and slid out of her chair. "I'd love to hear more about Nate—Bernie, not so much— but I'm meeting clients in half an hour. Let's do a quick check-in by conference call at the end of the day, okay?"

"Good plan. By then I should be finished painting and have the estimate on the glass rail for the pool."

"Fantastic. What about you, Kristi?"

"I'm shopping for storage baskets and boxes this morning, and then I'll be working at home. I need to finish the curtains." She had another project in mind for Nate's place and she needed to shop for supplies for that, too, but she wasn't ready to tell Sam and Claire about it. Not yet. Mostly because they were out of time, but also because it didn't exactly fit with her plan to take things slow.

Chapter 11

Kristi quickly cleared the junk mail, candle holders, dog leash and her morning teacup from the kitchen table, and then she set down the bag of supplies she'd brought home from the craft store. On the counter between the kitchen and eating area, she carefully spread the photo strips she had surreptitiously collected at Nate's place. He didn't seem to notice they were missing, and until she was finished with them, she was keeping her fingers crossed he wouldn't.

She picked up one of the most recent strips and turned it over. She was impressed that he had carefully noted the date, and sometimes the occasion, on the back of each strip. How many guys would think to do that? Not many. Certainly none she knew.

In Nate's case, these systematically labeled photo strips resembled the work he was doing in his gazebo-slash-greenhouse. She had watched him out there when he didn't know it. Every plant had an ID label attached to its pot, and all the data he gathered was entered into his computer and double-checked for accuracy.

He didn't apply the same level of detail to everything—the foyer closet attested to that—but he paid attention to the things that really mattered. She loved that about him. No, she *liked* that about him.

She set the photo back on the counter, faceup, and emptied the craft store bags. Four white shadow boxes. An assortment of scrapbooking paper, a package of miniature clothespins, a roll of twine. Plus the box of screws with little eyelets on the ends that she'd picked up at the hardware store.

She had never done anything like this for a client before, and she sincerely hoped she wasn't overstepping. It had taken a while for her to come up with a project to display the photographs without damaging them or altering them in any way. If he totally hated her idea, at least he could remove the strips and put them back on the fridge.

"Stop worrying about it." She loved to dream up DIY projects, and she was sure this one would be a winner.

She pulled the measuring tape out of her basket of sewing supplies and double-checked the widths of the shadow boxes and photo strips. Each box would easily hold six strips, with room to spare.

She planned to make two boxes for the girls' bedroom—one for each of them—and another for Nate's office. The fourth could go in the family room, or he might even want to have it in his office at the university. Did university professors do that sort of thing?

At the craft store she hadn't been able to decide on what to use for the backdrop in each box, so she'd purchased more paper than she needed. Now she spread the sheets on the table and studied them.

The polka-dot print in three shades of purple on white was an obvious choice for Martha. She was torn between two pink designs for Molly but finally settled on the peppermint-pink butterfly silhouettes, again on white. The two patterns complemented one another, fit the design scheme she'd created for their bedroom and still personalized each girl's keepsake.

For Nate's office she decided on a sheet with a mossy-green solid background and a plant motif in a slightly lighter shade. She compared it to the paint sample she'd chosen. Perfect.

She couldn't decide on a background for the fourth box, so she set it aside and turned to the photographs. Should she randomly choose six strips for each box? Unable to decide, she sorted them chronologically.

The first few were taken when the girls were about a year and a half old. Nate said he'd started taking them when his wife was in the hospital and too sick to visit with their young daughters. As toddlers, Molly and Martha were adorable with their wispy blond curls and innocent smiles. Martha was sucking her thumb in at least half of the shots.

Kristi's chest went tight. She had allowed these two little cuties to carve themselves a large niche in her life, and there would be a big hole in her heart when the house was finished and she and their father were no longer pretending they had a thing for each other. Ending the fake relationship would leave another hole. If she wasn't careful, her poor heart was going to resemble a piece of Swiss cheese.

"That has to be the dumbest analogy for a broker

heart I've heard." Besides, her heart could only be broken if she let it.

She laughed at her own nonsense and woke Hercules from his slumbers on a sunny patch of the floor near the patio doors. He cocked a quizzical ear, then scratched at the glass. She slid the door open for him, checking to be sure the gate to the common area was securely latched so he couldn't get away.

Setting her emotions aside and letting her creative instincts take over, she skimmed the strips again and selected six, each containing at least one photograph of the girls kissing Nate's cheeks. She set those with the green paper she'd chosen for Nate's shadow box and looked for similar themes for each girl. For Molly, some of the sillier pictures, like the one with the girls making bunny ears over their dad's head. For Martha she chose several of the more serious poses, including one in which they were looking at a book with dinosaurs on the cover.

The front door opened. "Mom?"

"In here, sweetie."

Jenna came through the kitchen, grabbing a bottle of water from the fridge on her way.

"How was the water park?"

"Fun. It's hot out, though." She flopped onto a chair, unscrewed the bottle cap and took a long drink. "Ah, I needed that. On the way home, Abbie's mom took us to the drive-through for ice cream."

"That was nice of her."

Jenna took another drink and capped the bottle. "What are you working on?"

"Shadow boxes for Nate's place."

"Cool." She picked up a photo strip, put it down and picked up another. "Wow. They have a lot of these."

"I know. Aren't they adorable? I've been finding them all over the house, so I decided to figure out some way to display them."

"So you're putting them in these frames?"

"Yes, I thought this would be a fun way to display them. I'm going to screw these little eyelets into the inside of the boxes." She opened the package and took out two of them. "Like this."

She measured and marked the inside of each frame, then with a small pair of pliers from her craft box, inserted the screws.

"Now I'll run a piece of this twine from one ring to the other to make a little clothesline. If you'd like to give me a hand, you could measure and cut four of those."

"Sure." Jenna dug a pair of scissors out of the sewing basket. "Oh, these are so cute!" She picked up the package of mini clothespins. "You're going to use these to hang the pictures on the clothesline? Neat idea."

"I thought so." She hoped Nate would agree.

While Jenna installed the twine clotheslines, Kristi glued the colored paper to the backboard for three of the boxes. Then together they hung the photo strips, attached the backing and stood back to admire their handiwork.

"What do you think?" Kristi asked.

"You always have such neat ideas. It'd be fun to make one of these for Abbie for her birthday."

"Good idea."

"And it's obvious you're totally into this guy."

"What?"

"You asked what I thought. I'm telling you." Jenna drained her water bottle, got up and nonchalantly tossed it in the recycling bin in the cupboard under the sink.

Smarty pants. "Nate and I hardly even know each other."

"You've been on three dates in less than a week."

"Three? How did you come up with that?"

"You went out Friday night. I babysat, remember? Then you went out on Saturday, and I babysat again."

"Saturday wasn't a date. We went to look at furniture."

"And then you went for lunch. That *totally* makes it a date."

Kristi let that slide.

"And there was Sunday brunch. Also a date."

Arguing would be pointless. The whole purpose of going together to these family events was so everyone would believe they *were* dating. She hated to deceive her daughter, but she hated the thought of having Bernie Halverson show up at Aunt Wanda and Uncle Ted's barbecue even more.

"Do you mind?" Kristi asked, steering the conversation in a different direction. "I know you were mad about the way Nate handled the whole makeup thing when you looked after the girls on Saturday."

"We talked," Jenna said. "He apologized, and now we have an understanding."

An understanding? "Um...what does that mean, exactly."

"He has to treat you well and not yell at you like he yelled at me."

Jenna's cat-that-got-the-cream smile had her feeling a teensy bit uncomfortable. "Is that what the two of you talked about in the kitchen?"

"Yep."

"And you said that to him?"

"Yep. I told him I'd be pis—" Jenna cut herself off. "I'd be *angry* if anyone does anything to hurt you."

Yesterday, after Nate and Jenna had talked in the kitchen at his parents' place, he had assured her everything was "better than okay." Nate had definitely looked more relaxed, even a little relieved, and she remembered thinking at the time how she would like to have been a fly on the wall for that conversation.

Kristi laughed and gave her daughter a hug. "Have I told you lately what a great kid you are?"

Jenna hugged her back. "Not lately."

"Well, I'm telling you now. You're a good kid, and I love you."

"I love you, too, Mom. And since I'm so great and you love me so much, maybe I should get a new cell phone. Abbie's getting an iPhone for her birthday."

"Nice try. You know we can't afford one."

"Yeah, well, it was worth a shot."

Hercules slipped in through the narrow opening in the patio door, skittered across the floor and yipped around Jenna's ankles.

"Hey, little buddy. Let's go upstairs. Can I use your laptop, Mom? I want to check email and Facebook."

"Sure. It's upstairs in my bedroom."

Alone again, Kristi took another long look at her handiwork. The three shadow boxes had been so easy to make, and she was sure Nate and the girls would love them. She was uncertain what to use for the background of the fourth box. It would depend on where Nate wanted to hang it. For either the family room or his office at the university, something more neutral would be best. That ruled out the other paper she'd purchased at the craft store. Unless...

She dug her camera out of her bag, took it out of the case and turned it on. She had taken some photographs at the birthday brunch yesterday, promising to email them to Britt as soon as she had a chance to download them. She scrolled through the photographs till she got to the one she'd taken of Nate, Molly and Martha. If she converted it to black-and-white, gave it a washed-out look and had a large enough print made to cover the backboard of the shadow box, it would be perfect.

"Brilliant, even if I do say so myself."

She would get it ready as soon as Jenna was off the computer. Instead of turning off the camera, though, she studied the photograph. Nate hadn't dressed up for the occasion, but he hadn't worn one of his science-geek T-shirts, either. He had attempted to style his hair—she could tell because it smelled so good—but a couple of wavy, finger-tempting strands fell over his forehead as though they had a mind of their own. As always, though, his eyes were what drew her to the photograph, to him. They were honest, intelligent and so, so blue. In this shot, he was looking at his daughters, not the camera, and the intensity of his love for them filled Kristi with longing. As a child she had ached for that kind of fatherly love, and since Jenna was born, she had ached for it on her behalf.

Molly and Martha were adorably cute in their party dresses, and while the loss of their mother at such a young age was heartbreakingly sad, there was no lack of love in their lives.

She clicked the camera off and hastily stuffed it back in her bag.

Get a grip. She'd met Nate less than a week ago, had broken every single one of her rules about setting a good example and not having a man in her life, and now—even though there was absolutely no logic to it—she was falling for this guy.

One thing was certain. Jenna did not need to worry about Nate hurting her mother. If Kristi ended up with a broken heart when this was all over and done with, she would only have herself to blame.

By the end of the week Nate had decided that if anyone ever needed anything done around the home, these were the women to call. More than once Kristi had insisted there should be fewer items in a room, and the things that were there should have more importance. Now, looking around, he could see she was right.

The week had flown by and today the house was a hub of activity, with Kristi putting the final touches on the family room and Sam outside, hammering and sawing and, at that precise moment, running a power tool of some kind. Jenna was here, too, keeping the girls entertained in their newly refurbished bedroom. He should be doing more to help, but after several years of managing on his own, his home was now overrun with women. There were feminine touches everywhere, and he liked it.

Kristi breezed in the front door with an armload of cushions and he stood there, breathing in her fragrance. He was used to it now, but every once in a while it sneaked up on him and set his senses on fire. He was going to miss that, too. A lot.

"Anything I can do to help?" he asked, not wanting her to disappear just yet.

She stopped. "There is. Two of these cushions, the blue ones, are for the guest room. Can you run them down there for me?"

"Sure." As he tugged on one, she lost her grip on the

entire armload and down the pillows went in a jumble of color and patterned fabric. Together the two of them knelt to retrieve the wayward cushions, but they ended up reaching for the same one. Pulling on it brought them closer together, the cushion caught between them. Kristi was laughing, her eyes more gray than green in this light, and he felt himself free-falling.

The condom incident flashed into his mind, then it was overshadowed by the prospect of kissing her again. The possibility had occupied most of his waking thoughts for the past week, and every dream for as many nights. He just needed to figure out a way to make it happen.

She was within kissing distance right now. All he had to do was lean in a little.

She went quiet and her eyes darkened.

Kiss her.

He wanted to, badly, but the happy voices of children playing down the hall and the sounds of backyard construction drifted into his consciousness, reminding him this was not the right time. One kiss wouldn't be enough, not now and not ever.

He let go of the cushion, stood and offered her a hand up.

"Thanks."

"You're welcome."

"I'll be right back." He scooped up the two blue cushions and left her to gather up the others.

Kristi had spent the week working her way from room to room, and she had started by turning the spare room into a guest room after the girls' belongings and the contents of his office were returned to their rightful places. Not that he ever had overnight guests, but this was meant to show the new owners they could. Or they might fill these rooms with more children. Now that he'd settled things with Alice and the house was looking so good, he was starting to regret his decision to sell it.

Before Kristi arrived on the scene, the bed in the spare room had been buried beneath boxes of Christmas decorations and an assortment of winter coats, and a treadmill had taken up a considerable bit of floor space. Now the room was, in his sister's words, "a study in beige and white."

He didn't know what Kristi wanted to do with the pillows so he tossed them on the bed. On his way back to the family room, he stopped at Molly and Martha's room. They were sprawled on the floor with Jenna, Gemmy and Hercules, and surrounded by LEGO.

"How's it going?" he asked.

"Good." Jenna offered a green brick to Molly. "Is this the kind you're looking for?"

"Yup." Molly held up two bricks and snapped them together. "Daddy, we're building a town."

Martha, head bent, was intent on choosing pieces for her construction project.

He was glad Kristi had suggested Jenna watch the girls while he helped her get the house organized. Now that school was out, she wanted to keep her daughter busy so she didn't spend her summer vacation hanging out with boys at the mall. Jenna was great with the girls, and they adored her. Seeing the three blond heads huddled over their LEGO village, it struck him that anyone who saw them like this might think they were sisters. There was a crazy thought. If Molly and Martha had a big sister, that would make him the father of a teenager. Definitely a crazy thought.

He shifted his attention away from the girls and

scanned their room. It had been finished earlier this week—Kristi had even sewn curtains for it—and Molly's and Martha's furniture had been moved back in. Sam's closet organizer worked like a charm, and so had Kristi's suggestion that they replace the mountain of stuffed animals with a few favorites and framed photos of the ones they weren't keeping. He never would have thought of that, and even if he had, he sure wouldn't have expected the girls to go along with it.

Kristi's curtains looked every bit as good as anything from a store. Probably better, but what did he know? They were plain white and the edges were trimmed with purple, pink and green ribbons sewn in horizontal and vertical stripes. The girls loved them, and his sister, Britt, claimed they were magazineworthy. He didn't know if home stagers normally sewed custom-made curtains for their clients, but he liked that this one did.

Molly and Martha had been reluctant to take down the tent in the family room, but Kristi convinced them to put it away, saying that when the new sofa was delivered, she needed their help arranging the furniture for optimal TV viewing. The tent had then been packed away with the same excitement as when they'd pitched it. Kristi was great with kids, and watching her with his girls was like taking a master class in parenting. And she'd managed to arrange the new sofa so it faced the TV and afforded a view of the patio.

Sam had spent most of the week working outside. She'd brought in a pool maintenance company to clean and fill the pool, treat the water and make sure the pump was in working order. True to her word, she had arranged to have a glass railing installed around the pool. It looked amazing, it was safe for children—his or those of a prospective buyer—and the glass virtually disappeared, leaving a clear sight line to the pool from anywhere in the yard. The place was starting to look more like a magazine spread than his home.

Yesterday he had collected the last set of data from his plants in the greenhouse. Then he had hauled the plants through the garage and out to the driveway, and Sam had been right behind him, stripping away the plastic off the pergola and sanding the wood in preparation for a fresh coat of stain.

The phone rang, and Alice's number appeared on call display. What now? He didn't want to answer it, but with so many people around he couldn't let it just ring until it went to voice mail. He sighed and took the call.

"Nate, how are things going with the house?"

"Good, thanks." He paused and waited for the other shoe to drop. When Alice called she never got right to the point.

"Is there much more to do?"

"I don't think so." He honestly didn't know, but Kristi definitely seemed to have things well in hand.

"We know you're busy so Fred and I decided we would help you out by taking the girls off your hands tomorrow night."

Instead of sounding like an offer, it was more of a demand.

"We'll pick them up around lunchtime and drop them off sometime Sunday morning before we go golfing."

He could decline their offer by making up some sort of excuse, but Molly and Martha did enjoy spending time with their grandparents. And having the girls gone for the evening would give him a chance to set something up with Kristi.

"That sounds good, Alice. I'll have the girls ready to go by noon."

"Oh." The surprise in Alice's voice implied that she had expected him to put up an argument. "All right, then. We'll be there at noon."

He set the phone back in its cradle and pondered the possibilities that had just opened up. He could offer to take Kristi out to dinner and a movie. No, that sounded too much like a traditional date, and despite what they wanted everyone else to believe, between them they were still taking the "we're not really dating" stand.

From the sliding doors in the family room, he surveyed the backyard, watching Kristi and Sam carefully position the patio furniture. Kristi stepped back, shook her head, and they moved a pair of lounge chairs closer to one corner of the pool.

"Much better," he heard her say. "This is a perfect spot for parents to sit and keep an eye on the children while they're swimming."

That's it, he thought. Dinner here, by the pool. He could barbecue something. Steak? No, better make it burgers. It would just be the two of them but he would keep it casual, make it sound as though it was his way of saying thank you for all the work she'd done.

Kristi had performed nothing short of a miracle. He hadn't realized that the cluttered and untidy house had been weighing him down, or that cleaning and decluttering would also sweep away some of the grief and much of the guilt that had been pressing in on him. She was walking around the pool, examining her handiwork from every angle, and he couldn't take his eyes off her.

She looked deceptively sporty in what he'd come to realize was her customary work attire. Trim black exercise pants cropped below the knee and low-cut white sport socks in a pair of canvas sneakers. Today's were red to match her pullover. Her hair was pulled back in a ponytail and held in place with a red-and-white scrunchie. No way did she look old enough to be the mother of a fourteen-year-old.

He slid the screen open and stepped out onto the patio. Kristi whirled around, smiled at him and tripped over an ottoman. Sam caught her and laughed, and Nate had a pretty good idea she was laughing at the two of them.

"I'll just run out to my truck to get the solar patio lights you want to use around the yard," she said. "If you need anything else moved, maybe Nate can give you a hand." She winked at him on her way to the house. "You don't mind, do you?"

He returned the wink. "Not at all. Happy to help." And more than happy to have a few minutes alone with Kristi. "What would you like me to do?"

"If you could set up the umbrella while I arrange the seat cushions, we'll be done."

Easy enough. He angled the umbrella pole through the centre of the table and anchored it in the base below.

"Would you like to come over for dinner tomorrow night?" He held his breath and waited.

She stopped what she was doing and stared at him for a full five seconds. "You mean like a family thing?"

"No. The girls will be at their grandparents'."

"So just the two of us. Like a…date."

She was avoiding emotional entanglements until her daughter was older, so this dating thing—real or not—was as new to her as it was to him. Best to take it slow. "No, not exactly. I was just thinking it seems a shame to have everything looking so good and not use it. So I thought, with the girls gone, we could throw some burgers on the barbecue, nothing fancy."

"That sounds nice." She arranged the last seat cushion and then looked up at him again. "Jenna has a sleepover tomorrow night. It's her friend Abbie's birthday."

Sleepovers were good. Molly and Martha were having one, Jenna was having one. That meant he and Kristi could spend all evening together. And sleepover suddenly took on a whole new meaning.

"Well, good," he said. "It'll just be the two of us."

"And the dogs. You don't mind if I bring Hercules?"

"Not at all."

"Okay, then. It's a…" She didn't finish the sentence, but they both knew what she had almost said. "What time?"

"How does seven sound?"

"Seven sounds great. I'll be here. And since you're making dinner, I'll bring dessert."

He liked the sound of that.

Sam returned with an armload of boxes and a sly smile. "I hope I'm not interrupting anything."

"Not at all." Nate had accomplished everything he'd set out to do.

Chapter 12

By six o'clock on Saturday, Kristi had tried on half the things in her closet and still hadn't found anything to wear. Jeans and a T-shirt looked too casual. It was a warm evening so she could get away with shorts, but they would show too much leg. A skirt and top made her feel as though she was attending a business meeting. Her eye kept straying to the vintage-inspired boat-necked dress hanging on the inside of her closet door. She'd made it to wear to her ten-year high school reunion a couple of years ago. It was a nice subdued shade of pale yellow, knee-length with a full skirt. It was a bit dressy, but was it too dressy? Not if she wore her white cashmere cardigan over it, she decided. She held up the jeans again and studied herself in the mirror.

"Mom, you can't wear jeans," Jenna said from the doorway.

"What's wrong with jeans?"

"Nothing. They're just not you. You wear jeans to do housework or take Hercules for a walk, but you'd never wear them on a date."

True. She loved pretty clothes and bright colors. That she would even consider blue jeans simply showed how desperate she was to convince herself this was not a date.

Oh, it was a date, all right. Her legs were shaved and everything.

"Wear the dress," Jenna said. "It looks great on you."

Kristi fingered the soft fabric. Her daughter was right. It was a very pretty dress, totally feminine, and she did look good in it. With a white belt instead of the silver one she'd worn to the reunion, flats instead of heels... Okay, she was definitely wearing the dress.

"What time is Abbie's mom picking you up?"

"They'll be here in a few minutes."

"And her parents are supervising the entire evening?"

"Mom! We've gone over this a hundred times."

Kristi made a face at the mirror. This was the second time they'd talked about this, maybe the third. Definitely not the hundredth. She still hadn't found the right time for her and Jenna to have "the talk," though, and there were going to be boys at this party. Only till ten o'clock, and then it would just be Abbie, Jenna and another girl for the sleepover. Still, a lot could happen between six-thirty and ten.

The doorbell rang.

"There they are. See you tomorrow, Mom."

Kristi reached for Jenna to give her a hug, but she was gone. "I'll see you tomorrow morning," she called down the stairs.

"Okay, see ya!" And that was all the goodbye she got before the front door slammed.

Jenna will be fine, she told herself. *It's you I'm worried about.* Not that anything would happen between her and Nate tonight. They were both too cautious and levelheaded for that.

She shrugged out of the housecoat she'd put on after her shower, slipped the dress off its hanger and held it up for one last look. Nate would like it, she was sure of that, but she hoped that by dressing up for a casual dinner of burgers by the pool, she wasn't sending the wrong message. Or maybe dressing up was the right message.

At five minutes to seven, Nate warned himself against checking the clock every thirty seconds and keeping track of how many minutes ticked by until Kristi arrived. They'd have the whole evening together. Just the two of them, no kids to offer up a distraction, no extended family keeping tabs on them. He could still hardly believe his luck.

He had given her a key so she could come and go as she needed, but tonight she rang the bell. She was right on time, and she took his breath away. He would have waited a lifetime for this woman. Hell, he already had.

"Come in." He reached for Hercules's travel bag and set it on the floor. The dog started yipping right away and a drooling Gemmy loped into the foyer to greet him. He opened the Yorkie's bag, and he skittered out, touching noses with the Saint.

"Looks like they have a date, too," he said.

Kristi laughed, and for once he wished he could take his lead from the dogs, shove propriety aside and kiss her. Right here, right now. Of course being a dog and acting like a dog were two different things, and tonight he was determined to do this right.

"You look amazing."

"Thank you. I was leaning toward jeans, but my daughter said I should wear the dress."

He wondered if it would be appropriate to thank Jenna the next time he saw her. Not likely. "I'm glad she did. Come in."

"Thanks."

They were both feeling awkward and overly formal, and he would be glad when they were sitting by the pool with a glass of wine.

Kristi was carrying a small box, and that's when he remembered the dessert.

"Would you like me to take that?" he asked.

"No, thanks. It's sort of a surprise, and I don't want to ruin the fun."

"Bring it into the kitchen, then."

They walked through the house together, and when they got to the kitchen, Kristi opened the fridge and tucked the container inside. "Whipped cream," she said. "It needs to stay chilled."

It's just dessert, he reminded himself, but the words *whipped cream* had his heart and his mind racing ahead to later in the evening.

Down, boy. It's just dessert.

"Let's go sit outside," he said. He slid the screen open and the dogs dashed out ahead of them.

Kristi followed and stopped just outside the door.

"Is everything okay?"

"Yes," she said. "More than okay. It's really beautiful out here." She laughed at her own words. "I'm really pleased with the way it turned out."

"So am I. You've done an amazing job." He couldn't remember ever meeting anyone like her. His entire adult life had revolved around the university. The women he met were smart, serious, studious. Heather included. Kristi was every bit as smart and creative, but with more joie de vivre.

She touched his arm, lightly, and the effect was electric. "I remember the first day I was here, thinking how unfortunate it was that you had this amazing outdoor space but it wasn't being used. Have you and the girls had a chance to get in the pool yet?"

"We had a swim yesterday afternoon before supper. They were so excited... I can't even tell you."

"I'm glad."

"Come on. Let's sit. Would you like something to drink? There's white wine in the ice bucket. I remember that's what you had at Britt's birthday party. I also have beer. A dark ale." He held up the bottle. "And a lager that's a little less...dark. And I'll stop talking now."

"The white wine sounds great," she said. "I'm not much of a beer drinker."

Good to know. He opened the bottle with as much flourish as he could muster while Kristi settled into one of the four club chairs she and Sam had arranged in the pergola. He handed a glass to her and took the chair next to her, grateful that the close proximity still afforded a view of her legs stretched in front of her and demurely crossed at the ankles. He could get used to this.

"So..." She smiled at him and he almost forgot what he wanted to say. "Ah, Jenna's at a sleepover tonight?"

"Yes, her friend Abbie is turning fourteen so it's a birthday-party-slash-sleepover. I had some misgiving about it."

"Why is that?" He was genuinely interested, sinc

someday he, too, would be navigating life with teenage girls.

"There'll be boys at the party. Just till ten o'clock, not for the sleepover, obviously."

He laughed. "A disappointing fact of life for them, I'm sure."

Kristi laughed, too, but there was little humor in it. "Tell me about it. Anyway, I spoke with Abbie's mom and she's assured me the party will be fully supervised, as will the sleepover after the boys leave."

"So no sneaking out to meet them once the parents have gone to bed."

"That's what we're counting on."

He debated whether or not to ask if they'd had "the talk." No, that would be way too personal.

"You're probably wondering if I talked to her about…"

"How did it go?" he asked.

"It didn't." She looked a little deflated. "I don't know why this is so difficult. We have a good relationship—we talk about all sorts of things, but this is really awkward. I'm afraid Jenna's going to think I'm lame and not take me seriously."

He could well imagine a safe sex demonstration involving a banana would seem lame to a teenager.

"You'd think there would be books on how to do this sort of thing," he said.

"Books?"

"Yes, books. Books for parents, books for teenagers."

"I'm not sure about parenting by the book. They can be helpful but I think it's up to parents to decide what they need to tell their kids, and when their kids are ready to hear it."

"Good point." He hoped he remembered that when his time came to make these decisions.

"And I'm not sure how effective a safe sex handbook for teens would be anyway." Her smile curved in a way that could only be described as mischievous. "Most kids wouldn't bother to read it. They'd just look at the pictures."

He laughed. "Girls, too? I'd have thought…hoped?… that maybe just boys did things like that."

"I wish." But she was laughing, too.

He set his beer on the table and stood up. "More wine?"

"Not just yet, thanks. Maybe with dinner."

Dinner. Right. "I'll start the barbecue."

"Were Molly and Martha excited about spending the night with their grandparents?"

"They seemed to be. I just hope they don't come home with more stuff. Alice likes to take them shopping."

"How has she been since you told her the girls weren't going to be in the pageant?"

He shrugged. "She hasn't said a word about it."

"Nothing?"

"Not one word. It's almost too easy, and I'm not sure if that's a good thing or a bad thing."

Kristi looked thoughtful. "I think you should just relax. This is what you wanted, right?"

She was probably right. If he was honest with himself, it had been a long time since he really thought about what he wanted.

"It's just that she has a mind of her own, and once she's made it up, there's usually no changing it." He didn't know why he was telling her this, except that she was easy to talk to, and he liked her levelheaded, no-non-sense approach.

"It can be hard to set boundaries with family. Was it like that when your wife was alive?"

Heather and her mother had been very different people. "Heather always made it seem as though she was going along with her mother, then she usually did whatever she wanted to do."

Even as he said it, he could see the flaw in that approach. He'd bet Kristi saw it, too.

"I can relate," she said. "It seems like an easy way to avoid conflict, and for a while it works, but eventually whatever it is you're trying to avoid will sneak up and bite you on the butt."

No kidding. Like Alice's crazy scheme to enter the girls in some kind of beauty pageant.

"How do you like your burgers?" he asked.

"Well done, and I mean really well done. Black on the outside and absolutely no pink on the inside."

More info to file away. He slid a patty onto the grill for her. He'd give it a couple of minutes before he started his.

"I usually have a head-on approach to setting boundaries," Kristi said. "Trust me, when Molly and Martha are teenagers, you'll get lots of practice. I've been putting off this talk with Jenna, but now that you and I have had this conversation, I know I can't keep doing that. She's a good kid, and I trust her, but it's time. As she gets older and becomes more independent, I want her to have all the information she needs to make the right choices."

"When Molly and Martha get to that age, I'll call you for advice."

For the life of him, he couldn't decipher the look she gave him. Probably wondering, like he was, if they would still be friends ten years from now. Ha. Even now he didn't want to be just friends. Taking their relationship to the next level would definitely rule out the possibility of them still being "friends" a decade from now.

"What I meant—"

"I think I know what you mean. I hope you do call."

"Oh, that's good." That was very good. He tossed his burger onto the barbecue next to hers.

She took a sip of her wine. "Here we are, spending a nice evening together, and we're talking about our kids and our families. Why don't you tell me something about yourself?"

He was all for it. "What would you like to know?"

"What you teach at the university, your research, how you got interested in studying plants."

"How much time do you have?" He was only half joking.

While he prepared their burgers and served the salad he'd made to go with it, he gave her the *Reader's Digest* version of his life as a graduate student and touched on the research he'd done for his PhD thesis while hoping he didn't sound too boring.

"What about you?" he asked when she joined him at the patio table. "When did you decide you wanted to be an interior decorator?"

"I'm not sure. I always knew I wanted to do something creative, and when I finally went to college after my divorce, I was seriously considering graphic arts."

While they ate, she told him how she had put herself through a two-year diploma program at community college while juggling single-parenthood, how she'd met Sam and Claire, and how they'd made the decision to open Ready Set Sold. He was already impressed by her, and now his admiration reached a whole new height.

"That was the best burger I've ever had. Are you ready for dessert?" she asked when he pushed his plate away.

"I can't wait to find out what's in that box." And what else was in store for them tonight.

She smiled coyly. "Why don't you sit here while I clear the plates and serve?"

"Sounds like a plan." He watched her walk toward the house, then refilled their wineglasses. She might not want any more, given that she had to drive home. Unless things went the way he hoped and her car spent the night in his driveway.

Kristi returned carrying a pair of bowls with both dogs following closely. "I thought they might like to have their dinner out here." She set the dogs' dishes on the patio. "Be right back."

This time she came back with two cupcakes on a single plate. Cupcakes? That was the surprise? Not that there was anything wrong with her cupcakes—they were delicious—but she had implied something a little less kid's birthday party and a little more grown-up. And then he saw them close up, a pair of chocolate cupcakes in red foil cups, generously topped with a swirl of whipped cream and a red maraschino cherry, stem and all.

Kristi slid her chair closer to his and sat down, wrapping him again in the fragrance he'd now come to associate with her.

"What are you wearing?" he asked. "That fragrance?"

"French lilac. Do you like it?"

"I do."

"Good answer."

He put her wineglass in her hand, picked up his,

touched his to hers. Then, from the top of one cupcake he plucked a cherry by its stem, but instead of eating it himself, he offered it to her.

Their gazes met and connected. She opened her mouth and accepted it, closing her teeth around the sweet fleshy fruit as he gently tugged the stem away.

"Mmmm," she murmured, chewing it slowly, washing it down with another sip of wine. Then she licked her lips, and he was a goner.

He kissed her, losing himself in the taste of the wine and her, and she kissed him back with a hunger that had nothing to do with dessert. He had planned to invite her to swim with him, hoping she would accept, hoping even more that she hadn't brought a swimsuit with her. Now he had only one thing on his mind.

He pulled back a little, reconnected with her deep green gaze and gradually became aware of hundreds of tiny white lights twinkling in the backyard shrubbery. It was magical.

Kristi was smiling. "Pretty, isn't it? Sam put the lights on a timer."

It was magical. So was she. "Stay the night?" he asked.

The answer he needed to hear came in the form of a kiss, and he was happier than he had been in a very long time.

Chapter 13

Kristi woke to the sound of running water. As she rolled onto her back and stretched, she drowsily thought how unusual it was for Jenna to be the first one up. Wait a minute…

Her eyes snapped open and she stared at the ceiling. Nate's ceiling. Nate's *bedroom* ceiling. She was alone in the bed and the shower was running in the en suite.

She held up the covers, took a quick look underneath and hastily pulled them down again. She was naked.

"Of course you're naked." Now wide-awake, she had a vivid recollection of Nate undressing her last night, of her returning the favor, of tumbling in his bed together.

How much had she had to drink? Two glasses of wine? Three? No, she was sure it was only two. Not enough to blame her impulsive behavior on being tipsy. And now she was in his bed without a stitch on and he could appear any minute and they'd be naked together, in broad daylight.

No way. She flung the sheet away, leaped out of bed and grabbed her clothes. She'd slept with a man she'd met a week and a half ago, and on their first real date.

Way to set an example, Mom.

What had she been thinking? And where was her underwear?

Screw it. Braless, she wriggled into her dress and zipped it up. On the other side of the bed she found her panties and pulled them on. From the back of a chair across the room, one bra strap peeked from beneath the shirt Nate had been wearing last night. She snagged the undergarment and ran, barefoot and silent, down the hall.

In the family room she found her shoes where she'd kicked them off as she and Nate had stumbled in from the patio, with only one thing and one destination in mind. Her handbag was on the kitchen counter where she'd left it. She grabbed it and stuffed her bra inside.

She was halfway to the front door when she remembered Hercules. *Where's your head?* His travel bag was in the family room and so was he, curled up next to Gemmy's head, sound asleep.

"Come on, boy," she whispered. Ignoring his whimpers, she whisked him into the bag and zipped it shut. "Sorry, Herc. We have to get out of here."

From the foyer she listened for sounds coming from down the hallway. Relieved to hear the shower still running, she slipped out the front door. She hated herself for taking the coward's way out, but she couldn't face him. Not this morning, maybe not ever. She was not the kind of woman who slept with a guy on the first date. Correction, she didn't used to be.

* * *

Nate cranked off the shower. He hadn't had the heart to disturb Kristi, she'd been sleeping so soundly, but as he dried himself off he contemplated how he would wake her after he slid back under the covers. There were a lot of options, and he liked every single one of them.

Or maybe she'd be awake by now, waiting for him. He fastened the towel around his waist but stopped in the doorway, taking in the rumpled sheets and empty bed. No sign of her clothes, either. Hmm. She must have gone into the kitchen, maybe to make coffee. Without bothering to swap the towel for his robe, he went to find her.

Several minutes later, reality slowly sank in. Kristi was gone. While he was in the shower, she'd taken her dog and snuck out. A quick check outside confirmed that her van was gone, too.

What the hell?

Last night had been amazing. At least, for him it had. It had been their first real date, and thanks to the previous fake ones, there had been none of those awkward first-date moments. Their conversation felt natural, comfortable, and by the time they got to dessert they were both ready to take things to the next level. He was damn sure of that. They couldn't get out of their clothes and into bed fast enough. This morning apparently the reverse had also been true, for her at least.

What the hell? he thought again.

Sure, he was a little out of practice, but sex was one of those things you never forgot. Like riding a bicycle. There was solid scientific evidence to prove how those memories were stored in various parts of the brain, and how the brain retrieved them.

"Seriously? You've just been dumped in the worst

possible way by the hottest, sexiest woman you've ever met, and all you can think about is some stupid scientific theory?"

And it wasn't an everyday, garden-variety dumping. He'd been dumped by the woman he was in love with, dammit.

He prided himself on being a practical man. A week ago, he'd have said love at first sight only happened in the movies, not real life, but the truth was he'd fallen for her that first day. She'd breezed through his front door, tripping on his kids' boots and spilling his dog's water bowl, and blazed a trail straight into his heart.

Straight into his heart. "Geez, when did you turn into a poet?"

Since last night, maybe. And now that the shock... and, let's face it, the hurt...of her unexplained departure had sunk in, he was damn sure that his performance in bed wasn't the reason she'd bolted this morning. No way she'd faked those orgasms, he thought smugly. Not a chance. Last night had been every bit as good for her as it had for him. He and Kristi were compatible in and out of bed, so it had to be something else.

Maybe Jenna was in some kind of trouble and she'd had to rush off to help her. No, that didn't make sense. She would have said something before she left.

As he filled the coffeepot with water and scooped grounds into the basket, he systematically reviewed the conversations they'd had since she'd started the transformation on his house.

She resented her family's matchmaking attempts as much as he did his, and together they'd found a solution to put a stop to it.

Her ex was a deadbeat, but they'd established that Nate wasn't.

She was anxious about having "the talk" with Jenna because she didn't want her daughter to make the same mistakes she had.

None of those unexplained her unexpected departure.

Then he remembered something Jenna had said, that she saw stuff and heard stuff, and had figured out that her mother avoided relationships because she wanted to set a good example for her daughter.

Was that it? It was okay to have dinner with him, but spending the night would send the wrong message? Jenna would never know she'd stayed if Kristi didn't tell her.

He grabbed a mug from the cupboard and set it on the counter, waiting for the machine to beep, and picked up the phone. There was only one way to find out. Ask her.

After five rings, her cheerful, upbeat greeting told him she was busy, apologized for not being able to take his call and invited him to leave a message.

"Kristi, it's Nate. Can we talk? Call me, okay?" He forced himself to hang up before he started to ramble.

"Busy my ass."

He poured coffee into his mug and carried it into the family room. Gemmy heaved herself up from her bed and ambled across the room to greet him. He opened the patio door for her.

"Go on. I'll take you for a walk after I get dressed." If Kristi had still been sleeping when he got out of the shower, he would have walked both dogs. Her little Yorkie and his huge Saint Bernard made an odd-looking couple, and their mutual infatuation was a humorous reminder that opposites attract.

Not unlike he and Kristi—the boring academic and the

beautiful, spontaneous interior decorator. And yet there was common ground, including single-parenthood and challenges with their extended families. Jenna seemed fond of the twins, Molly and Martha adored her, the dogs were smitten with each other. He'd be the first to admit that he didn't always pick up on these things, but even he could see they were good together. Why couldn't she?

Maybe he should try calling her again.

"Yeah, right. Because your number showing up repeatedly on her phone isn't going to look desperate." And definitely more loser than deadbeat.

He needed a better plan, but first he needed to get dressed and take Gemmy for a walk. That would give him a chance to think this through and figure out a way to convince Kristi that taking a chance on him was the right thing to do.

On the way to his bedroom, he stopped and looked into his office. Since she'd worked her magic in there, it was his favorite room in the house, and for as long as he lived here it would be a productive place to work. She had taken it from chaos to calm, and the room was organized and comfortable. It was as if she knew him better than he knew himself.

Five minutes later, as Nate was standing in the foyer, clipping the leash to Gemmy's collar, the doorbell rang. Kristi? Oh, yes. Please let it be her. He flung the door open and felt his smile fade. It was his mother-in-law, dropping off the girls an hour early.

"Alice, I wasn't expecting you. I was just going to walk the dog."

"Daddy!"

"Good morning, girls." He knelt and drew them in for a hug. "I missed you. Did you have fun?"

"Yup. Now we're going to build LEGO."

Molly pulled away, but Martha stayed close, with her head against his shoulder and her thumb in her mouth.

"Are you going to play with LEGO, too?" he asked.

She nodded and let her sister take her by the hand. He watched them disappear down the hall, each dragging a Hello Kitty backpack behind her. Then he stood and faced the woman at the door, who had yet to say a word, or even crack a smile. "Would you like to come in?"

She stepped in and closed the door, giving Gemmy a wide berth, not out of fear but because she simply didn't like dogs. She was carrying two clear plastic garment bags and the contents appeared to be dresses—one pale yellow, the other light purple. Dresses that Molly and Martha would have no occasion to wear, unless…

He didn't like the direction that thought was taking.

"Thanks for having the girls. Sounds like they had a good time."

Alice thrust the garment bags at him. "These are the girls' pageant dresses. They needed something for the evening-wear portion and I knew they wouldn't have anything suitable, so I took them shopping."

Nate stuck his hands in his pockets and stood his ground. He was having one of the crappiest mornings on record, and now this. "We've already discussed this, Alice. My daughters will not be entering a beauty pageant."

Her steely gaze didn't waiver. "You seem to forget that they're my granddaughters, and with Heather gone, they're all I have."

His temper was about to boil over when he remembered what Kristi said after he apologized for losing it over the girls playing with makeup.

Don't let this be about the pageant. Make it about your family—you and your daughters. She needs to know that you're open to her suggestions, but that in the end, you're the one who makes the decisions about what's best for them.

Kristi was right. He needed to put his foot down, once and for all, and he needed to do it now.

"Alice, you and Fred are an important part of the girls' lives, but you are not their parents. I am. I'm open to suggestions but I make the decisions, and I've decided there will be no pageant."

"But the girls want to do this, especially Molly. And Martha needs to get over her shyness—"

He hated to be rude, but this woman needed to learn how to take no for an answer. "I've already said no but you didn't seem to hear it, so let me say it again. *No.* The girls will not be in a pageant. And in the future, you will not discuss these things with my daughters until you've talked to me first."

He was on a roll now, and there was no stopping. "Molly'd never heard of these beauty pageants until you told her about them. And Martha's shyness is not a flaw, it's who she is. If you could accept that, then maybe you wouldn't feel the need to turn her into someone she's not." He stopped before he said *like you tried to do with your daughter.*

For the first time in all the years he'd known Alice, she was speechless. She opened and closed her mouth a couple of times before she managed to sputter, "Well, I never…"

No doubt that was true. She'd never heard these things, because no one had ever had the balls to say them. If not for Kristi, he might never have, either.

Gemmy, leash still attached to her collar, nudged the garment bags with her nose.

"For heaven's sake, get your dog under control," Alice said, jumping back a step and staring with disgust at the dog drool on her shoe.

Well placed, Gemmy. Nate tugged on the leash, lowering his head to pat the dog's back so Alice couldn't see his smile. "Sorry about that."

Without another word, Alice swung around and huffed out the door. She was furious, Nate got that, but she would come around. In the past, he would have felt like an ungrateful jerk but for the first time in what felt like forever, he was in control. Even Kristi's departure felt less about him, probably because it wasn't. He hoped she would have a change of heart but if she didn't, he would find a way to change it for her.

Instead of crawling into bed and having a good cry when she got home from Nate's—and she'd been so tempted—Kristi forced herself to keep busy. After a quick shower, she pulled on a T-shirt and pair of yoga pants, went into the kitchen and hauled out her baking supplies.

A long time ago, she had figured out what she needed to do to ensure that her life didn't become a blueprint for Jenna's. She'd made the right decision, she was convinced of that. Last night she'd had a lapse in judgment, had let her feelings and Nate's hotness get the better of her, but she wasn't going down that road. Not now. The timing just wasn't right.

She was taking the second batch of cupcakes out of the oven when Jenna arrived home from her sleepover.

"Mom? I'm home." The front door slammed and a moment later Jenna appeared in the kitchen. "Wow, that's a lot of cupcakes. Is something wrong?"

"Of course not. Why?"

"'Cause when you're upset, you bake."

Jenna knew her too well. "I'm not upset," she said, hoping she sounded more convincing than she felt. "I'm going to put these in the freezer so they're ready for Aunt Wanda's barbecue."

Jenna leaned on elbows on the counter and studied her from the opposite side of the peninsula. "How was your date?"

Kristi avoided eye contact as she carefully removed the cupcakes from the pan and set them on a rack to cool. "It was fine."

"Did you and Nate have a fight?"

"No, of course not." Time to change the subject. "How was the party?"

"Awesome. Abbie's so lucky, her parents gave her an iPhone." She paused for effect, then continued, "After everybody left, we spent ages figuring out how it works and getting a bunch of apps set up and texting our friends."

"That's nice." Kristi turned off the oven and started to wash her baking dishes, fully expecting yet another explanation of how badly Jenna needed a new phone.

"Are you sure you're okay?" her daughter asked instead.

"I'm fine, sweetie. What are your plans for the rest of the day?"

Jenna yawned. "I'm going back to bed. We stayed up super late, and Abbie's mom made French toast for breakfast so we had to get up early."

Ordinarily Kristi would insist she stay awake and go to bed early tonight, but if Jenna went back to bed now, she would stop asking questions.

"I told Abbie she could come with us to Nate's tomorrow. Now that the pool's done, we can go for a swim."

Kristi snapped. "Jenna, you can't just invite people over there."

"But Nate said—"

"No *buts*. You should have asked *me* and I would have told you it's not appropriate for you to invite your friends to my client's home."

"Geez, you don't have to bite my head off. And since when is Nate a client? You guys are dating."

Calm down. It isn't fair to take this out on Jenna. "We're not dating. We've had a couple of casual…things. That's all. And I won't be working there tomorrow anyway."

"Why not?"

"I'm starting another project in the morning. Sam will finish up at Nate's." Which wasn't completely true. Or even remotely true. She didn't have another job lined up, and she had yet to talk to Sam about finishing this one. The part about her not working there was true, though. No way could she face him. Besides, a clean break was always best. Like tearing off a Band-Aid. It might hurt like hell at first, but not as much as prolonging the agony.

Jenna wasn't buying any of it. "You and Nate did have a fight."

Kristi turned back to the sink. "No, we didn't." They hadn't known each other long enough to fight.

Her phone buzzed and Jenna grabbed it off the counter.

"Don't answer that!"

"It's Nate," Jenna said.

Of course it was. He'd already left one message, now he

most likely wanted to know why she hadn't called back. She reached for the phone and Jenna put it in her hand.

Kristi turned it off and tossed it aside.

"Why didn't you answer it?"

"I'm busy. I'll call him later."

"Right. 'Cause you're not upset, and you guys didn't have a fight, and you're just busy." Jenna rolled her eyes. "Whatever. I'm going to my room. Come on, Herc." She scooped the dog out of his basket and disappeared upstairs.

Once Kristi heard footsteps overhead, she quickly picked up her phone and checked her voice messages.

"Kristi, it's Nate. Again. Sorry to bother you. I want to make sure you're okay, and I want to tell you I had another talk with Alice. And this time she finally got the message."

"Daddy, I can't find my skipping rope."

"I'm on the phone, Molly. I'll help you look for it in a minute. Kristi? Hi, sorry about that. Anyway, give me a call when you get a chance. We should talk."

Kristi saved the message, then absently counted the rows of cupcakes cooking on the rack before they were blurred by tears. Then she opened a drawer, dropped her phone inside and closed it. Whatever she did, she would not call and tell him the skipping rope was in the toy box in the playhouse.

Chapter 14

Kristi dragged herself out of bed on Monday morning, feeling like hell. Looking like it, too, she confirmed as she stood in front of the bathroom mirror, brushing her teeth. She pulled a robe over the T-shirt and boxers she'd worn to bed and went downstairs. Hercules scampered out of Jenna's room and followed, barking excitedly until she shooed him onto the patio.

She filled the kettle and put it on to boil, then checked her phone for messages. There weren't any. After two attempts to reach her, Nate had apparently given up.

"Can you blame him?"

She was tempted to replay the two he'd left yesterday, just to hear the sound of his voice, but she knew better. Instead she perused the assortment of teas in her cupboard and decided on a nice soothing cup of chamomile.

She was sitting with her fingers curled around the cup,

staring at the four shadow boxes she'd made for Nate, when Jenna straggled down the stairs.

"Morning, Mom." She opened the fridge, poured herself a glass of orange juice and brought it to the table. "What are you doing?"

"Nothing."

"Are you still moping from yesterday?"

"I wasn't moping yesterday."

"Yes, you were, and you never do 'nothing.' You're always baking or sewing or working on some project on your laptop."

Kristi sipped her tea, which wasn't nearly calming enough. "I'm taking a day off."

"You said you were starting a new job today."

"I changed my mind."

Jenna sat across the table, gulped half the glass of juice before setting it in front of her, and leaned on her elbows. "Okay, spill. You've been grumpy as an old bear ever since you had dinner with Nate. What happened?"

"Nothing 'happened.' We just decided… I decided… that it's not going to work out."

"That's a bunch of crap."

A challenge sparkled in Jenna's eyes, but Kristi was too exhausted to take the bait.

"You like him, right? And he's totally crazy about you, so what's the problem?"

Kristi sighed. The role reversal caught her by surprise, but that didn't mean she owed her daughter an explanation. She was doing this for her, after all, but she was too young to understand why.

"It's not that simple."

"Seriously, Mom? You think I don't know what's going on here? It's like I said to Nate—"

Jenna talked to Nate? About this? And he didn't say anything? "When did you talk to him?"

"At the brunch thing when we were putting away the salads."

That's when he'd apologized for overreacting about putting makeup on Molly and Martha. She had no idea they'd talked about anything else. "What did you say to him?"

Jenna drained her juice glass. "I told him you hardly ever go on dates because you think that if you do, you'll be setting a bad example for me."

"Where did you get that idea? And why would you say that to Nate?"

Jenna grinned. "Mom, I'm fourteen. I'm not a little kid. I hear you talking to Grandma and Aunt Wanda when they try to set you up with blind dates."

Kristi wondered what else her daughter knew, and decided there were some things she'd be better off not knowing.

"I turn down most of those dates because I'm just not interested...."

Her daughter laughed and shook her head. "I also know you're worried that I'll end up pregnant like you did, being a single mom like you were."

This was all bordering on too much information, especially this morning. Lack of sleep was making her head hurt and her eyes itch. She was in no mood for a teenage pep talk.

"I'm not a bad kid, Mom." She got up and put her glass in the dishwasher. "I know all about sex and where babies come from...and how not to make one."

And now Kristi's head was ready to explode. "I've been meaning to talk to you—"

"I know." Jenna was actually smirking now. "And I already know about this stuff, everybody does, and I'm not going to let it happen to me. I'm a good kid, I get good grades and just 'cause me and Abbie are hanging out with Matt and Jordan doesn't mean we're going to have sex with them. We're not ready for that."

Kristi got up and hugged her. Some of the all-aloneness she'd been feeling was replaced with a little relief and a whole lot of pride. Her daughter was a good kid, and maybe she worried more than she needed to.

"So, you know what this means, right?" Jenna asked.

With the sleeve of her bathrobe, Kristi dabbed the moisture from the corners of her eyes. "What does this mean?"

Jenna picked up the phone and handed it to her. "You can answer all those messages he left. I'll even go up to my room, give you some privacy."

Was Jenna right? Was it time she gave someone a chance? Tore down that fortress Sam had talked about? Maybe she should call him. Her heart thumped in her chest and her mouth went dry, and then the shadow boxes lined up on the sideboard caught her eye. Forget the phone. She had a better idea.

After a lousy night of tossing and turning, Nate was in no mood to cope with anything, especially not two rambunctious girls clamoring to go swimming, to read a book about hippopotamuses, to put the tent back in the family room. He rarely asked for favors but while he waited for the coffeepot to do its thing, he called his mother and asked her to take the girls, using his work at the university and the final work on the house as an excuse.

He still didn't know what would happen this morning and that had him on edge. Would Kristi show up as though nothing had happened? Send someone else to wrap up the last things that needed to be done? He sure wasn't going to try calling again. If she needed time, he'd give her time. Even if it killed him.

From the kitchen, he walked through the dining room and into the living room. Except for the major pieces of furniture, these two rooms had been stripped bare and given a thorough floor-to-ceiling cleaning. Today they were to be staged. Kristi said they were her favorite rooms. When he and Heather bought the house, these had been his favorite rooms, too. And for some reason he had closed the doors and all but forgotten about them, as he'd done with other parts of his life. And then Kristi had come along and quite literally thrown the doors open.

Through the living room window, he watched Sam's truck pull up and park in front of the house. She didn't get out, though. She was on her cell phone, so he stood and watched and waited.

His patience was rewarded. Kristi's van pulled up behind Sam. In case they could see him from the street, and not wanting to be caught spying on them, he hustled back into the kitchen. Gemmy was sprawled on the family room carpet but the sound of the doorbell would have her up and running, so he opened the patio door and coaxed her outside.

The minutes ticked by. What were they doing out there? As he debated going to investigate, the bell rang. He rushed to the door, couldn't help himself, but he opened it slowly and did a terrible job of feigning surprise.

Kristi stood alone with the purple cupcake-printed purse slung over one shoulder and a big blue shopping bag in the other hand. After worrying this moment would never come, he wanted to pull her into his arms and not let her go for a very long time.

Play it cool, he told himself. "Hi."

"Hi."

"You didn't answer my calls. I thought you might not come."

"I almost didn't."

"Is Sam coming in?"

"Ah, no. She forgot to pick to the…widgets she needs to fix the…thingamajig." She couldn't keep a straight face and he laughed with her, grateful she'd found a way to break the ice and get rid of Sam so they could be alone.

"I asked her to give us a few minutes."

Good call. "Come in."

She stepped into the foyer and closed the door. "Where are the girls?"

"Spending the day with my mother."

"Good, because we should talk."

"Let's go in and sit down."

She set both bags on the family room floor and sat on the sofa. He joined her, thinking the last time they sat on it together was that day in the furniture store. She didn't say anything, and the only way he knew to start this conversation was to take the direct approach.

"Why did you leave yesterday? I was worried about you."

She folded her hands in her lap and stared down at them. "I'm sorry. I sort of freaked out."

"About us?"

"Yes. No. I mean, mostly about me. I've had this thing about setting a good example for Jenna." She glanced up at him. "She might have mentioned it?"

He covered her hands with one of his, and she didn't push him away. "She did."

"Why didn't you tell me?"

"I'm pretty sure she shared that in confidence and I didn't want to risk losing her trust. For all I knew, she was testing me."

Kristi smiled at that. "It's what teenagers do. And it turns out they're a lot smarter than we... I...give them credit for."

She told him about the conversation she'd had with Jenna that morning and while she did, he thought of ways he might thank the girl. She had hinted that her friends would think a pool party would be the coolest thing ever. *Well, Jenna. Prepare to be cool.*

"So to summarize," he said, "you think you need to set a good example, and she thinks you don't."

"Pretty much."

"Any chance you'll agree with her?"

She unfolded her hands and intertwined her fingers with his. A hopeful sign...he hoped.

"I want to, I'd like to, but..."

All he could do was hold his breath and wait.

"I need to take this slowly. The other night..." Her color deepened. "That was not slow."

She was right. If she'd said no, that it was too soon to take their relationship into the bedroom, it might have killed him but he would have stopped.

"I hope you didn't feel pressured."

"No! No, not at all. But we both have kids to think about, and even though Jenna says I don't need to worry about her, I do. You and I just met, and if she knew we were already sleeping together... Well, that's not the message I want to send."

She was right about this, too, and he was reminded of his mother's words of wisdom. *Blended families are a big adjustment. They take work, and patience.* It was too soon to talk about them being a family, but he needed to put the rest of her advice into practice.

"Listen, the last thing I want to do is send the wrong message to Jenna, or Molly and Martha. What if we slow things down, give them a chance to get on board with this? No more sleepovers until they get used to us being a couple."

"You'd be willing to do that?"

"For them, yes." *For you, anything.* He wanted to be in her and Jenna's lives, and he needed them in his and the twins'. He'd do whatever it took.

To demonstrate just slow it could be, he slid his hands up her arms and gently eased her in for a kiss, just a light touch of his lips to hers. As he pulled back, her eyelids fluttered open and her smile told him everything he needed to know. Well, almost everything. "I still have one question."

"What's that?"

"What's in the bag you brought with you?"

Her smile widened. "A housewarming present. Come on, I'll show you."

She stood and picked up the blue shopping bag, extending her other hand to him. He took it and let her lead him to the breakfast bar. She set the bag on the counter and after they'd each taken a stool, she pulled out a rectangular box wrapped in plain brown paper. "I made this for your office. I hope you like it."

He tore the paper away and stared at the framed photobooth strips until the lump in his throat subsided enough for him to speak. "I... Wow... I don't know what to say."

"If you don't like it—"

"No, I love it, thank you."

"I'm glad. I made two more for the girls, and one that you might want to have in your office at the university."

He liked that she would create something so personal. To him, it felt the opposite of taking things slowly, and he loved that. He loved her. And he thanked her the best way he could, with a kiss that let her know there was nothing wrong with speeding things up once in a while.

Chapter 15

The summer had flown by and it had been pretty close
to perfect in Kristi's opinion. Nate had decided not to
sell his home after all, and she and Jenna had spent many
happy hours there with him and the twins. Jenna was
teaching Molly and Martha how to swim. Kristi was re-
discovering the joy of having young children in her life
again, and her biological clock was ticking a little less
loudly. She'd learned the best example to set for Jenna
was being in a healthy, committed relationship. And Nate,
the same great dad he'd always been, was more confident and even more patient than ever. Nate had found the
nerve to have that talk with his mother-in-law, so Kristi
worked up the courage to have the talk with her daughter.

Today they were at the mall, all five of them, shopping for school clothes. Kristi was surprised that Jenna
had agreed to tag along, and even more surprised that her

daughter was cheerfully accompanying them from store to store, and not begging to go off on her own. Whatever the reason, Kristi didn't intend to question her behavior. She was too happy, strolling hand in hand with Nate, listening to Jenna's running commentary on outfits worn by other shoppers and keeping a close watch on Molly and Martha. This felt like a real family, as real as it got.

"Daddy, there's the photo booth," Martha said.

Molly hopped up and down. "Let's take our pictures."

Nate looked down at her. "You don't mind?"

Kristi smiled up at him. "You know I don't. Go ahead. Jenna and I will wait here for you."

Nate handed coins to the girls, who fed them into the slot, then he followed them into the booth and pulled the curtain closed. A couple of minutes later they appeared, the girls giggling over the new strip. Nate smiled and waved her over.

Kristi shook her head. She hated being photographed.

"Oh, Mom," Jenna prodded her. "Go have your picture taken. It'll be cute."

"Cute? Who are you, and what have you done with my daughter."

Jenna gave her a playful shove toward Nate. "Go. I'll watch the kidlets."

He took her hand, and while she smoothed her hair, he did that thing with his thumb on her palm that always made her shiver.

"You look beautiful." His credit card went into the slot, then he swept the curtain aside for her. "After you."

Kristi ducked inside and sat down. "I've never done this before."

"Neither have I." He settled in next to her, his thigh pressed firmly against hers.

What was that supposed to mean? He and the girls had done this dozens of times.

"This light lets you know when the next photo will be taken."

"What am I supposed to do?"

"Be yourself. Ready?"

The light blinked.

"I love you, Kristi."

That made her laugh. "I love you, too."

The light blinked a second time.

"Will you marry me?" Nate was holding a ring.

He was proposing? He was proposing! "Yes, I'll marry you."

He slid the ring onto her finger.

She blinked. So did the light. It was the most beautiful ring she'd ever seen.

And then he kissed her and she closed her eyes and saw something that looked a lot like fireworks.

"Our pictures are ready," he said a moment later.

Her hands were shaking, so he held up the strip so she could see it.

In the first frame, they were gazing into each other's eyes and wearing the goofiest smiles imaginable. In the second she was staring wide-eyed at the ring. In the third photo the ring was on her finger, and in the fourth his lips were on hers.

This was the most romantic thing that had ever happened to her, and now she was engaged—engaged!—and she still hadn't really looked at her ring. She held up her hand and got a little teary. A princess-cut diamond solitaire in a stunning art deco setting.

"Nate, it's beautiful. It looks…old."

"It is. Jenna helped me pick it out."

"She knows?"

"I needed to be sure she was okay with it."

The curtain whipped open and Jenna stuck her head in. "What's taking so long?"

"She said yes."

Jenna launched herself into the booth and the twins followed, and then everyone was laughing and talking at the same time.

"Do you like the ring?" Jenna asked.

"I love it."

"I knew you would. I helped pick it out."

Kristi looked from her daughter to her fiancé—she had a fiancé!—and her heart suddenly felt too big for her chest.

"Nate said I can have an iPhone," Jenna announced.

"An engagement present," he said. "Figured it was the least I could do for the help with the ring."

"And he's going to let me drive the Volkswagen!"

His arm tightened around Kristi's shoulder. "After you get your license," he said. "And if your mom says it's okay."

"You're going to spoil her." But Kristi knew he wouldn't. He was Jenna's dad now, every bit as much as he was Molly's and Martha's. Over the tops of three blond heads, she looked at Nate and she knew she had it all...the man, the family and the home of her dreams.

* * * * *

*When a guide dog trainer becomes a target
of a dangerous crime ring, a K-9 cop and his loyal
partner will work together to keep her safe.*

Read on for a sneak preview of Trail of Danger
*by Valerie Hansen, the next exciting installment
to the* True Blue K-9 Unit *miniseries,
available September 2019 from Love Inspired Suspense.*

Abigail Jones stared at the blackening eastern sky and
shivered. She was more afraid of the strangers lingering
in the shadows along the Coney Island boardwalk than
she was of the summer storm brewing over the Atlantic.

Early September humidity made the salty oceanic
atmosphere feel sticky while the wind whipped loose
tendrils of Abigail's long red hair. If sixteen-year-old
Kiera Underhill hadn't insisted where and when their
secret meeting must take place, Abigail would have
stopped to speak with some of the other teens she was
passing. Instead, she made a beeline for the spot where
their favorite little hot dog wagon spent its days.

Besides the groups of partying youth, she skirted
dog walkers, couples strolling hand in hand and an old
woman leaning on a cane. Then there was a tall man and

enormous dog ambling toward her. As they passed beneath an overhead vapor light, she recognized his police uniform and breathed a sigh of relief. Most K-9 patrols in her nearby neighborhood used German shepherds, so seeing the long floppy ears and droopy jowls of a bloodhound brought a smile despite her uneasiness.

Pausing, Abigail rested her back against the fence surrounding a currently closed amusement park, faced into the wind and waited for the K-9 cop to go by. His unexpected presence could be what was delaying Kiera.

"Come on, Kiera. I came alone, just like you wanted," Abigail muttered.

Kiera had sounded panicky when she'd phoned.

"Here. Over here" drifted on the wind. Abigail strained to listen.

The summons seemed to be coming from inside the Luna Park perimeter fence. That was not good since the amusement facility was currently closed. Nevertheless, she cupped her hands around her eyes and peered through the chain-link fence. It was several seconds before she realized the gate was ajar. *Uh-oh. Bad sign.* "Kiera? Is that you?"

A disembodied voice answered faintly. "Help me! Hurry."

Don't miss
Trail of Danger *by Valerie Hansen,*
available September 2019 wherever
Love Inspired® *Suspense books and ebooks are sold.*

www.LoveInspired.com

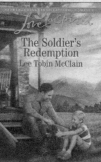

*After escaping her abusive ex, Cassie Zetticci is
thankful for a job and a safe place to stay at the
Gallant Lake Resort. Nick West makes her nervous
with his restless energy, but when he starts teaching her
self-defense, Cassie begins to see a future that involves
roots and community. But can Nick let go of his own
difficult past to give Cassie the freedom she needs?*

*Read on for a sneak preview of
A Man You Can Trust,
the first book—and Harlequin Special Edition debut!—
in Jo McNally's new miniseries, Gallant Lake Stories.*

"Why are you armed with pepper spray? Did something
happen to you?"

She didn't look up.

"Yes. Something happened."

"Here?"

She shook her head, her body trembling so badly
she didn't trust her voice. The only sound was Nick's
wheezing breath. He finally cleared his throat.

"Okay. Something happened." His voice was gravelly
from the pepper spray, but it was calmer than it had been
a few minutes ago. "And you wanted to protect yourself.
That's smart. But you need to do it right. I'll teach you."

Her head snapped up. He was doing his best to look at her, even though his left eye was still closed.

"What are you talking about?"

"I'll teach you self-defense, Cassie. The kind that actually works."

"Are you talking karate or something? I thought the pepper spray…"

"It's a tool, but you need more than that. If some guy's amped up on drugs, he'll just be temporarily blinded and really ticked off." He picked up the pepper spray canister from the grass at her side. "This stuff will spray up to ten feet away. You never should have let me get so close before using it."

"I didn't know that."

"Exactly." He grimaced and swore again. "I need to get home and dunk my face in a bowl full of ice water." He stood and reached a hand down to help her up. She hesitated, then took it.

Don't miss
A Man You Can Trust *by Jo McNally,*
available September 2019 wherever
Harlequin® Special Edition books and ebooks are sold.

www.Harlequin.com